"THEIR ATTACKS ARE SUDDEN AND TERRIFYING.

"If you're unprepared for them, they will paralyze you to your soul. Their basic soldier is the Legionnaire, the dead from our own battl̶e̶ cemeteries reanimated by th̶e̶i̶ ight with insane frenzy. necromutants, creatures storted by Legion tech war machines and can t dying."

"That's wha̶t we encountered in the hospital. No wonder we had to shoot it so many times before we killed it."

"Wounding these creatures will not stop them. You must use your firepower without mercy, Captain, to destroy them. For if you fail, they will succeed at what they plan to do to humanity. And what they wish to do is not to destroy us but to seize us, defile and pervert us into their own creation, and have billions of human souls in unquestioning service to their dark ends. . . ."

MUTANT CHRONICLES

THE APOSTLE OF INSANITY TRILOGY™

VOLUME TWO

FRENZY

by

John-Allen Price

A ROC BOOK

ROC
Published by the Penguin Group
Penguin Books USA Inc., 375 Hudson Street,
New York, New York 10014, U.S.A.
Penguin Books Ltd, 27 Wrights Lane,
London W8 5TZ, England
Penguin Books Australia Ltd, Ringwood,
Victoria, Australia
Penguin Books Canada Ltd, 10 Alcorn Avenue,
Toronto, Ontario, Canada M4V 3B2
Penguin Books (N.Z.) Ltd, 182–190 Wairau Road,
Auckland 10, New Zealand

Penguin Books Ltd, Registered Offices:
Harmondsworth, Middlesex, England

First published by Roc,
an imprint of Dutton Signet,
a division of Penguin Books USA Inc.

First Printing, June, 1994
10 9 8 7 6 5 4 3 2 1

For my mother,
Norabelle Ann Price (1922–1992)
She lived long enough to see me get this sale,
but would probably spin in her grave if she knew
I dedicated something like this to her.
What's that sound I hear?

CHAPTER ONE

"Master Ragathol, we're ready to enter Venus orbit," said the courier ship's pilot. "Do you wish to come forward and observe?"

The necromutant had barely finished his advisory when the cockpit hatch slid open, allowing in the ship's lone passenger. Ragathol limped slightly and held one of his arms at his side as he made his way forward. He stopped when the increasingly narrow cockpit would no longer accommodate his massive frame and looked up.

What had hours before been only a bright point of light in the heavens was now a majestic swirl of white, blue, and green. It filled most of the cockpit's front and overhead windows. For a few moments even Ragathol was transfixed by the planet's beauty.

"It's ... it's green, Caliqabaal," said the nepharite, scanning his destination through the overhead windows. "And blue. This is so unlike the world the humans created out of Luna. It resembles the description of what their original Earth once looked like."

"In centuries past this world was uninhabitable, even to us," Caliqabaal replied, his maneuvers for orbital insertion over; he could afford a brief gaze at their destination. "Its atmosphere was pure carbon dioxide, it rained acid, and the surface temperature made metals run liquid. The humans are to be respected for the ways they've changed this world."

"Yes, their machines and their worlds are to be coveted. But the humans themselves are irritating fools. Like all similar races we've encountered, their fate is to be conquered and turned to serve us. What maneuver are you completing now?"

"Entry attitude positioning. We'll only do a fractional polar orbit, my Master. If we were to remain aloft any longer, we would attract sustained attention from the human military forces. This way we'll arrive at the Citadel before any human even asks us for our registration number."

Instead of entering equatorial orbit like all other arriving spacecraft, the tiny *Gamma*-class courier dropped into Venus orbit over its north pole. Caliqabaal immediately rolled the ship off its back, and raised its nose until it was skimming across the Venusian atmosphere on its belly. It skirted the planet's terminator line between night and day. For the moment not visible to anyone on the ground attempting to track it; and by the time it finished landing at the Citadel night would have fallen.

"We are approaching the atmospheric interface," Caliqabaal continued. "You should return to the passenger cabin for the rest of the re-entry."

"No, I will see it from here," said Ragathol, moving to the back of the cockpit and lowering one of the jump seats. As he did so he glanced out the port windows at the sparkling field of lights that spread across the planet's night side. "Millions ... a thousand million humans and more. The conquest of this world will be our greatest triumph. If we win it for Algeroth, then he'll stand alone among the Apostles. Not even Ilian could challenge his power."

Minutes later, the view from all the windows on the spacecraft was lost as it became enveloped in a plasma sheath of ionizing gases. For the next dozen minutes it plunged through the Venusian atmosphere like a glowing meteor. It was readily visible against the evening sky; however, most of this occurred over the planet's equatorial oceans and barren deserts. By the time it emerged from the blackout layer, its undersurfaces no longer glowed; and the black technology that corrupted its basically clean design rendered it all but invisible to radar. The courier arced over the cities of the southern hemisphere, and descended to land in a remote Antarctic region claimed by both Capitol and Mishima, yet occupied by neither megacorporation.

"Brother Ragathol, we congratulate your escape from Luna," said the nepharite leading the arrival delegation. "It's fortunate this ship was available to facilitate it."

"Yes, the Fate of the Apostles favored me," said Ragathol, descending from the ship's main hatch. He scanned the desolate terrain from the stairway and found little to see beyond the service towers that surrounded the pad the ship had taxied to. "Brother Azurwraith, I thought your Citadel was more developed in its construction than this."

"Below ground it is almost complete. The aboveground structure will be its final stage." Azurwraith's response grew colder with each word, yet he was able to retain his official civility with his guest. "Do not think Their Fate will be kind to you. . . . Algeroth is 'displeased' with your failure."

"It was not my fault. The humans I faced were better than I had been lead to believe."

"He isn't interested in your excuses for failure. Neither am I. He has no desire to punish you further, but if you wish to regain His favor you must work for it."

"Like you, I am but His servant," Ragathol answered. He stepped up to Azurwraith and faced him briefly. Then backed away and, with difficulty, lowered his head. "What task does He wish of me?"

"The human female I sent you?" said Azurwraith. "The Receptacle of Visions? For some reason the humans have returned her to this world. In His beneficence, Lord Algeroth tasks you with retrieving her. He further orders that you be given sufficient forces to accomplish this end."

"This is a task for a necromutant, or even some heretics, not me. I wish a task more worthy."

"You lost the woman. You lost all your forces on Luna. Algeroth considers it appropriate for you to retrieve her and bring her to His Defiled Castle."

"To His Castle . . ." said Ragathol, mulling over the words. And slowly, a smile crept onto his face. "To be at His seat of power. Yes, such a small task can have great consequences. I accept. Where is the woman located?"

"Capitol has her," said Azurwraith. As he responded, he signaled to his necromutants; and moments later the massive, circular pad the courier ship and those around it stood on began to lower silently into the ground. "They picked her up at their spaceport and moved her to a hospital not far from it. As of yet, they're unaware of her importance. You should be able to accomplish this task quickly."

ZULU TIME: 11:23 hours.   MISSION TIME: 8:45 hours.

TO: Battle Station Lucas 1138, Senior Military Advisor C. Hart.
FROM: Dirk Bamble. Advisor, Special Forces squad Trident.
ENCRYPTION CODE: Capitol Fox Alpha 973 Sierra.
MISSION SUMMARY: Supplemental.

By using unorthodox jamming strategy and assault tactics, Captain Mitch Hunter successfully attacked the Cybertronic observation post at grid reference 4A6/7X7. The newly completed facility had an improved defense system, but this proved ineffective against our new, extended range CGA-12 grenades. The Liche CAR-24smg assault rifles proved very capable in firing this new munition. They did not jam or misfire during the entire combat phase of this operation. We are now awaiting egress at our evac point. If Lieutenant Alverez is following a standard deviation flight path we shouldKnvoIeru90wQrhedsioDb8k90 sS3dexxzgadlkf045847ergaeri0q----------------------------
------------ .

"Damn it, Hunter! You'll die for this!" Bamble shouted, leaping away from the briefcase-size transceiver set. The spray of plastic shards from its exterior shell and fragments of silicon chips was still falling and mixing with the dust raised by the six-round burst. "What the hell's the matter with you?"

"We're still in hostile territory, Bungle," said Mitch Hunter, the spent shell casings from his rifle still bouncing around his feet. "And the ban on everything except essential radio traffic is still in force."

"What did you call me, Captain?"

"I'd like to call you Missing in Action. But your directorate would only assign me someone else just like you. And the men have grown fond of you."

"Yeah, who do you think gave you the name 'Bungle' in the first place?" Sergeant Leo Venneti added. He was standing closer to the plateau's edge and was busy scanning the western horizon with a pair of electronic binoculars. "The captain's busy with other things, such as where we'll dump your body if you keep disobeying his orders."

"Combat has ended, Sergeant," said Bamble, turning his

attention to the enlisted men. "And according to corporate protocol I'm entitled to transmit battle reports. And even if Cybertronic were monitoring the frequency I use, they still can't read what I send because of the encryption system I have."

"Don't go quoting protocol out here," said Hunter. "We're still a hundred and twenty clicks from the Capitol frontier. We just blasted the latest Cybertronic observation post and Julia hasn't picked us up yet. It doesn't matter if Cybertronic can read what you sent or not. They can pinpoint where you sent it from, even if it's a burst transmit."

"Captain, I got movement," warned one of the other squad members, Sergeant Jacob Shacker. Unlike Venneti, the stoutly built black man scanned the same horizon with his weapon, a Vampire SR-50 sniper's rifle. Ponderously large, its weight was partly lessened by the absence of a clip and the four pounds of ammunition it carried. Shacker moved the weapon slowly, mostly to prevent the image from blurring in his digital scope. "Aircraft, max range."

"Leo, do you confirm?" said Hunter.

"Not yet, Captain. I got too much heat distortion at distance," said Venneti. "God, how I hate the desert."

"Captain, you want me to set up the portable radar?" asked Lieutenant Raymond Rogers, grabbing his backpack.

"Never mind," said Hunter. "By the time you set it up we'll be able to eyeball whatever's out there."

"Captain, they're helicopter gunships," said Shacker. "Cybertronic Sky Witch-class and there's a lot of 'em."

"What ... what does that mean?" Bamble nervously requested.

"Protocol this!" Hunter spun around and punched his military advisor on the left side of his chin. Bamble's head snapped to the right, the rest of his body followed it, and he collapsed to the plateau's sun-baked surface, raising a brief cloud of fine dust. "Troopers, we are leaving! Sun Burst, Sun Burst! This is Lone Wolf. We need evac, now! Over."

"God, Captain. You wanna be the next Bob Watts?" said Theodore Halston, the squad's fire-support specialist, rising wearily to his feet. "How are we gonna explain this?"

"One of these desert dung beetles must've wanted to lay eggs in his head," said Hunter, motioning for his squad's medic to check Bamble. "I think it made an overeager approach."

"Captain, your request did the trick," advised Diane Parker, scanning the southern horizon with her own SR-50. "I got Julia inbound and closing fast."

"I have 'em now, Captain," said Venneti. "Twelve Sky Witches in two groups of six. They're doing sweeps, and they're all heading this way."

"It sounds like lock and load time," said Halston, grabbing his heavy machine gun by its twin pistol grips. Despite the fact the Tempest was almost the same size as the Vampire, Halston lifted it easily and in seconds had its breech open. "How come we're always nailing Cybertronic whenever they set up somewhere?"

"No. Only Diane and Jake are to arm weapons," Hunter ordered. "We're withdrawing, not fighting a pitched battle. The rest of us will prepare to board the gunship when it lands."

"Captain, you only put his lights out," said Sergeant Wendy Levin, still crouching over Bamble's crumpled form. "You want me to wake him up?"

"No, give him something that'll keep him out. He can whine and be a thorn in my side later. Not now."

Of the ten members in the Special Forces squad, only two loaded their weapons, while most of the others grabbed the equipment they had stripped off in order to rest. It took them just over a minute to slip on the camouflaged armor, helmets, and backpacks. They spread out and used what available cover they could. However, the barren plateau offered only rock outcroppings and depressions, sculpted into their bizarre forms at a time when the planet's surface temperature would melt lead and the atmospheric pressure was ninety times that on Earth. Even now the air felt heavy to the squad members, in spite of their position atop one of the terrain's numerous plateaus. It deadened the first rumble of helicopter rotorblades to reach the squad.

"Captain, that first group of Cyber choppers is at two thousand meters and closing," informed Shacker, deploying the bipod legs on his rifle. "We can nail 'em with DUDSAP rounds."

"Open fire on the flight leader," said Hunter. "That should

confuse them long enough for us to evac. Julia's dropped into the valley, she'll be here any moment."

"Corporal, you got the leader?"

"Yes, Jake," said Parker, now lying next to Shacker and with her SR-50 similarly readied. "DUDs loaded and locked."

"Three-round burst. Fire at will."

In unison, Parker and Shacker opened fire on the drone helicopter formation closest to the plateau. Even in the bright sunlight the sniper rifles had visible muzzle flashes; and each 15mm round they unleashed raised a veil of dust from the surrounding rocks. Twenty yards in front of the weapons, the plastic casings shed by the Depleted Uranium Discarding Sabot Armor Piercing shells clattered across the ground. What remained of each bullet was a solid uranium arrow, two-thirds the size of the original round.

With no human crew to accommodate, the Sky Witch had a narrow, impossibly angled fuselage with a skeletal tail boom and stub wings full of weapon pods. Head-on it presented a tiny silhouette of sloped armor plate; but the uranium arrows were too heavy and moving too fast to be deflected. They punched small holes in the lead Sky Witch's skin, causing it to shudder visibly. Thin wisps of smoke curled out of the holes, the result of the helicopter's electronic systems short-circuiting. It wavered and began to slow, and moments later ejected all its external weapon pods, as did all the other aircraft under its command.

"Good God, talk about a silicon fizzle," Shacker remarked. "Captain, did you ever see anything like this?"

"Not often, but it's better than what I could've hoped for," said Hunter, studying the disabled flight with his own binocs. "They'll be paralyzed until either the leader explodes or finishes its run through its logic tree. We'll be long gone by then!"

The heavy air suddenly became filled with the thump of rotorblades and the growl of noise-suppressed turbines. Leaping over the plateau's far edge, the sharklike CFAH-3 Cutlass bore down on the squad like a predator homing in on prey. Its camouflage pattern of green, black, and yellow made it difficult to track against the desert background, until it slowed and briefly reared into the air.

From their streamlined recesses the helicopter's main

landing skids extended to a preselected length. When it set down, it did not raise the choking cloud of sand it had done earlier on the valley floor. Almost at once the squad was up and running for it. They dragged what they could not carry, and when they reached the helicopter, they found the main cabin doors at exactly the proper height for easy entry.

"What happened to Dirk?" said the cabin's lone occupant, Military Advisor Lynn Sutter. She moved to one of the open hatches and helped drag Bamble's limp body inside.

"He ran into something solid!" Hunter answered, sliding into the cabin next. "C'mon, let's hurry it up! This cab's got a fast meter!"

In seconds the nearly empty cabin was filled with sand, exhausted soldiers, and their battered equipment. As the hatches rolled shut, the sand and rotorwash ended, but not the noise. There were still the turbines, and now the shouting became more audible.

"You gonna help me lock Bamble's harness or not?" asked Corporal David Redfield, Halston's weapons' assistant.

"What do you think?" said Halston. "Let 'im bounce around a little. He won't feel it."

"Julia, this is Mitch," said Hunter, plugging his headset into a cabin intercom link. "Nail those Sky Witches before they get their act together."

"We copy," said Lieutenant Julia Alverez, pushing the throttle levers forward. "You got 'em, Jefferson?"

"Locking targets into the Autofire system," replied the sergeant in the gunship's first cockpit. Jefferson Taylor touched each of the hostile symbols on his tactical screen and switched his forward turret to computer control. "Just give me some altitude and I'll dust them."

A burst of power lifted the Cutlass off the ground, and as Julia swung it to the left, the nose-mounted Gatling gun instantly began tracking the still-hovering Sky Witches. The turret stopped just long enough on each to unleash a burst of several dozen 20mm shells. They were just enough to critically damage the robot helicopters, only the last of which had started to maneuver before being raked with fire. In seconds the entire flight was spiraling out of control. The last to go down was the leader, its damage control program having finally run its course.

"Lieutenant, we're being laser tracked," Taylor continued. "It's that other flight. They're going to launch missiles."

"Decoy 'em," said Alverez. "I'm taking us to the deck."

Its landing skids retracted, the Cutlass accelerated rapidly toward the plateau's southern edge. Just as it crossed it, a series of white-hot flares were ejected from either side of the machine. They burned intensely enough to attract the short-range, infrared guided missiles unleashed by the second flight of Cybertronic aircraft. They were still exploding while Alverez was leveling off just above the valley floor.

"They're still after us," said Hunter after the cabin's roof-mounted tactical terminal had been rolled down its track to him. On its screen he could see a tactical map of the area, with the Cutlass and the Sky Witches moving erratically across it. "And they got more forces joining in. Where the hell's our Air Force?"

"Probably still waiting around the frontier," Venneti offered. "If we'd climb, they'd have to spot us and step in."

"We can't do that with these drone ships after us." Hunter had since changed the screen to the gun-sight camera for the aft turret. After switching between its view and the tactical map, he activated his headset link. "Julia, this is Mitch. Take the side canyon on the right. Arm cluster bombs. Set dispersal altitude for one hundred meters. Set dispersal pattern for maximum spread. Set detonation time for impact plus ten seconds."

To confuse the pursuing robots, Alverez had kept her ship on the deck and gracefully S-turned it, raising a pall of fine sand behind it, effectively obscuring their optical and infrared aiming systems. It took them several seconds to realize the Cutlass had broken hard to the right—enough time for the Capitol Fast Attack Helicopter to enter a smaller auxiliary valley.

"Lieutenant, here they come," said Taylor, watching a swarm of dark specks appear on one of his screens. "Range, four thousand meters."

"Have you programmed the cluster bombs?" said Alverez, glancing at the same tail camera view.

"Roger, when do we drop them?"

"I'll find out. Mitch, this is Julia. When do you want the fireworks?"

"Soon, when the width of the valley approximates the dispersal pattern for the bomblets," Hunter replied, surfing rapidly between the tactical map, weapons' data, and various external camera views. "I'll let you know when that happens."

"Captain, the Cluster Bomb Dispenser is an antivehicle, antipersonnel weapon," said Lynn Sutter, trying to stop her unconscious teammate from bouncing out of his seat. "How will you use it to bring down airplanes?"

"Not directly. But if we throw enough trouble at those drones, we'll defeat their logic trees. I just—"

A sharp explosion deadened all other noises in the main cabin, except for Sutter's screaming. The helicopter lurched sharply to one side, then climbed as Alverez compensated. A more familiar chattering quickly followed; Taylor was returning fire with the aft turret.

"I was going to say I hope we can do it before the drones close to cannon range," Hunter continued, before checking again on what the terminal showed. "A few more hits like that and they'll penetrate our armor."

"Mitch, this is Julia. If we're gonna spring your trap, we better do it soon," said Alverez. "This is a box canyon, and its sides are getting mighty steep."

"I know. Just stay with me a few more seconds."

"A few more seconds he says," Taylor remarked while he snapped out short bursts with the 15mm tail gun. "I hate this kind of flying. Lieutenant, I hope you know we'll have to climb to get above the bomb dispersal pattern."

"I do," said Alverez, twisting the gunship across the increasingly narrow canyon floor. "C'mon, Mitch. I don't like this kind of flying either."

"Now, Julia, now! Up and to the left! Eject weapons and keep firing that tail gun!"

Hunter was still giving his orders when the Cutlass reared onto its tail and swung to the canyon's southern wall. An instant later the two gray pods on its outboard wing racks were kicked away by the ejectors. They barely had time to unfold their stabilizing fins and clear the ship before compressed gas charges ripped them open. Freed from more than half a ton of ordnance, the CFAH-3 leaped out of the canyon as hundreds of bomblets scattered across its floor.

In place of short bursts, Taylor hosed the pursuing Sky Witches with a continuous stream of armor-piercing and explosive-tipped shells. Their delicate rotor heads suddenly vulnerable, the drones immediately began jinxing more erratically. Two collided, and their fireball was still expanding when the formation reached the freshly sown carpet of bomblets.

They detonated in a surging wave of explosions, filling the canyon with shrapnel, more clouds of sand, and countless shock waves. All the while more shells continued to be sprayed from the retreating Cutlass, and collision debris started to rain down. The surviving drones did not remain so for long.

Their programming overwhelmed by so many threats at once, they either crashed into the ground, the canyon walls, or each other. The Capitol gunship hovered just beyond the canyon rim, waiting for any to appear. When all it was greeted with were rising columns of smoke, it turned once again to the south and increased speed.

"Is that it, Captain? Are we in the clear?" asked Halston.

"Not yet. We're still eighty kilometers from our own frontier," said Hunter, switching back to the tactical map.

"Julia, this is Mitch. Keep us low. They may not be pursuing us, but Cybertronic can still track us."

"Will do. Though I don't think they'll be paying much attention to us," Alverez replied. "Take a look at the incoming data traffic. The Air Force has finally decided to show up."

With a few strokes of the terminal's keyboard Hunter increased the map's scale until it included the frontier line. Crossing it were formations of symbols he recognized as standing for Capitol fighters and attack bombers. There were several dozen of them, moving at different speeds and altitudes, and appearing like a major strike force. In place of the gunship, they now received the lion's share of Cybertronic's attention, as evidenced by the terminal's tactical readouts on missile battery status, radar operating modes, and the movements of airborne Cybertronic aircraft.

"So long as we don't attract attention to ourselves, we'll be across the frontier in thirty-five minutes," said Hunter, rotating the overhead terminal for Sutter to see.

"And about five minutes after that, we'll be landing at our designated forward base," she said, "where you'll be refueled, and Dirk and I will send our reports up the line. I have to tell you, Captain, that some of the things you did were highly unorthodox, and I'll have to report them. I must also report what happened to Dirk. I doubt he'll say he ran into something."

"This sounds familiar," Parker noted, a resigned tone in her voice. "We've been successful in our mission, and we're in trouble again. When is this going to end?"

"When they stop assigning military advisors to operational units," said Venneti, growing angry. "We don't need someone looking over our shoulders all the time and quoting us corporate protocol."

"All right, Sergeant. Don't get worked up," said Hunter. "You might say something that'll have to be 'reported up the line.' Let's just wait until we reach the forward base before we start worrying or griping over what kind of trouble we're in."

CHAPTER TWO

"Thank you, Mr. Bamble, Ms. Sutter," replied Senior Military Advisor Calvin Hart. "I expect full reports from both of you later. Especially with regard to Captain Hunter's tactics and behavior. Good day."

The diminutive civilian waited until his subordinates acknowledged his sign-off before he ended the video link with the Capitol forward base. The scene on the monitors of the spartan base and its hot, dusty environment contrasted sharply with the room Hart stood in. Its lighting was subdued, not blinding, and its air-conditioning allowed everyone to work in their uniforms without sweating through them.

"I wonder, what drugs did they give your advisor?" Colonel Rebecca Vardon said absently; she could not help the sly smile crossing her face. Fortunately, the subdued lighting helped hide it. "From the way Mr. Bamble was talking, I'm not sure he even knew what planet he was on."

"All right, Colonel. Don't try that flippant attitude on me," Hart continued, turning to the command officers standing behind him. "General, do something about her."

"Sorry, Mr. Hart. You can't *make* Special Forces respect you," said Brigadier General Richard Cyrus, district Army commander. "And in my father's time the regular Army learned not to try controlling the Special Forces. You have to earn their respect."

"My position should earn their respect. Colonel, this is a serious matter. Even if it doesn't concern the Air Force, I would like your attention on it."

"Yes, Mr. Hart. I'm sorry," said Colonel David Joel, the district's Air Force commander. He immediately swung away from the air defense/surveillance consoles he had been called to and returned to Hart's conference. "But we had a brief appearance of what we think were aircraft. We detected them moving along the boundary line between us and District Landis."

"Then inform them of your sighting and let them deal with it. We have a serious problem of insubordination here, and I'd like everyone's attention."

"I hardly think you need Colonel Joel's participation," Vardon observed, her smile disappearing. "The Air Force part of this operation was the diversion and nothing more."

"Wrong, Colonel," said Hart, moving over to the one commander he could look in the eye. "You may think of Lieutenant Alverez and her navigator as your people, but they were reassigned from the Air Force's Silent Vengeance units on Mars. Should it prove necessary, I can advise they be returned there."

"I don't know if their original units would want them back. You have to be a real troublemaker in order to be seconded out of Silent Vengeance," Joel said incautiously. A withering look from Hart caused him to cut short his reply and retreat.

"I don't believe the incident, if there was one, is serious enough to warrant a transfer," said General Cyrus, stepping into the conversation. "Or any major disciplinary action. Until we learn otherwise, we should accept Captain Hunter's explanation of what happened to Mr. Bamble's SatCom transceiver and his injuries."

"You seem more interested in these side issues than in the results of the operation," Vardon added. "May I remind you that the observation post Hunter's squad destroyed was very different from anything else Cybertronic has ever deployed. It could've served as a hub for a new command and control net—something that would've allowed them to launch an offensive against us."

"I'm well aware of the post's military significance," said Hart. "I wish you would be equally aware of the significance good discipline and respect for corporate protocol plays in a smooth functioning military . . . Colonel, will you get back here. I insist on your undistracted attention; those transient aircraft are someone else's concern."

"I'm growing tired of this tour, Echmeriaz," Ragathol told one of his newly assigned necromutants. "I know well the construction of our Citadels, and this one isn't even mine . . ."

"Your tour is almost at an end, Master," said Echmeriaz, avoiding Ragathol's glare when their eyes met. "This is your residence."

The high-ceilinged hallway was dimly illuminated, and vibrated softly from the dark technology labs and weapon production rooms below it. Ragathol was at the head of his entourage and nearly walked past the tunnellike door his chief necromutant had motioned to. Just inside it was an antechamber where most of the entourage waited. Only Echmeriaz accompanied him into the Nether Room itself.

"We constructed it while you were in transit from Luna," Echmeriaz explained while his Master walked to the room's center. "We had to rush its completion. We all hope it meets your approval."

"Its construction does not show it was hurried," said Ragathol, smiling. "And it's in perfect alignment with the forces of the Dark Symmetry."

The nepharite stood in the middle of the domed room, his legs spread and his arms, with some difficulty, raised to its apex. His smile became a soft, confident laugh, and the exposed areas of his skin glowed dimly with an electric green light. The glow ended when he moved out of the stance he took.

"I can feel the strength of those forces," he continued, "their purity. They will help heal me . . . Yes, by what reason do you violate the sanctity of my residence?"

"I bring you good news, my Master," said the necromutant appearing behind Echmeriaz. "Our heretics have found the human female, the Receptacle of Visions. She's on a special floor of a medical dispensary at a Capitol District Base called Roswell."

"Roswell? Is this near the spaceport where she returned to her home planet?"

"It is, Master. The heretics report the floor the Receptacle is on has high security, but she can be taken."

"Of course she will," said Ragathol, a little anger showing through his serenity. "Echmeriaz, ready a plan for her immediate abduction. Let me rest now. And when I arise, I'll want to review those plans."

* * *

"Captain, this is Julia. Our ETA to Roswell is twenty minutes," said Alverez, responding to a question from those in the gunship's main cabin. "We're just entering its air traffic management zone."

"Thanks, Julia. Let me know when we begin our preliminary descent," Hunter answered. "All right, we got enough time to go over our stories for the debriefing crew."

"I think we could better use our time considering employment outside of Special Forces," said Diane Parker, glancing out the port hatch at the passing landscape. It had grown progressively less desertlike and more tropical since the gunship's departure from the forward base.

"What? You don't mean going back to the regular Army, do you?" said Halston, incredulous. "Give up all this fun for monotony, poor leadership, and bad weapons? Not me."

"No, Ted. I don't mean the Army."

"The Air Force?"

"I mean cutting free of the military entirely and going free-lance," Diane replied hesitantly. She got the surprised looks she expected, from everyone except Hunter. "Captain, you got friends who've done it. Tim Small left Security and then there are those Martian Banshees."

"I know it's frustrating to deal with behind-the-line-chain-snappers like Calvin," said Hunter. "But I tried free-lancing once and didn't like it. If you like regular paychecks, good medical care, and good food you won't like it either."

"But Tim's already got a detective agency set up. He could provide us with a base for operations, and Wendy'll take care of us."

"Don't get caught in the romance of being a free-lance mercenary. It isn't what they show in the movies. Pam Afton and Lane Chung spend most of their time at the Midnight Star, hoping to snag a contract. If you're desperate, and you usually are, you'll work for anyone. Imperial, Bauhaus, the Brotherhood, even Mishima."

"Forget that," snapped Shacker, waving a hand at Parker and those who were nodding in agreement with her. "I'm not working for no slants. I'll go hungry before I do that."

"And Lane would tell you, if you're hungry enough, you'll work for anybody," said Hunter, getting a faraway look in his eye as he thought about distant friends. "I must admit, after the problems Stutter and Bungle have given us,

I've had passing thoughts about being a free-lancer again. And I've let them pass right on by."

"I hate to interrupt your future employment seminar," said Alverez. "But something strange is happening at Roswell."

"Something strange is always happening at Roswell," grumbled Venneti. "I think that's why we were assigned there in the first place."

"No, this is ominous-type strange. The automated air traffic management net just went down. The emergency hasn't booted in yet, and I can't raise anyone at the tower."

"Take us to the deck," said Hunter, his daydream abruptly ending. "Now. Don't worry about getting permission or violating air traffic rules. Everyone get your headsets back on."

"It's easier to ask for forgiveness than get permission," said Alverez. "Here we go."

Those who had released their restraint harnesses were just relocking them when the Cutlass dropped its nose and fell out of the sky. The dive's acceleration held everyone in mid-air, pulling them against their straps, until the gunship leveled off and everyone crunched back into their seats.

"Switching air surveillance and terrain-following radar to Discreet mode," said Taylor, his hands flying over the myriad of knobs and switches in his cockpit. "Fire control system, activated. Weapons, armed. You know, we don't have a lot left."

"Believe me, I know," Alverez replied as she glanced at the changing status lights on her own instrument panels. "I asked them to rearm us at the base and they refused. Seems as though the corporation wants only heavily armed aircraft near the frontier."

"Yeah, we're not fighting anybody. Lieutenant, smoke at ten. Looks like we got us a crash."

By the time Alverez caught it, the dissipating plume of black smoke was off her port wing. She was forced to climb and double-back to reach the crash site, located in a grove of fruit trees. Upon reaching it, she circled the area slowly at five hundred feet to give everyone in the main cabin a good view.

"Captain, look. Over there," said Halston, pointing at a more distant pillar of smoke as it slid into view. "What gives?"

"Captain, that looks like the remains of a Grendel attack chopper down there," Alverez added. "And from the way those civilians are signaling, I don't think its pilot survived."

"Those helicopters usually patrol in two-ship teams," said Wendy. "You think they collided?"

"If there had been a midair, they'd be closer together," Hunter finally said. "Taylor, you picking up any crash locator beacons?"

"No, sir. Nothing on the emergency frequencies," the sergeant answered.

"Then these two were shot down, and some kind of jammer dropped in the area."

"Are you saying an attack is happening?" Lieutenant Rogers asked. "Why aren't we getting an alert transmit?"

"It's a commando operation," said Hunter. "And from the feel of it, a pretty big one."

"You may be right, Mitch," said Alverez. "I just got a garbled message about the base and main hospital being attacked."

"Julia, get us in there. Everyone, arm your weapons and attach safety lines. Ted, ready that hatch mount."

The Cutlass orbited the first crash site one more time before breaking to the east and diving for the deck again. Alverez increased its speed, and in minutes the landscape changed from farmland and scattered buildings to a neatly organized small city. Except for the military base at its outskirts, the largest buildings were at its center. Around them could be seen orbiting groups of helicopters.

"We got Python One Hundreds and Long Rider fast transports," said Alverez, reading off the attacking helicopter types on the tactical screen.

"Yes, this is a Bauhaus operation," Hunter added, glancing at the same information on his terminal. "And they appear to be gathered around the hospital. They've hardly touched the base except to destroy flight-ready aircraft."

"This is more than I'd care to take on. What do you want me to do, Captain?"

"Think of it as a target-rich environment. Take out as many ships as you can with missiles and get us in close, where smart weapons won't be of much use."

"Roger. Switching fire control system to missiles," said

Julia, tapping one of the largest switches on her armaments panel. "Jeff, let's designate some targets."

On the tips of the gunship's stub wings were pairs of ten-foot-long tubes. Each tube contained a Sidewinder CX missile, and once their seeker heads had locked onto their designated targets, all were launched. As they broke through the transparent nose caps, their control fins unfolded and they immediately veered off to the individual Bauhaus helicopters.

They crossed a dozen miles in seconds and were closing to proximity range before most could react. Three of the missiles exploded beside or behind their targets, bringing down two Python gunships and a Long Rider transport. The third targeted Python managed to eject a series of flares in time to decoy the missile burning across the sky toward it. By the time it swung around to locate and face its attacker, the Cutlass was entering the canyons of the city center.

"Didn't we just do this?" said Taylor as he armed both of his turrets.

"Yes, and if anything this'll be more dangerous," said Alverez. "Mitch, this is Julia. Are you ready back there?"

"We're ready," Hunter answered, doing a final check of his safety line. "Now remember, only those at the hatches are to do any talking. All right, open 'em up!"

The moment the side hatches cracked open, the main cabin was filled with noise and cyclone-force winds. Halston and Shacker swung the port and starboard gun mounts into position and clicked the safeties off their weapons. Even though Shacker's SR-50 was a sniper's rifle, it fired the same rounds as Halston's machine gun and had been loaded with an extended clip.

"You got the rocket pods, I got the turrets," said Taylor.

"Roger. Mitch, Long Rider coming up on starboard side," said Alverez. "I'm going after a Python."

The sleek transport stayed in Shacker's field of fire for only a few seconds; still, he managed to squeeze off half a dozen rounds, and Venneti added a full clip from his Liche assault rifle. However, they had little apparent effect on the helicopter, except to force it into evasive maneuvers.

Alverez and Taylor had better luck with the Bauhaus gunship. Momentarily frozen by the destruction of its leader, the second aircraft of the element did not react until it was raked by a burst of 20mm cannon fire. Damaged, it pivoted rapidly to bring its own turreted cannon to bear on its attacker, giving Alverez a perfect broadside silhouette to launch a volley of two-inch-high velocity rockets against.

The first two hissed past their target, missing it by a few feet. The third rocket exploded at the juncture between the Python's fuselage and its streamlined tail boom. The fourth blew off its port landing gear pod, and the fifth hit the port engine housing. The turbine disintegrated instantly, causing the aircraft to shudder violently enough to snap off the weakened tail boom. Alverez leaped her gunship over the doomed, rapidly spiraling, machine and dove behind the hospital's opposite side.

"God, it looks like they really wasted Security," Taylor exclaimed when he noticed the wrecked police cars and light armored vehicles scattered along the street in front of the hospital's entrance. "Who would they want that badly in this place?"

"Julia, this is Mitch. Python closing on our port side!"

The gunship that escaped destruction earlier was hurtling up the canyon formed by the hospital complex and the buildings facing it. The last of the machine's dual-purpose missiles burned off its launch rail and homed on the laser light reflecting off the Cutlass.

"We're being laser-scanned!" said Taylor, reaching for his ECM panel. "Firing smoke rounds!"

"Keep firing! Maybe we'll distract the gunner!" Hunter ordered, changing clips on his rifle.

Halston's machine gun scarcely let up its heavy chatter and kept scoring hits until the ECM mortars next to the hatch fired their salvo. The shells scarcely arced a dozen yards before exploding into oily black clouds of chemical smoke. They effectively blinded the laser designation and homing systems. Even so, the missile barely missed the Cutlass, shooting under the rapidly ascending helicopter. And the moment it cleared the smoke curtain of its own creation, Alverez was launching another salvo of rockets.

"Take it easy on those, Lieutenant," Taylor warned. "We don't have many left."

"We don't have much left of anything," said Alverez, glancing at her own weapon status screen. "Where did he go?"

"Starboard side! Evasive! Evasive!"

Alverez reacted on Taylor's words; only later did she see the dark blur streak past her machine's right side. Its nose cannon flared brightly, but the two aircraft were too close for it to score anything except a few hits along the tail boom.

"Damn! That pilot had blond hair and blue eyes!" Shacker exclaimed. "I could see the curls under his helmet!"

Before Diane or anyone else could challenge him, the Cutlass lurched sharply to the right and spun around. The centrifugal force generated by the maneuver had everyone in the main cabin hanging at the ends of their safety lines. Any spent shell casings and empty clips still inside it were hurtled out the hatches. By the time it ended, and the squad members were picking themselves up, the helicopter was dropping back into the canyon.

"Go ahead, Lieutenant. You got a clear shot," said Taylor, watching the Python fly up the avenue.

"I can't!" said Alverez. "The damn fire control system's fizzling! You take the shot."

"Well, get me closer. He's moving out of range."

Alverez advanced the throttles and was overtaking the Python when it cleared the city's central core buildings. As the airspace opened up, it turned hard left and climbed, hoping to catch its pursuer while it was still confined in the artificial canyon.

"I know what he's attempting," Alverez concluded. "I'd try the same thing in his position."

"What should we do?" said Taylor. "Why are we slowing down?"

"We're low on fuel, and we got less than a hundred rounds for the nose gun. Give me control of the nose turret; you watch our tail."

The Cutlass slowed to a hover, then swung around quickly. While Taylor concentrated on the aft turret, Alverez took control of the nose mount. She folded the sighting glass of her cockpit's fixed gun sight, then flipped down the sighting eye piece mounted on her helmet. By the time she had full operation of the turret, the Python had reappeared.

"It's gonna be a difficult shot, sir," said Taylor, glancing up from his CRT screen. "You got lots of smoke in the background. Maybe you should try laser targeting?"

"It's too late," said Julia. "I'll go with what I got."

The black-and-green helicopter blended in too easily with the landscape of dark smoke building in the city center. Alverez was unable to accurately track it, and the bursts she fired were too long in duration. By the time it was lining up on her ship, she had run out of ammunition.

"Lieutenant, what are you doing?" Taylor asked when he noticed the Gatling gun's cluster of barrels being raised. Then a warning light flashed on his weapon status screen. "You just jettisoned the rocket pods!"

"If we can't use them, why keep 'em?" said Alverez. "It'll lighten our girl, and maybe we can avoid being shot down awhile longer. I'll wait until the last second before breaking left."

The final seconds of the Python's attack run never came. After the Cutlass dropped its rocket pods, the Bauhaus gunship visibly slowed and raised its own nose gun. It continued to slow until it came to a hover, a few dozen yards in front of the Capitol ship.

Its jagged, splintered, camouflage pattern of dark green and black was readily seen, as was all the service stenciling and an incongruity—a painting of a small, red airplane with three wings under the pilot's cockpit. For a moment he and Alverez exchanged glances; then he saluted her and lifted his gunship out of the canyon.

"Now that the damnedest thing I've ever seen," Taylor finally remarked.

"Not for me," said Hunter, switching his tactical terminal to a nose camera view. "Some of the Mishima elite forces on Mars believe in the code of the Bushido. They will not kill a helpless adversary."

"Since when do the slants have a code of honor?" Shacker asked, lifting his rifle off the door mount as the hatch rolled shut.

"A few of them do, and this Bauhaus pilot obviously does. And it was a good idea for him to leave now. Our surveillance radar indicates the rest of his strike force is withdrawing."

"We gonna chase 'em down, Captain?" asked Halston, loading the last belt of ammunition into his M606.

"And do what?" said Hunter. "Hope they'll fly up our tail so we can shoot them down? We'd probably run out of fuel before we overtook them. Julia, this is Mitch. Are we cleared to land at the base or not?"

"They're just clearing us," Alverez responded. "And they want us to land at the Security Forces hangar, for questioning."

"Not at the Special Forces hangar?" asked Venneti. "What're they doing to us?"

"Whatever it is, it's not good," said Hunter. "Note we're going to be 'questioned', not 'debriefed'. Something tells me the rest of this day will be a lot harder than the beginning."

CHAPTER THREE

"First to leave, last to return," remarked Colonel Rolf Kriegler, running through various calculations on a hand-held computer. "According to this, he ran out of fuel a minute, forty-five seconds ago."

"Did you factor in single-engine flight?" said the strikingly beautiful woman standing next to the base commander. First Lieutenant Anna Lindholm smiled as she talked, but it did not hide her anxiety.

"I'm well aware of your friend's tricks. I figured in single-engine operation. He's been out of fuel now for two minutes."

"Then declare an emergency. Activate our own radar and send out the rescue ships. We know what his bearing was from the last base up the line. We have to—"

"Do nothing," Kriegler completed. "As my security officer you're well aware of our mission orders. We're to maintain complete electronic emission control until new orders are received. We didn't communicate with our aircraft when they left, we can't as they return."

"Colonel, we have something on the motion scanners," said the base Air Defense officer. He emerged from his control center near the base's flight line and approached the group of officers waiting beside the newly returned helicopters. "An aircraft, at high-altitude and descending. These storms are interfering with our optical systems. We won't be able to identify until it's almost on top of us."

"What about its infrared signature? Maybe you can't identify the individual ship, but you can tell its type."

"I'm sorry, we can't. The approaching aircraft has no infrared signature. It's like a glider."

"Put your defenses on alert," said Kriegler. "We may have a Capitol scout ship."

"No. It's him," said Lindholm, smiling again. "It's Maximilian."

An anxious minute later, a Python helicopter dropped through the cloud deck of the storm front advancing on the Bauhaus jungle base. Except for the armed hovercraft and other gunships sitting on its hangar apron, Base Aquila looked like a civilian research station set deep in the Venusian jungle territory controlled by Bauhaus. Most of its other military equipment was hidden either in its buildings or in the surrounding rain forest. Its active missile launchers and air defense guns tracked the helicopter until it could be visually identified.

The only sound the Python made on its approach was the whisper of its main rotor windmilling. Its sink rate appeared dangerously high, until the last hundred feet, when it pitched up and flared out. With a solid thump the autorotating helicopter hit the base's manicured flying field. Its main wheel struts were compressed fully, and the wheels themselves were almost buried in the turf. By the time the rescue vehicles and base personnel reached the gunship, its pilot was climbing down from the command cockpit.

"I knew it was you!" Lindholm shouted, rushing into his arms and embracing him. "Why were you the last to leave the target?"

"I had to hold off the one serious threat to our mission," said Capitaine Max Steiner, releasing Anna and stripping off his helmet. His long hair matted with sweat, it stuck to his neck and forehead, though it still managed to curl. "We lost four aircraft, three of them gunships, to a lone Capitol Special Forces Cutlass. Its crew was good; our only serious losses were to them. And we would've lost more, had they not run out of ammunition."

"So we heard, Capitaine," said a civilian, using Steiner's rank. Olton Pearson wore no rank insignia on his white jacket, except for the gold Bauhaus emblems on its lapels. The military personnel swarming over the gunship gave him a wide berth as he walked up to Steiner and Lindholm. "Our agents in Roswell transmitted a curious report. That you ended combat when you could've destroyed this ship, and departed after saluting its crew."

"They were helpless, Mr. Administrator. I'll not wantonly kill such soldiers. And by occupying their attention, I achieved the same goal as I would have by killing them. The remainder of our strike was able to successfully withdraw— not only from Roswell, but across Capitol lines as well."

"And you nearly lost your own machine for this act of chivalry. You're no doubt an excellent pilot, but I question your tactical ability in light of your adherence to such ideals."

"And I question the tactical need for this entire mission," Steiner countered, his eyes narrowing, as if he were looking through a weapon aiming system. "We lost those planes and all those people, for what? To kidnap a lone mental patient of no apparent stature with us or Capitol?"

"Maximilian, this is best discussed later," said Lindholm, stepping between the two antagonists, "at your debriefing."

"No, Anna. This question won't be answered later. I've been at enough debriefings to know what happens. I want this question answered now."

"If you were any other pilot, I'd have you relieved of duty for making such a demand," said Pearson. "But I'm aware of your connections with corporate board members. So you'd learn this soon anyway. Come."

Pearson motioned for Lindholm and Steiner to walk with him to the base's flight operations building. They were joined by Kriegler, and while there were personnel running around them, they were largely left alone.

"That woman, Lorraine Kovan, is the most important nobody amongst our populated worlds," Pearson continued, involuntarily glancing over at the base's small hospital. "She may be the only human to have been captured by the Dark Legion and escape relatively intact."

"What? Them? Those ghosts the Rangers keep claiming they're fighting?" said Steiner, incredulous. "We risk starting a war with the only MegaCorp that can defeat us, for some mental patient who claims she was kidnapped by ghosts?"

"She claims nothing," said Kriegler, already breathing heavily and sweating in his effort to keep up with the others. "Doctor Reissner told us she's virtually comatose. It'll be some time before she tells us anything."

"What we know about her was gathered by Intelligence," Lindholm added. "She may be the only survivor of a Dark Legion attack on a Capitol settlement here. On Luna she was

rescued by an elite team of mercenaries working for Mishima. For some reason they sent her back here where Capitol Security picked her up at their Atlantis spaceport. That
was ten days ago; now we have her."

"What next? Will Imperial or the Brotherhood steal her
from us?" said Steiner, still incredulous. "I know several
members of our Duke Elector families. And they're openly
disdainful of this 'Dark Legion'. They believe it's some deception the Brotherhood's using to gain control over us."

"In the past the Duke Electors and the board has been disdainful of *any* external threat to us. That attitude has cost us
greatly, and now at last it's changing. Our Rangers have
fought too many skirmishes with this shadowy Legion for its
threat to be dismissed any longer. We must be ready to accept any risk and make any sacrifice to stop it."

"If anyone but you had told me this, I wouldn't believe
it," Steiner admitted, catching Anna's hand and getting her
to look him in the eye. "Perhaps this Legion is real and dangerous enough to be taken seriously. I only wish we had a
better way to get information than attack Capitol for it."

"Now wait just a damn minute," Hunter responded
sharply. "Accusing us of interfering with these two is one
thing. Accusing us of failure to stop the Bauhaus attack is
another game, and we're not playing it."

Hunter briefly pointed across the black polished table at
Sutter and Bamble. Washed and dressed in fresh gray suits,
they hardly looked as if they had spent any time in the desert. By contrast Hunter and his squad still wore their dusty,
sweat-stained fatigues. In the hours since the debriefing began, piles of fine sand had collected on the squad's side of
the table. A small puff of sand lifted off its surface when
Hunter dropped his hand.

"If you'll recall, you specifically ordered my ship not be
rearmed after I requested it," said Alverez, picking up the attack the moment Hunter stopped. "We would've at least had
full munitions loads for my ship."

"If you'll recall, 'Mr. Hart,' " Hart corrected. "This session is being recorded, I insist you use correct protocol."

"Protocol . . . here we go again," muttered Venneti. "How
I hate debriefings."

"Yes, Sergeant. You have something to add?"

"Yeah, Calvin, I got something. You may want everyone else to think of you as 'Mr. Hart', but to us you'll always be Calvin."

"Captain, control your men. We've had it with their cheap cracks," Bamble said angrily. His rage built until he snapped the pen he'd been bending, its ink running all over his hands.

"Hey, Bungle, we sure named you correctly," said Shacker. "What're you gonna do next? Chew on a shoe?"

"You call this is a Special Forces unit?" Hart questioned. "Captain, this is insubordination. It's contempt for authority."

"Well, maybe if this were a *real* debriefing and not an interrogation, you wouldn't have this problem," said Hunter. "We executed our mission successfully, and we were the only ones to provide any effective opposition to the Bauhaus attack. I'd like to know how they could get this far inside our own territory without being picked up on our defense net."

"For a time they flew along the boundary between our district and District Landis," said Rebecca Vardon, deciding to join in instead of merely enjoying the fight. "However, at our battle station we had some administrative troubles and were unable to coordinate with Lucas."

"Colonel, I warn you. If you think you can blame this attack and the loss of a valuable asset on our earlier discussion, you're mistaken," Hart said defensively.

"What do you mean 'our' discussion? As I recall, it was mostly your tirade over Captain Hunter's actions on the mission."

"Now I know where your soldiers get their insubordination. It comes from the top down instead of the bottom up. Your example and Hunter's are detrimental to good discipline."

"Mr. Hart, please. This line of questioning is pointless. And as Captain Hunter would say, this should be a debriefing, not an interrogation."

The remark caused everyone at the table to stop and look toward its source. Lighting in the room was kept low everywhere except directly over the table. The figure who prowled the shadows around it had been there since shortly after the debriefing began. Until now it had not spoken, and

the light beyond the table was so dim Hunter could not tell
if the figure was a man or a woman. The deep, masculine
voice that grabbed everyone's attention resolved that question; but the man behind it refused to step out of the shadows and reveal himself.

"Too little has been said about your actions during the
Bauhaus attack," he continued. "You showed great skill and
courage, Captain. A more cautious man would've stayed out
of the battle entirely. A more reckless one would've charged
in with weapons blazing and no battle plan. You showed an
excellent combination of aggressiveness and skill."

"The rest of my people did their jobs well," said Hunter,
squirming uncomfortably at being the object of so much
praise. "I only wish I had asked for external fuel tanks when
we were at the forward base."

"You also share the results of your success with your men
and accept full responsibility for any failure your unit
makes." The shadow man paced back and forth behind Hart,
the other advisors and military officers lining one side of the
table. He was close enough for the soft crunch of his shoes
on the room's carpet to be heard. Even so, very little of his
features could be seen. "Excellent. Very professional."

"If it wouldn't be too much to ask ... Could you tell us
something about this asset Bauhaus kidnapped? We heard it
was a female patient at the hospital. It's very unusual for
Bauhaus, or any other Megacorporation, to mount a kidnap
operation on this scale."

"That, Captain, would be telling too much. At least for
now. Gentlemen, I think this debriefing has run its course.
These soldiers are tired and deserve a well-earned rest."

"Yes, sir," Hart said quickly, first looking over his shoulder; then he turned to face Hunter. "Captain, we'll have dis-
cussions about these matters later. For now you're
dismissed."

"Good afternoon, Captain," the shadow man added as the
squad rose from their seats. "I believe we'll meet again."

Hunter had only enough time to say a quick thank you before Capitol Security guards escorted him and his squad out
of the room. When the main door slid shut behind them, the
room's lighting was increased and the man at last came out
of the shadows to take one of the recently vacated seats.

"Mr. Wood, I really would've liked to continue this debriefing for a while longer," said Hart. "We need to hear much more about what went on."

"And I've heard enough," said Noah Wood. He did not wear a military uniform or an advisor's light gray suit. Instead he wore a dark blue suit, matching tie, and white shirt. Out of place for the semiarid, semitropical climate of Roswell, but the accepted dress for a major stockholder on Capitol's board of directors. "That squad is probably the best small unit in Special Forces service. They're experienced, unorthodox, and aggressive—behind both enemy lines and, apparently, our own."

"Mr. Wood, they need to learn more discipline, respect for authority, and corporate protocol. Surely a man who's risen so quickly to a position like yours will understand this."

"I understand that in our past the maverick has accomplished more than the conformist."

"Yes, Mr. Wood. But we don't live in the past," Hart instructed, trying not to make it sound like a criticism. "We live in the present and build for the future."

"I understand that as well," said Wood, his voice growing sharp. "Who do you think reviews and approves of the corporate line in the first place? I now believe if we're to have a future at all, we must entrust it to people like those who built our past."

"Mr. Wood, as Captain Hunter's superior, what would you like me to do with him?" Rebecca asked. Unlike Hart, she met his gaze instead of trying to avoid it. "The charges before us are serious enough to have him taken off duty, even relieved of command."

"Quite right. But the situation we face is serious enough for him to be kept on duty and his squad to be given a new assignment. I want them on the rescue of the kidnapped VIP."

"Mr. Wood, please. You would only be rewarding their insubordination," said Hart, for the moment gaining enough courage to challenge the decision.

"I fail to see where giving these soldiers an even more dangerous assignment is a reward for them?" said Wood, a puzzled look on his face. "I'm not sending them to a seaside resort or some pleasure house in the Athena metropolis. This mission will take them into the heart of Bauhaus territory. Chances they'll all return from it are slim. My decision stands. General, Colonel Vardon, see that it's carried out. I'll get on to our Intelligence and Strategic Reconnaissance services to track down where this raiding force fled to."

"Hey, the shadow guy was right," said Venneti, the first member of the squad to step outside the operations center. "It is afternoon."

"Yes, midafternoon by the feel of the heat," Hunter added before he checked his watch. "A shame we're not near the ocean, I could use a swim."

"Who do you think that man was?" asked Alverez, quickly slipping on her aviator sunglasses. "I say he's some corporate VIP, way up the line."

"Yeah, did you see the way Calvin jumped at his word?" Shacker remarked. "He sure got his chain snapped. I bet he's a board member, maybe even a stockholder ... Hey, why you all looking at me like that?"

"Because everyone knows there ain't no stockholder who's ever gonna visit this place," said Corporal Mark Harris, Venneti's assistant and the youngest member of the squad. "They all stay on Mars or Luna. And when they come to Venus, the closest they ever get to Roswell is when they land at Atlantis."

"Whoever he is, he's certainly powerful," said Hunter. "And he's not military. He was civil to Calvin and could hardly care less about what he thought."

"Whereas we constantly insult Calvin, but eventually have to do what he demands," said Alverez, stopping at the base of the stairs leading to the center's entrance and looking back up at Hunter. "Maybe Jake's right; maybe our friend is big time corporate. Why don't you have Tim investigate him? If anyone could do it, he can."

"Actually, I have someone else I want Tim to investigate. Someone you're all forgetting."

"Who? Bungle?" Taylor suggested, pulling off his own pair of sunglasses. "You wanna find something bad about him and blackmail the jerk?"

"No. That would be too easy," said Hunter, irritated. "The woman. Our shadow friend ended the debriefing when I asked about her. If she's important enough for Bauhaus to kidnap this way, then she must be *very* important to us, and I'd like to know why."

"So what should we do, Captain?" said Venneti.

"Go back to your quarters and get washed, get some rest, something to eat, and meet me off-base at Tim Small's apartment. We'll be able to talk freely there, and if I know Tim he'll have a lot to tell us about this morning's adventure."

CHAPTER FOUR

"How many aircraft do you think we'll need?" Ragathol asked, studying a projected map of the route the Dark Legion raiding force would take from the Citadel to deep inside Capitol territory.

"Not many, my Master. Unlike Azurwraith's original annihilation of the settlement, ours will not be a frontal attack," said Caliqabaal, sitting at the controls of the wall projection system. "It's not a demonstration of our power, but rather a demonstration of infiltration skills. We'll steal into the city, take back the woman, and return here in a single night. We won't need many aircraft, we have more than enough Capitol machines available for use, and more than enough heretics ready to help us."

"Excellent, excellent . . . Yes, what is it?" Ragathol smiled serenely at the plans being shown him, then turned to face a heretic seconds before he entered the Nether Room. Because he was unsummoned and unexpected, the human's presence irritated the nepharite, and he did not choose to hide it. "By what reason do you intrude in my most sacred residence?"

"I bear you news, Master Ragathol," the heretic said nervously. "New . . . News that will not please you."

"I will decide if the news displeases me," Ragathol snapped. "What is it?"

"The woman, the Receptacle of Visions? She's no longer at the Capitol location."

"You mean she's gone? She's been lost to us! That the humans outsmarted us!"

With each response Ragathol's anger grew, as did the electric green sparks that danced over his body. The power he generated began interfering with the projection system, and Caliqabaal hurriedly shut it down.

"You jeopardize my triumph!" Ragathol continued. "The Wrath of the Apostles be upon you!"

The moment he pointed at the heretic, Ragathol had him pinned against the wall beside the entrance. The same green sparks that first appeared on his body now covered the heretic's. They had him writhing in agony and seemingly unable to catch his breath. Were it not for the power Ragathol used to keep him pressed against the wall, he would be a twitching heap on the floor.

"Ma ... Master, please!" he managed to scream. "We ... we know who's taken her!"

"Very well ... speak," Ragathol ordered. The moment he lowered his hand the torture ended, and the heretic collapsed to the floor. For the first few, irritating, moments all he could do was gasp heavily. "I said speak! Or do you wish me to summon the Powers and rip the information from your mind?"

"No! No, Master Ragathol!" said the heretic, finding the strength to barely raise his head. "It's Bauhaus! They raided the Capitol location and took the Receptacle of Visions from them. She's now in their territory, but we don't know where."

"That will be easy to find." The anger flowed out of Ragathol, as did the sparks it generated. His mouth curled into a hellish smile, and he laughed softly. "Of all the human organizations, we've had our greatest success in corrupting and infiltrating Bauhaus. Their leadership is arrogant and believes no outside force can threaten it, human or Legion ... Caliqabaal, a change in plans. Alert those who serve us in the Bauhaus organization to hunt down where it's hiding the Receptacle of Visions. Tell them to be quick, I grow tired of these delays. You ... you have served me well, now leave my presence."

"Yes, my Master," the heretic answered, picking himself up and staggering to the entrance. There he was grabbed by several tekrons who silently carried him off.

Ragathol waited until they had all left before turning and walking to a seat in front of the wall projector. His limp was more pronounced than before, and he held his injured arm instead of just letting it hang oddly at his side. When he sat down, he virtually crashed into the seat, the heavy thud forcing Caliqabaal to notice it.

"Are you tired, my Master?" the necromutant asked hesitantly.

"I'm not as completely healed as I thought," said Ragathol. "The humans on Luna inflicted more than mere nuisance injuries on me. They interfere with my ability to use the Dark Gifts. Leave me now, I wish to rest. And when I bid for you to return, I'll expect to see new plans for stealing the Receptacle of Visions from Bauhaus."

"You should visit me more often than you do, Mitch," Tim Small tried to casually remark, though he could not hide the glee in his voice. "Especially when you bring such gifts."

He fairly sprinted to his apartment's tiny kitchen where he unwrapped the layers of plastic from the package Hunter had given him. Beneath them was a layer of heavy wax paper, and under it a mound of finely ground red meat in a Styrofoam tray. After smelling it for a moment, Small put the tray beside the sink, where he washed his hands and cleaned a few of the utensils lying in it.

"How much of that did you give him?" said Alverez, looking at the mound of fresh meat.

"A full kilo," Hunter answered, pausing when he noticed the surprised look on Alverez's face. "Why not? What we need him to do isn't just expensive, it could also be dangerous."

"There's just something about the smell of fresh hamburger that the veggieburgers and nukepatties can't ever capture," said Small. "Delicious. You know the way to my heart, Mitch. You want one?"

"We had plenty in the Officers' Mess. Enjoy yourself."

"Don't worry, I will."

Cupping a small amount of the ground beef in his hand, Small worked it first into a ball, then flattened it into a patty, and dropped it onto the skillet he had on rapid heat. The moment the hamburger landed on the hot surface it sizzled loudly, and moments later, juices began running from it.

"Leo, close that door," said Hunter. "If the rest of the people in this building smell what Tim has, they'll beat the door down for it."

"I don't think anyone in this place but Tim knows what real hamburger smells like or can afford to buy it," Venneti replied, only turning to look at the door instead of closing it. Seconds later, Redfield came through the apartment's entrance and closed it. With the exception of Rogers, the entire squad had at last arrived.

"Excellent, Mitch. It's the real McDonald," said Small, after taking the first bite of his hastily made dinner.

"It may be real, but is that healthy for you?" said Taylor, sarcastically. "Nuke Foods have replaced most of the fat in a burger with soy meal."

"Yeah, and you know why Nuke Foods packages its burgers in plastic?" Shacker added. "It's because they hope some of the plastic will rub off on them and double their nutritional value."

"It looks like you haven't used this since the last time we were here," said Hunter, examining the neural link helmet and finding a fine layer of dust on it. "You know how much this cybersuit cost us?"

"More than the computer, but I prefer doing my work the old-fashioned way," said Small, moving out of the kitchen. "At a computer keyboard. Cyberspace is for kids. Always has been, always will be. And I'm twenty years too old for it."

"So how do you expect to find anything about this mystery woman Bauhaus kidnapped?" said Alverez. "Everyone knows all the latest info is floating out there in cyberspace."

"So's a lot of rumors and false reports. It'd take forever to sort through it all. Watch closely, and I'll show you how a pro works."

Small took his well-worn seat in front of a computer as he finished his luxury hamburger. Already activated, all he had to do was stroke a few keys, and data blocks immediately began appearing on its screen. Not surprisingly, they were all from Roswell's central hospital.

"Now none of the news shows gave a name to this mystery VIP," Small continued. "And your cyberspace is filled with all sorts of fiction about her being the wife of a board member or a spy. Instead of putting up with that, I went right to the source through my favorite back door."

"The hospital's Nutrition Planning and Service Center?" asked Hunter, leaning closer to the screen.

"Just a fancy name for a kitchen. Hey, everyone's gotta eat, even if it's by IV tube. As you can see, only one woman

matching the description of the kidnapped VIP had her nutrition program canceled today."

"But this says she was discharged," said Wendy Levin,
joining Hunter behind Small's back, and effectively blocking
off what he was doing from the rest of the squad.

"Of course, since when is there a computer code for 'kid-
napped'?" Small replied, glancing over his shoulder at
Levin. Then he tapped another key. "But take a look at this.
If she were discharged, why doesn't the hospital's Account
Department have any bill made up for her? Especially con-
sidering the amount of care she's been given."

With the stroke of another key, Small brought up a file on
the medical services and treatments lavished on the woman
from the day she was admitted to the hospital until practically the hour of her kidnapping. After he started scrolling
through the pages, Wendy asked him to slow down so she
could examine the course of treatments.

"Sarah Smith ... is that the patient's real name?" asked
Hunter.

"Heck, no. It's a code name used to keep VIPs anonymous," said Small. "The hospital must've used it more than
a dozen times in the past year. It was one of the first things
I looked for after you called me. Eventually, I'll get her real
name."

"Captain, I've seen this course of treatment before,"
Wendy advised. She had since taken over the scroll keys and
was busy sifting through Small's newly acquired file. "It's
used to rehabilitate patients who've suffered long-term imprisonment or torture. Some of the best psychiatrists Capitol
has on Venus were here to treat her. And I should know, I've
studied with most of them."

"Maybe this woman was some kind of an agent or free-
lancer working on a covert operation?" questioned Alverez.
"Perhaps Bauhaus wanted revenge for something she did to
them?"

"If so, it's mighty expensive revenge they settled for,"
said Hunter. "How many 'copters did they lose? Four? And
almost that many damaged. Not to mention nearly two dozen
men and women killed. Tim, what else can you tell us about
the mystery woman? Anything on her background?"

"Nothing," Small admitted. "In fact, it's what I can't find
about her that tells me more than what I have. Usually, you

can discover an anonymous VIP's identity from the type and origin of the communications they get. What medical plan or bank account is paying for their stay and so on. However, for the mystery woman there's nothing. She has no apparent social status, wealth, or connections with any of the corporation's top levels or the military. And for the quality of care she got, you have to have connections like those."

"She's becoming a bigger mystery by the minute. You mean you got nothing else on her?"

"I do have one thing. Excuse me, Wendy."

Once he got his keyboard back, Small brought up another file. This time it was a passenger manifest from Inner System Spaceways, the largest of the Capitol-affiliated spacelines. It listed all recent arrivals at the nearby Atlantis Spaceport. Seconds after bringing up the file, Small had it narrowed down to one section.

"Our mystery woman may not be from this planet," said Small. "She matches the description of a passenger taken off an ISS liner by spaceport security. Notice the arrival date? It matches to the day her admission to the hospital. And here's the security report on her. The physical description is a perfect match."

"Indeed it is," said Hunter. Now it was his turn to take control of the keyboard. "And the flight's point of origin was the Capitol spaceport on Luna. You could be right, Julia. Remember hearing about that recent covert operation against a Bauhaus weapons plant on Luna? It was carried out by a free-lancer, a woman."

"She must've done some real heavy damage to warrant this kind of revenge," Venneti observed, standing beside the desk everyone had crowded around. "What'll we do about it?"

"Look into it further and see if a rescue operation can't be mounted."

"Why, Captain?" Halston asked. "If she's a free-lancer, then she knew the risks when she contracted for the job. It's not like she's one of us."

"You're forgetting, Sergeant. Some of my friends are now free-lancers," Hunter said sharply. "This could be one of them. Though the description doesn't exactly fit Pam Afton."

"There's one place in Roswell where her true identity and

complete background would be listed," said Small. "The protected files in the hospital's computer system. But to get to them I'll have to use one of the terminals in the hospital itself or hook a portable one directly to the data base."

"I know how that can be done," Wendy offered. "Especially in this hospital. What do you say, Captain?"

"Rule number one of free-lance ops," said Hunter. "Don't get caught. I want both of you to be careful going in there. Security's bound to be paranoid after today's attack."

"You have any other advice, Captain?"

"Rule number two. If you get caught, act innocent."

"Real cute, Mitch," Small commented, looking up from his keyboard. "Don't worry, I have no intent to spend so much as a night in a detention cell. If we do it right, it'll be a quick in-and-out."

"Captain, what should the rest of us do?" asked Shacker.

"Go back to our quarters and rest," said Hunter, checking his wristwatch. "If this mystery woman is as valuable as she appears to be, then she'll have to be rescued, and I'm gonna do a little planning toward that end. Afterward, I'll enjoy a full night's sleep. And after all the time we've spent in the field, we deserve it."

"Does anyone know why they attacked the central hospital at Roswell and not the air base?" asked Captain Miranda Jackson, one of the technicians at Venus Command's Tri-Services Satellite Reconnaissance Office.

"The brass down the hall and up the line know," said her commander, Colonel Michael Toren. "But ours is not to reason why. Our task is to find and verify. Have you had any luck?"

"Nothing yet, though this is just the beginning of the last sweep."

The black woman waved a hand at her console's display screen. Two feet wide and two feet high, the screen was slowly running through the still images taken by the Oracle on its latest orbit. The satellite was Capitol's principal strategic reconnaissance platform and occupied a high equatorial orbit, allowing it to photograph all of Venus except for its extreme polar regions.

While Jackson's console ran the still images, the one next to her ran the images created by the satellite's side-looking

radar system. Less than a dozen feet away, a third console
was busy running the scans made by its infrared sensors.
The digitalized radar data was presented in one continuous
scroll of what appeared to be a high-resolution black-and-
white photograph.

"God, when is this going to end?" muttered the radar-
imaging specialist after Colonel Toren had moved to another
part of the office. "I bet slave-driver Toren is gonna keep us
here for the whole night."

"And I bet you think that's real deprivation," said Jackson, matching her sarcastic remark with a sharp look. She
caught Lieutenant Josh Webber's eye and quickly turned his
pained expression into one of embarrassment. "For someone
who eighteen months ago was wasting his time in
cyberspace, I bet it is. You should spend a tour of duty at a
forward base, where you're either being bored to death or
getting your butt shot off by some Mishima commando
squad. After that, spending a night in a comfortable, air-
conditioned room with a fully stocked cafeteria downstairs
won't seem so bad."

"Yes, but if we're tired, we could miss something important," Webber said meekly. "Why do we have to rush this?"

"Because who knows what interrogation or torture they're
inflicting on the woman they kidnapped. Bauhaus can be
pretty nasty to its prisoners if they're not military— Wait,
this looks different. Colonel, I think I got something."

Jackson's warning brought Toren running back to her console, shouting orders for the other imaging specialists to
freeze their searches and coordinate with the frame she had
stopped on. By the time he reached her, Jackson was magni-
fying an innocuous-looking smudge on the frame until it
filled the screen.

"This is the maximum enhancement I can coax out of the
computer," she said with Toren standing behind her. "What
you're looking at is a scientific research and conservation
base. It's the largest in the area and supervises the operations
of many smaller stations. Because of that, it has a well-
equipped airfield, hospital, and headquarters' facilities."

"It also has a small detachment of Venusian Rangers for
defense," Toren added. "So if you're going to say military
activity drew your attention to it, then it's a false alarm."

"Not this kind of military activity. These aren't standard

equipment for a small garrison force." Jackson pointed to the many helicopters sitting on the airfield, some of which looked as though they were caught in the process of being moved into the base's lone hangar. "Long Rider Two-twenties and Python One Hundred gunships—the exact type of aircraft used on the Roswell attack."

"Yes, they certainly look like them." Toren studied the fuzzy images and was able to count the number of rotor blades on each machine and could see which had stub wings. "But it's not conclusive enough, Miranda. These ships could be part of a training exercise. We have to prove these are the same machines used in the attack."

"Digital resolution will make these machines a lot clearer. We could even read their military registration numbers. Footage from the hospital security cameras and that Special Forces Cutlass should help us identify a few."

"All we'd really need to do is ident one. Lester, what are you reading on this site?"

"The thermal sensors aren't too effective at this slant range," said the officer at the infrared imaging console. "But what I can tell you is all those 'copters were recently flown. Their engines are still warm, and one of 'em looks like it took some damage in an engine pod."

"Hardly the sort of thing you get on a training flight," said Jackson. "Battle damage should show up even better than registration numbers."

"It should," Toren mused before he looked at the back of the room. "Major, what does Tactical have to say about this site?"

"Bauhaus military calls it Base Aquila. Which means 'Eagle' in some ancient Earth language," said an Air Force major assigned to the Reconnaissance Office. He glanced down at his tactical display screen just long enough to check its latest information. "And from what my computer is showing, it's just within range of Long Riders and Pythons flying from Roswell—provided they launched from a Bauhaus forward base."

"I think we can safely assume that. Miranda, how long will it take to refine what you have?"

"The rest of the night, at least," said Jackson, checking on the progress her console was making. "It would help us if the satellite could be respositioned on its next orbit. Especially Lester at infrared."

"Yes, a more direct view of this site would help greatly," Toren admitted. "But it could give away what we're up to. Oracle is closely watched by all the MegaCorps, and changing its orbit could arouse Bauhaus suspicions. It's too important to risk that way. You know what the Brotherhood calls Oracle? The Great and Only Surveillance Eye of the Sinisterium. Even they think the information it provides is too important for it to be risked or threatened. I'm sorry, we'll just have to put up with refinement and enhancement. Lieutenant, you were saying?"

"Noth . . . nothing, sir," said Webber, stifling a groan while still in the middle of it. "We'll work through the night to resolve this problem if we have to."

"Good, get on it. Miranda, you're in charge. I'll tell the cafeteria to send up some coffee for us, and some whine-suppressant pills for Mr. Webber."

CHAPTER FIVE

"Was this chamber originally a natural formation?" Ragathol asked after he entered the Citadel's main hangar by its aft portal.

"Yes, my Master," said Echmeriaz, stopping and waving his hand across the cavern's vast interior. "We believe it was created by the planet's plate tectonic movements in its ancient past. We started Azurwraith's Citadel by burrowing into this structure. And from here we spread out, using the mining technology we corrupted from Mishima, until we completed the other halls, tunnels, and chambers you toured."

"What you've done is impressive. May Azurwraith be as successful above ground. Wait, you have not sent the courier ship away?"

"It's being prepared for your trip to the Defiled Castle, my Master. Algeroth has ordered it so."

Ragathol slowed perceptibly as he passed the *Gamma*-class spaceship that brought him to Venus. Instead of resting on its landing gear, it now stood on its tail. Around it was a stacking gantry that nearly reached the roof of the cavern. A horde of tekrons worked inside the skeletal structure, busily attaching liquid-fuel booster rockets to the roof and belly of the spaceship's fuselage. Mounted atop a transporter/launch pad vehicle, the whole assembly dominated the main hangar. And in its shadow Ragathol found Caliqabaal tending to a small fleet of captured Mishima aircraft.

"We salvaged these off a battlefield between the Mishima and Bauhaus entities," informed the necromutant, pointing to the helicopter gunships and medium assault transports. "The humans considered them too expensive to recover and repair. But the tekrons under Shaguhl created wonders with their Dark Technology. These machines are now operational."

"These craft are not infused with the same degree of Dark Technology as the ones we obtained from Capitol and Bauhaus," said Ragathol, stepping up to one of the Mishima gunships. He had to lower his head to avoid striking one of its high-mounted stub wings and ran his hand over the long, oval-shaped canopy that covered its pilot and gunner seats.

"Internally they are more complex machines," said Caliqabaal. "They're also different in operation. This one has its pilot sitting in the front seat and the gunner in the back one. The exact opposite of similar Bauhaus and Capitol aircraft. We don't fully understand why, except it does have something to do with the gun turret. It can fire in a full, three-hundred-and-sixty-degree arc."

"Master Ragathol, this raiding force can be ready in a matter of hours," said another necromutant, hesitantly approaching the nepharite and his entourage. "The Legionaires and Centurions are ready for battle; when will we be unleashed?"

"Soon. Our minions are tirelessly searching for where the humans have hidden the Receptacle of Visions," Ragathol answered, at first calmly. "And only when her location has been revealed will you be sent. Until that time, learn patience! Do what Caliqabaal does. Learn the weapons of those we shall one day conquer and subvert to the Darkness. Above all, learn from my example. I, too, must be patient to heal completely and win back favor and power from He whom we must obey."

For a change, Venus's Great Equatorial Ocean was calm, the sky was clear, and not even a distant storm marred the horizon or roiled its surface. The beach was marbled with yellow and pale orange sand, a distinctive feature of many Venusian shorelines, and filled with customers from the Nova Miami resort.

For Hunter this was the way to acquire a rapid suntan. Even thought the lapping surf beckoned for another swim, he refused. His muscles were tired, and he was looking forward to the drink he had ordered. When he glanced at the resort's beachfront bar, he found the waitress who took his request bearing down on him. The tall glass on her tray was already sweating from the heat, and the young woman bounced enticingly in her scant swimsuit.

"Captain Hunter?" she said once she reached him. "Wake up, we need you."

"Why is she asking me to wake up?" he thought before a blinding white light dissolved the scene and Hunter found himself struggling to surface from his dream, like the swimmer he had just been.

"Captain? Mitch, wake up," repeated one of the two Security officers standing over his bed. Her voice was firm yet feminine, and all-too-familiar.

"Oh, God. Couldn't you have waited?" said Hunter, rubbing his eyes and trying to shield them from the harsh room light. "Judith, what's going on?"

"We need you at Roswell General," said the other Security officer, a hard look on his face. "One of your people was arrested there."

"Hospital Security caught her gaining access to a secured area with forged orders," added Lieutenant Judith Fowler. "I thought we should bring you in on it before the incident gets too serious."

"All right, let me have a jumpsuit," said Hunter in place of asking who Security had arrested, even though he already had a good idea of who it was. "Looks like I won't be getting much sleep tonight."

Fowler's partner shot a fresh uniform from the room's closet at Hunter while he was still getting out of bed. He managed to catch it without being knocked off balance, or surprised at the typical rudeness of the Security officer. Hunter decided to let him stew a little longer by taking extra time to find his boots, fresh socks, and his identity wallet. He knew he had succeeded in raising the man's frustration level when he was grabbed seconds after finishing and virtually dragged out of his quarters.

"If you had anything to do with this, Hunter, you'll pay for it," the partner, Senior Lieutenant Brian Nordley, threatened.

"Brian, please," said Fowler. "We need his cooperation and you're treating him like a criminal."

"That's because I know these Special Forces types. They're what Command calls 'Unit Cohesive'. They always know what everyone else in their unit is up to. We should just take him to the Security annex and interrogate him. Let his friend stay in one of the hospital's padded rooms for a few days."

"Good idea, Nordley," said Hunter. "With an attitude like that no wonder you're the oldest lieutenant in Security."

"And . . . and you're the oldest captain Special Forces has ever had," Nordley stammered. "They'll never let your ass rise above major."

"Better to retire on a Special Forces captain's pension than a Security lieutenant's."

"I can see this is gonna be a *long* ride to the hospital," Fowler grumbled.

For the most part the trip into Roswell proved to be a silent one. While nowhere near as large as the sprawling metropolises of Venus, Roswell had the same imposing, dehumanizing architecture in its center core. Though the wrecked Bauhaus helicopters had since been removed to the air base, repair crews were still at work fixing the damage the attack had wrought. It took nearly half an hour for the jeeplike Security car to reach the shell-marked entrance to Roswell General Hospital. Throughout that time Hunter spoke as little as he could and answered the questions from Nordley and Fowler as neutrally as possible.

"You mean I gotta submit to fingerprint scan, too?" said Nordley when he realized the door to the hospital's security office wasn't unlocking for him.

"Check reality, Brian," answered the desk sergeant. "We just suffered a major attack. Of course we're going to have increased security procedures."

"But you know Judy and me."

"It'll mean my job if you don't. Or, you can wait out here until Judy and Captain Hunter are finished."

"Haven't you heard of leading by example?" said Hunter, placing his right hand on the deck's scanning plate and waiting for a bar of green light to sweep under it. "Do you still wonder where the rest of us get the idea to be insubordinate?"

A moment later the authorized entry chimes began sounding and Hunter pushed the door open. Fowler submitted to the scan next, and finally her partner slammed his hand on the plate so hard Hunter thought it would break. He was not allowed to enter the detention waiting room until his escorts joined him, giving Hunter a few seconds to prepare for the expected.

"Julia? What the hell are you doing here?" he said, not having to act surprised at whom he found in the room.

"We caught her in the morgue," explained the duty watch officer sitting next to Alverez at the table. "Trying to steal the Bauhaus casualties from yesterday's raid."

"Why on earth would you want to do that for?" Hunter waited until Nordley and Fowler were in the room before making his remark; he wanted them as witnesses. "They're the enemy."

"They're also soldiers and warriors like us," said Alverez. "Perhaps even more like us. And they deserve honorable burials."

"But Bauhaus will do that themselves, once the Brotherhood arranges for their transfer."

"No, Captain, that won't happen this time," said Fowler, taking a seat beside the duty watch officer and glancing through his report. "The latest signal from Venus Command says Bauhaus denies responsibility for the attack. They claim it was an unauthorized operation by a free-lance company associated with them. They've sent their apologies and have even offered to search for the renegades."

"These were no renegades or mercenaries," Alverez replied before turning to Hunter. "Mitch, you saw how they fought. They didn't turn tail when we attacked, they hit back. And since when have you heard of a chivalrous mercenary?"

"I know a few," said Hunter. "But they're on Luna, not here. Judith, what'll happen to these soldiers?"

"Since they'll not be claimed, they'll be buried in the Dispossessed Field," said Fowler. "And from the looks of this report, cremation and burial have already been approved."

"Thanks, Judy. Sergeant, could I use one of your secure line phones?"

"Yes, Captain. I'll have one brought in," said the watch officer as he pressed a button on the table's intercom box.

"I don't see why you'd be so interested in burying these guys," added Nordley, after trying hard to think of something intelligent to say. "After all, you killed most of 'em."

"That makes it even more imperative for us to act," said Alverez. "They fought us honorably and spared us when they had us cold. The least we can do is respect their dead."

"Colonel Vardon? Yes, this is Captain Hunter," said Mitch, the handset from a bulky, wireless telephone pressed against his ear. "I'm sorry for the hour, but an urgent problem has come up. My pilot wishes to have the Bauhaus Rangers who were killed yesterday buried properly. May I suggest room can be found for them at our base cemetery?"

"I don't believe you, Hunter," Nordley commented. "We brought you here to help interrogate your officer, and you end up siding with her."

"Shut up, Brian," said Fowler. "This may be the best way to resolve our little problem."

"Yes, Colonel. I think they would do the same for us," Hunter continued, sticking a finger in his other ear to block out the conversation. "No, I don't think we need anything elaborate. Yes, I'll let them know to expect your orders. Thank you, Rebecca, and good night."

"How'd you get away with calling a colonel by her first name?" said Nordley. "That's insubordination anywhere else."

"Brian, stop it. You're just doing it to be argumentative," said Fowler before she turned to Hunter. "What are we to do with your pilot, Mitch? She did try to steal the bodies with falsified orders. Those charges are serious enough for a court-martial."

"Colonel Vardon will talk with the base commander about them," Hunter answered while the portable phone was lugged away by a Security patrolman. "Julia's orders won't end up false so much as 'premature'. And if it's okay with the sergeant, the remaining charges will be dropped."

"Believe me, with all that's happened in the last twenty-four hours, nothing would make me happier." The duty officer grabbed the report Nordley had been fumbling through and with much relief tore it up. "This incident never happened. Just one thing, would you want us to cremate the bodies before we officially turn them over to you?"

"What? So the bogeymen or the little-green-things won't raise them from the dead?" Julia scoffed. "I don't think anyone's gonna invade a military cemetery and rob our graves."

"Sorry, Lieutenant, but I had to ask. Rules from the Brotherhood, you understand. If there's nothing else, Lieutenant, then the prisoner's free to go."

"Thank you, Sergeant. We owe you one," said Fowler. "Mitch, why don't you take your pilot back to the ride? We'll finish off the rest of the paperwork here."

"Thanks, I owe you on this one, too," said Hunter, rising

from the table and shaking both the sergeant's and Fowler's hands. "And I owe you as well, Judy. Taking Julia back to the car will give me a chance to explain the finer points of creating 'premature' orders. Julia?"

The sergeant quickly unlocked Alverez's handcuffs, and rubbing her sore wrists, she left the waiting room with Hunter. They spent a few more minutes in the Security Office as its staff hurried through the release procedure. They did not speak extensively to each other until they were out of the office and far down the corridor from it, where their conversation was lost in the normal clamor of hospital operations. Even so, they still only spoke in hushed tones.

"You've no idea how relieved I was to see it was you they caught," Hunter whispered, "not Wendy. What happened to her?"

"She and Tim were busy while I was getting caught," Julia said quietly. "I know nothing of their plans. But they knew mine and planned their ops around it. We all knew I wouldn't get away with swiping more than a dozen bodies from the morgue. But the confusion I'd create would easily cover a far smaller break-in."

"So, you did this just to run interference for them?"

"No. I felt for some time we should do something like this. And when I heard those men and women would be cremated and buried with the Dispossessed, I decided to act. That it helped Tim and Wendy was a fringe benefit. I would've done so even if it didn't help anyone else."

"I see. And did you count on Colonel Vardon and me rescuing you when you got caught?" Hunter asked as they approached the hospital's main entrance. "And forgiving you in place of getting permission?"

"Yes. I know you too well, Mitch Hunter," said Julia, now smiling. "And Rebecca's reputation is known to everyone who serves in Special Forces on this planet. If one of you didn't help me, I knew the other would."

"I hate it, but I guess we're all predictable. So when will the rest of us learn if the other ops has been successful?"

"Wendy will advise us tomorrow, and it looks like that'll be at the funeral we'll arrange."

CHAPTER SIX

"All right. Here it comes," warned Miranda Jackson when a familiar, innocuous-looking smudge appeared at the top of her screen. "I'm initiating enhancement. Corporal, you better go get the colonel."

While one of the enlisted staff slipped out of the Strategic Reconnaissance Office for the nearby crash quarters, Jackson programmed her console to magnify the smudge until it nearly filled the screen. Webber repeated the same procedure at his radar-imaging station, and by the time both were nearly finished, Colonel Toren staggered back into his command.

"This had better be good to interrupt the dream I was having," said Toren, yawning and still rubbing the sleep from his eyes. "What do you have? Captain."

"Latest images of Base Aquila," said Jackson. "And, as expected, all those helicopters are gone."

"Well, they certainly didn't take off, or our long-range surveillance radar would've detected that. Lieutenant, are they still there?"

"Yes, sir. They're sitting in rows along the airfield perimeter," Webber answered. "Let me match the magnification scale, and I'll transfer this to Miranda's console."

Moments later, a black-and-white image almost identical to what Jackson had on her screen appeared on it in an insert frame. Its chief differences were a lack of obscuring clouds and concealing vegetation. With a stroke of a few keys, Jackson had the radar image enlarged and superimposed on her original optical one. And clearly seen along the airfield's jungle perimeter were single rows of Python and Long Rider helicopters. Hidden from optical surveillance by camouflage nets, the Oracle satellite's Side-Looking Radar easily scanned through the artificial canopies.

"That's almost all of them," said Toren, finishing his count of the rows. "What we don't see must be in the hangar."

"It would've been dangerous for anything to fly in or out of the base," said Jackson. "The storms blasting the area are quite violent. We're lucky we got a partial break in 'em on this pass."

"It looks like this base has been secured to ride out the storms. No activity. What have you heard from the E.R. team?"

"Nothing since you crashed out down the hall. They must've finished something by now."

"Contact them. Let's see what they have," Toren responded.

Located at the back of the Strategic Reconnaissance Office, the Refinement and Enhancement Team was squeezed in next to the Tactical Team. For the last several hours, ever since they received the data from the initial pass, they had been quietly busy. They strained, divided, and reconstructed the images until they had something that could be identified.

"This looks familiar," Jackson commented, pointing to the helicopter appearing in the next series of refined shots. "It's the Python gunship that appeared to have landed hard."

"Looks like it had reason to," said Toren, grabbing one of the console's headsets. "E.R., this is Toren. Do you have any enhancements of quadrants fifty-seven through sixty-three?"

"Yes, Colonel. We'll put them up now," said the team leader. A few seconds later, the spine of the Python 100's tail boom appeared in exacting detail. The images ran from where the boom attached to the fuselage back to its midpoint, where the irregular pattern of buckled and rent open outer skin panels ended.

"That doesn't look like any kind of damage you'd get on a training exercise," Jackson noted.

"It's what you get when armor-piercing cannon shells explode against kevlar," said Toren. "It's battle damage. And from what I recall of the gun camera recordings from Roswell, I think we can match this helicopter with one of those involved in the attack. I think we have our ident."

"Does this mean we can go off-duty?" Webber asked, eagerly and incautiously.

"Not yet, Lieutenant. Not by a long shot." Toren's wither-

ing look was laser-hot and seemingly melted the junior officer into his console. "I need as complete an identification of
this machine as we've done in the past before I'll take it up
the line to the command staff."

"We have had a long night, Colonel," said Jackson, rubbing her eyes. "Not to mention a long day before it."

"I know," said Toren, glancing at the Office's chronometer and mildly surprised at the time it displayed. "Even
though we've all had a couple of hours in the crash quarters,
it *has* been long. I promise this won't take much more time.
I can have our relief crew arrive soon, and if we don't finish
identing this gunship, they'll do it for us. Then it goes up the
line."

"Who's this coming up?" asked Shacker, pointing to yet
another vehicle approaching the base cemetery.

"Some of the Air Force fighter jocks," said Hunter. "They
tried to track down the remaining Bauhaus choppers, but
their radars were jammed, and the choppers stuck to the
floor until they reached the border. Those guys were good,
and our pilots respect them."

"Yes, it's a damn sure bet there won't be many people
from Security attending this service," said Venneti.

More than a dozen Capitol Air Force pilots and their
weapon systems officers joined the Special Forces personnel
and the Tri-Service military honor guard already in the cemetery. They had all just finished introducing themselves
when a small convoy of trucks finally arrived at the lushly
planted, somber location.

"There's something about a cemetery," Julia remarked as
she stepped off the lead truck. "No matter how they landscape it, it always manages to feel like one."

"Did the Brotherhood missionaries perform their rituals at
the hospital?" asked Hunter.

"Yes, then they gave the bodies over to our keeping. And
now it's time for ours."

At Hunter's signal the honor guard came to attention and
part of it marched up to the trucks. One by one they gently
off-loaded the lozenge-shaped metal coffins and laid them in
a perfect row in front of a freshly excavated mass grave. The
assembled guests snapped to attention when the first arrived
and remained so until Alverez and Hunter joined them.

"Fellow officers and soldiers," Julia began once Hunter ordered everyone to 'at ease'. "We gather here today to honor our adversary's dead, in the hopes that should we fall in similar circumstances, we'll be accorded the same rights. I will now recite the Air Warrior's Farewell.

"You have flown your last mission. You have fought your last battle. And your orders are to slip these bonds that hold you to the Earth, and dance the skies on laughter-silvered wings. Sunward you climb, to join the tumult of sun-split clouds and footless halls of air, where you can do all the things we have only dreamed of. Wheel, arc, and climb. Up the windswept heights you soar, where never hawk or even eagle flew. And with silent, lifting mind you slip to the untresspassed sanctity of space. Put out your hands and touch the face of God. We are but born human and can only hope to die that way. We give you your final salute and bid you your last farewell."

When Alverez finished, the honor guard's armed section pulled the bolts back on their rifles simultaneously and snapped them forward. They raised the weapons to their shoulders and fired a series of volleys while everyone else came to attention and saluted. As the last ripple of explosions echoed in the distance, Alverez stepped forward and laid a dollar coin in a shallow well on the first coffin's lid. The remaining attendees repeated the ceremony until all the coffins bore the same symbolic payment for burial. Only then did the honor guard lead the procession out to the parking lot, where it would disband.

"I'm glad the lieutenant didn't carry on for too long," said Halston, marching directly behind Hunter. "Or else she would've sounded like a damn Brotherhood missionary or mystic."

"That'll be enough, Sergeant," Hunter warned, turning his head just far enough to look over his shoulder. "Wendy, you got anything to say about last night?"

"Yes, we better meet at Tim's apartment later," said Levin, speaking in a softer than normal voice so only the squad could hear her. "Our search was very successful, and very disturbing."

"I . . . I mean no disrespect, Master Ragathol," the heretic quickly and nervously replied. "But Lord Algeroth has taken great interest in your activities. I ... I have journeyed far through the worlds of Man to deliver His message to you. The Receptacle of Visions has taken an increased importance to His plans, and He wishes to know of your progress in recapturing her."

"Progress? As of yet there's been no progress!" said Ragathol, making predatory circles around the newly arrived heretic. "The human organizations keep stealing her from each other. And each time we must track her down again and create anew plans for her recapture."

"I understand your frustration, Master Ragathol."

"Understand ... you understand nothing! What am I master of here? This is Azurwraith's Citadel, his domain. I am but master of an operation. I must go begging to him for every resource I need. This is growing more humiliating than I had reckoned. Yes, Shaguhl ... what is it *you* wish?"

Ragathol turned to the hulking form which had suddenly appeared in the entrance to his Nether Room. As he motioned with his uninjured arm, the lead tekron silently entered and bowed respectfully to his master. For a few seconds they both ignored the trembling heretic as the giant worker opened his mind to the nepharite and allowed him to probe his thoughts.

"Indeed ... our minions have been successful much faster than I had thought," said Ragathol, smiling at first. Then he broke into a blood-chilling laugh which echoed through the main chamber of his Nether Room. "Inform Echmeriaz and Caliqabaal of this and have them report here. We must complete our preparations to steal the Receptacle of Visions back. Now for you, messenger ... journey back through the worlds of man and report to Lord Algeroth that the human female has been found, and this time we'll act too swiftly for her to be stolen by anyone else. Leave me now, I wish to enjoy the serenity of this moment."

"Okay, is that gonna be everyone?" Small asked after Harris and Taylor slipped into his apartment.

"Yes. Rogers won't be joining us," said Hunter. "He's kissing up to Hart and his staff at their dinner tonight."

"That doesn't surprise me, even though Raymond does remind me more of me than anyone else in your squad."

While he spoke, Small pulled an old model sonic disruptor out of a desk drawer and sat it on his living room table. He dialed in a radius roughly equal to the room's area and activated it. Anyone outside the disruptor field would hear an unintelligible mumble and a static buzz. He made sure his telephone, television, and various radios stayed outside the radius, and as a final security measure he attached a motion detector to the front door.

"You know, Tim, they make portable models of these things," said Alverez, pointing at the saucer-shaped disruptor. "The Cybertronic ones are especially good."

"And really expensive," Small countered. "Besides, I like being a dinosaur. Now the disruptor will cover only this room—not the kitchen, bedroom, storage room, or bathroom. So don't carry a conversation from here into one of them. What I have to tell you is for your ears only."

"What's got you spooked?" said Hunter after nodding in agreement. "You're acting like a Cybertronic Infiltrator is on your tail."

"Believe me, I think I'd prefer one of them to what may really be out there." Uniquely, instead of turning to his personal computer and calling up a file, Small produced a series of printout sheets and handwritten notes from his attaché case. "Your kidnapped VIP was nothing of the kind. She was an amnesiac picked up by spaceport security after being alerted by the crew of ISS spaceliner *Copernicus*. She boarded, or was put on board, the liner at its Luna stop. However, if you think she's from Luna, she's not."

"Her name is Mrs. Lorraine Kovan—a married mother of two young children, a member of one of Capitol's smaller agricultural settlements, and a lifelong resident of Venus. She's never been to any other world, and there's no record of her recently leaving the planet. In fact, the last record I could find of her prior to being picked up at Atlantis was a Ground Forces report. It listed her as 'Missing and Presumed Dead' when her village was attacked and massacred by an Unknown Force. Mrs. Kovan is apparently the only known survivor of the attack, and Wendy knows her examination by the doctors had just begun when Bauhaus kidnapped her."

"It was probably Bauhaus who attacked the village," Venneti suggested, "and they kidnapped her to silence her."

"If Bauhaus had wanted to silence her, they would've sent

an assassination team," said Hunter, "not a major commando strike group of Air Cavalry and Venusian Rangers."

"Perhaps it was Mishima," said Shacker, studying one of Small's printouts. "The settlement was closer to slant territory than anyone else's. It'd just be like the slants to sneak up and wipe everyone out."

"Then why was this woman left alive?" Taylor asked. "And why would Bauhaus help them? Don't be a fool, man. Bauhaus hates Mishima even more than you do."

"Corporate politics have made stranger alliances. Even Cybertronic and the Brotherhood have cooperated."

"None of you are even hitting close to the mark," said Wendy. "It's the Dark Legion."

Her quiet voice cut through the more raucous conversations like a knife. They stuttered to a halt, and a few even laughed, but in seconds the room was silent.

"You mean the little green aliens?" said Julia, incredulous. "The bogeyman? Sure we've all heard about 'em—the Brotherhood talks about nothing else—and we all know the story of the Nero disaster. But have any of us actually seen one of these creatures? Or even a heretic?"

"I have," Small answered, cutting short the nervous laughter. "The work I've done for the Brotherhood has brought me into contact with those claiming allegiance with the Legion."

"Those who claim? There are nuts out there who claim to own a majority of Capitol stock." Julia's response rapidly grew more mocking and strident; she even tried to laugh. "I want more proof than the crazed mutterings of those in need of a psych adjustment."

"If it's proof you want, Lieutenant, I'll give you some," said Wendy, her quiet voice growing cold. "While Tim was raiding the hospital's protected files, I was analyzing them. The medical and psychological reports on Lorraine Kovan carried an Eyes Only secrecy rating. I've never seen that level on anyone's medical report, not even a major stockholder's. And what they detail is a form of chemical mind alteration unlike anything anyone's ever even attempted before—a literal brainwashing. The doctors were surprised Mrs. Kovan was still alive; and the reports suggested nothing of her original memory still exists."

"So she's a zombie? The walking brain-dead?" asked Halston.

"No. There was higher-function brain activity all right. The doctors think it was some sort of artificial memory that has literally been programmed into her brain."

"The she's the victim of some Bauhaus mind control experiment," said Alverez. "No wonder they wanted her back so badly."

"No, Lieutenant. What was done to Mrs. Kovan is beyond every MegaCorp's medical technology," said Wendy. "We're talking about restructuring the human brain. In our ancient history we once compared it to a mechanical watch, and for centuries now we've likened it to a digital computer. Neither analogy is true; the brain is far more complex than anything it can build. However, a report based on evidence gathered by the Brotherhood indicates an alien science called Necrotechnology can literally wash and reprogram the human brain."

"You had me, but you lost me. Now you're talking about things out of some dark fantasy movie."

"No offense, Julia. But I happen to believe that something alien and evil was uncovered out there on Nero," Taylor interrupted. "But it was always 'out there'. Maybe it reached as far as the moons of Jupiter or even the asteroid belt. But here? This far into the solar system?"

"You haven't said much so far," Small noted, turning to Hunter. "Are you willing to believe, Mitch, or are you eager to dismiss?"

"The military has always been a society unto itself," said Hunter. "And Special Forces is an especially insulated world. This is one of those times I wish I were a free-lancer roaming the streets of the Luna cities. I'd be much more in touch with what's happening in the real world and could tell if what we're listening to is spook stories and rumors or the real thing. No, I'll not dismiss what we've just been told. But I'd like some more information about it. Tim, can you arrange a meeting with your Brotherhood contacts?"

"If you want it, sure. It may take a little while to set it up though."

"Don't worry, I'll have plenty of other things to keep us busy."

"You mean your rescue operation?" said Alverez.

"That, and something else," Hunter answered, paging through the notes and printouts of Small's report. "Bauhaus took Mrs. Kovan because they obviously thought she was valuable. Perhaps she's also valuable to the Dark Legion? She could be just as dangerous to possess. Perhaps in addition to planning on rescuing her, we should also make plans to warn Bauhaus about the threat from the Dark Legion."

"Not only would it be illegal, Captain," said Venneti, "but I think the Duke Electors in Heimburg would laugh your warning right off the Com Net."

"It doesn't hurt to think about it. I'd like to have as many options open to us as possible. It'll save us from being stuck on one course of action."

"What makes you think Venus Command will use your squad for the rescue?" asked Small. "The guys who came in before you told me what you did to that idiot advisor. You should be up on insubordination charges. You could be demoted or kicked right out of the military for it."

"I know," said Hunter, looking up from the report. "But I haven't been charged yet, and my unit is still on active duty so there's a chance we'll be selected. All right, I want everyone to go over this material and memorize as much of it as you can. No photocopies or computer copies will be made of any of it. This is our own private operation, and no one needs to know anything about it. You're not even to discuss it with anyone outside of the people you see here."

"Drone Nagato, change to course one-eight-one degrees on my mark and change to terrain-following mode. Proceed on new course for one hundred kilometers before pop-up and evasive return maneuvers to original course. Mark, mark, _mark_."

Mishima Trooper Momoko Watanabe watched on her tactical screen as one of the Warhead reconnaissance drones she had airborne responded to her new orders. After skirting the unofficial frontier to Dark Legion territory since its launch, it now deviated sharply from its preset patrol pattern. It flew toward the frontier and dropped to the deck, following the contours of the jungle-covered terrain. The drone's sudden change was in response to a dramatic increase in electronic emissions from a site called the Citadel.

"Drone Yamamoto, increase altitude to five thousand meters," Momoko ordered while she studied the status panel to the other drone she had airborne. "Reduce speed by sixty percent and change to holding pattern Alpha on my mark. Analyze hostile electronic emissions in conjunction with Nagato maneuver. Mark, mark, *mark*. Computer, analysis of latest hostile emissions."

As with most of her other watch tours, Momoko staffed the outpost's observation tower alone. She sat before its immense communications and control console, monitoring the activities of the Warhead drones she had airborne and the outpost's electronic surveillance systems. In addition to covering the frontier with Capitol, she also watched a remote area occupied by the Dark Legion. It was in territory contested by both Capitol and Mishima and did not usually occupy much of her time. Lately, however, the times were unusual, and most of her tours were spent recording all activities at the distant Citadel.

For a few moments her tactical computer silently worked on its analysis of the newest transmissions from the Citadel. When it finished, the analysis was displayed on one of the console's data screens:

98% probability that emissions were of an area surveillance/air traffic control radar last detected at 19:53 hours. Duration was two minutes, thirty seconds. An increase in 60% over previous transmission time. End analysis.

Momoko immediately realized what was happening; the Citadel was preparing to launch either aircraft or a spacecraft, and she had just enough time to prepare for it.

"Drone Nagato, emergency cancellation order Archimedes," she said. "Maintain current terrain-following mode and heading. Reduce speed by thirty percent. Prepare for evasive maneuvers and return to original course and position on my mark."

Even though her first drone's speed had dropped to less than two hundred miles an hour, it would reach the Citadel's outer defense perimeter in a matter of minutes. Though its stealth properties and tiny radar signature would probably allow it to escape detection, it would be deeper inside restricted territory than officially allowed by Mishima Military Command.

However, the drone never even closed to proximity warning distance of the perimeter before activity at the Citadel jumped dramatically. The outpost's long-range radar detected the liftoff from its spartan surface facilities of slow-moving aircraft. They circled the location just long enough to join formation, then headed northwest at increasing speed.

"Drone Nagato, change to intercept course of hostile formation," Momoko ordered. "Maintain current terrain-following mode until nominal safe distance from formation, then climb to one thousand meters and maintain surveillance. Drone Yamamoto, change to intercept course of hostile formation and maintain surveillance at nominal safe distance. Execute all commands on my mark. Mark, mark, *mark*."

In unison both machines broke away from their previous headings and closed on the distant formation of unidentified aircraft. Even though Watanabe soon ordered the Nagato warhead to increase speed, its closure rate was still far slower than Yamamoto's, mostly because it continued to hug the increasingly rugged terrain the formation was crossing.

"They're not just airplanes, they're helicopters," said Momoko, studying the warheads' initial sensor scans. "Computer, analyze Nagato and Yamamoto data and identify aircraft types."

The formation was still more than fifty miles from either drone, but already they were scanning it with their sensor arrays and transmitting the data back to the outpost. Seconds later, the computer's analysis of it all appeared on the same auxiliary screen:

Hostile formation consists of three MMAT-3 Kyokko assault transports and five MLRG-15 Hayabusa helicopter gunships. External configuration of all aircraft has been altered, but not severe enough for them to be unrecognizable. End analysis.

Line drawings for the two Mishima warplanes appeared next on the data screen and the back-up one below it. The formation's Kyokko transports had the familiar boxy fuselage, triple tail fins, and short span wings with tip-mounted turboprop engines.

But there were also the melted deformations, the thorn- and spike-shaped projections that told Watanabe she was looking at a Dark Technology–corrupted ship. The Hayabusa long-range gunship bore similar alterations to what had been a slim, streamlined fuselage with only the belly-mounted gun turret to mar its clean design.

Yet in both aircraft the corruptions were not as extensive as what she had seen on Bauhaus- and Capitol-designed weapons. And this time, because the sighting involved stolen Mishima aircraft, she felt her superiors would not mind if she bent the surveillance rules a little.

"Drone Yamamoto, increase speed by twenty percent and close to optimum observation distance," said Momoko, studying the tactical screen and the original Time To Intercept flashing beside the symbol for her second drone. "Prepare for evasive maneuvers if threatened during surveillance. Execute on my mark. Mark, mark, *mark*."

The moment the drone received its new orders, it was accelerating and changing course slightly to make the quickest interception. Once it reached the optimum distance, it would no longer be necessary to observe the Dark Legion formation through radar and infrared systems. It could do so with its optical system and might be able to read any unit markings still on the aircraft.

"As I had hoped," said Momoko, studying yet another screen on her immense console. "Computer, run analysis of partial Sentai markings on third Kyokko trans—"

A light started flashing atop the tactical screen, and the blaring alert horn caused Momoko to almost jump out of her seat. But it was all superfluous; she could already see what triggered the alarms. The two Hayabusa gunships on the formation's starboard side had broken away and were closing on the warhead.

"Drone Yamamoto, immediate evasive maneuvers!" she shouted.

The second airborne drone had just finished rolling on its side and was diving for the jungle when the gunships opened fire. It tried to dive under them, but their gun turrets continued to track and snap out short bursts, even when fully depressed. The inhuman crews worked closely with each other, almost as if one mind were directing them. It did not take many hits for them to disable the drone. Soon it was spiraling out of control, instead of just maneuvering frantically.

"Drone Nagato, emergency cancellation order Archimedes," said Momoko as the other warhead crashed through the thick jungle canopy and exploded. "Execute evasion and escape program on my mark. Mark, mark, *mark.*"

With some satisfaction she watched her remaining airborne drone end its intercept course with the Dark Legion formation and swing back for the frontier. She then ordered the outpost's computer to timeline all events for the last thirty minutes in preparation for a report she would send to her superiors before her watch ended. Perhaps now they would take her warnings about the Dark Legion more seriously. And maybe they would at last send the additional reconnaissance drones and personnel she repeatedly claimed the outpost needed.

CHAPTER SEVEN

"Captain, you're needed at headquarters," said one of the figures standing over the bed. "Captain, emergency briefing—"

"Pam, watch it! Incoming!" Hunter blurted out, briefly thrashing around in his bed. Then the Martian battlefield evaporated in front of him and his private quarters returned. In place of the friends fighting for survival, he now saw the two officers looming over him. "Judy? What gives now? Can't you guys let me have a full night's sleep?"

"Sorry, Captain. This isn't Security. It's Major Charles Tower, Capitol Intelligence Service."

"Yes, Major. Now I recognize you." Hunter rubbed his eyes and shielded them from the room's harsh glare. "What's going on? Why's a briefing being held at this hour?"

"Your questions will be answered at the briefing," said Tower, already growing impatient. "Not now. Get one of your best uniforms on. We'll wait for you outside."

Unlike the previous night's rousing, Hunter did not have to get dressed in front of those who awakened him. He grabbed one of his more formal uniforms and had the time to get properly dressed. Major Tower and his subordinate led Hunter to a command staff car in place of a Security vehicle and drove him a short distance across the base to its operations center.

"Wait a minute. I thought this was to be a briefing?" said Hunter upon entering a familiar room and confronting a familiar group of officials. "Not a repeat performance of my squad's interrogation."

"I can assure you, Captain, that it's not," Rebecca Vardon answered. "A critical situation has developed, and your unit is the best and only answer to it. Please, have a seat."

Rebecca motioned toward the same table where Hunter and his squad had been grilled less than two days before. This time the lighting over it was softer, though it still did not fill the room. And as before, while most of the officials took seats around the table, there was one who preferred to remain cloaked in the shadows.

"We know you've been asking questions about the VIP Bauhaus kidnapped from here," said General Richard Cyrus sitting at the head of the table. "So for that and other reasons we felt it appropriate to call you in. Do you recognize this place?"

On the wall screen behind Cyrus, a small base cut from the heart of the jungle appeared. From the jungle's lush foliage Hunter concluded it was at least on Venus. Mars scarcely had anything that could be called a jungle and Luna had no forests whatsoever. Not until he took a closer look at the helicopters on the base's airfield could he identify who owned it.

"Those are Long Riders and Python One Hundreds," said Hunter. "This is a Bauhaus base."

"Very good, Captain," Cyrus added. "Perhaps this machine will be more familiar to you."

A magnification grid appeared on the screen and focused down on one of the Pythons. When it stopped flashing, the area outlined by the grid was blown-up until it filled the screen. The slim, angular gunship in the center was fuzzy until a digital enhancing bar wiped over the image. Then it became sharp enough for Hunter to recognize some of its markings and all of its battle damage.

"Good Lord, I think that's the Python we had the duel with," said Hunter, the shock evident in his voice. "Lieutenant Alverez would probably be more definite."

"It is, and we'll bring her in later," said Tower sitting next to General Cyrus. In front of him were a series of folders and data disks with the emblems of the Strategic Reconnaissance Office. "This is Base Aquila. Base Eagle. It was originally a science research station, and believe me, only an eagle can reach it. There's no way into it by land; it's so remote you can only reach it by air. And we believe this is where the VIP is being held. We've accounted for virtually every surviving helicopter from the raid and have concluded they made no stops anywhere else."

In addition to the magnified image of the Bauhaus gun-ship, a series of inserts were added to the screen. They showed the jungle base in various infrared and radar-imaging views. Finally, everything was wiped from the screen and replaced with a tactical map showing the base's location inside Bauhaus territory, together with a line snak-ing from a Capitol forward base into Imperial territory be-fore looping back on Aquila.

"Are you certain she's still there?" Hunter asked. "And not at some base in Heimburg?"

"There's been no air traffic into Aquila or out of it since the arrival of the raiding party," said Tower. "And our agents in Heimburg report no activity that would coincide with the arrival of our VIP."

"From the looks of this map, you're going to repeat our operation against Cybertronic. Except you're staging the di-version near the start of it, instead of at the end. When will it be launched?"

"Later today," Cyrus answered. "A fast response is essen-tial, which is one of the reasons why we brought you in. Your unit is the only Special Forces Independent Action Squad that hasn't suffered any recent casualties. You're at full-strength and can be deployed in a matter of hours."

"General, there are other such squads available," said Hart, speaking up after a prolonged period of agitated si-lence. "And we can have one of them flown here in a matter of hours."

"What? Bring someone in from halfway around the planet?" asked Rebecca, giving Hart a sharp look. "And ex-pect them to go into action immediately? On top of that, none of the other units have had extensive experience oper-ating from the local districts. No, you're creating a scenario for disaster."

"And you're rewarding Captain Hunter's insubordination. Charges should still be laid against him for what happened to my advisor, and I would like his subsequent activities in-vestigated as well."

"Sorry, Mr. Hart, but the gravity of the situation overrules disciplinary concerns."

The deep, familiar voice ended the argument between Vardon and Hart before it really started. Everyone turned to the man in the shadows, who was now standing so close to the table that he grazed the field of light circling it. The details of his suit were visible; however, his face was not.

"The funeral service you organized for the Bauhaus dead was commendable," Wood added. "It shows you have respect for the enemy, Captain. This is good, it's something soldiers once did."

"Thank you, sir," said Hunter. "How much time do we have before this operation is launched?"

"Approximately eight hours. We'd like to get you into the drop point by early afternoon. The storms that move continually through the target area should provide you with excellent cover."

"Good. Will the ops briefing start now?"

"No, this has merely been a preliminary one," said Wood. "You appear to be eager to join it. Though if you wish to withdraw, you may do so now."

"No. I can promise my entire squad will want to be part of this," Hunter responded. "I'd just like to have my officers with me for the ops briefing."

"Then collect them. Lieutenant, take Captain Hunter back to his quarters."

Tower's adjutant officer led Hunter from the conference room, and the moment they disappeared through the main doors Wood finished emerging from the shadows. He took Hunter's seat at the table, one directly across from Calvin Hart.

"General, have you had any problem coordinating the operation with District Landis?" Wood continued.

"Only in the requisition of fuel stocks for the decoy ops," said Cyrus. "They'll just have to restrict some of their training flights. How have negotiations with Imperial fared?"

"They owe us for warning them about the Cybertronic assassination attempt earlier this year. They'll allow one helicopter and one transport-tanker to cross their borders unchallenged. It wasn't even necessary to mention the Dark Legion."

"A mission like this is so sensitive," Hart interjected. "I dread to think how a unit as undisciplined as Captain Hunter's may ruin it."

"If this were a diplomatic mission, you'd be right," said Wood, growing irritated. "But it's not. It's a very dangerous rescue, and we need the best Special Forces unit available.

Be grateful for the one concession I did give you. If any diplomatic problems arise, your advisor team should handle them."

"Greetings, Timothy. Peace be with you," said the middle-aged black man wearing the robes of a Brotherhood mystic. "Congratulations in again selecting another appropriate meeting place."

After making his announcement, Portius slid into the restaurant booth Tim Small had reserved and found his lunch already waiting for him. The crock of soup was still hot to the touch, as was the round loaf of wheat bread in the middle of the table. Small had already taken a wedge from the loaf and was dipping it into his own soup. A large carafe of iced tea also sat on the table, and it was this Portius first helped himself to.

"I always wondered how hot you mystics got walking around in robes like that," Small said after standing up to greet his contact man.

"Sometimes it's very hot," Portius answered after drinking down nearly half the glass he had just poured. "But not so much as I can't enjoy your offering of sea food and vegetable soup. I see yours is beef."

"At least it's what they call beef around here. And it does taste somewhat like it."

"You never stray far from hamburger, do you? So, my friend, what's this report you're so eager for me to view?"

Small slid a folder out of his attaché case and up onto the table so quietly it almost appeared like magic to Portius. In between slicing off a piece of bread and buttering it, he opened the folder and began reading the report as he ate. He had not gone far into the printouts and handwritten notes before he stopped eating. When the bread he'd been holding fell into his soup, Small knew he had something the Brotherhood was greatly interested in.

"We've heard of this woman," Portius said in a hushed voice. "She was the object of a Mishima covert operation on Luna. We heard she'd been a prisoner of the Dark Legion, and that the Mishima operation did rescue her. But the ending was confused. We believed Mishima still had her on Luna. We put no faith in the reports she had returned here. In our arrogance we were foolish."

"You mean Capitol never told you they had her?" Small asked, keeping his voice just above a whisper, in spite of the restaurant's noise from its other guests.

"We heard Capitol had some*thing* which would help us in our struggle against the Dark Legion. We never heard it was some*one,* most particularly this woman."

"Well, Bauhaus has her now. Maybe your people in Heimburg can find out where she is."

"Indeed. We'll also warn them that possession of the woman risks an attack by the Dark Legion," said Portius as he resumed eating his meal.

"That's weird. Mitch said pretty much the same thing when he saw this report," Small said, remembering.

"You mean your friend, the war hero?" Again Portius stopped eating, and this time the look on his face was not of shock but mild surprise. "Captain Hunter is concerned an adversary may be attacked by the Dark Legion? This isn't weird, Timothy. It's good."

"Funny you should mention that. One of the reasons I asked for this meeting is to see if Bauhaus can't be warned. The other reason is Hunter wants to know more about the Dark Legion. He'd like for you to meet with him and his squad."

"As to the first, I'll see what can be done through our Directorates. For the second, the Captain can view our broadcasts and learn much from them."

"Those are generalized for the average citizen to understand," said Small. "And they're designed to frighten. Mitch and his crew are professional soldiers; they're not interested in being scared by a spook show. They want to know the facts."

"The facts," Portius repeated in between spoonsful of soup, "the facts, Timothy, are more frightening than any spook show could possibly be. We wish to warn humanity of the growing threat, not strike them with mortal fear. Though it's against our rules to discuss such secrets with outsiders, I agree to meet with your friends. I hope indeed they are professional soldiers. They'll need to call upon such professionalism when the threat's true nature is revealed."

"Thank you, Portius. I'll contact them when I can and arrange the meeting."

"When will that be?"

"I honestly can't tell you," Small admitted. "I tried Mitch's private line before coming here. But all I got was a prerecorded message saying he was unavailable. I got the same message for other squad members, which means only one thing. They're on an operation. I only hope they'll survive it."

"Dave and I are done with our weapon and equipment checks, Lieutenant," said Halston. "If you need any help we'd be glad to give you a hand."

"Good, we got touch-up work that needs to be done fast," said Alverez. "Use these to spray over the yellow sections of the camouflage."

Alverez handed the squad's fire support specialist and his assistant several large aerosol cans, then led them over to her Cutlass and indicated some of the areas on its surface she wanted covered with new paint.

"How come, Lieutenant?" Redfield asked, puzzled. "Your ship just got touched up a couple of weeks ago."

"This here's a jungle operation, not a desert ops," said Halston, responding first. "And yellow don't mix too well with jungle."

"Just make sure you don't overspray any of the armor-glass," Alverez added. "And don't touch the areas you've sprayed. Otherwise they won't dry evenly. Now get to work, and don't try to be 'flitter' artists."

Of the several Cutlass and Grendel helicopters sitting in the Special Forces hangar, only the one assigned to Hunter's squad was receiving any major attention. The fuel and ordnance crews had just finished loading its internal and external tanks, and arming it with belts of cannon shells, rocket pods, and Sidewinder CX missiles. Unlike most weapon-loading procedures, which required the aircraft to taxi out to an open-air service point, this would allow the CFAH-3 to depart as soon as it left the hangar. All it needed now to become operational was its crew and their personal equipment.

"Squad, attention!" Alverez barked when she noticed a sizable entourage of officers and civilians entering the hangar. Work on her gunship and the tables of infantry weapons beside it came to an abrupt halt. Loose cartridges were still rolling and clinking against each other when the entourage arrived.

"Colonel Vardon, I believe you already know my officers and men," said Hunter, turning to the highest-ranking officer in the group.

"Yes, they're becoming the best known unit in my command," said Rebecca, who in turn introduced the squad members to the Army and Air Force officers accompanying her.

"You could also call them the most notorious in the Special Forces," Hart added, just as the round of introductions was ending.

"Thanks, Calvin. You really know how to throw cold water on something," said Hunter.

"Yes, Mr. Hart. We conceded on one of your more important requests," said Rebecca. "You should be grateful higher authority didn't reject everything you put forward."

"What request is this, Colonel?" said Venneti, hesitantly and suspiciously.

"A military advisor team will accompany you on this mission. I know it's unusual for such a deep penetration raid, but this is an unusual mission to begin with."

"Who's it gonna be, Colonel?"

Before Venneti's next question could be answered, a crash of plastic storage containers caught everyone's attention. The hard clacking seemed to spread across the back of the hangar before it ended, by which time Sutter and Bamble had finally appeared.

"Dirk. Lynn. It's good to see you again," said Lieutenant Rogers, looking up from his backpack of communications gear.

"Raymond. I should've guessed you'd be the only one who'd be happy to see them," Alverez observed sarcastically.

"I'm sorry we didn't get to your office in time, Mr. Hart," Bamble apologized. "But as I told you on the car phone, we got lost."

"That figures," said Hunter, the tone in his voice matching Alverez's attitude. "And I suppose in all this rushing around neither of you had the time to go over the mission plan? That one of us is going to have to waste time briefing you?"

"Following our takeoff from Roswell, we're to cross into District Landis at low altitude," said Sutter after she scanned the hangar and made sure the only people in it were either high-ranking officers or Special Forces personnel. "We'll maintain minimum altitude as we cross the Imperial frontier and until we rendezvous with our tanker. Once we're refueled, we'll slip across the Bauhaus frontier while the Air Force stages more large-scale maneuvers just inside our airspace."

"It's nice to see someone's done their homework," Hunter responded, impressed. "All right, get out of those suits and into some jungle fatigues. If your partner has to be briefed, Lynn, you do it. We synchronize our chronometers in thirty minutes. Julia, conduct your tour of the Cutlass later. What gives? Haven't you guys ever seen a *real* gunship before?"

After shooing the Air Force officers out of their helicopter, Hunter's squad began loading their weapons, munitions, and other equipment into it. Half an hour later they paused briefly to set their watches and the mission event timer in the cockpit. Once the squad and their advisors boarded it, the Cutlass was finally towed out of the hangar.

Its auxiliary power unit was whirring loudly by the time the tractor had finished pulling it out to a spot on the apron marked for helicopter launches. Alverez waited until the ground crew had just cleared the area around it before firing up the main engines and engaging the rotors.

Buzzing furiously, the CFAH-3 lifted off the trolley used to move it around and headed across the airport. Alverez did not use any of its runways or taxiways to make her departure; nor did she enter its sparsely populated traffic pattern. She never contacted its control tower or acknowledged any instructions. Officially the sortie did not exist.

The Cutlass retracted its landing skids and darted away from the field on a southwesterly course. Behind it, standing in front of the Air Force hangars and filling the arming service points, were most of the F/A-99 fighters based at Roswell. Already a supporting force of Hercules IV cargo/tankers were marshaling on the taxiways. By the time they were disappearing over the horizon, the fighters would be assembling in a massed formation over the field.

CHAPTER EIGHT

"Mr. Hart, welcome back to Station Grace THX," said the senior coordinating officer when a large group of civilians and military officers entered his tactical center. "Have you been following the updates on the operation?"

"Except for the last fifteen minutes," Hart replied, visibly relieved to be in out of the oppressive heat and humidity he encountered on his trip from the helipad. "What's happened?"

"Has there been any more problems with the battle station in District Landis?" asked Noah Wood, being more specific.

"No, sir. They stopped arguing with us over command jurisdiction more than an hour ago," said the coordinating officer. "We now have complete operational control. Thank you for your assistance, Mr. Wood."

"You should thank General Powers. He's the one who I called. Now, is the operation still on schedule?"

"Yes, sir. Force Trident's gunship has caught up with the tanker and is climbing to rendezvous with it. The deception maneuvers are just beginning. The lead formations are entering Bauhaus air defense radar coverage."

The coordinating officer turned to the center's wall of display screens and pointed to its largest one. The tactical map showed the boundary line between the two adjoining Capitol districts, and the frontier split between Bauhaus, Imperial, and Cybertronic territories. It also showed the wide swath of Imperial and Capitol airspace covered by the Bauhaus air defense net.

Just entering the net were the first flights of F/A-99 Feline multipurpose fighters. They flew at high altitude and in loose, weaving formations that indicated they were acting as air superiority escorts. At a more medium altitude was a far smaller formation of Felines operating in the defense suppression and electronic jamming roles. Hugging the terrain, even at their distance, was the largest group of Capitol aircraft, F/A-99s armed and operating as strike fighters.

"Very good. To Bauhaus this'll look exactly like a retaliatory strike for the Roswell attack," said Wood, standing behind the console operators. Then he glanced over at Hart, who was still wiping sweat off his neck and face. "We must find some way of air-conditioning that walk from the helipad to the station."

"Would it be possible, Mr. Wood?" Hart queried, believing the casual remark to be serious.

"Indeed. I'll mention it at the next building improvement conference. Major, has Bauhaus started to react?"

"Yes, their radars are changing modes," said the coordinating officer. "To track-while-scan. They'll put up their own fighters next, then activate their missile batteries. Soon their attention will be entirely focused on this frontier."

While the tactical map showed the wave of fighters continuing to advance on the border, the auxiliary screens on either side of it finally started showing some activity. They recorded the radar stations that were changing modes, the status of the various groups of Capitol aircraft, and even which Bauhaus airfields appeared to be readying aircraft for takeoff. On only one of the side screens was displayed the most important part of the operation; deep in Imperial territory two symbols were linking up.

"Mitch, our tanks are nearly full," said Alverez. "I'm breaking the connection."

Less than a hundred feet in front of the Cutlass loomed a CCTL-5 cargo/troop lifter. Normally used as an Army assault transport, this version was a tanker variant for the Capitol Air Force. Its high cruise speed and VTOL characteristics enabled it to refuel a wide variety of combat aircraft, from supersonic fighters to helicopters. Unfortunately, they could only hook up to a single hose and reel unit mounted in its tail because its diminutive, high-set wings were occupied by massive engine pods.

A brief plume of fuel spilled from the hose's cone-shaped receptacle a few seconds after Taylor waved to the reel operator to end the transfer. As the fueling probe retracted into a housing beside Taylor's cockpit, Alverez rolled the gunship to the left and dove for the jungle. It was the first time in over five hundred miles that the helicopter had climbed higher than a hundred feet. Now it was back down on the deck, hugging the treetops as it set course for Imperial's frontier with Bauhaus.

"And if it all works out, the worse reaction we'll get from Imperial is an official complaint about an unauthorized border violation," Sutter commented, once the hard maneuvers ended. "In a few days' time."

"Let's hope it goes that way," said Hunter. "Bamble, what are you examining?"

"Electronic surveillance readout on Imperial's reaction to us," said the team's other military advisor. He had the roof-mounted terminal at his side of the cabin and was surfing through its tactical displays. "They haven't even changed modes on their air defense radar. This warrants—"

"Don't even think about sending a report. Not until we're on departure from the target area. Julia, this is Mitch. Do you have the river yet?"

"Got it in sight," Alverez responded. "Hold on, this looks like it's gonna be a fun ride."

Apart from the plateau line in the distance, the only major terrain feature in mile after mile of dense jungle was a meandering river. Called the Diana Majoris River, it was one of the largest rivers on Venus. Amazon-like in its vast network of tributaries, it drained the rain forest basin of the southern continent into the Great Equatorial Ocean. Hundreds of miles from its delta, the river snaked its way around the terrain's rolling hills and was wide. Even at this stage in its journey it was easily wide enough for Alverez to drop the Cutlass over it and fly its winding course back to its headwaters, and deep into Bauhaus territory.

"Finally, after all this time our schedules allow us to have lunch together," said Max Steiner, visibly pleased to encounter Anna in the officers' cafeteria. "I do hope this chair isn't reserved for someone else."

"No, Maximilian," Lindholm answered, motioning to the empty place beside her. "I knew you would break away from your duties at this time. Sometimes you're very predictable."

Once Steiner sat his tray down, all the seats at the oval-shaped table were filled. Relatively small, the cafeteria was quickly filling with both officers and high-ranking civilian officials—so much so that Steiner soon found it difficult to look out the room's windows at the base's hangar and flight line.

"To you I'm always predictable," he said, laying an affectionate hand on one of Lindholm's. "I guess that's the way I'll always be."

"You're predictable to more than just your fiancée," the base administrator quickly added. Pearson sat across from Steiner and had just been finishing his lunch when he arrived. Instead of rising to leave, he stayed in his seat, and his expression took on a cold, official look. "Your request to do local training flights is on my desk again. This will save me the time of preparing an official reply. Rejected, Capitaine, and you know the reasons."

"Max, you didn't?" said Lindholm, pulling her hand out of his. "You know we must have as little activity at this base as possible."

"Don't act so surprised, Anna," said Steiner. "I thought I was predictable? I examined Aquila's flight logs, and your regular schedule would allow for a few training flights."

"We can't do anything that will draw attention to ourselves," Kriegler added, barely looking up from his plate. "Even this far from the border, Capitol can still watch us."

"I would say permitting absolutely no flying would draw attention to us, Colonel. We should present the appearance of normal activity."

"If you wish, Capitaine, you could fly the transport helicopter when it arrives later," said Pearson.

"I'm a warrior, not a bus driver," Steiner replied, trying to keep the irritation out of his voice. "What you're suggesting wouldn't give me the chance to examine the local terrain and decide how to use it should I have to fight here."

"The Virtual Reality simulators should allow you to do that, Capitaine," said one of the other officials at the table, Dr. Helga Reissner. The middle-aged woman was Aquila's senior doctor and in charge of the VIP's examination. "They're rare and expensive machines, brought here specifically for you and your people."

"I know, they're wonderful machines. But they're only as good as their programming, and even with the best there are drawbacks." Steiner grabbed his fork and plunged it into the middle of his steak, then lifted it off his plate. "The scientists who work on Virtual Reality can put me in one of their neuro-sensor machines and make me believe I'm actually looking at a real steak. It would even smell and taste real. But would it give me the same sensation and nutrition as eating a real one? I don't believe it could."

"Eating a steak won't get noticed by Capitol surveillance," said Pearson. "Flying a warplane like the Python One Hundred would. Request denied, Cap— Yes, what is it?"

"Sorry to disturb you, Mr. Pearson," said the lieutenant who stepped up to the table, holding his salute until Pearson returned it. "But Armed Forces Command in Heimburg reports our southern frontier was crossed by a force of unidentified aircraft some hours ago."

"Yes? And what does this have to do with us? Think hard about this, Lieutenant."

"No need to, sir. After losing track of this force, Air Defense has since relocated it in our sector and heading straight for us."

"Where are they, and has Air Defense been able to identify them?" asked Kriegler, pushing away his half-finished lunch.

"Approximately ninety kilometers from us," said the lieutenant. "And no one's been able to identify the aircraft. We think they're Mishima, but we're not positive."

"Looks like I'll be flying whether you want me to or not," said Steiner, taking one large cut out of his steak and wolfing it down before rising. "Lieutenant, alert my squadron's personnel. Arm all flyable gunships at once."

"You're overreacting, Capitaine," said Pearson, growing more irritated with the interruption. "Wouldn't you like to know who these people are before you intercept them?"

"I'm afraid I must agree with Maximilian," Lindholm advised, also rising from her seat. "This is a threat, no matter who it is. Max, I'll get one of the portable links from Operations and meet you at the hangar. Good luck."

"Captain ... Captain, your catnap's over," said Wendy, raising her soft voice until it could be heard above the muted thumping of the helicopter's rotor blades. "Something's up."

"I'm never gonna get any sleep," Hunter mumbled, rubbing his eyes, then his stiff neck. "We're still a couple of minutes from drop time. What's going on?"

"It's Jeff and Julia. They say something strange is happening in the target area."

"I don't like this. The last time Julia told us something strange was happening was when this whole crazy ride started."

Hunter slipped his intercom headset back into his ears while the terminal was rolled down to him. On its screen was a view from the helicopter's forward infrared scanners. Adjusted to compensate for the jungle's heat, it nonetheless showed intense heat sources floating on the horizon. Only after he plugged in did Hunter realize the Cutlass was no longer flying up the river and, in fact, was hardly flying at all.

"Julia, this is Mitch. What do you have on the FLIR?" he continued. "And how come we're moving so slow?"

"That's Base Aquila," said Alverez. "And from the look of it, I'd say it's under attack."

"I'd say you're right. Have you detected anything else?"

"Some garbled radio transmissions on the frequencies used by Bauhaus," Taylor answered in place of Alverez. "Some coded, some in the clear. A couple of emergency locator beacons went off briefly, but everything's been silent for the last forty seconds. Ground-based missile fire control radars were also briefly activated. That's what stopped us in the first place."

"From the sound of this, our target's been hit by a surprise attack," said Hunter, checking a tactical map of the area, as well as the mission log showing the events Taylor described. "And a pretty good one."

"Well if it ain't us, then who?" Bamble asked nervously. "Cybertronic? Imperial?"

"You don't want to know who we think it might be." Hunter glanced around the terminal at Wendy. His hard look caused her to stop speaking before the word *Dark* was finished.

"What about our original operation?" said Sutter. "Will you go ahead with it?"

"We'll change it. Julia, this is Mitch. Take us to within ten clicks of the base, then drop us off. Head for your ground holding point and wait there for further orders."

"Roger. Heading for new drop point," said Julia, advancing the throttles a little and increasing airspeed by twenty miles an hour. "Get your rappel gear ready."

"Ten kilometers?" said Bamble, attaching a metal clamp to his safety harness. "That's a lot farther than we had discussed at the briefing."

"We weren't expecting to find the base under attack then," Hunter responded. "I'd like to drop us even farther out, but we have to reach the target area in a reasonable time. Arm weapons, stand by for deployment."

Even at its new speed, the CFAH-3 crept along, barely skimming the jungle's upper canopy as it hugged the terrain. It came to a full stop when it slid into a shallow depression where the canopy was partially broken by several fallen trees. Almost at once the main hatches slid forward and the pylons for the automated rappel system snapped out.

There were two such pylons for each hatch, and after they finished extending from the roof, they began unreeling their lines into the jungle. Those squad members nearest the hatches locked their waist clamps around the nylon lines and waited a few more seconds for them to finish dropping.

In unison, the first four soldiers pushed off the cabin seats and slid down the lines. Using their padded, friction gloves to control their descent rate, they dropped into the clearing and were nearly swallowed up by it. They spread out, armed their weapons, and established a perimeter while the rest of the squad joined them. Last to arrive was Bamble, who slipped off the fallen tree trunk he initially landed on and crashed the last five feet to the jungle's swamplike floor. He was still picking himself up when the rappel lines retracted and the cyclone of rotorwash ended.

"You delay us like this again and I'll put Ted behind you and have him kick you out," said Hunter, standing over Bamble while Rogers was helping him to his feet. "Raymond, I want you and Wendy to watch over him. And keep him out of my hair."

"Captain, I know this is a sore point with you," said Bamble, straightening up and promptly sinking into the soft ground. "But this attack is something unexpected. A brief report should be sent up the line."

"You so much as open the lid on that SatCom unit, and I'll feed it to you one precious microchip at a time. Then I'll have you staked out for tiger bait. Don't cross me, Bungle. This ops is suddenly a lot more dangerous than even I thought it could be. All right, we move out. Heading, one-nine-one degrees, south-southwest. Diane, you have the point."

"Mr. Wood, something's wrong," warned the coordinating officer, intruding on the private discussion the corporate officials were having. "There appears to be heavy military activity at Base Aquila, well ahead of schedule."

For the last hour the civilians in the tactical center had been clustered near its administrative desks and entrance. There the light was better, and the hum of conversation among the military personnel was softened. It allowed Wood to talk freely with the various managers, and it kept Hart from interfering with the operation—until now.

"Heavy military activity," Wood repeated, scanning the main screen's tactical map and the information shown on the auxiliary ones. "This is combat and looks like one hell of a fight."

"Well I can't say I'm not surprised by it," said Hart, a small, vindictive smile on his face. "Hunter's squad was too undisciplined to have slipped into the target area unnoticed and freed the VIP. They've been discovered and destroyed."

"I don't believe what we're seeing was caused by them, or even involves them," said Vardon, turning to look Hart in the eye. "Fragmentary transmissions from Base Aquila indicate they're being attack by several aircraft, not one. And the volume of fire we're seeing from this distance far exceeds what a lone Special Forces squad can deliver, no matter how well we equip them."

"I would expect you'd believe that. After all, they're your people."

"*I* believe it as well, Mr. Hart," Wood offered, catching the senior military advisor and several other civilian officials off-guard. "You can't deny what the infrared and radar images are showing. Captain, can you identify the type of aircraft attacking Aquila?"

"We think some are helicopters," said the commander of the radar-imaging team. "But I'm sorry, we can't be any more specific."

"What do you mean, you can't?" said Hart, growing angry. "Do you realize what percentage of the Army's budget is spent on your training and your equipment?"

"Mr. Hart, please. This type of arguing is useless," Wood declared. "There must be something better for you to do."

"Yes, Mr. Wood. Major, open a secure channel to Squad Trident and keep broadcasting a hail until you hear from them."

"No! Belay that order, Major." After he finished giving his countermand, Wood turned and glowered angrily at Hart. "We're to make no attempt to communicate with them. The situation Hunter's squad is in is a lot more dangerous than anything we considered. I don't care what protocols it breaks, we'll wait until they're ready to contact us."

CHAPTER NINE

"This looks like the spot," said Alverez, swinging the Cutlass back over a stretch of the Diana Majoris River. She matched its contours with an enlargement of a topographic map on one of her CRT screens. "What does the depth look like?"

"Less than a meter right below us," Taylor answered, trying to interpret the readings from the radar altimeter. "And this section looks about as firm as any other area of riverbed."

"Okay, we'll do it. I'd prefer getting close to one of the sides, rather than in the middle. Raise the gun barrels and retract all the sensors and antennas you can. Extending landing skids."

The fuselage-mounted skids extended from their streamlined pods and dropped to their maximum travel limits. Alverez easily brought the helicopter to a stop, and maneuvered it slowly until she was comfortable with its position over the river. She eased off the throttles and kept it from drifting as it settled toward the muddy gray waters.

Spray generated by the rotorwash heavily coated both canopies, until Alverez and Taylor activated their wiper blades. The landing skids slipped into the water easily, encountering no resistance until they entered the first layers of soft mud. It rapidly grew firmer, and when Alverez felt the riverbed could take the weight of her aircraft, she cut both engines. Though it would take time for the main rotor to finish windmilling, the sheets of spray quickly ended, and the stream flow soon returned to its eddying, turbid state.

"Ju . . . Julia, this is Lynn," Sutter informed, finally hitting the transmit switch on her intercom headset. "Are you shutting everything down?"

"No, our auxiliary power turbine is still on," said Alverez.

"And so's our passive surveillance systems. If anyone comes our way, we should have just enough warning to lift off and meet them."

"You think we should send out a report on what's happening at the base? As Hunter said, we didn't expect to find it under attack. Our superiors must be wondering what's going on."

"They can just wait to find out like the rest of us. Really, Lynn. That's an idea I would've expected from your partner, not you."

"All right, everyone hold," Hunter ordered when he noticed Diane freeze ahead of him and signal. "It looks like our point man found something."

After the squad had moved out of the clearing, they did not have to go hacking through much jungle before they found a well-traveled path. Cleared by personnel from the base, debris on the trail indicated it was probably used by scientists and other civilians. Not until now had the squad come across even a hint of military equipment.

"It's an automated laser trip wire," said Parker, indicating the two small devices mounted across the path from each other. "These goggles just barely picked up their beam. We have to get some better ones."

"Save it for the debrief," said Hunter, the only other member of the squad to have joined her. "You think they got motion scanners in the area, too?"

"If this base is following standard Bauhaus security practices, then they'll have 'em a little farther down the trail. Motion scanners use a lot of power, so they wouldn't be activated until one of these trips is set off. If we avoid triggering this, we won't have to worry about them later."

"What about microphones?"

"Not in a jungle, Captain," Parker advised. "Animal noises make 'em virtually useless."

"Animal noi . . . that's it," said Hunter, rising out of a crouch and scanning around him. Involuntarily sweeping with his M50 assault rifle, the action also caused Parker to rise and sweep with her Improved M89. "That's not what we're hearing."

"Well, the sounds of the battle we're heading into scared 'em off."

"Those ended almost ten minutes ago; since then we've heard nothing." Hunter lowered his rifle and continued to scan; all around his unit an otherwordly silence prevailed. "Not a bug, not a bird, not a monkey, anything. They've been scared off, all right. It's as if we're the only things left alive in this place."

"Captain? What's going on?" asked Halston, moving close enough so his whisper could be heard. "What did ya find?"

"A laser trip wire," said Hunter. "If we can avoid setting it off, we'll be able to penetrate fairly deep into the base perimeter."

"Yes, sir. And what did you hear? From the way you were looking around, you heard something."

"Nothing. I heard nothing, and that's the problem." Hunter motioned for the rest of the squad to join him and made sure they all saw where the laser trip was located. "Ted, load a belt into your M606, now. I want you and Redfield with me. Jake, you join Diane on point. Leo, I want you and Harris behind me. Rogers, you, Wendy, and Bamble will stay in the rear."

Sure thing, Captain," said Venneti, unslinging his own CAR-24 submachine gun and, not only clicking its safety off, but also loading a grenade into its integral launcher. "God, how I hate fighting in the jungle."

"This time I'm inclined to agree with you. I want everyone to arm *all* your weapons, sidearms included. You too, Bamble. And don't blow your toes off with that Bolter. We got another two kilometers before we reach the base itself."

After avoiding the laser trip, the squad moved down the trail as Hunter ordered. This time everyone except Bamble and Wendy carried their main weapons unslung and cautiously swept the surrounding terrain. No one spoke, which only added to the eeriness, and occasionally the sky could be seen through breaks in the canopy. As the squad drew closer to the base, clouds of dark smoke filled the breaks, and the smells of burning drifted through the jungle. Minutes after the first whiff, they thoroughly permeated the area. And with them came the first sounds beyond the clink of belted ammunition and the shuffle of boots on soft ground, the muted crackling of multiple fires.

"It feels like we're marching into a funeral pyre," Halston finally whispered.

"It does," said Hunter, for the first time wishing he had something more powerful in his hands than an assault rifle. "Wait, Diane's found something again."

Once again Hunter moved forward while the rest of his squad halted and attempted to blend in with the cover. This time both Parker and Shacker knelt beside an object just off the trail.

"It's a Bauhaus Impaler Seven antipersonnel mine," said Parker, answering Hunter's question before he could ask it. "With a remote detonator."

"What the hell happened to it?" said Hunter. "Did it spontaneously explode?"

"It looks like it spontaneously melted," Shacker countered, hesitantly reaching down to touch its warped, distorted casing. "It still feels warm, and so does the ground."

"I wonder what melted it?" asked Parker.

"We're going to find out," Hunter said softly. Then he straightened and motioned for the squad to move off the trail. He did not bring them up to view the melted weapon. He guessed they would soon be finding enough on their own.

Less than ten feet away the path had disappeared from view, and already the squad was discovering melted infrared sensors, motion scanners, and more antipersonnel mines. Hunter moved from one team to another as the initial discoveries were made, speaking briefly to them, then urging them forward. For a time nothing further was needed to keep them advancing until they discovered the missile launcher.

Like the mines, the launcher was a standard Bauhaus defensive system. Mounted on its hexagonal base was a rectangular tray holding a dozen transport/launch tubes for short-range surface-to-air missiles. Or at least it should have been there. Both the tray and the targeting radar associated with it were obliterated, their support arms bent and melted. The base took some of the force of what had been a direct hit and was blown open. The entire structure still smoldered, and some of its electronics were still shorting.

"This is kevlar armor plate," Bamble whispered, touching one of the base's hexagonal sides. "Whatever this was hit with melted right through it."

"Maybe it'd be advisable to retreat," said Rogers. Though his voice was quiet, his suggestion cut through the silence like an explosion.

"We got a job to do, mister," said Hunter, looking at his subordinate officer as if he had been betrayed. "We either find Lorraine Kovan and rescue her, or we report back she's dead. Now let's move it. Ted, you have the point. Jake, you and Diane cover us."

Now the squad was within a few hundred yards of the base. They crept the rest of their way forward as silently as they could. To communicate, they snapped their fingers and gave hand signals. The closer they moved, the more pervasive the sounds of burning grew. The smoke they had at first only smelled was now thick enough to be seen drifting through the foliage. Finally, at less than a dozen feet from the clearing's edge, the squad caught sight of the base—what was left of it.

Though their view was still limited, not a single building appeared to be undamaged, and not a single vehicle or aircraft was left intact. Beyond the fires, no other movement could be seen, though there were plenty of bodies. After letting his men pause for a moment, Hunter snapped his fingers and signaled them to move out.

He was the first to step into the multiacre clearing and swept it with his rifle, before taking what cover he could beside a furiously burning T-32 Wolfclaw tank. He covered Halston's and Redfield's appearance, and in turn all were covered by Shacker and Parker. They were the last to emerge from the jungle, and continually swept what was left of Aquila's buildings for any signs of activity.

"Captain, we get any closer to this thing and we'll cook with it," Redfield warned, raising a hand to shield his face against the heat from the mangled tank. The fires in it were burning so fiercely its jungle camouflage paint was boiling off it.

"I know, but it'll help hide us from infrared sensors," said Hunter. "Rogers, you detecting any electronic activity?"

"Nothing, Captain," said Rogers, sweeping the base with a hand-held scanner. "No radio, radar, or laser emissions of any kind. Whoever hit this base did a good job blasting it."

"You think these Bauhaus guys put up much of a fight?" Halston added.

"Not for very long," said Hunter, kicking at one of the few empty shell casings that had been ejected from the tank. "Fat lot of good their triple auto-cannons did. They should've gone with a single, larger caliber gun. All right, let's fan out. Keep your weapons ready and don't bunch up if you find anything."

Singly or in pairs, the squad spread out from the Wolfclaw and moved toward the base's small complex of buildings. As they did so, the damage to them became more apparent. None of their upper stories were intact—twisted steel girders, remnants of building materials, and frayed bundles of electrical and fiber optic cables. Their debris had mostly fallen in on the lower floors, adding to their carnage. Scattered around them, the wrecked vehicles, and aircraft were the bodies, and the squad was soon coming across them.

"Captain, here's another!" Venneti shouted. "And he ain't like the rest!"

Moving rapidly from one team to another, Hunter rejoined his demolition expert and assistant as they stood beside what was left of a Long Rider helicopter. Next to it lay the remains of something that may have once been human. Beneath its helmet was a grinning, cadaverous face, and under the armor plate was a body rapidly decaying, except for its artificial limbs.

"Now we know who attacked this place," said Harris. "Cybertronic."

"Cybertronic never turned out anything so grotesque as this," said Hunter, studying the body before it completely melted into the ground. "It looks like something out of a bad fright movie. Only they never made special effects this detailed. What's that you have?"

A glint of metal in the corporal's hand drew Hunter's attention away from the body. What he held looked like an assault rifle. Some of its design stylistics Hunter recognized, but could not place because its basic frame was distorted by thornlike projections. They appeared to have grown out of the weapon, instead of being additions to it, and made it difficult to handle.

"I think it's an Invader assault rifle," Venneti declared. "Standard issue to Imperial's Blood Beret forces. But I don't understand what happened to it. You think the fire could've melted it?"

"I doubt it," said Hunter, glancing at the still burning remains of the Bauhaus helicopter. "A fire hot enough to partially melt that gun would've cooked off its ammunition.
Does it still function?"

"Yes, sir. You can detach the clip," said Harris, unlocking
the magazine from the weapon. "And I can pull the bolt
back. Ow, damn it! Damn it!"

Harris had scarcely finished working the rifle's action
when one of its metal thorns dug into his hand, causing a
spurt of blood and forcing him to drop the distorted weapon.

"Wendy, get over here," Hunter ordered. "And break out
the most powerful antibiotic you're carrying."

"Captain, if this stuff's too weird for even Cybertronic to
have invented," said Venneti, "then are you thinking what I
think you're thinking?"

"That it's the Dark Legion? Unfortunately, yes. Rogers,
hold it up. Open a channel to Julia. Let's bring in some air
support."

"I don't see why you're getting so nervous about this,"
said Alverez, growing irritated. "Our original plan was to sit
here as long as we needed, maybe even past nightfall."

"And I don't see why you can't accept that this attack
changes everything," Sutter shot back, her anger overriding
her hesitancy. "We have to send a report."

"Okay, girls. Cat fight's over!" said Taylor, speaking loud
enough to drown the other two off the intercom. "The captain's on the line."

"Thanks, Jeff. Saw Blade, this is Eclipse," said Alverez,
switching her headset from Intercom to one of the mission's
assigned frequencies. "Go ahead, over."

"Eclipse, this is Saw Blade. You're cleared for arrival,"
Hunter answered. "Priority evac not needed. Sweep area for
hostile forces before landing. Over."

"Understand, Saw Blade. Can you describe target area
condition? Over."

"I'll explain it when you get here. Saw Blade, out."

"Activating number one turbine," said Alverez, after the
conversation ended. "Jeff, stand by to arm weapon systems
and radars."

"Julia, what do you think we'll find when we get there?"
Sutter requested.

"All I hope to find is our guys still alive. I'm not going to think about anything else."

Above the whine of the auxiliary power unit, a deeper rumble shook the helicopter as its main engines were restarted. Instrument panels in both pilot's and gunner's cockpits came back to life, and by the time Alverez was ready to engage the main rotors, she and Taylor had checked out all the other systems.

The placidly flowing waters were once again roiled by the downwash and minutes later exploded into blinding spray as full power was applied. After standing in mud for well over an hour, the heavy machine had settled in deeper and needed sustained application of full power to break free.

Slowly, the landing skids became unstuck from the gluelike mud, helped along by Alverez wiggling the gunship through the use of its tail rotor. With a final tug it leaped clear of the river and gained more than a hundred feet before it was brought under control.

Alverez circled the ground holding point for several minutes while the Cutlass's tail-mounted surveillance radar scanned the immediate area for other aircraft and Taylor ran the fore and aft turrets through their tests. Only when both were satisfied did she set course for Base Aquila.

"If that sign's correct," said Parker, "then this is the hospital."

Still sweeping the area with her heavy sniper's rifle, Parker nodded at the bullet-riddled sign lying on the ground. Hunter, Wendy Levin, and Bamble clustered around it briefly until Hunter noticed most of his squad was joining them.

"God, whoever did this could put me out of a job," Venneti remarked, impressed at the level of destruction the hospital had been subjected to.

"All right, this isn't the place for a conference," said Hunter, waving away most of the other squad members. "Leo, I want you and Harris to check the operations center. Ted, check the hangar. And tell Jake to find a place where he can be a lookout."

"You want me to do the same, Captain?" said Parker, finally clicking on her SR-50's safety and letting its stock rest on the ground.

"Yes, but I want you to stand guard here while the rest of us go in."

"What do you mean by the rest of us?" Bamble asked nervously while the others Hunter had given orders to fanned across the base.

"I mean you, Wendy, Rogers, and me," said Hunter. "This is the most likely place Bauhaus kept the woman. If we don't find her, and I doubt we will, we might at least find her records. Your computer skills will prove useful there. Maybe you'll be good for something after all, instead of good for nothing."

"Captain, that remark's uncalled for. And it's going in my report."

"Yeah, I know. I'll pay for it. Raymond, motion scanner."

"What? Where do you see one?" said Rogers, glancing over the rubble-strewn grounds.

"No, idiot. I mean *our* motion scanner," Hunter barked. "Break it out and leave your backpack with Diane. In fact, I want everyone to take only essential equipment in there. No backpacks and no weapons except sidearms. Wendy, just bring your med kit. Bamble, your SatCom unit. Fold down your helmet goggles and slip on your friction gloves. Their kevlar liners should protect our hands."

Following his own orders, Hunter left behind his CAR-24smg rifle, backpack, and even his Harker combat harness in Diane's care. The debris piles in front of the hospital entrance were large but not insurmountable. Hunter lead his team over them and through the one door not blocked or crushed. Inside, the receiving room and lobby were heavily damaged though passable. One of receiving's computer terminals was still intact, and Bamble went to work trying to retrieve information from it while the others spread out to search the immediate area.

"Captain, I got movement!" Rogers shouted, sweeping his scanner over the crumpled remains of an outer wall. "I think someone's alive in here!"

"Start digging, damn it!" said Hunter, rushing over to the site with Wendy. "C'mon, Rogers, use your hands! Get 'em dirty for a change!"

Scrambling in unison, the three started pulling out scraps of wall panels, chunks of precast concrete, electrical conduits, and shards of glass. They raised a veil of dust as they worked and threw or tossed away the debris wherever they could. In just over a minute they had made a sizable dent in the pile, then it exploded.

"Back off! It's going for you, Wendy!" said Hunter, pushing himself off the pile and grabbing his medic by her arm. "Back off! It's not human!"

From the rubble a dark, twisted body sprang up. Its matted hair was silvery white, and it emitted a wailing, inhuman shriek. Only that its legs and lower torso where still trapped by the debris prevented it from attacking its rescuers. Even so, it was still able to hurl pieces of rubble at them.

"Open fire! Open fire!" Hunter continued, rolling to avoid getting hit by volleyball-size chunks of concrete. "If it bleeds, we can kill it!"

While Bamble dove for cover, the rest pulled their sidearms and opened up on the creature. The heavy, Ironfist automatics unleashed deafening claps of thunder and two-foot-long muzzle flashes as they sprayed the creature with .55-caliber slugs. The teflon-coated, hollow point rounds easily penetrated the necromutant's leatherlike skin, though most wounds appeared to seal up almost as soon as they were made.

However, in addition to the grave injuries already suffered, it could not withstand the heavy barrage for long. One of the necromutant's hands was shredded by multiple impacts as he raised it to shield his face. His neck and lower jaw disintegrated in much the same way. And so complete was the destruction that, when the head rolled to one side, the remaining tissue connecting it to the body rapidly separated.

"What in heaven's name is this thing!" Rogers shouted, as much from fear as from the temporary deafness caused by firing large-caliber weapons inside a building.

"Heaven's got nothing to do with this monster!" said Wendy, checking her gun's LED display to see how many rounds it still held. "We just killed something from the Dark Legion!"

"What did she say it was?" Bamble asked, peering over the counter he had been hiding behind.

"Never mind!" said Hunter. "Have you found where the woman's located?"

"I . . . I think so. The computer's memory wasn't damaged, and it's apparently operating on emergency power. She's on this floor, west wing—suites seven and eight."

"Good work. Now which one of these is the west wing?"

"Captain, I think it's this one!" said Wendy, pointing down a hall that appeared to be in slightly better condition than the others.

"Hunter, is there anything else you'd want me to do?" Bamble asked, raising his voice loud enough to be heard by the others.

"Yes, tell the rest of the squad what happened when they come charging in," said Hunter after the stamp of boots in the hospital's entrance caught his attention. "Then order them back to their assignments. Whatever this thing was, we killed it."

Hunter led Wendy and Rogers out of the lobby just as Parker stumbled into it, carrying his assault rifle instead of her SR-50. They only had to go a few dozen yards down the hall to find the rooms that had been used to treat Kovan. What they discovered was relatively undamaged, compared to the rest of the hospital, free of blood and empty.

"This is obviously where they had her," said Wendy, approaching the lone bed in the two suites. She quickly examined the intravenous tree and the medical monitoring equipment scattered around it, as if by a tornado. "And from the look of these drugs Bauhaus was taking good care of her."

"It looks like they were recording everything they were doing," Hunter added, checking a video camera still mounted on a tripod though its lens had been sheared off. "Raymond, is there anything in those recorders?"

"Some audio-visual storage discs," said Rogers. After hitting the eject buttons and finding none of them worked, he resorted to prying open the access doors on the machines and manually pulling out the disc trays. "If you want, I can set up some of these machines and play back what's on them."

"No, we don't have the time. We'll let Intelligence work on 'em. Take whatever else you think we'll need for evidence and let's clear this place. I think I hear our air support."

Unlike the hospital's lobby, where the few windows had been demolished and filled or covered with rubble, the two suites still had their windows partially intact, and through them came the muted thumping of rotorblades. Making their way back to the entrance and collecting Bamble from the receiving desk, they emerged in time to see the Cutlass finish circling the base. It maneuvered around the pillars of smoke and landed on one of the clear patches of flying field big enough to accept it.

"Good Lord, Mitch! What on earth happened here?" said Alverez, taking Hunter's signal to kill the engines and pop open her canopy. "I've never seen an attack this devastating."

"Exactly," said Hunter, standing next to the helicopter. "This isn't an attack, this is a massacre. We haven't found a single Bauhaus soldier or civilian alive."

"Captain, what about the VIP?" asked Sutter, climbing out of the main cabin.

"She's gone. Whoever hit this base took her, I think alive."

"Dirk, is this true?"

"If Hunter says it's so, then it's so," Bamble muttered, staggering out to the aircraft as if in a trance. "We haven't found anyone alive. Except for that thing . . ."

"Thing? What thing?" asked Sutter.

"The thing he killed." Bamble pointed to Hunter as he walked past him, then leaned against the gunship in an effort to remain standing. "You know what happened to it after you blew its head off? It melted—right there before my eyes."

"Melted? How could someone melt?"

"It just did! Oh God, I'm gonna be sick."

Bamble reeled away from the ship and managed to stumble a few feet before dropping to the ground. Sutter and Wendy joined him as he began heaving while Hunter and Alverez were joined by someone else.

"Captain! Captain, you better get over here!" Halston shouted, stopping within hailing distance of the Cutlass. "We found someone alive!"

In response both Hunter and Alverez came charging around the ship's nose and followed Halston back to the hangar he had been ordered to search. Like every other building at Aquila, the hangar was demolished and had largely collapsed. However, it had collapsed around the helicopters inside it, and since none were armed and fueled, they had not exploded when hit.

Near the front of the hangar, the more robust Python One Hundred gunships had withstood the attack well. The metal and composite structure had draped around them like a blanket, which helped hide the two bodies under one from the Dark Legion scavenger search.

"I'm afraid she's dead, Captain," said Redfield. "But this guy's still alive."

The woman, dressed in the uniform of the Bauhaus Military Security Corps, still lay facedown in a pool of her own blood. Her blond hair was stained with it, and it covered the uniform of the Air Cavalry officer Redfield was kneeling beside.

"We heard this one moaning and pulled him out from under her," said Halston, pointing first to the Air Cavalryman, then to the woman. "She caught most of the burst in her back, while he took only one round in that helmet of his."

"It's almost as if she were trying to shield him," Alverez remarked, looking over the scene.

"Let's not get romantic, Julia," said Hunter. "How badly wounded is he?"

"He'll have one hell of a headache when he wakes up," said Redfield. "Other than that, I think he's okay."

"Diane, get Wendy over here." Hunter turned briefly when he sensed someone else was approaching the hangar and discovered one of his snipers. "If Bungle's only tossing his food then he can do it by himself."

"My God. Mitch, we know this man," said Alverez, the shock registering clearly in her voice. "Look."

She pointed to the side of the Bauhaus gunship that had sheltered the two bodies. On it, in addition to the usual service stenciling, was the painting of a small, red airplane with three sets of wings. Below it was the legend VON RICHTOFEN ELITE.

"He's got the blond hair just like Jake said he had," Hunter observed. "I think you may be right. Dave, wipe the blood off that nameplate."

"Max Steiner?" said Julia, once Redfield had finished cleaning the flight jacket's metal identity tag. "*The* Maximilian Steiner. We fought him?"

"What gives, Lieutenant?" said Halston, incredulous. "You two know each other?"

"He's the best combat pilot in the Bauhaus Air Cavalry. And he was the one we fought over Roswell."

"Considering his stature," said Hunter, "he probably led the attack."

"Well, Captain. I say that's the last attack we should let him lead," Halston suggested, pulling the bolt back on his M606.

"No! We owe him our lives!" Julia shouted, pushing the Sergeant off-balance. And by the time he recovered, he found her standing between him and Steiner. "If you want him, you'll have to go through me."

"Cripes, what is it with this guy? Getting women to defend him all the time?"

"Enough, Sergeant. Not even your hero would do something like this," Hunter said sharply. "Not even Bob Watt would call this 'pulling a Watt'."

"Looks like I can't have no fun on this ops," Halston sulked, clicking on his machine gun's safety and turning away from the hangar while Diane and Wendy came running to it.

"My God," said Wendy, coming to stop just short of the blood-soaked bodies. "Diane, I thought you claimed one of these was alive?"

"This one is," said Redfield, sliding out of the tentlike space created by the gunship's port stub wing. "The only thing I think he has is a head injury."

"Can you bring him around?" Hunter asked. "I'd like to find out what happened."

"Let me have a minute or two," said Wendy, kneeling beside Steiner and pulling her med kit in after her. "I won't guarantee anything."

"How much time will you give this?" said Alverez as she and Hunter moved away from the hangar's entrance. "Even though Jeff and I didn't detect any aircraft on our sweeps, it's only a matter of time before some arrive. Military command in Heimburg must already be trying to raise this base."

"I know. I'd like to be long gone before any rescue forces arrive," Hunter responded after thinking for a moment. "In the meantime, there's a few things we can do. Diane, I want you to go around and collect some Dark Legion weapons and artifacts. Try to load 'em in the chopper without Stutter and Bungle seeing you. These'll be for our own use."

"I'll also make sure Rogers doesn't see me," said Parker, before slinging her rifle over her shoulder and heading across the field.

"I'd like to see some of these Dark Legion things," said Alverez. "If that's who attacked this place?"

"No other explanation fits what we've encountered," said Hunter. "These things aren't ghosts or little green aliens. They're real."

"Captain! He's coming around!" Wendy shouted, looking up from her patient. Seconds later both Alverez and Hunter were towering above her and blotting out the sun. "He's got a concussion and a couple of bruised ribs. I think some of the bullets that killed the woman passed right through her and hit him. He's lucky his jacket's got a kevlar lining."

"We'll see if he thinks so," said Hunter, dropping to his knees and crawling forward until he was almost on top of Steiner. "Capitaine . . . Capitaine Steiner, can you hear me? Can you hear me? I'm Captain Mitch Hunter, Capitol Special Forces squad Trident."

"Captain? Am I your prisoner?" Steiner asked after mumbling something inaudible. He opened his eyes and looked at both Levin and Hunter, but was unable to focus on them.

"No Capitaine. I lead a recon squad. We detected your base being attacked and came to help. Can you tell me what happened here? Who attacked you?"

"We . . . we got, warning. I came. Ready guns . . . Then they came." Steiner's eyes rolled and like his speech he made disjointed efforts to get up. So much so that Hunter and Wendy had to hold him down. "They came. Demons! Wild creatures! They attacked . . . Anna, where? Anna!"

"Tell him, Mitch," Alverez requested, kneeling just behind Hunter and looking over his shoulder. "Please?"

"All right," said Hunter. "Capitaine Steiner, your Anna is dead. I'm very sorry. Did the demons kill her? Steiner, did they kill her?"

"They came. We were in hangar," said Steiner, his speech becoming more lucid. For a moment his tear-filled eyes focused on Hunter. "They swarmed, everywhere at once!

Screaming, they never stopped screaming. Even as they died . . . I got some, then Anna was in front of me. Anna . . . Why? Why?"

"It looks like he never got a chance to reload," Wendy informed. She pointed to an MP105 handgun lying far under the Python. Most notable about it was the absence of its unique, angled clip.

"Mitch, I'm getting a report from Jeff," Alverez warned, pulling down her helmet's microphone. "He's got aircraft, at max range."

"Time for us to leave. Tell Jeff to warm up the ship," said Hunter, glancing over his shoulder, then turning back to Steiner. "Capitaine, we have to leave now. Your forces will be arriving soon. We're all sorry for Anna. I promise, if we can, we'll avenge what happened here. Wendy, give him something that'll let him sleep."

"Anna, please . . . Just one more time," said Steiner, and as Hunter backed off him, he caught sight of her body lying at his feet. His tears flowed freely, and his body convulsed with deep sobs. "No. Just once more, I wanted to kiss . . ."

"This'll not only knock 'im out; he'll think we were part of a dream," said Wendy, pulling the autoinjector from his arm. "It'll take effect in a few minutes."

"Then there's just enough time," Alverez remarked helping Wendy out from under the stub wing. Then, peeling off her helmet, she crawled inside and kissed Steiner on the lips. "One last time, my love. Remember me as I was."

"C'mon, let's move it!" Hunter shouted, standing in front of the Cutlass. "This cab's got a fast meter! Julia, what's been keeping you?"

"Something I had to do," said Alverez, trying to slip her helmet back on as she ran. "If Jeff has her ready, we'll dust off in two minutes."

Climbing back into the gunship's second cockpit, she found all its systems checked and the main engines idling. The moment she engaged the rotors they began turning, a final signal to the squad members to board the aircraft.

With the downwash swirling the pillars of smoke, the helicopter lifted off the field and climbed through the pall. Setting course for the Capitol frontier, it dove back to treetop height and would hug the jungle canopy in an effort to avoid detection by the approaching Bauhaus aircraft. Not until it crossed the frontier and was closing on one of the forward bases designated to receive it would the gunship climb and establish radio contact for the first time in the entire operation.

CHAPTER TEN

"From the sound of your chamber, you're quite busy, curator," said Ragathol as his entourage approached the entrance to one of the Citadel's prisoner processing chambers.

"Yes, my Master. Busy," responded Chief Curator Praecor, a soft giggle running through his answer. "The raid has been most successful; we have much to work with. Come, I'll show you the prize."

The noises Ragathol made note of were the moans and screams of the Bauhaus prisoners, at least those who were still alive. Inside the cavernous chamber were row after row of beds, giving it the appearance of a giant hospital ward. But the beds were slabs of stone, and the medical personnel were Dark Legion curators. Their tattered, blood-stained clothing and medieval-looking implements were grotesque parodies of humanity's versions.

For the most part the curators appeared interested in giving pain, not relieving it. For those prisoners still alive, if just barely, they were busy giving injections that started screaming fits, or attaching sluglike black hearts to their chests. And for the dead, they were being "harvested" instead of autopsied. Their limbs and vital organs were hacked from their bodies and carried from the cavern.

Of the hundreds of prisoners taken from Base Aquila, there was only one the curators left relatively alone. The stone slab she lay on had been provided with a thin mattress; she was not restrained with heavy steel manacles; and the equipment hooked into her appeared to be sustaining her life, instead of killing her or driving her mad.

"Greetings, Receptacle," said Ragathol upon reaching Lorraine Kovan's bed. "I've been waiting for you, expecting you. Do you remember me?"

"She will not answer you, my Master," said Praecor, a

sickening lyricism to his words. "She's aware of her sur-
roundings, but we have her in a trancelike state. We think
she never rose out of the one you maintained her in on
Luna."

"I think she'll respond to me." Ragathol bent his massive
frame until his face was only a few inches from Lorraine's.
"The humans who rescued you on Luna thought they could
hide you here, didn't they? Well, there's no place you can
hide from the servants of Algeroth and the Dark Legion. We
have need of you, Receptacle, and soon you'll serve Him as
well. You're beyond the reach of humanity now. Perhaps if
its various entities had united, they could've saved you ...
But now there is no chance."

All the while he spoke Lorraine's blank eyes seemed to
stare through Ragathol to the chamber's ceiling, where the
cries and screams of those around her seemed to gather and
echo. Only when he finished did the eyes blink a few times
and tears roll out of them.

"Good ... I see you understand," Ragathol concluded,
raising his head and laughing triumphantly. "And soon you
will accept. Caliqabaal ..."

"Yes, my Master?" said the necromutant, moving to the
front of the entourage. "What do you wish?"

"Complete the courier ship's preparations for launching.
Be sure there's enough provisions for the flight to Algeroth's
Defiled Castle. We leave when everything is ready."

"What else would you wish done with her, my Master?"
said Praecor. "Do you wish for the attachment of a Black
Heart for the journey?"

"No. She may look frail, but there's no need to reanimate
her," said Ragathol. "Have her moved to one of the Isolation
Chambers close to my Nether Room. The sounds and smells
must be upsetting to her. I want her state to be serene before
we leave. See to it personally, Praecor. From now on she is
your only duty."

"I see the news reached here ahead of us," Hunter grumbled as he, Alverez, and Rogers stepped inside the officers'
barracks. Instead of being greeted with cheering and words
of praise from the other Special Forces personnel, they got
silent, sympathetic stares and a few acknowledging nods.
"So much for the security net thrown around the mission."

"We were in debriefing for so long, it's no wonder they know about us," said Rogers. "By now it must be old news."

"I *still* don't see where Calvin got off calling us failures," said Alverez. Like Hunter she was tired though still defiant. "All of us got back alive, and we didn't create a major incident with Bauhaus. What do you say, Raymond?"

"That I need a shower and a lot of rest. If you don't mind, guys, I'm all argued-out."

"I understand," said Hunter, stopping at the barracks' elevator core and pressing the wall button. "We all need what you mentioned. Go crash the showers, Ray. We'll see you later. Julia, let's find out if our friends left us anything?"

Fortunately, Hunter and Alverez did not have to share the elevator they got with anyone else. On his floor the reception was scarcely any better than what they received in the lobby, a few "I'm sorrys" mixed in with the sympathetic stares. And it was not until they were in his quarters that either felt safe to speak openly.

"I bet we'll be taken off duty now," Alverez warned. "Calvin's been looking for an excuse to do so. We just handed him the best one he'll ever get."

"The debrief would've gone easier if our shadow friend had been there," Hunter said idly, hitting the replay toggle on his message recorder. "I hope Jake's right about him and he was at some sort of stockholders' meeting."

"Well, he was right about our adversary having blond hair. Maybe we should pay more attention to his wild claims. Mitch, is that one from Tim?"

"They're all from Tim. There must be half a dozen messages on this machine."

"Why's he talking like that?" said Alverez. "It sounds like nonsense."

"Quiet. It's supposed to," Hunter informed, leaning an ear closer to the recorder, as if he needed to hear every word in the brief messages. "And from what I can gather, it sounds like Tim's arranged the meeting we wanted with his Brotherhood contact."

"When? Don't tell me it's tonight?" Alverez groaned, and literally had to peel her flightsuit's sleeve back to the chronometer on her wrist. "Ray is right about us. We all need a good shower and a long rest. This hasn't been one of our better days."

"Go get your shower and skip the rest until later." Hunter switched off the machine and picked up the telephone's handset. Without having to think, he began punching in a series of numbers on the keyboard's heavy buttons. "Wendy can give us a booster shot to keep us going for a few more hours. I'll get a hold of Tim. You let the rest of the squad know there'll be a meeting. After I set it up with Tim, I'll phone everyone to let 'em know when."

"All right," Alverez sighed. "Just let me know first. Most of those artifacts are still in the Cutlass, and I'll need some time to retrieve them. If we're gonna meet with the Brotherhood, I'd like them to explain the evidence we gathered."

"From the sound of your debriefing with Hunter's squad, I should've been there," Wood commented, circling the living room's array of sofas and chairs, making sure everyone was comfortable with what he or she had to drink before ordering the servants away. "You browbeat the military commanders and conducted a witch hunt."

"Against someone who claims their failure was the result of an attack by little green aliens?" said Hart, incredulous at Wood's accusation and trying not to show his anger. "You bet a kilo of casino chips I would. This is what you get when you support the insubordinate, Mr. Wood. I tried to warn you about it."

"The evidence your own advisor team and the squad collected points conclusively to the Dark Legion having attacked Base Aquila. Our surveillance efforts were able to sporadically track the raiding force. We finally lost it in the south polar region in an area known for Dark Legion activity."

"Surely you don't believe in the Dark Legion, Mr. Wood," said the Roswell city manager. "We all know there was some sort of alien encounter on Nero. But this Dark Legion 'spook' talk is an invention of the Brotherhood in order to justify their existence."

"I see you've not been to Mars recently," Wood answered, waiting for the executive suite's main doors to close behind the last servants before speaking. "Seen the Dark Legion's Citadel grow in the wastelands. Even in San Dorado, you could feel the towers shake from the battles we and the Brotherhood have fought with the Legion."

"We know of the battles," said Vardon, surprised at Wood's revelation. "But we thought the enemies were Bauhaus and Mishima."

"In a few of the battles they still are. But most are against the Dark Legion. So far, we've been unable to drive them out, and they're impossible to defeat once they've established a Citadel in an area. I think the same thing is happening here, and I've advised Charles Colding of this."

"You've spoken to the Chairman of the Stockholders?" said Hart, so stunned that his glass slipped out of his hand.

"What did he have to say?" General Cyrus asked.

"That we must prevent what's happening on Mars from happening here," said Wood. "I'll be flying to Athena tomorrow to help the command staff prepare a major operation against this infestation."

"And what about the woman?" Vardon requested. "The VIP Hunter's squad was supposed to rescue?"

"The Dark Legion has her," Wood said somberly. "She's deep inside their lair now. We could rescue her from Bauhaus, but not from them. The only escape for her and the others captured by the Legion is death. Mr. Hart, gather all the evidence your team and Hunter's squad collected from Aquila and prepare it for me. Include *everything*, no matter how trivial you think it may be."

"I should've guessed you'd be the last one to show up," Hunter noted, responding to a sharp knocking on the apartment door.

"The security at our hangar makes it difficult even for us to enter it," said Alverez, holding up a canvas bag, "let alone take things out of it."

With her arrival the entire squad was in Small's apartment, except for Rogers. If anything, it was even more crowded than before. Portius and his flowing mystic robes filled up most of one of the living room's sofas. It forced many of the squad members to stand if they wanted to be in the room and part of the conversation.

"There, we can talk freely now," said Small, setting the radius on his sonic disruptor and activating it. "I believe everyone's already met you, Portius. Except for you, Lieutenant. Portius, this is Lieutenant Julia Alverez, the squad's pilot."

"Yes, the former Silent Vengeance pilot," Portius noted, rising and bowing in Alverez's direction. As he did so, his eyes focused on the bag she held and seemed to look right into it. "Like your compatriots, I'm pleased to meet you."

"How'd you know I was once in Silent Vengeance?" said Alverez, immediately defensive and suspicious, mostly because of the drugs Wendy had given her earlier.

"Don't be shocked, Lieutenant. The Brotherhood archives are the most extensive in humanity. We have some information on virtually everyone, especially military personnel."

"Let's not get off on an antagonistic stance," said Hunter, accepting the bag from Alverez. "We're here to exchange information, not renew old suspicions."

"Agreed," Portius added, retaking his seat. "Timothy has explained to me your belief that you're facing the Dark Legion, and I've seen his evidence. Now I hear on your latest operation you had a more direct confrontation with the Legion. Can you illuminate?"

"We can do better than illuminate. We can do what they called in my school Show and Tell."

Hunter opened the bag and carefully removed what looked to have once been a Bauhaus MP-105 handgun. While it still had the basic design, its appearance was distorted by the thornlike projections growing out of it. Hunter gingerly worked the action, to prove to Portius it still functioned and to show it was empty, then laid it on the table in front of him. All the while it was being handled, Portius's eyes showed a mixture of repulsion and fascination.

"We think this is a Dark Legion weapon," Hunter continued, "obviously based on the Bauhaus MP-105. We found it at the base where Bauhaus had been keeping Lorraine Kovan."

"And what of the woman?" said Portius, taking his eyes off the weapon for the first time since its appearance.

"Gone. The base had been torn up by some type of Legion assault. We think they took her back to wherever they came from. Our superiors think we're crazy. They think the base was hit by Cybertronic, and weapons like this might be of their manufacture."

"I can assure you this abomination did not originate with Cybertronic." Portius's gaze returned to the weapon. He hesitantly reached out to it, running his fingers carefully over the projections. "You are partly right, Captain Hunter. This is a Dark Legion weapon, but it's no copy. This was once the human weapon you mentioned, until the Legion seized and corrupted it with their hideous necrotechnology. You see, the Legion builds very little of its own equipment. They prefer to take what man has created and pervert it to their own use. As they shall one day do to us, if they're not stopped."

"What about these thorn-things?" Venneti asked. "What good are they? My assistant cut his hand up on them."

"Has his hand been looked after? Treated?" said Portius, glancing up and catching sight of Harris waving his bandaged hand. "Have you received antibiotic injections?"

"Injections?" said Harris sarcastically. "At the base hospital they practically turned me into a human pincushion."

"Good. With a wound delivered by a Dark Legion implement, one must be careful of spreading corruption. The exact purpose for these projections is unknown. But they do provide the weapon with many cutting edges, making it even more dangerous in a close-quarters, melee attack."

"That could explain the appearance of the Bauhaus dead we found," Wendy concluded. "Except for those in inaccessible areas, they were not only shot, they were torn up."

"Torn up, there's that phrase again," said Portius. "The evil patterns of the Dark Symmetry are becoming even more apparent."

"All right, here we go," said Shacker, throwing his hands up. "The spook show starts. I knew we'd get to this, only I didn't think it'd be so soon."

"Hold it, Jake. Let's give him a chance to speak," Hunter suggested. "Portius, we discovered a lone survivor of the attack. He described it as being 'wild', that the Legion soldiers were everywhere at once, swarming and screaming. They moved so fast they apparently were unstoppable. Is this how the Dark Legion fights?"

"For the most part, yes," said Portius. "Their attacks are sudden and terrifying. If you're unprepared for them, they will paralyze you to your soul. Their basic soldier is the Legionnaire, the dead from our own battlefields and cemeteries reanimated by their necrotechnology. They fight with insane frenzy, but are mindless. They need to be led by a Centurion or necromutant, or will not act at all. The creatures I mentioned were once human as well, but were alive when captured. Distorted by Legion technology, they're monstrous living war machines and can take great injuries before dying."

"That's what we encountered in the hospital," Wendy blurted out. "No wonder we had to shoot it so many times before we killed it."

"Wounding these creatures will not stop them. They must be destroyed. There is no glory in confronting them in close-quarter combat. If they get that near to you, it's likely you'll be killed. You must use your firepower without mercy, Captain. For those humans corrupted by the Legion, annihilation is their only release from living death."

"And who's behind them?" Parker requested. "So far you've only told us about the humans who are turned into monsters. Who does the turning and why are they out to destroy us?"

"The heart of the Dark Legion are the creatures our explorers and settlers released from imprisonment on Nero," said Portius after taking a deep breath to help compose himself. Even so, beads of sweat started appearing on his black forehead and glistened softly in the room's light. "The Apostles of the Dark Symmetry and their generals, the nepharites. All the others, from tekrons to Legionnaires, are either beings created by their hideous technology or perverted through it to serve their purpose. Where they came from and who imprisoned them on Nero is unknown to the Brotherhood. In reality those questions are irrelevant to the struggle that lies before us. And no, my child, they're not out to destroy humanity. *This* is what they plan to do with us."

After studying it for so long, Portius was able to slide his fingers around the corrupted weapon and lift it off the table without getting cut.

"They wish to seize us, defile and pervert us into their own creation, and have billions of souls in unquestioning service to their dark ends. Perhaps then we'll learn the reasons why they were imprisoned and who did it. The cost, however, will not be worth the answers."

Portius let the weapon fall from his hand, and though it only had about half a foot to drop, the momentum it picked up caused its sharp projections to embed in the table's sur-

face. That left the gun positioned awkwardly and menac-
ingly, its muzzle trained on Hunter.

"Nice trick. But your point has already been driven
home," he said, glancing around the room at the rest of his
squad. He found the incredulous and mocking smiles they
had worn at the start of the meeting were replaced with more
sober expressions. "I think you have a squad full of believ-
ers."

"I hope it has, Captain," Portius warned, leaning against
the sofa's back and relaxing a little. "The Dark Legion is a
threat that humanity has still only half awakened to. After
countless centuries of being our own worst enemies, we're
now confronted with an adversary whose threat far exceeds
anything we can do to ourselves. I hope you understand well
the gravity of all this and will steel yourselves for combat
the likes of which you've never experienced before."

"We must plan my arrival at His Defiled Castle to coincide with a period of light activity for Algeroth," said
Ragathol, studying a map of the solar system displayed on
his wall screen. A line arced around the planets, the path his
courier ship would take to reach its outermost fringes and
Nero. "That way, He can personally welcome me in triumph
and glory."

"A difficult task, my Master," responded Echmeriaz,
seated at the controls to the wall projector system. "It could
be accomplished by changing certain aspects of your flight
plan. I'm not experienced or skilled enough on these matters
to accomplish what you need. Our most experienced pilot
should be here."

"Ah yes, Caliqabaal. I sense his presence growing stronger." Ragathol smiled and turned to the entrance to his
Nether Room. Moments later, the massive, hulking form of
the anticipated necromutant appeared in the dim light spilling from the room's antechamber. Ragathol continued to
smile until his servant was close enough for him to sense his
anxiety. "Yes . . . what is the trouble?"

"A problem has arisen in the courier ship," said
Caliqabaal, a slight tinge of fear in his voice. "Critical components in its main engine have failed and need to be replaced."

"Then do so," Ragathol ordered, becoming irritated.

"Command Shaguhl to manufacture replacements and see to it that my departure isn't delayed significantly."

"It's ... it's not that easy, my Master. The parts are manufactured out of molecularly bonded uranium alloy. They're beyond the capabilities of our necrotechnology to replicate."

"You mean to tell me something this insignificant will deny me my triumph?" Rising from his thronelike chair, Ragathol glowered at Caliqabaal, then his skin glowed with an electric green light. "The Wrath of the Apostles be upon you!"

The moment the nepharite raised his arm, the green arcs dancing over his body sparkled on Caliqabaal's body. A little more slowly than the heretic, the necromutant was lifted off his feet and pinned against the wall. His face wracked with pain, he did not bellow or scream. Instead, he concentrated his energy on giving an answer.

"Master, this needn't delay you for long!" he said. "We can obtain the parts we need from outside sources! We can steal them from Capitol!"

"Very well ... explain," said Ragathol, lowering his arm. And the instant the sparks stopped dancing on the necromutant's body, he landed on the floor with a resounding crash. "What military base will we have to raid now?"

"No military base, my Master. The parts we need are common to all Capitol-built spacecraft, both military and civilian. The Atlantis Spaceport will have large quantities of these parts. If we could organize a cell of heretics to steal them, then only a small raiding force need be used. It could be as small as a single Capitol gunship."

"Very good ... arrange it immediately."

"Yes. Yes, my Master," Caliqabaal responded, lifting his heavy frame off the floor. "I'll see to it at once. I promise it won't delay you for long."

"Wait, before you leave," said Ragathol, massaging his injured arm and finding he could still easily move it. "The pain you experienced when I summoned the Powers ... What did it feel like?"

"It was ... exquisite, my Master."

"Excellent, I've regained my abilities. I am healed!" Ragathol moved to the center of his room where he spread his legs and raised his arms without difficulty to the apex of its domed ceiling. He laughed joyously as his body once again glowed with the power of the Dark Symmetry. "I've triumphed over those who violated me on Luna! Go now, both of you. And when I bid your return, I expect to hear that our minions are preparing for the raid we'll launch."

CHAPTER ELEVEN

"Well, you look bright-eyed and on-line today," Alverez noted when the warning knock on her door was followed by Hunter entering her quarters.

"I should," he answered. "It's now the middle of the afternoon. I must've slept for almost twelve hours. Wendy, what are you doing here?"

"Going over some of the revelations Portius told us about last night," said Levin, seated at the room's small table, which was piled with many of her medical and psychological texts. "We were discussing these spells the Dark Legion creatures can cast on us. We're trying to figure out if there's a way to neutralize them."

"That depends on if you believe these creatures can actually do it." Hunter moved over to the table and glanced at the titles of the various books. "I think some of it may just be what Jake said it was, Spook Talk. Not even Portius could claim everything he told us was factual."

"I know, but it would go a long way in explaining why so few Dark Legion incidents are reported. It may also explain the reports of so many insanity victims found at the scenes of crimes and even military clashes."

"You remember the stories flying around that assassination of big-time Mishima officials?" said Alverez, joining the others at the table. "That many of their bodyguards were raving nut cases when Lord Heir's police arrived. This could explain it."

"Oh yes, from earlier in the year," Hunter recalled, snapping his fingers as the memory came back to him. "I thought that was explained away as a Cybertronic attack?"

"It seems everyone wants to blame Dark Legion activity on Cybertronic. If you haven't heard, the latest news reports from Heimburg are blaming them and Mishima for the Aquila attack. I wonder, who does Cybertronic blame when the Legion hits them?"

"The Brotherhood. Those two rarely get along. So, what have you two decided will help defend us against these spells the Legion can cast?".

"Except for the Dark Gifts Portius claims can warp time and space, the rest must work on some principle of auto-suggestion or mind control," Wendy advised, closing the book she had been studying. "What could work against them might either be a strong determination or certain strong emotions. However, the countering effects may only be transitory."

"So your answer is get angry, stay angry, and kill 'em fast," said Hunter, glancing away from the books and catching sight of some framed documents on the nearby wall. "What are these, Julia? Original shares of Capitol stock?"

"No, something I think is much more historically important," said Alverez. "Why don't you read one?"

"You're on. You think I can't read this old-style script?" Hunter leaned against the wall and studied one of the frames before reciting its contents. " 'We the People ... of the United States, in order to form a more perfect union, establish justice, insure domestic tranquillity ...' This sounds a little familiar, what is it?"

"The Constitution of the United States of America. The other is the constitution for something called Canada. Together they represent the foundations of the principal countries that eventually became Capitol. There was once a time in our ancient past when people pledged their allegiance to nation-states, not MegaCorporations—when the ideals of individual rights were codified under the law—when armed forces swore to defend the freedoms and interests of those people, not the corporate bottom line. Maybe it wasn't perfect, but it's better than what we have now."

"Some of what's in here is familiar," said Hunter, reading farther into the document. "Now I know where parts of Capitol's corporate creed come from."

"A lot of what we say and do has origins in the past," Alverez replied. "Only we don't know it. They haven't taught ancient history in the schools for generations, just corporate history. Does anyone know when we say 'the real

McDonald's' that it refers to an ancient company of restaurants that specialized in serving hamburgers?"

"That's a rather trivial matter, but I understand what you're getting at. None of the MegaCorporations want us to know much about the past—especially our ancient past on Earth, where life may have been better before the great crumbling of civilization. How'd you come across these things if history is discouraged?"

"My father gave me these. His collection of ancient artifacts was divided among my brothers and me when he died. He told me he could trace our family's military service back through dozens of generations—to something called the United States Marines."

"Capitol may not teach history," Wendy added, "but they don't ban it or try to rewrite it, like Mishima or Bauhaus. The colleges teach some ancient history courses, and there are curiosity shops where you can buy items like those, or replicas."

"Curiosity shops," said Hunter, while Alverez went to answer her phone. "Things like these should be in museums. Perhaps one way to debase history is to turn it into something insignificant. Yes, Julia, who is it?"

"It's Tim," said Alverez, waving the handset at him. "And it sounds urgent."

"He's probably run out of hamburger." Like all quarters for officers below the rank of major, this one was tiny and Hunter easily crossed it in a few strides. When he reached the desk, Alverez tossed him the handset and returned to Wendy. "Yes, Tim, what's new? Portius? What did he call you about?"

The mystic's name caused both Julia and Wendy to stop leafing through the text books and turn to Hunter. For the next few minutes he gave only a few terse replies and hurriedly wrote whatever Small was telling him on one of the notepads scattered across the desk.

"Well? What was that all about?" Alverez finally asked when the telephone's handset landed back on its cradle.

"There's activity in the local heretic groups," said Hunter. "Portius is hiring Tim to help watch the one here. But the informants the Brotherhood has in the groups indicate the main action will be at Atlantis."

"That spaceport? What would the Dark Legion want there?"

"Maybe another assassination?" Wendy blurted out. "Most Capitol VIPs go through it instead of the old port at Athena."

"No, Portius doesn't think so," said Hunter, walking back to the table. "The number of heretics being organized is too large for assassins and a support team. He and Tim think they may be trying to break into the place."

"What would they want from there?" said Alverez.

"The Brotherhood doesn't know. Try as they may, they can't look into the minds of those who control the Legion. But whatever the heretics may be after, the one thing the Brotherhood does know is it's been ordered by their Legion masters on Venus."

"You mean that nepharite-thing Portius told us about?"

"Yes, apparently there is one on Venus," said Hunter, enjoying the surprised reactions. "He may be the nepharite who's reported to have escaped from Luna."

"What're you gonna do with this tip, Mitch?" Alverez requested. "Stopping this operation would be a major coup for us, especially after being blamed for the 'failure' of the ops we did yesterday."

"What do you mean 'us'? This is an internal matter. I'll advise Judy Fowler about the heretics, and she can alert Spaceport Security."

"Mitch, they won't be able to handle this. They're a private police force trained to stop smuggling and petty crimes at the port. They're not us, they're not even Capitol Security Service. At least *they* have access to regular infantry weapons."

"And I'll remind you that we are a military force," Hunter protested, growing defensive. "We can act only on orders from our local commanders or Venus Command. If we do anything else, it's illegal. You got away with stealing those Bauhaus dead, but we won't get away with conducting a private operation *inside* Capitol territory."

"But this is the Dark Legion," said Alverez. "They're more powerful than any organized crime family—more serious a threat to humanity than anything we've done to ourselves. Mitch, listen to me. The future of mankind is at stake."

"She could be right, Captain," said Wendy, trying to be more diplomatic. "This isn't an act of petty theft, or even grand theft, we've been warned about. It's an act of war—covert war, what they once called guerrilla war, but war just the same. We're the only force who can stop it."

Hunter turned away from Julia and Wendy and stared at an almost blank wall, blank except for the framed documents. After staring at them for a few silent moments, he reached out and laid his hand on the American document.

"Let's contact the rest of the squad," he said. "Since we all keep our weapons and some munitions in our quarters, those won't be a problem. However, transportation *will* be. We'll have to work on that when we meet. Which will have to be someplace secluded, but far larger than this."

"The gunnery range," Alverez suggested. "It won't look unnatural for us to go packing all our weapons to it. This time of day there won't be many people in it. And it's right next to the base motor pool."

"Good point, let's do it. If this blows up in our faces, I hope you realize Rebecca won't be able to save our asses. I doubt this'll be something where we can get forgiveness in place of permission."

"Kyle, this is a surprise," said the woman who opened the door. "But a wonderful one. What are you doing here?"

Sarah Roberson planted a heavy kiss on her lover's cheek, then led him into her home by the hand. At thirty-eight she was some fifteen years older than Kyle Mortus, though she did not look it, even when dressed in the sexless, one-piece worksuit of her employer, Inner System Spaceways. In the living room she gave him a much longer and more affectionate kiss, not allowing him to talk until their lips parted.

"What I came here for are your spaceport and company security cards and the access passwords to the ISS computer system," Mortus answered, the warm smile on his face rapidly cooling into a mask of ice. "My friends and I need them."

"What? Friends?" said Roberson, the soft gleam leaving her eyes. "Who are these people?"

Roberson had not closed the door after greeting Mortus, allowing in nearly a dozen people, none of whom she recognized. By then she had released Mortus and was trying to move toward the kitchen telephone without it being obvious.

"I want them, my love," Mortus continued. "Now!"

As he spoke, he extended his hand and Roberson staggered to her knees in pain. She landed partway on the sofa and tried to use it to get back on her feet. But all she succeeded in doing was rolling down its length, all the while being tracked by Mortus.

"What's . . . what's happening?" Roberson screamed. "What are you doing to me? Stop! Please!"

Her lover dropped his hand, not because of her pleas so much as the weakness he experienced in using his Dark Gift against so strong-minded a victim. Within seconds of the pain's cessation Roberson managed to stand and found herself hemmed in by a semicircle of strangers.

"What are you?" she said. "One of those monsters from the Brotherhood shows?"

"You can resist much better than I had expected," Mortus said, his ice-cold look somewhat negated by the sweat running down his face. "We'll have to take what we need in a more typical way."

The gun he drew from under his jacket shocked Roberson; she had not felt it when she embraced him, and in their yearlong relationship he never mentioned owning guns or even liking them. The weapon itself looked like a miniature version of the automatics the Atlantis Security Force carried, except for the extra tube on its barrel.

"Kyle, please," Roberson pleaded when she realized the clicking she heard was the weapon's safety being removed. "You love me."

"I also love those I serve." Mortus brought the gun up to chest height and pointed it in Roberson's general direction. At the distance he stood from her, there was little need to aim it precisely. "And they promise greater rewards."

Unlike the side arms used by the military or security forces, the automatic Mortus held was not .55-caliber, 10mm or some other large bore. It was .25-caliber, a pirated copy of a Mishima target pistol with a shorter barrel and no fore sight over the muzzle. Otherwise, the silencer could not have been attached.

The first shot struck Roberson in the stomach just below the rib cage. The next in the right side of her chest, causing her to spin into the sofa as she doubled up. The third hit her in the neck below the left ear, releasing an immediate spurt of blood from the severed artery. When it smashed through the neck vertebrae, it disintegrated, severing the spinal cord so completely Roberson crashed into the sofa and did not move from where she landed.

"Mortus, she's still alive," said Rich Dorr when he noticed Roberson's labored breathing. In response he drew his own weapon, a Bauhaus MP-105.

"Don't bother finishing her," Mortus ordered, looking up from the handbag he was going through. "She'll die soon enough. If we haven't found what we need in this or her bedroom, we can search her body later when it won't bleed on us as much."

"Kyle, the time," said yet another heretic. Monica Lewis checked the chronometer on her wrist, then held it up for her leader to see its flashing display. "If you delay us any further, we won't have the time to make this look like a robbery."

"Don't worry, if we can't do that now we'll have someone come back later to complete it . . . Wait, I have them! Check to see if these are the correct ones. Shayne, check her bedroom just in case."

The stiff plastic box he pulled from the handbag held several credit card–size security passes, each emblazoned with the logo of either the Atlantis Spaceport or Inner System Spaceways. Also in it was a slightly smaller file card on which all the latest computer access codes for the spaceline's flight vehicle maintenance and repair department.

Upon finishing a cursory exam of the small tract home, Mortus ordered his group to leave it. He never looked back at it or the body of the woman he had repeatedly claimed he loved. Instead, his eyes and attention were now focused on the spaceport visible beyond the residential area where the home was located. For the most part Atlantis was a vast field of ethereal light with only a few of its largest buildings and tallest launch towers discernible in the otherworldly glow.

"How fast are you pushing this thing?" Hunter asked, finally returning to the driver's cockpit.

"A hundred and thirty clicks an hour," said Parker, glan-

cing up at the LED displays mounted on the top of the wind-
shield. "I know she can do more, but I don't want to push
it in this traffic."

The highway connecting Roswell to the Capitol communities along the coast of the Equatorial Ocean was a wide,
four-lane affair. A thousand yards on either side of it were
the high-speed rail tracks that constituted the principal mode
of transport for most of the people in the region.

This usually left the highway lightly traveled, except for
now. The coming weekend meant those who had leisure time
were going to spend it at Nova Miami or the other beach resorts. And seemingly all of them were jamming the north-
bound lanes at this hour.

The bulky, Imperial-designed Riot Wagon towered over
most of the other vehicles on the road, and its drab, military
paint scheme made it an even more conspicuous sight. Despite its size, lack of aerodynamic design features, and six
massive wheels it was also the fastest vehicle using the
highway. Parker was forever weaving it around the slower-
moving traffic and honking it out of her way whenever it
presented a temporary block.

"Damned electric cars," Venneti grumbled, glancing out
one of the observation slits in the main hull. "Why can't
these people use the turbo-trains or shuttle liners?"

"Because everyone has the right to use the most conve-
nient form of transport available to upset Leon Venneti,"
said Shacker, enjoying the slow-burn look he got from the
demolitions expert. "Captain, when do we arrive at the
spaceport?"

"A half hour to forty-five minutes," said Hunter. "That's
if we don't run into more traffic congestion, an accident, or
base security finally figures out someone's acquired one of
their Riot Wagons and puts out an alert on us."

"Captain, what if we do run into an accident?" Parker requested. "Or a road block?"

"Go around it if you can. Imperial designed this thing for
both all-terrain use and crashing barricades. So if you can't
do one, try the other."

"Think you should try contacting Julia and Taylor? They
should've gotten something by now?"

"They should," said Hunter, glancing at the front instrument panel's tactical radio set. "But no, we'll stick to our

plan as agreed. It's a lot more difficult to steal an airplane than even an armored personnel carrier. I'll open up a channel at the arranged time and let them contact us. I hope they can get something. I'd like to have some air support; you can never have too much of it, even in a situation like this."

Continuing to weave sharply around the slower-moving civilian vehicles, the Riot Wagon maintained its illegally high speed. It almost kept pace with the turbine-powered train cutting through the groves of fruit trees some three thousand feet off to its right.

"Will this allow all our vehicles to enter?" Lewis inquired when she handed over the Atlantis security pass to Mortus.

"Yes. Sarah told me how to program the toll bar terminal to admit more than one vehicle," said Mortus, slowing their car to a stop. "She and her co-workers would do it when there was a crush during shift changes."

The moment he slipped the plastic card into the control post's slot, he was tapping out commands on its key pad. An anxious moment later, the card re-emerged, and the toll bar lifted. It remained raised until the last vehicle in the five-car convoy had entered one of many service crew parking lots dotted around the spaceport.

"All right, you guys. How many times have we told you not to gang crash the entrance?" said an overweight, tired Security sergeant. "Hey, what gives with the street clothes? Where are your uniforms?"

The sergeant and his assistant had reached the parking lot before they realized none of the people climbing out of the newly arrived cars were wearing the blue-and-white jumpsuits of the spaceline. At the moment they decided to go for their side arms, paralyzing fear washed over them. Their Bolter heavy automatics slipped from their hands, and they turned to run, only to stumble and fall. They never tried to rise; they barely had the strength to crawl out of the heretics' way.

"You see how easy it is to use your Dark Gifts against the weak-minded?" said Mortus, glancing at those who had been granted the power to invoke terror. "The rest inside the maintenance center will be just as easy."

"How long will they be, 'incapacitated'?" asked one of the other heretics.

"At least an hour, and for some it's forever. Those with weak hearts will suffer cardiac arrest and die. I wish we could have time to practice our skills on them further, but the Master didn't send us here for that."

Inner System Spaceways maintenance and repair center was a simple, two-story blockhouse set behind the much larger storage warehouses and deport hangars. Because they relied on the spaceport's security service, the company provided for none of its own security, apart from the pass cards. The terminal in which Mortus inserted Roberson's pass did not even have the capability of matching the identity of the person using the pass with the one to whom it was issued. Within minutes of entering the facility, the heretics had its entire staff cowering in terror, unable to think coherently enough to even press an alarm.

"How many were here in total?" asked Mortus, sitting down at one of several on-line computer terminals.

"Fourteen in all," answered Shayne Silva, the heretic who led the assault on the second floor. "And all have been neutralized. Would you like me to help you with that? In my job I work with computers all the time."

"So do I." The terminal started beeping and flashed a message on its screen that there had been a mistake on the command input. "This, this is just different than what I'm used to."

"You work in a livestock slaughterhouse. Where do you interface with computers?"

"I just do!" Mortus shouted, glaring angrily at his subordinate until the terminal beeped once instead of repeatedly. "There, we're in! Now all I have to do is call up their inventory of spacecraft spare parts, and we'll soon locate what the Citadel needs from us."

"Yes, Mr. Hart, how may we help you?" said the desk sergeant at the Special Forces barracks. He only needed a moment to identify the civilian standing in his lobby.

"I need to see your log," Hart answered, grabbing the prominent book on the desktop and turning the volume around before it had been offered. "I must round up the members of squad Trident, and so far all I've been able to locate is their communications officer."

"Last time we saw any of 'em was when they packed off

their weapons to the gunnery range. And that was hours ago."

"So I see." Hart stopped leafing through the log's pages and ran his finger down one column of names. "And they all checked out within fifteen minutes of each other. Didn't you think that unusual?"

"No, sir. We often get whole squads booking time at the range," said the sergeant.

"Didn't you think it unusual for a squad just back from an operation would want to fire their weapons again?"

"From what I heard, they didn't do a lot of shooting on that sortie. I'm not part of Security or Intelligence, Mr. Hart. If you want someone to answer those questions, why don't you ask the lieutenant."

The sergeant pointed to the latest arrival in the lobby. Judith Fowler was standing only a few feet behind Hart, yet he was not even aware of her presence until informed of it. She came to attention and saluted him when he spun around and immediately began her report.

"My watch officer said I'd find you here," she started. "There's been a break-in at the corporate hangar on the other side of the field and a theft."

"I'm aware of the hangar's location," Hart said sharply, making the nervous lieutenant even more so. "What was stolen from it? And who did the stealing?"

"Unknown, sir. But what they got away with was an executive transport helicopter. The Star Cruiser, sir."

"What? That was the best in the whole fleet! Is the air defense net tracking it?"

"Unable to, sir," Judith answered. "Whoever's flying it is staying just above the trees and has the ship completely blacked out."

"What do you mean 'whoever'?" Hart asked, his slow burn speeding up. "If you won't say it, I will. This theft sounds like Hunter and his crew."

"How can you be certain, sir? No one knew it was a theft until the helicopter took off."

"Because the Star Cruiser is based on the Cutlass gunship. Only Special Forces pilots would be able to safely fly it. It sure sounds to me like one of them is flying it now, and there's only one unaccounted for. Alverez."

"Why would they want to steal an executive transport?" Fowler asked. "It don't make sense."

"Why should it? This is the Special Forces we're talking about," said Hart, a vindictive smile beginning to cross his face. "Noah Wood can ask them when they're arrested. He wanted them sent to Athena. Well, now he'll get them, in chains. Put out an arrest alert for Mitch Hunter and all the members of his squad except for Rogers."

"Yes, sir. I'll do that as soon as I pick up my partner."

"You mean Lieutenant Nordley? What's he doing? Why isn't he here with you?"

"He's at the motor pool, sir," Fowler informed. "One of our Riot Wagons is missing."

"Oh? And what next is going to be stolen from this base, Lieutenant?" said Hart, the tone of his voice calm but sarcastic. "An F/A-99 fighter? The control tower? You'll find me in the Operations Center. If it's still there."

The highway's weekend traffic continued to be a hindrance to the Riot Wagon, until reaching the Atlantis exit. There most of the traffic continued heading north while the Security vehicle turned east and picked up speed. In minutes the vast, glowing complex appeared.

First in view were the launch gantries, vehicle assembly buildings, and the approach lights to the spaceport's three-mile-long main runway. Later the hangars, passenger terminals, and control tower could be discerned from the smaller buildings, a seemingly haphazard and confusing arrangement to anyone driving up to it.

"Are you sure we're on the right road to the Security Annex?" said Parker, trying not to sound critical.

"This time I'm positive," Hunter promised.

"Captain, you certain this is what we should be doing?" said Venneti, leaning into the Wagon's cockpit. "Roswell's gotta be missing this tin can by now. Suppose we drive up there and they got an arrest warrant waiting for us.?"

"If they do, then we'll have to rely on your charm and Ted's diplomacy. This is the only way we can do it. None of us has any contacts here, and we scarcely know our way around the spaceport. It's the size of a small city, and we're not going to do much sneaking around in a military vehicle.

If we can't be stealthy, we'll be obvious. Maybe we'll find out just how famous I'm supposed to be."

The Atlantis Security Annex was a sparkling new building—a squat pyramid a few stories tall and with an exterior of polished basalt and nearly indistinguishable black armored glass. The Riot Wagon slowed to a stop in front of its main entrance, which brought an immediate, if shocked, response.

"Hey, I know you," said the first patrolman to reach the vehicle. He slipped his automatic back into its holster and snapped its safety strap over it. "You're that Special Forces guy I've read about. Captain Hunter."

"This may be easier than we thought," Hunter whispered to Parker and the others still in the Wagon. "Yes, Officer, you got me. Why are you greeting my men and me with your gun drawn? I was told you'd be expecting us?"

"You? No, sir, sorry. We weren't expecting anyone, let alone someone military."

"God, they screwed up again," said Venneti, picking up on Hunter's question. "I suppose we should be lucky we got here before they attacked. Otherwise these guys would be firing on us."

"We're gonna be attacked?" asked the patrolman in front of his other startled colleagues. "By who?"

"I need to talk with either your commander or your watch officer," said Hunter, trying hard to maintain a serious look as the bait was swallowed. "Whoever's on duty."

"Well, Major Mullen's retired for the night. But Captain Stewart's right inside."

"Then take us to him; obviously there's been a mix-up in communications, and we need to work as fast as possible."

Hunter and his squad were led past the metal scanners at the entrance and straight to its most sensitive offices before being asked to even show their identifications, just moments before meeting the highest-ranking security officer at the spaceport.

"If I were a suicidal assassin, this would be a perfect setup to destroy Atlantis's defense," Hunter said quietly to Shacker. "They haven't even asked us if our weapons have been safetied. I could cut everyone down with a single clip."

"This isn't the military, Captain," Shacker replied, surveying the rooms. "Just a bunch of military would-bes and has-beens."

"Well we better treat 'em nice or we'll get nowhere. Yes, Captain. Thank you for seeing me."

"No, Captain Hunter, the pleasure's mine," said Doyle Stewart, stepping from his office to the ready room where the squad was being held. "We always get VIPs through here, but real war heroes are a rarity. I'm having our communication logs checked, but I'm fairly certain we didn't get the warning you claimed."

"Don't worry about it," said Hunter. "I'll find out what happened at Roswell later."

"Oh, it's not a problem. It'll only take a few minutes to contact Roswell."

"No! The violator units may already be in the spaceport." Hunter tried to keep the nervousness out of his voice, and a smile spread on his face when his warning had its desired effect.

"Violators? You mean Cybertronic Chasseurs?" Stewart asked, stopping cold in his tracks. "What are they doing here?"

"We don't know. All we do know is a Cybertronic Special Operations Unit is in our territory and its target is Atlantis. Now we just wasted a lot of time we don't have, so I suggest we get looking for them immediately."

"I'll put the whole spaceport on alert. If necessary, I'll stop everything except arriving flights."

"No, we can't let the unit know we're on to them," said Hunter, becoming exasperated with the misguided enthusiasm. "This isn't a gang of smugglers we're dealing with. It's a MegaCorp military unit. Let's start with a computer sweep."

Hunter pointed to the ready room's dormant computer terminal, which Stewart had powered up and on-line in about the same number of minutes as he earlier claimed it would have taken to put a call through to Roswell. He instructed the computer to do multiple tasks at the same time. Prime among them was ordering all sub-stations to report in and a sweep for any computer-related unauthorized activity.

"Hold it, Captain," Stewart advised. "I got an anomaly in ISS flight vehicle maintenance."

"Spaceships?" said Hunter, at first puzzled. "Now what would they be wanting there?"

"Spare parts, from the look of it." Stewart nodded at the screen, which he was splitting between two separate files. "Spares are being removed from inventory for which no request has been made by any repair crew. And not just any spares, we're talking critical engine . . . Wait a moment."

A shrill beeping sounded on both the ready room's terminal and in several offices outside it. The immediate response was a lot of personnel running around, with some entering the ready room to ask Stewart what they should do.

"It's like everyone just got official orders to panic," Venneti observed. "What gives, Captain?"

"Sub-station Seventeen-Zero-One-D hasn't answered the automated call," said Stewart. "And none of its crew are manning it. No one can raise them. The station covers the ISS maintenance and repair center and their warehouses. I think we've found your violators, Mr. Hunter. We better move fast."

CHAPTER TWELVE

"Even with the section and lot numbers, they're still difficult to find," Mortus grumbled, stamping down the main aisle between the orderly rows of aircraft and spacecraft parts.

"Perhaps we should've brought the woman with us," said Dorr, "instead of killing her as you did."

"That was no mistake. Her resistance to the Dark Powers would've made her very difficult to control. We would've needed to physically restrain her, and we haven't a large enough crew for that."

Approximately the length and width of a football field, the warehouse was a windowless building with just enough sodium vapor lamps to bathe the interior in continual twilight. It required the heretics to use flashlights, and many of them began shivering in its temperature and humidity-controlled atmosphere.

"Kyle, I have them!" Lewis shouted, the first time she raised her voice since the group entered the warehouse. The rest quickly gathered around her in one of the narrow side aisles.

"Yes, exactly what we need," said Mortus, playing his own flashlight beam over the plastic crates. "Start moving them; we'll have time later to enjoy our triumph."

"Damn! We'll need time just to move them, Kyle," said Dorr after he grabbed one of the crates by its handhold and succeeded only in pulling it off its shelf. "What are they made of?"

"Molecularly bonded depleted-uranium. It's the only alloy that can take the heat and stress of commercial spaceship engines."

"These aren't too bad," one of the stronger heretics replied, lifting the crate Dorr barely moved in a single, clean motion. "But I don't think any of our vehicles can take this much weight, plus passengers."

"Don't worry," said Mortus, smiling. "Our masters will provide us transport. And soon."

"Take the next left and we'll be there," said Stewart, pointing to the intersection signs about a hundred yards ahead of the Riot Wagon.

"Kill the lights," Hunter ordered. "The interior ones as well. Safeties off, everyone. Be ready to deploy the moment I give the command."

At both the intersection and the parking lot entrance, the armored vehicle slowed only enough to negotiate them. It did not come to a full stop until it had crossed the parking lot and driven up to the main entrance of the Inner System Spaceways maintenance center. It's rear hatch had scarcely finished lowering when Hunter's squad and a tiny contingent of Security officers spilled out. While most charged into the building to sweep it, a few were drawn to the thin wails coming from the landscaped knoll near the parking lot.

"Captain, I've found one of my men!" said Stewart, crouching next to a palm tree. "He's alive. But I think he's injured."

"Wendy, you're with me," said Hunter, stopping in midstride and swinging around. "Leo, you're in command. Sweep the building and report back to me."

In seconds Wendy and Hunter had joined Stewart on the knoll and had become the only people still standing outside while everyone else disappeared inside the maintenance center—everyone except for the patrolman they tried to pry off the palm tree.

"God, Keller, you were never this strong," Stewart swore. "Well, at least we know he isn't wounded. What could make someone this scared?"

"An auto-hypnotic suggestion," said Wendy, also giving up trying to pull the man off the tree. She turned to her med kit and removed an injector and several vials of drugs. "I'll give him a muscle relaxant, then something to knock him out."

"You mean someone hypnotized my officer? Check reality, Sergeant, this isn't a trick."

"Captain, is that another of your men?" Hunter asked,

pointing to a body lying behind a lamp pole. He then waited until after Stewart had moved out of earshot before turning to Wendy. "Whatever you do, don't mention Dark Legion or spells. I don't think he'd believe it. Hell, I wouldn't believe if it weren't for what Portius told us."

"That'll be tough," said Wendy. "A Dark Legion mind-control spell is about the only thing that can explain this. We've found our heretics all right. Captain, I think he wants you."

Hunter glanced over his shoulder and found Stewart waving frantically at him. Sweeping the area with his CAR-24 rifle as he moved, he charged off the knoll and hesitantly entered the pool of light created by the lamp. Even though it made him a perfect target, what lay in it compelled him to take the risk of becoming one.

"He's dead," Steward advised, rolling the sergeant's body onto its back. "Dead and not a mark on him, except for the way his face is twisted. Are you gonna tell me this was caused by hypnosis, too?"

"Cybertronic obviously has a new weapon of some type," said Hunter, surprised at the degree to which the man's face was contorted by fear, even in death. "When we find 'em, you better let us deal with them."

"*This* is what my systems woke me up for?" Coral Beach said to himself, lowering the night vision scope from his almost human-looking eyepiece. "An industrial theft? What'll we be blamed for next? Robbing the guests in a retirement center?"

Parked almost half a mile from the ISS maintenance center and warehouse complex, Beach was using one of several observation points he had earlier scouted around the spaceport. He used this one, the parking lot to a derelict restaurant, and the others to spy on Atlantis when Cybertronic needed a report on it.

However, this time it was not his MegaCorporation that ordered him into action, but his own internal surveillance systems. Even when he slept they still performed certain tasks; one of them was monitoring radio frequencies used by Capitol military and security forces. And when those systems had noted a transmission from Atlantis Security about a possible Cybertronic attack, they awakened him.

"If a Cybertronic unit was involved in this, I would've been notified," Beach continued, growing irritated over the sleep he was losing. He felt like disconnecting as many of his systems as he could and going back to sleep. But he only felt like doing so; he chose instead to watch the event unfold. It wasn't usual procedure for Capitol to respond to an industrial theft with what looked like a Special Forces squad.

"Mortus, we've been discovered," announced the heretic who had been left to watch the warehouse entrance. Denton Landis pointed through the Plexiglas outer door at the lone figure barely visible in the shadows and shrubs at the maintenance center's corner.

"It's one man," Mortus dismissed. "Arm your weapon and kill him."

"No, there are others. I've seen them in the building windows. And before that a Security vehicle of some kind drove up to its front. There must be a dozen of them."

"They've cut us off from our vehicles," Dorr said angrily. "And they'll be impossible to fight through. What are we to do now Master Planner?"

"Take the parts to the back entrance," said Mortus. "When you're ready to leave, we'll open fire on them and join you. Jared, I want you and Tony to proceed us and set up sniper posts in the next office building. It's empty, and these passes will get you inside."

"What good will this do?" Lewis demanded as the two men grabbed rifles and weaved around her. "If we go that way, we'll end up at the spaceship hangars and taxiways. Where will we escape to then? Orbit?"

"Our transport will be provided for." Mortus tried to sound serene, but could not keep all the anger out of his voice. "You'll see . . . Now, prepare for our diversion."

"I've seen some movement, but not a lot," Diane reported when Hunter finished crawling up to her position. "Where's Stewart and his patrolmen?"

"With Wendy," said Hunter. "They're examining the ISS people in the center. We found his sub-station crew; they're either scared like the people you saw or dead."

"I take it that's convinced Stewart we're facing a Cybertronic attack."

"It's convinced him we're dealing with someone his forces can't handle. We'll have a free hand in stopping this attack."

"When do we do that, Captain?" asked Diane.

"Soon. You and Jake will provide the rest of us with covering fire when we—Hit the deck!"

Hunter was still giving his orders when a burst of movement caught his attention and Parker's. A group of heretics appeared in the entrance to the only warehouse computer records had showed was recently opened. They separated just far enough to give everyone a clear field of fire, then the muzzle flashes started sparkling.

The barrage not only peppered the two corners where the squad members were gathering, but the entire back facade of the center. The chatter of automatic weapons was accompanied by sounds of glass shattering and falling to the ground. And then it was over. Hunter was raising his weapon to his shoulder when he realized the heretics had fled back inside the warehouse.

"God, Captain. They could've found a nicer way of letting us know they knew we were here," said Venneti, his voice overriding everyone's else's on Hunter's headset.

"Cut the comedy," Hunter ordered. "That was a diversion. They're not following it up with an attack or any kind of suppressing fire. We go as briefed, only don't enter the warehouse. We have to get to its back door and cut 'em off."

"Good. *Very* good," said Beach, watching the squad advance on the warehouse. "After contending with police amateurs for so long, it's refreshing to watch professionals."

Beach did not have much time to enjoy the operation; he soon lost the squad when they moved in between the warehouses. He resumed sweeping the general area with his night-vision scope and did not have to wait long before he located more activity.

"So, you're the ones who committed the theft," he continued, scanning the people who emerged from the other end of the warehouse complex. "You look like a street gang, but Capitol wouldn't deploy an elite military unit on an internal operation if you were. Who could you be?"

His internal systems analyzed every possibility in seconds, far faster than his human brain alone could. He could almost feel them working, evaluating every piece of evidence he had so far gleaned. And all reached the same conclusion.

"The Dark Legion," said Beach. "But Capitol doesn't believe in you. Could it be they're finally awakening?"

Another movement caught his attention, this time in an office building that had a commanding view of the warehouse complex, the ISS hangars, and taxiways. This time his instinct beat out his computer-generated analysis; it would be the perfect location for a sniper. Beach fixed his scope on a corner office, where a man was using something to cut circular holes in all its windows.

"No, there'll be no triumph for you tonight," he said, turning to his car and hitting the trunk release.

"Watch it when we get near the end," warned Hunter. "They could have someone fighting a rearguard action."

Shacker was the first to reach the warehouse's opposite end, skidding to a halt and pressing himself against its side. From his position he could sweep only a limited sector. Though by the time the rest of the squad had joined him, he had located the heretics.

"They're carrying a couple of things in small storage boxes," said Shacker, studying the image on his scope's tiny view screen. "Looks like they got whatever they came for."

"What's the range?" asked Hunter, unable to discern anything more than tiny silhouettes moving against the distant hangars.

"Scope says just shy of two hundred yards. These people can move fast, too."

"That's at the limit of effective range for most of us. Jake, you, Diane, and Ted are to unload on 'em. And make sure you aim carefully. People are still working in those hangars."

As an executive marketing consultant, it was not unusual that Beach should drive a Bauhaus Vinciano-Traffaux heavy convertible. The luxury car was a highly coveted status symbol by the officials of all the MegaCorporations; and since Cybertronic built no such vehicles of its own, it looked entirely natural that he was provided with one. What Beach enjoyed most about the car was its interior space and the modifications Cybertronic did to it. He only had to open a small hatch in its trunk in order to pull out an SR3500 sniper rifle.

The heavy, long-barreled weapon had an integral bipod that most operators felt the need to use. Beach, however, had mastered the art of firing the rifle without such support. As he walked back to his observation point, he completed activating the sighting system and interfaced with it.

"Just one machine talking to another," he grumbled, yet he found a cold pleasure in the way he and the rifle interacted. He was already letting it know the range over which it had to shoot and the lighting conditions to optimize the scope's performance. With a reassuring clink the bolt pushed the first 15mm round from the clip into the breech; a moment later he took the safety off.

Back where he had stood earlier, Beach planted his feet in a firing stance and raised the SR3500 to his shoulder. He did not have to rescan the distant office building to relocate his target. He knew exactly which floor and which corner to aim at. Already focused, light-enhanced, and set at maximum magnification, he placed the scope's aiming grid on the heretic, who was also raising a rifle to his shoulder.

"Your luck has ended, heretic," said Beach, squeezing the trigger and lowering the gun a few millimeters, compensating perfectly for the rise it took when the heavy bullet rode down the barrel.

"Damn! What was that?" Shacker demanded, swinging out of what he imagined was the line of fire and slamming his back against the side of the warehouse. "Who's shooting at us?"

But the explosion he and the rest of the squad reacted to was not gunfire; it was more shattering glass. They all looked up in time to see a body finish ejecting from the fifth floor of a nearby office tower and begin its fall. Around it shone a fountain of glass shards, sparkling in the light from the hangars. The body tumbled as it fell, but did not flail around. Its movements were limp, and Hunter realized he heard no scream coming from it. He concluded whoever it had been was already dead, just before the body and rifle accompanying it crashed resoundingly in the parking lot.

"Who the hell got him?" asked Halston seconds after the heretic's flight ended.

"I don't know. Maybe some of these Security guys aren't too bad after all," said Hunter. "Jake, can you still nail 'em?"

"I'll give it a try, Captain," Shacker replied, reshouldering his Improved M89. And moments after he reacquired the even more distant targets, the muzzle of his weapon erupted with a blinding flash.

"Kyle, help me!" screamed one of the heretics who was helping carry the spare parts. He let go of his side of the crate and grabbed his right thigh. "They've shot me!"

The case thumped loudly when it hit the ground, as did the others. The heretics made less noise when they fell, except for the one whose leg was nearly torn apart by the artillery-size bullet. He continued to scream for help and rolled about in agony.

"Silence him!" Mortus ordered, and a moment later a sharp crack echoed across the open ground. When the echoes faded, the crying was no longer heard. "Did anyone see where the fire came from?"

"It must've come from the warehouses," said Lewis, raising her head just enough to see above the grass and weeds they were all lying in.

"I want to know what type of weapon they're using," said Dorr. "At this distance the side arms and submachine guns Security has shouldn't reach us."

Dorr raised his head higher than the others to get a better view of the warehouse they had just fled from and was rewarded with a sputtering muzzle flash. He ducked in time to avoid the shells whistling over him; they dug a line of dirt plumes a few yards beyond the heretics.

"That's automatic weapons fire," Dorr belatedly informed. "Someone a lot bigger than Security is after us, and they got us trapped."

"Not for long," said Mortus. "The Legion will be here soon. They promised they would."

"I got 'em pinned down, Captain," said Halston, looking up from the sights on his M606. "But at this distance, I won't be too effective at hitting 'em."

"We can nail them," Parker offered. Unlike Halston, she and Shacker were standing and bracing their weapons against the corners of the warehouses the squad was hiding between.

"No, shoot the crates they came for," said Hunter. "Only shoot the heretics if they fire on us. I'd like to capture a few for questioning. Coordinate with Ted; the rest of us will move out and surround them."

At Hunter's order, most of the squad assembled behind him and cautiously moved out. They had yet to proceed more than a dozen yards before one of them noticed a formation of lights, low in the night sky and heading into the spaceport.

"That has to be Julia," Venneti guessed. "Looks like she and Taylor found something they could fly."

"I don't know," said Hunter, more cautious. "She hasn't contacted us, so how would she know where to find us?"

The aircraft quickly became visible in the glow of the spaceport's lighting. It was a huge helicopter, more than twice the size of the Special Force's Cutlass, with twin fuselage booms, broad-chord stub wings, and large external fuel pods. The overall design was readily identifiable, yet it was bizarrely deformed, with many spike and thornlike projections marring its surface.

"Weird," said Harris. "It looks like those weapons we discovered at the Bauhaus base."

"Bauhaus," Hunter repeated, the shock of recognition in his voice. "Take cover! That Guardian's now a Dark Legion ship!"

The AH-19 was the standard helicopter gunship of the Capitol Air Force, though it looked more like something that would be deployed by the Capitol Ground Forces. It was a flying tank, slow and cumbersome, yet heavily armed and armored. It displayed all these aspects as it ponderously circled the field where the heretics had been trapped.

Between the scream of its engine and the thumping of its main rotor blades, all other sounds were drowned out in the area. Even the firing of its own turret-mounted auto-cannons and Gatling gun were muted to barely discernible chatters. Fortunately, the muzzle flashes were very prominent and gave Hunter's squad just enough warning before a storm of shells lashed the warehouses where they had taken refuge.

After the storm passed, the gunship's sound was still omnipresent. And when they peered out from where they were hiding, Hunter's squad discovered it had landed.

"Move it! Move it!" Mortus shouted, even though his words were lost more than two feet away from him. More effective was his waving his people onto the massive helicopter's tail ramp. "He won't give us much time!"

Mortus pointed at the top of the ramp where the looming form of a necromutant stood. He started moving when he noticed the slowest heretics were the ones lugging the spare parts. In a few strides he was at the ramp's base and grabbing the crates from them. Cradling three in his arms, he charged back up the ramp, each footfall seemingly shook the entire aircraft. Moments later the ramp's hydraulic struts were pulling it flush with the fuselage pod's tail, cutting the noise level back to a constant rumble.

"I have two men stationed in the flight reservations center," said Mortus. "Will we pick them up?"

"No. We've made no provision to pick up anyone else," said the necromutant, grumbling loud enough to be heard. "They'll delay whoever was attacking you. Should they survive the operation, we'll rescue them later."

"But they're risking their lives for us."

"The Legion appreciates their sacrifice, and they'll be rewarded for it. If not in this life, then the next. Now, sit down, we're lifting off."

Analysis of target aircraft indicates a 100% probability that it is Dark Technology corrupted. End run. End run . . .

"Suspicions confirmed," said Beach, smiling as his systems reached a unanimous conclusion. "Only the legion could so defile a machine and yet still have it operate."

He held the SR3500's sight on the helicopter, trying to study it even though the reservations building partially blocked his view. When he had been completely human, the weight of the rifle would have quickly tired his arms. Now, with the latest cybernetic implants, he could hold the weapon for hours and not feel any exhaustion.

A movement in the sight's view screen caught his eye. It

was not the AH-19, or anywhere around it, but on the building that obscured his view. A normal human would have dismissed it, or not even noticed it in the first place, but he tracked it. And the moment he decided it warranted closer inspection, the sight zoomed in on the building's roof and refocused.

Beach immediately recognized the human form in the silhouette and the long barrel of the rifle it held. He had a clear shot at the distant sniper, but decided not to take it, yet. Even with his digital enhancement system he could not tell if what he had centered in his aiming grid was a Capitol soldier or a heretic.

"Don't bother shooting at it," Hunter advised, walking among the twisted pieces of sheet metal and concrete rubble blasted off the warehouse by auto-cannon fire. "You'd only get it angry at us."

A sharp increase in rotor noise heralded the take off of the giant gunship. It rose slowly, scarcely moving forward at all until its landing gear sets were retracted. Its multiple turrets continued to sweep the spaceport, but did not fire. Its crew was now more intent on escaping than fighting its way in. Even though it moved slowly, inside of a minute it had become just another constellation of lights low in the night sky.

"Damn, we blew it," said Venneti, emerging from the alley between the two warehouses. "This is becoming a habit."

"I think they're gonna start calling us Squad Bungle," Shacker added, "along with our advisor."

"Don't give up yet," said Hunter, pressing one of his headset earphones a little deeper into his ear. "I got Julia."

"I know who you are now, heretic," said Beach the instant his target pointed its rifle at the Capitol soldiers. "Join your friend."

He again lowered his SR3500 a few millimeters before pulling the trigger. The barrel snapped back up as a powerful flash erupted from its muzzle. The report of the heavy, high-velocity bullet starting its flight was deafening. But half a mile away no one heard it or saw the flash. Just the way Beach wanted it.

"Don't think I feel sorry for you, heretic," Beach remarked, keeping his sight on his last target. "You willingly gave up your humanity, I had no choice in the matter. And you serve evil, I've found the perfect enemy. Computer, end interface."

"Captain! Here comes another one!" Parker shouted, motioning to the office building.

A much larger movement caught her attention, that of a human body spasming and falling off the roof. Once again there was no report of gunshot, no scream from the victim. He arced through the air as if he had jumped, or been thrown, and landed with a snapping crash in an ornamental tree. The accompanying rifle made more noise when it hit the parking lot.

"Who's doing that?" asked Venneti, dropping to a low crouch and sweeping the area with his submachine gun. "It sure ain't' us."

"And whoever it is, he's not in this area," Hunter added. "I don't hear any gunfire. I don't see anyone but us and the copter Julia stole."

"What'll we do about those bodies?" questioned Harris.

"Leave it for Security. We have a gunship to catch."

Like the AH-19 before it, the newest helicopter circled the expanse of open ground before coming in to land. However, it did not lay down a devastating barrage of cannon fire; it didn't even brandish any weapons. The sleek machine was far smaller and maneuvered faster. The moment it finished settling onto its landing gear, its main cabin doors swung open.

"Good God, you stole a Star Cruiser!" said Hunter, first to climb inside and clearly impressed at what his pilot had managed to steal. "How does she fly?"

"A lot like a Cutlass!" Julia answered, seated in the cockpit's left-hand seat. "But I don't like this side-by-side arrangement!"

"This sure is fancy!" said Halston, climbing in next, and even more impressed with the cabin's lush fittings. "We're gonna get to ride like real executives!"

"Yeah, but how are we gonna fight like soldiers from this thing?" said Shacker.

"We'll figure it all out later!" Hunter advised, then lowered his voice as the cabin doors swung shut. "Julia, get us in the air."

"Wait, Captain," said Taylor, looking over the cabin behind his seat. "Where's Wendy? What happened to her?"

"Don't worry, she's safe. She's helping Security with the casualties. Julia, move this thing."

Rocking slightly, the executive transport leaped off the ground and pitched its nose down steeply to increase speed. By the time it leveled off, it was departing the spaceport at nearly two hundred miles an hour, twice the speed of the Dark Legion AH-19.

"Those people after us, you think they were military?" Dorr asked, walking up to the cabin's front row of seats.

"With the kind of weapons they used against us?" said Mortus. "Of course they were. We not only outsmarted Atlantis Security, we beat the Ground Forces as well."

"Our pilot, Caliqabaal, would tend to agree with you," said the necromutant controlling the cargo deck crew. "But don't be so quick to announce our success."

The massive creature pointed to the monitor screen directly above the front seats. On it was a tail camera view of Atlantis. Already the spaceport was an island of light retreating toward the horizon; all around it the far smaller communities similarly glowed against the velvety black background. Above the landscape moved a cluster of flashing lights, which were all extinguished as soon as the helicopter moved beyond the spaceport's immediate vicinity.

"Do you wish us to man the gunnery stations?" asked Mortus.

"No, I want all of you to stay in your seats," said the necromutant. "We'll deal with this interference ourselves."

Similar in overall design to the Special Forces Cutlass, the Star Cruiser had a conventional tail rotor in place of the ducted fan unit and a much shorter, broader nose to accommodate a pilot and copilot in side-by-side seating. It also did away with the retractable landing skids and stub wings in favor of conventional landing gear mounted under the nose and in external sponsons. All of which gave the helicopter a distinctly less predatory look, yet it still retained the speed and maneuverability of its military cousin.

"Not only don't we have any weapons on this bird," Alverez warned. "We have no way to mount any. There's no mounts on the hatches and there's no way to open 'em in flight."

"Then what good is this thing?" asked Halston. "It'll get us there but won't let us fight."

"Don't sweat it. We got power windows," Taylor added. "After all, this is an executive ship."

"All right, I'll take the port hatch," said Hunter, checking the munition load status of his M50 rifle. "Ted, you take the starboard one. Leo, you'll back me up and Redfield will back up Ted."

"What about us, Captain?" Shacker complained. "We can hit harder than your rifles and submachine guns."

"What good would we do?" inquired Parker. "The 'Nineteen is the most heavily armored warplane in our inventory. What we have are infantry weapons, and they won't bring it down."

"The new dash-twelve rifle grenades might," said Hunter, holding up a sharp-nosed munition the size of a ten-gauge shotgun shell. "They worked pretty good on that Cybertronic observation post and it was heavily armored. Julia, what type of attack do you want to try?"

"Diving attacks," Alverez replied. "That Grapeshot may be heavily armed and armored. But it doesn't have much armor on its topsides, none of its turrets point up, and we can fly circles around it."

"Grapeshot? I thought the Air Force called these things Guardians?" said Redfield, confused.

"Never mind," said Hunter. "We'll do aircraft recognition later. Is everyone ready?"

"Captain, should I continue broadcasting to Air Defense that we're chasing a hostile?" Taylor asked.

"If they haven't answered you by now, don't bother. Everyone set? Open the windows."

Tapping a couple of rocker switches, Taylor popped open the windows on the main doors. The roar and rotorwash flooded the cabin, though not to the expected level. By bracing their weapons against the window frames, both Halston and Hunter were able to steady their weapons, until Alverez dropped the Star Cruiser into a steeply turning port dive.

By now it was several thousand feet above and moving

ahead of the Dark Legion helicopter. The maneuver put it
slashing across the AH-19's line of flight, just a little too
high for the various turrets to track it properly. However,
they still threw up a heavy curtain of tracers, making the return fire from Hunter puny by comparison.

At full automatic his rifle burned through its thirty-round
clip in the first seconds. After it he worked the pump to the
grenade launcher; with its safety off and a round in its
breech all he had to do was squeeze the trigger and the
weapon kicked hard into his shoulder.

The first round passed safely though the AH-19's rotor
disc and exploded in the second cockpit. It killed the primary gunner instantly, causing all the turrets to fall silent.
The second grenade was hit by a rotor blade and spun out of
control. The third hit the fuselage above one of the forward
auto-cannon turrets. It penetrated an armor plate, but did little damage to internal systems.

"Julia, take us closer!" Hunter shouted after Venneti replaced him at the window behind the pilot's seat. "I think
we killed their NEW Guy! We can do some real damage before the turrets go independent!"

Swinging low behind the twin tail booms, Julia fought to
keep the Star Cruiser level and give Venneti the best firing
arc. Like Hunter before him, he went through his clip of
10mm rounds in the first seconds. Firing the caseless rifle
grenades took a little longer, though by then Hunter had still
not finished reloading to replace him.

"Outta my way, Leo!" Halston advised. "I'll show you
some real damage!"

Rocking the helicopter with each step he took, the fire
support specialist crossed to the cabin's port side and pushed
the barrel of his machine gun through the open window. He
fired as he took his stance, scoring a few damaging hits but
mostly getting spectacular ricochets off the AH-19's armor
plates and rotor blades.

Slowly, the huge ship wheeled to the left, a clumsy attempt to evade its more nimble adversary. It banked steeply,
forcing the Star Cruiser to climb and stay above it in order
for its fire to hit the more vulnerable areas. Without warning, and much sooner than expected, its starboard auto-
cannon turrets began to track.

"Julia, get us outta here!" shouted Hunter. "The turrets are going independent!"

Alverez dramatically tightened the turn she had been holding the helicopter in as tracers flashed perilously close to it. In seconds she had pulled it beyond their travel limits, but it was too late. The executive ship jarred heavily from several cannon shell hits along its tail boom.

"My M606!" said Halston, losing his grip on the heavy weapon, and watching it sail out the window. "What gives, Lieutenant?"

"I can't control the tail rotor!" Alverez replied. "We're going down!"

"What? We only got hit a few times." said Hunter, trying to hold onto the pilot's seat.

"This isn't a warplane, Mitch! We don't have armor plate or any redundant systems! Rig for crash landing! Jeff, trip the locator beacon!"

While she managed to get the Star Cruiser level, Alverez was unable to stop it from slowly spinning in the opposite direction of the main rotor blades. She finally uncoupled the rotor from the engines and guided the machine to an auto-rotation landing among the desolate foothills south of the Atlantis Spaceport.

While some of the squad members were able to strap themselves into the cabin seats, most dropped to the cabin floor and waited for the impact. In the last minutes of flight Alverez shut down the engines and activated the few crash systems the executive ship had. She had just lowered the landing gear when the radar altimeter's readout began flashing a ground proximity warning.

Alverez completed the auto-rotation maneuver, drastically slowing its descent rate as it made contact with the treetops. Still spinning sedately, the Star Cruiser flipped on its side, causing its main rotor to buzz-saw through tree branches until shattering on contact with the ground. The fuselage made several impacts, rolling down a hillside and losing momentum until it came to rest against a large tree.

"Move it! Evacuate now!" Hunter ordered, pulling the emergency release lever, then pushing the starboard door out of its frame. "I smell gas! Hurry, toss me your weapons if you can!"

Climbing out the one door not blocked by the tree or

jammed tight in its frame, Hunter remained standing atop the fuselage, helping the rest of his squad out and tossing clear whatever weapons they had handed him. Only after the last was out did he jump free of the wreck and scramble for cover like the rest. As omnipresent as the smell of jet fuel was the deep growl of the Dark Legion AH-19.

"Why are we leaving?" asked Mortus, noticing the helicopter was settling back on its original course, instead of heading for the crash site. "We won! Now we can destroy those who hindered us."

"Air combat was not the goal of this mission," said the necromutant, growing angry. "The theft of those replacements was. Getting them to the Citadel has priority over everything else. The humans are finally responding to our presence in considerable numbers. If we stay here any longer, we could be overwhelmed. Not only would our successful mission fail, but events far more important to our Masters would be hindered. Those will be explained to you later, at the Citadel."

"A 'copter, finally," said Alverez when a muted thumping became sharper. "Mitch, we're gonna be rescued."

"Light the flares," Hunter responded. "Maybe we'll find out if the Dark Legion was stopped."

Not one, but several helicopters appeared in the night sky and descended toward the clearing marked with the flares set by Hunter's squad. Two were standard light executive helicopters, outfitted with external turbojet pods. The third was a former Capitol Air Force troop transport, seconded to Atlantis Security Service. All three swept the clearing with their searchlights, and the first to land was one of the smaller executive ships, not the transport.

"Captain Mitchell Hunter?" demanded the Atlantis Security officer who stepped out of the idling machine.

"I'm Captain Hunter." Hunter moved forward wearily, then snapped out a crisp salute. And he was not surprised when he did not get one in return. "I wish to report all my people are alive, if a little bruised."

"I can see they are. I'm Major Lawrence Mullen, commander of Atlantis Security. By order of the Senior Military

Advisor at Roswell and Venus Command headquarters, I'm placing you and your squad under arrest."

"For what?" questioned Venneti, jumping to his feet and laying a hand on the submachine gun that had been lying beside him on the tree trunk. "We just tried to stop a Dark Legion attack."

"I don't know what you tried to stop," said Mullen, barely hiding his hostility. "But you've been charged with theft of a military vehicle, theft, and destruction of an executive helicopter and conducting an unauthorized military operation."

"Well, maybe we should conduct one more operation, just for the fun of it."

Venneti did not have to say anything else; the moment he grabbed his weapon the rest of the squad was doing the same with whatever had been salvaged off the Star Cruiser. Even Alverez chose to draw her side arm.

"Knock it off," Hunter barked. "I said knock it off! We've lost enough fights for one day. And even if we were to win this one, we'd still lose. Disarm your weapons and drop 'em. I surrender my squad, Major."

"Good. This will go easier for you," said Mullen as he gave a signal to his helicopter. Its idling engines rapidly increased power; in minutes it would be ready for lift-off, clearing the area for the transport to land. "Actually, Mr. Hart thought your surrender wouldn't be this easy. He told us to be prepared for a fight."

"Leave it to Calvin to make things difficult for us anytime he can. Did he have anything else to say?"

"Yes, he did. He wanted me to tell you, 'You'll die for this, Hunter.' "

CHAPTER THIRTEEN

"That Dark Legion technology must've changed the 'Nineteen's fire control system," Alverez said idly, sprawled across one of the benches in the detention room. "Those turrets switched over to independent operation a lot faster than the original system. It's something we better remember the next time we encounter 'em."

"Who says there'll be a next time," Halston replied, pacing wearily up and down the room. "C'mon, Lieutenant. Will ya give up a little space?"

"Sorry, rank has its privileges."

"What rank?" said Hunter, glancing at one of his shoulder boards to reconfirm its grade badge had been ripped out. "What privileges? We're prisoners now. Stripped of everything that identified us as military men and women. I'm sorry I got you guys involved in this. I really didn't expect it would end this way."

"We all volunteered for it, Captain," said Wendy, speaking up for the first time since they were reunited. "And if you ask me, this was one of the best operations we've been on."

"Yeah, Captain. Don't try hogging all the blame for yourself," Shacker added. "There's plenty to go around."

"They're right," said Alverez, finally relenting and giving over part of the bench to Halston. "This time we weren't fighting for the corporate bottom line, or against some territorial threat by another MegaCorp. We were fighting for humanity, for the fate of all mankind. And what we were fighting was an evil more threatening than anything any army has yet encountered."

"Noble sentiments, Lieutenant," said Parker, leaning despondently against the wall. "If only we could get Calvin and the rest to believe us. We might as well be telling 'em we were battling the Bad Elves of those fantasy movies."

"Colonel Vardon would believe us," Harris offered. "If we could only get word to her. She'd take our story to the generals at Venus Command and make 'em listen."

"The Colonel would believe us if we told her we *were* fighting the Bad Elves. Her defense of us would be dismissed, and it'll be Calvin's word that carries the day."

"Captain, we're gonna get some visitors," Venneti warned, moving back from the room's one door. "Real soon."

Venneti had barely completed his sentence when the prominent surveillance camera above the entrance made several noisy sweeps of the room. The armored door swung open next, and through it came several Atlantis Security officers, some of whom were familiar.

"When you came here, I thought you were a hero," said Doyle Stewart, stepping up to Hunter. "Now I don't know what to think of you, but you ain't no hero. Heroes don't wear these."

Stewart nodded to the patrolmen in his detail; they carried the traditional handcuffs, legcuffs, and attached steel balls, as well as the latest-model personal locator beacons. There were enough to provide every member of the squad with a complete set.

"Good God, they're really gonna do it to us," said Halston, the shock growing through his exhaustion. "Now, you saw what we fought. Don't tell me you believe the charges they've dumped on us."

"Whatever we fought, it wasn't the Cybertronic force your captain claimed it was," Stewart answered, motioning to his detail to spread across the room. "Are your men going to give us any trouble?"

"No," said Hunter. "We'd only be bigger losers in the end for it. Where are be being taken, Captain?"

"To Venus Command in Athena. A Hercules troop carrier is arriving here just for you. I'd say if you were lucky, you'll come away with suspended sentences and dishonorable discharges. I'm sorry it has to end this way for you."

"Sounds to me like being a free-lancer on Luna has gone from option to being our only viable alternative," said

Parker before the locator beacon was slipped around her neck and locked. "Midnight Star, here we come."

"Your name is Landis?" Ragathol noted as he was being introduced to the newly arrived heretics. "Why is that name familiar . . . Is there not an area of Capitol territory that bears it?"

"Yes, my Master. The district was controlled by my family for generations," said Landis, his voice growing sharp. "Until corporate politics forced my father out and ruined him. Now it's being avenged."

"I sense your anger . . . Learn to refine it and you'll serve me well. Now for you, Kyle Mortus. I congratulate you on a most successful mission; your success will ensure that I'll have mine."

"My pleasure is to serve you, my Master," said Mortus, the last heretic the nepharite greeted. "What shall we do next for you inside Capitol?"

"Nothing. None of you can return to your former lives," said Ragathol, glancing over the heretics gathered in his Nether Room. In some he felt shock and pain at his announcement, a peculiar mix of emotions he knew the humans called sadness. "Don't feel weak and sorry for this. For your sacrifice you'll be granted additional Dark Gifts, and you will serve directly under me. I promise, you'll become exalted among the heretics who serve the Legion."

"Will those we left behind also be rewarded?" Lewis asked hesitantly, lowering her head when Ragathol glanced at her.

"Unfortunately, no. They were killed by the same force that interfered with your mission. As many of you suspected, it was no police unit, but a Capitol Special Forces squad."

"The military, my Master?" asked Mortus. "How did they happen upon us? Was it by accident?"

"It was no accident this squad happened upon you," said Ragathol, his voice rumbling with anger. "I suspect the Brotherhood discovered your plot and revealed it to those in Capitol who are sympathetic to them. When your troubles were reported to me, I ordered those who hindered you to be tracked and destroyed if possible. Yes . . . what have you to report?"

Ragathol turned away from the heretics and confronted

the tekron standing in the entrance to his Nether Room. As he had before, Shaguhl opened his mind to his master and allowed him to sift through it for the latest news. Faster than it could be verbally reported to him, Ragathol had located and digested the information. The result was a growing roll of hellish laughter that echoed through the room, and for a time even drowned out the noises from the rest of the Citadel.

"What's happened, my Master?" Mortus inquired, once Shaguhl had left. "Is it something that pleases you?"

"It amuses me," said Ragathol, still smiling. "Our minions have learned the fate of those who interfered with you. It was indeed a Special Forces squad, one of the best Capitol had ... They're no longer a threat to us. They've been arrested by their own army for theft and carrying out an unauthorized operation. They're being taken to the Athena metropolis, where they'll stand trial for these crimes and likely be found guilty."

"If they end up in prison, or thrown out of the armed forces, they'll be an even easier target for us to kill," Landis noted.

"They'll not be touched; I've rescinded those orders. They're of no threat to us now, and killing them would only arouse unneeded suspicion. Letting them live will allow them to serve as a lesson for those who would cooperate with the Brotherhood. They'll have nothing to gain from such acts and much to lose. I could never have predicted such a stupid reaction. If Capitol and other such organizations continue to act in such a way, then they'll be all the more easy to defeat. Go now, make preparations to receive your Gifts. And after the ceremony there'll be much to do for my departure. Echmeriaz will show you to your quarters."

Not quite as large as Heimburg, the Bauhaus seat of power, or San Dorado on Mars, and nowhere near the scale of the globe-encircling cities of Luna, the Athena metropolis was nonetheless a major city in its own right. Like Heimburg it was one of the earliest settlements on Venus, but its age was shown more in its haphazard sprawl and disorganized architectural styles than in ancient, well-preserved buildings.

Nothing more epitomized Athena's lack of planning than its original spaceport. Long since surrounded by the sprawl, it was rarely used by even small spaceships and served mostly as a staging point to the Atlantis Spaceport and other communities in Capitol territory. When the Hercules IV entered its traffic pattern, little notice was given to it, not even when it landed at the Capitol Security Service hangars instead of the Armed Forces hangars.

The small convoy of vehicles that met it were CSS, with only one military staff car at its head. After the prisoners were taken off the troop carrier, the convoy left the spaceport and drove into Athena's congested city center. There they disappeared through a side entrance to one of the city's newest and largest buildings, Venus Military Command headquarters.

Even inside it Hunter and his squad were still escorted by CSS guards, instead of the Armed Forces' own Security Corps. It made them feel even more like criminals, as they were taken from one elevator to another and down seemingly endless corridors. They soon lost sense of what direction they were being taken in, except the elevators continued to take them up. Just as it seemed they were being taken on an interior forced march, they were delivered to a room with an imposing view of the city.

"We've been expecting you, Captain Hunter," said a figure sitting in the shadows, whose voice was immediately familiar. "And in case no one's said it before, welcome to Athena."

"Remove that gear," ordered another figure, who emerged from the room's shadowed area. "All of it, and bring up the lights."

First to be unlocked were the handcuffs on each prisoner, allowing Hunter to salute his superior officer.

"General Powers. This is a shock," he uttered, getting a return salute from the black man wearing the major general's insignia on his shoulder boards. "I'd thought you wouldn't want to be associated at all with us."

"We hope that's the impression the world outside these walls has," said Vernon Powers, commander of Capitol Special Forces on Venus. "The operation we're planning must have the most complete security possible in order to succeed. And you're a critical part of it."

"I'm sorry we had to bring you in this way. But your 'independent' operation provided us with such a perfect opportunity we couldn't pass it up. Now, no one will suspect why you're here."

As he spoke, Noah Wood turned his chair around and rose out of it. At first most of the squad were more interested in massaging their sore ankles and wrists. And when they glanced at Wood, most did not initially recognize him, except as the visitor at their debriefings.

"Hey, he's the shadow man," said Venneti.

"He's more than that," Shacker added, recognition brightening his eyes. "He's Noah Wood. He's a major shareholder, just like I told you he was."

"I'm glad I could finally meet you," Wood continued, "and to do so out of the shadows."

By the time he made his full appearance, the Security officers had withdrawn from the room, leaving only Hunter's squad and the military commanders with him. Wood first approached Hunter and shook his hand. He proceeded to do the same with the rest of the squad, regardless of rank, then motioned for them to take seats at the table. As they did so, the room's windows were locked behind steel shutters and the lights lowered just enough so everyone could view the wall screen.

"Actually, your operation in Atlantis gave us several important clues to what is apparently a major Dark Legion operation," said Powers, taking a seat.

"Dark Legion?" Hunter repeated, his shock returning. "You mean you're accepting that they're real, and not some invention of a Brotherhood spook show?"

"They're quite real," said Wood. "Everyone on Mars knows they are, though we don't talk much about them. The Dark Legion was behind both the massacre at the Bauhaus base and the raid on Atlantis. Based on that raid, and the video records you brought back from Aquila, we now feel the VIP you were to rescue is still alive. Her name is Lorraine Kovan, and she's the only survivor of a Dark Legion attack on one of our settlements earlier in the year. But then, you already know this."

"I'm not sure what you mean, Mr. Wood." Hunter glanced away from the wall screen, which was showing an identity

photograph of a petite, dark-haired woman, and tried to look
innocent. "All I know was in the mission briefing."

"Captain, please. You know far more than what we gave
you. You used the woman's name while searching for her at
Aquila. Dirk Bamble may not be very bright, but he is me-
thodical. However you got the information, I don't consider
it a crime. Instead, I think it shows your degree of professionalism."

"Very well. We know who the woman is," Hunter admitted. "What we don't know is why the Dark Legion spared
her, why they took her to Luna, how she got back here, and
why they still want her."

"Neither do we," said Wood. "Except for some of what
happened on Luna. Overlord Mishima learned of a Dark Legion presence on Luna, what the Brotherhood would call an
'infestation'. He also learned that a survivor of a Legion attack on Venus had been sent to Luna. For what reason he
didn't know, but he recruited a force of mercenaries who
were ultimately successful in locating and largely destroying
the presence. Mrs. Kovan was rescued by the mercenaries,
who briefly put her in one of our hospitals. Then, for some
reason we don't know, they removed her from the hospital
and put her on a Venus-bound spaceliner. We don't know
why the Dark Legion wants her, though because of the ex-
traordinary lengths they've gone to in recapturing her, she
must be valuable to them."

"And does their raid on Atlantis tie in with her?" asked
Alverez, confused.

"We think it does. This spacecraft was stolen sometime
ago from us. It's visited Luna at least twice and was seen
about a week ago, entering polar orbit around Venus. The
spare parts stolen from Atlantis are critical components to its
main engine."

The wall screen's pictures and data blocks on Lorraine
Kovan were replaced with a single photograph of a Capitol
Gamma-class interplanetary courier ship. Its somewhat
scruffy appearance indicated it had been in service for a long
time. The data block inserted next to it confirmed this and
showed in the last entry when it had been presumed lost.

"Where did it land?" Hunter asked.

"Unfortunately, the ship only did a fractional orbit before
entry," answered one of the command officers, Major Gen-

eral Varley Summer, commander of all Capitol Air Force units on Venus. "We were unable to track it properly before it disappeared. But we believe it landed in the South Polar wasteland claimed by Mishima and us."

"We both call the area the Citadel, and for good reason," said Wood, the tone of his voice growing noticeably somber. "We believe much more than a Dark Legion presence is there. We believe one of their bases called a Citadel is being constructed in it. One of these Citadels already exists on Mars at the exact antipode to San Dorado. We recently tried to destroy it, but the raid was miscoordinated between us, Bauhaus and Imperial. Most of our strike aircraft were shot down by Imperial antiaircraft guns. What got through did heavy damage to the Citadel, but not enough to aid a Bauhaus ground offensive against it. Now the Citadel is complete and probably beyond our capabilities to destroy it. We don't want the same thing to happen here."

"Will Mishima cooperate with us?" queried Hunter.

"The Mishima officials we were negotiating with were assassinated not long ago—we suspect by the Dark Legion. It's too late to resume them, though we do at least have a promise that Mishima won't consider our operation a threat and won't interfere."

"Are you sure you want us, Mr. Wood? Calvin Hart can make a very good case that we're insubordinate, and we did fail in our last two missions."

"Oh yes, I'm positive," Wood immediately replied. "You've displayed initiative, resourcefulness, and you've had the most contact of any Capitol unit on Venus with the Dark Legion, and lived to tell about it."

"What part will we have in the operation?" asked Alverez.

"You and three other Special Forces squads will be the strike's pathfinder force," said General Marcus Brown, commander of all Capitol Armed Forces on Venus. "We think the Mars attack might've failed even at full strength because of the heavy defenses in place around the Citadel. So you and the other squads will neutralize parts of their defense grid, allowing clear paths for the fighters and troop carriers."

"And after you've accomplished that, you'll still have one more mission to perform," Wood added. "You're to rescue the woman if you can. The confusion of the attack will be your cover, and the Citadel is such a massive complex, both above and below ground, it's doubtful it'll be destroyed in the opening assault waves."

"Excuse me, Mr. Wood. But the odds of us doing all that are pretty long," said Venneti. "If I were a gambler, I'd bet a kilo of casino chips against us."

"It's this or face a court-martial, Leo," Hunter concluded. "And after coming up short against these creatures twice in a row, I want a little payback. Mr. Wood, when do the briefings begin?"

"When you're reunited with Lieutenant Rogers," Wood answered. "We're having him flown out from Roswell as we speak. We don't have much time, my friends. The Dark Legions horde has just started to build the aboveground portion of this Citadel. Completion isn't far away, and we'd also like to attack before this spaceship is repaired and lifts off. Ladies and gentlemen, you deserve either a very late supper or a very early breakfast. You're dismissed. We'll meet again in a few hours."

CHAPTER FOURTEEN

"What is this place?" asked Alverez as the staff car finished pulling up to a group of dilapidated hangars and service buildings. "The rattiest crew of free-lance cargo haulers wouldn't want to fly outta here."

"That's what we're hoping everyone will continue to think," General Powers replied. "This is the place every pilot thinks exists only in fables or tall tales. This is the Dreamworks."

The mechanics working idly on the ancient turboprop freighter scarcely looked up at the Special Forces personnel emerging from the staff car. The old hangars were set far away from the much newer complex at Athena's largest military air base. They were far enough to almost be in another district, adding to the desired desolation of the site.

Powers stepped up to a side door on the first hangar, one which looked like it was about to fall off its rusted hinges until Powers inserted his identity card and placed his hand on a scanning plate beside it. The moment he was cleared, the door snapped back into its frame and slid sideways. It remained open long enough for Powers, Hunter, Alverez, and Taylor to enter the hangar. By the time the door closed, the staff car had driven into a nearby service building.

"My God, how deep did you dig this place?" said Hunter, moving backward a few feet when he blundered into a guard rail around the entrance and realized the hangar's true floor was several dozen feet below it. "And what did you do it for?"

"This is nearly three stories deep," said Powers, opening the gate to a steeply inclined stairway. "We dug it so we could join all three hangars together, to facilitate moving the prototypes from the production complex, and then there's this."

Only when he mentioned it, did his guests realize that the interior space they were viewing was far larger than the single hangar they had entered. It was over five hundred feet wide and filled with the prototypes of the latest Capitol helicopters and jet fighters. At the centerline of the massive bay was the entrance to a rectangular tunnel. It was large enough for any of the aircraft in the bay to be towed through it, minus their wings or rotorblades. And hovering over the bay was an undulating roof of segmented armor plates.

"This is half a meter of the latest chobham armor," Powers continued, pointing to the roof as his party descended under it. "We decided to install it on the new center after the Mishima attack of thirty years ago leveled the original Dreamworks."

"If you don't mind my saying so, General, that *was* a bit before our time," said Hunter.

"I know. It seems as though all we've ever considered as history was what's contained in those 'Whatever Became Of' stories about old actors or music stars." Powers grew quiet for a moment, though before Julia could respond to his observation, they reached the bottom of the stairs, and he led his guests over to a familiar-looking machine. "Now I'm sure Lieutenant Alverez and Sergeant Taylor think they know this aircraft by heart, but they don't. This is the CFAH dash Four, Advanced Cutlass."

Externally, there appeared to be very few differences between the prototype of the newest Special Forces gunship and the models already in the field. Taylor quickly pointed out the more smoothly contoured nose bulges for the terrain-following radar, laser designator, and infrared sensors. But it was Alverez who noticed the shape of the rotor blades.

"They're not shaped like a conventional airfoil," she said. "And the tips are more sharply swept back then before."

"We've finally been able to use the Low-Radar-Return design of the Feline's wings on rotor blades," Powers responded. "While it doesn't make this version radar invisible, it is much harder to detect, especially when you use the electronic warfare suite's new 'shrouding' system."

"What else does it have, General?"

"More efficient and powerful engines, and improved armor plating. In that aspect she's now almost as good as the old Grapeshot."

"How long do my men have to familiarize themselves with it?" Hunter asked while Taylor walked up to the prototype and opened the canopy over the gunner's cockpit.

"You'll have only today to test-fly it," said Powers. "By this evening you'll be on your way to Forward Base Threshold. And by early tomorrow morning the operation will be under way."

"Sounds like you'll have just enough time to do a test hop this morning and some more extensive flights this afternoon." Hunter turned to Alverez and caught her just before she was enveloped by a group of military and company test pilots. The moment after she acknowledged his remarks, she was virtually surrounded and carried off by them. "Well, General, I think those two can be left alone for the rest of the day. If we could recall your staff car, I think it's time we find out what the rest of my squad is doing."

"You've taken the craft out of the launch position," said Ragathol, a rare touch of surprise in his voice. "Why was this done?"

What had once almost touched the roof of the Citadel's main hangar now sat beside the transport/launch pad on its landing gear. An engine service frame surrounded the tail of the *Gamma*-class courier. The tekrons working on it were busily replacing the spaceship's external panels, indicating the repairs had just been finished. For a few seconds Ragathol was frozen at the hangar's back entrance by the sight, causing Caliqabaal to move several feet ahead of him.

"It was necessary, my Master," he answered. "The main engine had to be completely removed to replace the affected parts. Now it's finished, and we can put the craft back into launch configuration."

"How long will it take?" asked Ragathol, carefully watching the activity of the tekron crew. "I sense there are fewer workers under your command than before ... Why is this so?"

"The courier will not be flight-ready until midday tomorrow. I'm sorry, my Master, but that's the best schedule we can attain with the service force we now have. Azurwraith has need of all the workers he can muster. He's even using Legionnaire units to complete the Citadel."

"Yes, for once there seems to be more noise filtering

down from above us, instead of coming up from below."
Even though the sounds in the hangar negated the more ambient background noise, Ragathol still glanced up at its roof,
where he could almost see it vibrate minutely from the
ceaseless heavy construction above it. "I understand
Azurwraith must finish his Citadel quickly; this is its most
vulnerable time ... But drawing tekrons away from us will
only slightly increase his work force and greatly delay us."

"Will you go to his Command Nexus and request more
tekrons released to us?" asked Caliqabaal.

"No. That is his domain," said Ragathol, maintaining his
serenity. "I will not enter it unless he invites me to do so.
Such is the tradition among us who command His armies.
I've suffered enough delays on this task already. One more
will only be a further small hindrance on my journey to
Algeroth's Defiled Castle."

"I don't suppose they call this the Dreamworks as well?"
Hunter asked as he entered a much smaller facility on Athena's outskirts than the air base.

"No, just the Special Forces Experimental Training and
Production Facility," said Powers, last to emerge from the
staff car. "There can only be one Dreamworks, and infantry
munitions isn't exotic enough to justify it."

Unlike the air base, the Special Forces site did not occupy
hundreds of acres of land beyond the sprawl of Athena. Its
compound was just large enough to hold an enclosed obstacle course, a firing range, and a factory for the production of
specialized munitions. Also unlike the air base, there was no
sign at its entrance identifying what the facility was for and
who ran it, even though it was well known.

Powers's staff car drove up to the factory's administrative
building where his passengers were met by the site's managers and commanding officer. They were quickly escorted inside and taken to one of the production lines, where Hunter
found part of his squad.

"Captain, you remember that idea I had for a napalm grenade?" said Venneti, once the greetings for Powers had
ended.

"I remember your attempt at being a weaponsmith nearly
burned down the Roswell gunnery range," Hunter recalled.
"Don't tell me they actually took your crazy idea seriously?"

"Seriously? Hell, they perfected it. They call it the Type Fifty-One. I'd like to call it the Flamer."

Venneti held up one of the completed hand grenades from the production line behind him. It had the same apple-shaped, hard plastic shell as all the other grenades used by Capitol's armed forces, but the identifying stripes on it were bright yellow. When Hunter examined it, he discovered it weighed somewhat less than the standard high-explosive grenades.

"We'll use it to replace our standard white phosphorus munitions," said Powers. "In spite of its craziness, we found in field trials it's a lot less dangerous to use than phosphorus or magnesium. I remember waiting a long time for those things to burn themselves out before taking a position."

"I see we can also set the detonation time," said Hunter, paying closer attention to the grenade's arming system. "So we can use it as a delayed action charge. Yes, Sergeant? What new toy do you have?"

"A new armor-piercing incendiary round," Halston offered, holding up a belt of newly manufactured 15mm bullets. "If we encounter any of those necromutants or razor-things, these should stop 'em. They're teflon-coated, have tungsten-carbide tips, and phosphorus charges atop rods of hardened plastic explosive."

"These Dark Legion creatures either have body armor or very tough skin," one of the civilian managers quickly added. "These rounds should be able to punch through 'em and cause fatal injuries by making the plastic explosives burn explosively."

"That's great for the sniper rifles and Ted's machine gun," said Hunter, examining the heavy belt and the multicolored markings on each shell, which indicated the rounds were both armor-piercing and incendiary. "But what about those of us with assault rifles and submachine guns? You got any kind of monster-killing munitions for us?"

"Ten millimeter is too small of a round for this munition design." The manager pointed to the shells Hunter was examining, then opened the notebook he had been carrying and leafed through the diagrams of the ammunition types the facility manufactured. "The best we can do is this, an experimental tungsten-carbide tracer round. The material in its recessed base has a high magnesium content, and it should continue burning long after it's entered the target."

"Good. I just hope they don't go melting the breeches and barrels when they're fired."

"I don't think so, at least with this latest batch," the manager said idly until he noticed the shocked expressions Hunter and the members of his squad wore. "I mean, we're really certain we worked out the faults in the previous lots."

"You better hope so," Powers warned. "I'll not send my people into a battle like this with weapons that'll get them killed because they fail."

"General, how long do we have before we gotta leave?" asked Halston, accepting the belt from Hunter.

"You're to depart from Athena Air Base at five o'clock. At max cruise you should reach your forward base in about two hours. Get as much rest as you can then, because you'll get very little of it tomorrow."

"Mr. Wood, Mr. Hart, welcome to Battle Station Avenger TBM," said the station's on-duty coordinating officer. He spun around when he heard the main doors hiss open and snapped out a salute when the expected VIPs finally arrived at his center.

"Thank you for allowing us in, Captain," Wood responded, shaking the officer's hand. "Can you tell us when General Brown and his staff are due in?"

"Yes, sir. If you'll follow me over to the main screen."

The captain led the civilians from the security and administrative desks near the entrance to the center's curved wall of display screens. On the largest screen was a tactical map of the district controlled by the battle station and the hostile territory several hundred miles beyond the frontier. When the captain whispered an order to one of the console operators, two of the many aircraft symbols flying inside district airspace were surrounded by glowing rings. Beside them were displayed their speed, altitude, heading, and Estimated Times of Arrival.

"General Brown's ship will arrive in the next fifteen minutes," said the captain. "General Powers left Athena later; his ETA is about an hour and a half."

"Sounds like Vernon was briefing his squads a bit more

extensively than he expected," said Wood, reading off the more distant aircraft's data block.

"And I still can't believe one of them is Hunter's squad," Hart commented, a resigned tone in his voice. "And they've been assigned the most important objective in the entire operation."

"It's also the most impossible objective. They're going to have to penetrate deep inside the Citadel—a complex we know nothing about—and locate one human being in its teeming population. The only thing that'll help us locate her is she's as valuable to the Dark Legion as she is to us."

"I'm certain one of the other squads we've assigned to the pathfinder force could do just as well, Mr. Wood."

"They'd have to be briefed on the woman," said Wood, his temper growing short. "Between what Hunter's squad has dug up on their own and the information we've given them, they know her more intimately than anyone else on this planet. No, Mr. Hart, there's isn't enough time to brief anyone else on the woman, and I'll not change the assignment. You've had your input on the matter, and the decisions have been made accordingly. Captain, can you show us how the aircraft assigned to the operation are marshaling?"

"Hey, Sergeant, listen. I think it's another one."

The private's warning caused only a few of the enlisted men on the exercise field to stop their work and scan the sky. In the afternoon's waning hours there was still enough light outside for them to work by, and the heat that had built up over the day made even the air-conditioned barracks at the forward base too stifling to stay in.

Those who did look up caught sight of a rare, though suddenly familiar, helicopter entering the base's traffic pattern. Its sharklike silhouette was immediately recognizable, as was the muted growl of its turbines. For a few seconds it was in clear view, then it disappeared behind the palm trees, and the soldiers went back to cleaning and reassembling their weapons.

"You're right, son. It's another Special Force's Cutlass," Sergeant Bob Watts answered, more concerned with finishing the reassembly of his M606 machine gun.

"Don't you think it's odd that we hardly see one of those

things for months," said the private. "Yet in the last twelve hours we've seen four."

"The kid's got a point, Big Bob," a corporal added. "With all the other activity that's been happening here, I say something big is up."

"Yeah, some fancy Special Forces show I'll bet," said Watts, smiling as he finally got the action on the M606 to function smoothly. "And when they blow it, the brass'll have to send us regulars in to rescue them."

"Who do you think the enemy is?" the private asked. "Mishima or the Dark Legion?"

"I'll believe in those little green aliens when I see 'em. I'd prefer Mishima; slants are just as good to kill as anyone else."

"You really hate 'em, don't you, Sergeant? Is there anyone else you hate more?"

"Don't get Big Bob started," warned the corporal, grinning mischievously. "You show him the right officer and he'll deck 'im for you right here."

"Is that true?" asked the private. "Why don't you like our officers?"

"Because they made me one once," said Watts, growing irritated. "But I soon fixed that. What I really hate are those map watchers in the battle stations. The only time they come to the frontier is with an armed escort."

"Is there any officer you like?"

"Well, the lieutenant we got ain't too bad. And there was this Special Forces captain I heard about. I like what I heard, until yesterday's news. Security arrested him at the Atlantis Spaceport. It seems as though you can't even trust a hero these days. Enough questions, kid. Let's see what the mess has for supper."

CHAPTER FIFTEEN

"I suppose some forward bases are more primitive than others," said Alverez as she and Hunter entered the briefing room and discovered several computer monitors sitting in front of the wall screen. "Don't you guys have repair crews?"

"This building was heavily damaged in the last Mishima attack," answered Major Gaines, the base's intelligence officer. "We just installed the display system, but the Corp hasn't sent anyone to program it yet."

"At my base we sometimes don't even have this," said the Special Forces captain entering the room next. Scott Hogan gave a sneering glance at Hunter and Alverez, then moved past them without even a perfunctory greeting. "C'mon, Hunter. If you can tolerate failure, you can certainly take this."

"Cheerful tonight, aren't you?" said Hunter. "Your reputation is well-deserved, Hogan. I hope this attitude changes after your first cup of coffee."

"You'll have breakfast later," said Gaines. "Take your seats, and let's keep this civilized."

Rogers joined Hunter and Alverez moments later, and with him came the main body of Special Forces officers. When they were all accounted for, the briefing room was locked and Gaines instructed each group to cluster around one of the monitors.

"As of twenty-four hours ago, this is what the area called the Citadel looked like," he began, then paused long enough for everyone to study the first image the screens showed. "And here's what it looks like within the past hour."

Taken by a long-range reconnaissance camera, the first was of a desolate landscape with only a runway, a bare launch pad, and some service towers to mark the Dark Le-

gion facility. The second image showed a massive building
under construction. Its design had no symmetry; it appeared
octagonal, but none of its sides were of the exact same
length or angle. Some looked like steeply sloped battlements, others were huge staircases that led to gaping portals.
Already giant statues were being erected in niches beside the
portals, and on every smooth surface there were work details
carving the runelike characters of an alien language. The entire structure looked like a monstrous perversion of an ancient castle. The first responses to it were gasps of awe and
fear.

"Are you sure this is the same site?" asked one of the
other officers, recoiling in shock from what she saw on her
screen.

"The very same," said Gaines, "at a slightly wider angle.
If you'll notice in the upper right corner, there's the launch
pad and service towers."

"How long before it's completed?" asked Hunter.

"We estimate another day. And the trenches you see being
dug around the Citadel will also be finished at that time."

"And you expect us to attack this thing?" Hogan asked,
incredulous. "Why, it would take a full division of ground
forces and every warplane we got on the planet to do so."

"That's the job for the forces being gathered at this and
other forward bases," Gaines responded, "and the airfields
behind us. Your job is to neutralize as much of the Citadel's
defense grid as possible, to allow those forces to be effective."

A tactical map replaced the nightmarish image of the un-
completed Citadel. It showed the layout of the site's outer
defenses, which began just south of the low mountains that
stood between the Citadel and Capitol's frontier. The map
not only had the positions of antiaircraft artillery and missile
batteries, but mine fields, power lines, observation posts,
and major sensor stations.

"I know it looks extensive," said Gaines, "and it is. However, based our own intelligence reports, and those from the
Brotherhood and Mishima, the whole system is vulnerable to
sabotage. The trick will be to insert you into the outer perimeter undetected and to make sure you stay that way."

"If I can sneak my men past Venusian Rangers undetected, I can get 'em past these creatures," Hogan quickly declared.

"I hope you can, Captain. Now before I begin a detailed explanation of each squad's mission, I'd like to introduce you to your new members. Since this is the first time Capitol has launched a major attack against a Dark Legion outpost on Venus, military advisors will be assigned to each squad."

"Something tells me I'm not gonna like who we get," Hunter groaned, and he had barely finished his warning when the main door reopened. Into the darkened room filed a shadowy group of figures; none were immediately recognizable until one stumbled into a chair and sent it crashing against some others. "Bungle. Well, I hope Stutter's with you. I'd sure hate it if the team were broken up."

"Yes, my Master? You wish to see the patient?" said Curator Praecor, an obsequious laugh running through his question.

"What other reason would bring me here?" said Ragathol, standing in the entrance to the Isolation Chamber. "Leave us. I wish to see the Receptacle alone."

The answer to Ragathol's order was an extended giggle as Praecor and his underlings moved out of the chamber while he strode in. Within seconds only the nepharite and Lorraine Kovan remained in the chamber. The bed she was tied to this time was more comfortable than the one in the processing hall; and she did not have to endure the screams and cries of other patients, only the soft buzzing and crackling of the computerlike necrotechnology machines lining the wall behind her. A cap of thick wires and two intravenous lines connected her to the life-support system, which kept her in a half-conscious, half-dream state. She opened her eyes when Ragathol spoke, and the system's blue and orange status lights registered an increase in her pulse rate and brain activity when he approached her.

"Greetings again, Receptacle," he said as he towered over Kovan. "I sense you're feeling much better. At least the part of you that can still feel ... I've come to tell you to enjoy these last few hours on your home world because you'll soon be leaving it. Forever. You'll be my gift to He who must be obeyed and responsible for elevating me to the more powerful circles in the Dark Legion. What do you think of that?"

The system's heart and pulse rate monitors registered Kovan's response, and seconds after more of their lights began flashing, a few tears rolled out of her eyes. Carefully, Ragathol brushed one of his fingers over her face and caught some of the tears in his clawlike nail.

"Enjoy these as well while you can," he warned. "For soon you won't have enough humanity left to even shed them. Praecor, return and prepare the human for transport. I'll leave with her in a matter of hours."

"So, these are the Flamer grenades you guys claim you invented," said a fire support specialist from one of the other Special Forces squads. He held the grenade gingerly, as if it would explode even though the safety pin and green safety flags were visible around its top.

"No. He didn't invent it," said Venneti, stepping into the conversation Halston was having with his opposites. "*I* invented it, and you can verify that with the SF training guys."

"Hey, Ted, what's with the midget? Is he your 'boom' guy or your mascot?"

"Yeah, he's our explosives specialist," Halston replied. "You got a problem with that?"

"Not really," said Halston's new friend. "It's just that boom guys always seem to be short, pushy types."

"All right, I know a fight brewing when I hear one," said Hunter, bearing down on the group with Scott Hogan in tow. "Save it for the Dark Legion. Right now you still got work to do."

"And so do you, Bryant," Hogan added. "I want everyone in their jet chutes before they board the Cutlass."

"You see, Mitch. Every other squad on this operation is using jet chutes," said Bamble, trailing behind the officers at a safe distance. "Why do you refuse them?"

"Because I prefer to use the antisensor technology in our new Cutlass to insert us closer than the other squads will be," said Hunter. "And I've never liked the jet chute; its infrared signature is too obvious for me."

"Well, whatever that signature is, it's certainly a lot smaller than what a Cutlass will put out," Hogan sarcastically declared. "And I don't care what fancy cloaking system your ship has."

"And I don't care that you don't care." Hunter's voice

grew more belligerent with each word until he realized both Hogan and himself were building the same antagonisms their men had been displaying moments before. "I've thought out my squad's part of this operation as carefully as you have yours. I know what my people are capable of, and a little nighttime hiking isn't unusual for them."

"Then we'll meet you at the Citadel, Hunter. I hope the hike will give you an appetite for combat; you'll need it. All right, Bryant, let's gather up the others."

"Mitch, I know we've had our differences," said Bamble after Hogan and the members of the other squads had left. "But this mission is different, and I think you should be more flexible in your mission plan. Your entire squad was recently recertified on jet chutes; changing to them shouldn't be that much of a problem for you."

"I get the feeling the *real* reason you want jet chutes is to cut down on the hike in," said Hunter. "Just remember what you are, Bamble. You're an advisor, not commander of this unit, and the plan won't be changed to make it easy for you. I want to enter Dark Legion territory the most covert way possible, not the most popular or easiest way. So get ready for the hike, and one more thing, don't call me 'Mitch'."

"Squad commanders, may I have your attention please," Gaines requested, his voice blaring over the hangar's speakers. "We're twenty minutes and counting to departure. Finish loading your helicopters, stand by for prestart signal."

Hunter and Bamble returned to their Cutlass just as the rest of the squad finished boarding it and Alverez completed her walk-around inspection of it. Of the four gunships that filled the hangar, theirs was the only one to appear in factory-new condition and did not wear the three-tone camouflage of a combat machine. It wore the standard midnight blue prototype finish, though the high-visibility fuselage markings had at least been removed.

"She checks out perfectly," said Alverez, popping the canopy on the second cockpit. "Not a single malfunction anywhere. We even managed to load all those extra munitions you wanted."

"Good. I got the feeling we'll be using them," said Hunter. "If we don't melt our guns first. Let us know when you get the departure command."

Moments later the last hatch slid shut on the last gunship.

While the pilots and their Navigator-Electronic Warfare/ Gunners did their prestart checks, the hangar lights changed to soft red to prepare everyone's night vision. And when the main doors started to slide open, they were extinguished.

"This is Threshold Tower to Special Forces flight. The mission event clock will commence running in one minute, twenty-seven seconds. You are cleared for departure. Weather conditions are nominal. Winds are out of the southwest at fourteen kilometers. We're holding all traffic until you leave. After this you need not acknowledge any further transmissions. From everyone here at Forward Base Threshold, good luck."

The first helicopter to be towed from the hangar was Hogan's. Among the last to come out was Hunter's, its rocking on its trolley a little more pronounced due to its increased weight. All four machines were lined up on the apron in front of the hangar, and the first had its rotorblades turning before the last finished emerging.

With its anticollision and running lights flashing brightly, Hogan's Cutlass lifted off its trolley and moved across the field. It climbed just high enough to clear the surrounding buildings, and its external lights remained on only until it cleared the base perimeter. Then they were extinguished and the night swallowed the machine. The rest of the gunships departed the same way, fanning out on individual courses, but all heading due south, where Venus's aurora australis undulated and sparkled brightly on the horizon.

Behind them the forward base was rapidly coming to life itself. Its arming service points were filled with AH-19 gunships and its taxiways with Hercules IV transports. The soldiers in the barracks just beyond the airfield were also preparing for the operation and would soon be marched out to the aircraft. Because of its short runways and its proximity to the frontier, there were no F/A-99 fighters at Threshold. They were marshaling at bases deeper inside Capitol territory, operating on their own timetable and awaiting the success of the Special Forces.

"There they go," Wood uttered soberly, watching the symbols for the four helicopters depart the forward base marker and spread across the tactical map. As each moved farther into the frontier, they started to flash and fade, indicating their radar returns were growing progressively weaker. "Now, it all depends on them."

"The other elements appear to be on schedule, Mr. Wood," said Hart, motioning to the readouts on all the side screens. "Shouldn't we hold everything on the ground until the Citadel's defense net starts going down?"

"That would be safer, but this attack needs split-second timing to succeed, and we're not going to change the operational plan at this stage."

"It's a shame you couldn't get the Cartel to release some Doomtroopers to us," said the battle station's senior coordinating officer. "They would've been a great help to the Special Forces."

"I know, but the Cartel has yet to fully and officially appreciate the threat of the Dark Legion," Wood answered, a rumble of irritation in his voice. "Too many bureaucrats, too many diplomats meeting over so many useless things. There are Doomtrooper teams and squads who know about the threat and take it seriously. If only we could convince their superiors."

"Do you think the success of this attack will convince them?" Hart asked.

"I hope it does. To borrow a Brotherhood term, this could be an Awakening to the threat."

"We'll need a lot of information to do so, Mr. Wood. And if my advisor teams will be allowed to follow corporate protocol, we should soon be receiving reports from them."

"Mitch, this is Julia. Approaching Citadel outer defense perimeter."

"I see it," said Hunter, watching a tactical display on the main cabin's terminal. "Stand by to activate 'shrouding' system. And I want you to deactivate all your radar systems, even your radar altimeter."

"Wha ... What? Why do you want to do that?" Sutter demanded, stammering out her question before Bamble could even start his.

"Julia and I read enough reports on the Dark Legion shooting down aircraft and drones to indicate they may be able to 'see' radar better than any of our equipment. This'll give us one extra advantage in penetrating their net."

"Mitch, this is Julia. Deactivating air surveillance radar," said Alverez, "terrain-following radar, fire control radar, and radar altimeter. Jeff says he can use the laser designator as an altimeter, and I'll switch over entirely to the low-light-level and infrared systems."

"Good work, you two," said Hunter, switching the overhead terminal to a schematic of the Cutlass, which indicated all the systems being shut down. "Don't push your airspeed anymore than you have to. As it is we're running ahead of schedule."

The gunship's airspeed dropped by more than fifty miles an hour immediately afterward. In part this was due to its climbing the northern slopes of a low mountain ridge that marked the unofficial beginning of Dark Legion territory. The nearer it got to the craggy summits, the sparser the vegetation became, until they were practically barren.

"Captain, in light of your decisions," said Bamble, trying to peek around the terminal in an attempt to get Hunter's attention, "I feel at least a brief message should be sent to the battle station so as to explain them. And since we're still outside of Dark Legion territory, I'll point our that I still have the authority to do so."

"You're right, Dirk, they should be explained," Hunter responded, getting shocked expressions from the rest of his squad, until he gave Halston a brief nod. "Break out your SatCom set. Julia, this is Mitch. Bring us to a hover when we reach the summit."

In the last few hundred feet of its ascent, the Cutlass slowed until it barely crawled up to the mountaintop, then came to a complete stop. In spite of the wind buffeting it, Alverez kept it so close to the peak its rotorwash flattened its thick patches of moss.

"I'm ready to transmit," said Bamble, just as his hands stopped flying over his SatCom's keyboard. "What are you doing, Captain?"

"The southern aurora makes transmissions difficult," said Hunter, unlocking the main cabin's port hatch. "You'll have to do yours with as little interference as possible. Just point your set out the hatch when I open it."

With the press of a button the hatch slid forward, filling the cabin with rotorwash and blade noise. Since Bamble was among the last to enter the gunship, he had the last seat on the bench and only needed to lean over slightly to clear the hatch. His attention was so focused on making the transmission and not losing his grip on the SatCom set, he did not initially notice Halston unlocking his restraint belts.

"Wait! No!" Bamble managed to shout before two giant hands slammed into his right shoulder and hip. Whatever he said afterward was carried away on the winds, as was he.

The drop from the helicopter to mountaintop was just over a dozen feet, enough to stun Bamble and smash the SatCom terminal. Moments later the hatch rolled shut, and the Cutlass rose higher into the air before dipping its nose and sliding down its opposite slope. By the time Bamble staggered to his feet, the aircraft had disappeared, even though the aurora australis cast an eerie, moonlike glow over the landscape.

"Captain Hunter, how could you order that!" Sutter raged, temporarily drowning out the laughter from the rest of the squad. "Dirk could've been killed by that stunt! I insist we go back and pick him up immediately!"

"If we go back, we'll leave you with him," Hunter said coldly, his icy stare extinguishing her anger. "This operation's too important for it to be jeopardized by some corporate protocol freak. I suggest for overall operational security that no more transmissions be made until I authorize them."

"As a military advisor it's my duty to report on the performance of Capitol Armed Forces, weapons, and those we encoun . . ." Sutter's counterattack trailed off when she finally noticed the equally frigid looks she was getting from all the other squad members. Even Wendy Levin's normally sympathetic expression had vanished. "I me . . . I. I understand, Captain. There's no need to make any transmissions until you clear them."

"Good. I knew you'd accept our intellectual reasons for it," said Hunter before he hit the intercom switch. "Julia, this is Mitch. How long before we reach outer defense perimeter?"

"Two minutes, fifteen seconds at current airspeed," said Alverez. "I'm reducing our altitude to fifty meters."

"Keep us low and slow, Julia. And when we cross the perimeter line, activate shrouding system. Everyone, ready your safety harness rigs. Arm weapons and stand by for deployment."

CHAPTER SIXTEEN

"Mr. Wood, we have a problem," Hart warned, moving through the circle of officers and civilian officials around the stockholder. "All of our Special Forces squads have reported in, except for Hunter's."

"Are you still tracking their helicopter?" asked Wood, turning his attention to the center's main screen.

"Intermittently until about a minute ago. We think they may have activated their antiradar system."

"Then I don't see a problem. I didn't think Hunter would allow his advisors to send any messages. He has to penetrate deeper into the Dark Legion's territory than the other units. Are you trying to contact him?"

"As per your instructions, no," said Hart, trying to keep his irritation hidden.

"Good. Keep it that way," Wood ordered. "Unless you see obvious signs of all the pathfinder squads getting into trouble, the operation proceeds as planned. General, advise the strike squadrons to start their final checklists."

"Mitch, this is Julia. We're approaching the drop point," said Alverez, steadily retarding the throttles. "Stand by for rappel system deployment."

"Roger," said Hunter, slipping on his friction gloves. "After we're down, head for your ground holding point. Good luck, Julia. See you soon."

The gunship's deceleration was so smoothly executed, few noticed it until they realized the landscape outside the hatch windows was no longer moving. With a sharp crack both hatches rolled forward, and the pylons for the rappel system snapped out. Their nylon lines were still unreeling into the jungle when the squad members at the hatches attached their clamps to them.

In unison they swung out of the cabin and hung on the lines for a few moments, until the Cutlass had restabilized. Then they slipped down into the jungle and disappeared from sight. The next four repeated the procedure seconds later, and the last squad member, Wendy Levin, was sliding down her line while the other three sets were being retracted.

As its main hatches slid shut, the CFAH-4 lowered its nose slightly and began to move forward. It rapidly picked up airspeed and gained a few feet in altitude before turning sharply for the northeast. In minutes it would be back across the perimeter line and descending for its ground holding point. If all went well, it would be landing just as its experimental shrouding system was in danger of burning out.

"This is about the quietest jungle I've been in," Shacker remarked, once the noise from the helicopter's main rotors had trailed off to a distant popping. "I thought the jungle was supposed to come alive at night with all sorts of critters."

"I think you're right," said Venneti in a hushed voice. "This is creepy. God, how I hate fighting at night."

"You hate fighting anywhere, anytime, Leo," said Parker. "I get the feeling there isn't anyplace you'd like to fight."

"Of course there is. I wouldn't mind invading one of those beach resorts along the ocean. Wouldn't you like to take Nova Miami, Captain?"

"I'll think about it later," Hunter advised, moving around his squad, "a lot later. Standard deployment, troopers. Jake, you'll be point man for now. Diane, you're the rear guard. Wendy and Rogers will be with me. Ted, you and Redfield will be ahead of me. Leo, you and Harris will stay behind me. Now even though we have a point man, I want all of you to be on the lookout for *anything* unusual. We're about to enter combat with an enemy the likes of which no army in mankind's history has ever encountered. I can't really tell you what to expect, but you're all professionals, and I'm counting on you to remain that way. Move out, our trail awaits us."

The rest of the squad nodded in agreement with Hunter, then quietly fell into the line of march he had ordered. In the polar regions the Venusian jungle was not nearly as lush and had few tropical plants. It was more of a temperate rain for-

est of various scrub pine and spruce trees. This made it easy
for the squad to march, even without trails to follow. Soon
they were deep inside a forest little visited by man, even
though he had originally seeded it. The anxiety of the mission and the eeriness of moving through a silent landscape
bathed in auroral light made them hold their weapons a little
tighter and pay closer attention to their motion detectors, as
well as infrared and electromagnetic sensors.

"Thank you for inviting me, my brother," Ragathol announced, stopping at the entrance to the Citadel's Command
Nexus and bowing respectfully. "For what reason do you
bring me here?"

"We've detected human activity," said Azurwraith, motioning to the row of terminals staffed by necromutants, and
each showing a wedge-shaped sector of the Citadel's defense
grid. "Of a type not seen in our area before."

Ragathol approached one of the terminals that displayed
the intruders. The group being tracked was moving low
across the terrain and at a relatively slow speed. However,
the infrared sensors in the grid were readily able to follow
them.

"Do you feel they're a probing mission of their own?"
asked Ragathol, moving down the row and glancing at the
readouts of the other two intruder groups. "Like the manned
aircraft and drones ... Or could they be precursor forces to
a much larger mission?"

"Whatever they are, my brother," Azurwraith serenely answered, "I feel they must be destroyed, and it will be easy
for us to do so. They're so puny, their threat to my Citadel
is almost nonexistent. But I shall deal with them."

"I see you already are." Ragathol glanced at the tactical
response board looming over the terminals, and could see
most of Azurwraith's ezoghoul forces taking flight to intercept the intruders. "My departure ... do you think they'll interfere with it?"

"No, my brother. They haven't the numbers to interfere
with your launch, and I'll not let them. Go. Return to the
main hangar and complete your preparations. You can expect
to depart with minimal delays. My forces will soon have a
glorious triumph over these pitiful intruders."

"If it would not displease you," said Ragathol, "I would

like to stay and watch your triumph unfold. In so doing, I could personally report to Algeroth your success in holding off any human interference."

"Yes ... I can see where that would please Him," said Azurwraith, his initial expression of anger giving way to elation. He smiled as if he were about to kill something, then broke into a hideous laugh that rolled and echoed through the high ceiling. "Stay then, my brother, and watch the triumph. Did you know, the humans once called themselves 'Earthlings'? Back when they lived exclusively on their home world. I must remember that. It makes them sound so ... pathetic."

"I knew it wouldn't take us long to find something," Hunter said quietly after getting tapped on the shoulder by Rogers. "What bearing is it?"

"It's ... over there," Rogers finally advised, pointing to his left. Due to their proximity to the south pole, his EM scanner was unable to give an accurate heading. "And the electromagnetic field is pretty strong. It's gotta be something a lot bigger than a power line."

"Wendy, what are you reading?"

"Just us," she said, swinging the motion detector in a slow arc. "I got this thing set so sensitive it'd pick up tree squirrels if there were any."

"All right, let's move," said Hunter, "to the southeast. Signal if you spot anything."

As the squad changed direction, it switched from a single-file march to a skirmish line. They had not advanced more than a few dozen yards when they came upon a nonsymmetrical crosswork of electrical lines. They surrounded a transformerlike device that glowed and sputtered softly.

"It's a power node for their sensor array," Rogers identified, getting within a foot of it. "We knock it out and we'll disrupt the outer grid."

"Until a backup kicks in," said Hunter. "I hope we'll find most of those as well. Leo, mine it."

"Sure thing, Captain," said Venneti, signaling Harris that he wanted to look in his backpack. "A hundred gram charge will do it. Shall I arm it with a remote detonator or a time fuse?"

"You better make it a time fuse. From the way the aurora

looks, solar flare activity is pretty strong tonight." Hunter
straightened up and glanced at the patches of night sky visible through the forest canopy. The curtains of ionized gases
were multicolored instead of pale white, and the soft crackling had now become as sharp as distant thunder. "I don't
think your transmitter is strong enough to break through this
interference. Set this charge to go off at H-hour minus five
minutes."

Venetti acknowledged his orders and in minutes had a
charge of plastic explosive assembled and armed. By then
the squad's other teams had spread out from the site and discovered other targets.

"There's another power node," Shacker informed, in-
structing Hunter where to train his night scope. "And that is
an observation post."

The pyramid-shaped structure was expertly hidden among
the conifer trees, making it all but invisible from the air. On
the ground, however, it was far more obvious, especially
when the heretics manning it had the interior lights on and
their glow spilled through the slit windows on every face of
the structure.

"A couple of three-second bursts will shred the place,"
said Halston, joining Hunter and Shacker. "Just give the
word, Captain."

"The word is no, Sergeant," said Hunter. "Remember
what the briefers told us? Any kind of military activity will
attract Dark Legion attention, and gunfire most certainly
qualifies. Since he's done with the first power node, get Leo
up here. We'll mine both the second node and the observation post. Jake, get Diane. If anyone can sneak up to that
post, she can."

"At last, the crash site," Alverez remarked, her tension
easing. "Jeff, deactivate the shrouding system. Deploying
skids."

Nearly twenty miles east of the drop point, and just inside
Dark Legion territory, lay the wreckage of what had been a
civilian-owned Hercules III cargo lifter. The giant aircraft
had strayed off-course during a routine flight, and without
any of the jamming systems on the military models, it had
been an easy kill for the defense grid. In the months since
then the site had been scavenged by the Legion, but the larg-

est pieces of wreckage still littered the site and would provide the perfect cover for the gunship.

Having already seen reconnaissance images of the area, Alverez made a straight-in approach and set down beside the intact tail section. There were no trees to interfere with the landing, not even partial stumps, and the rotor wash kicked up deposits of fine ash from the forest fire touched off by the crash. The gray veil spread across the site, though would be dispersed by the wind once the helicopter stopped generating it.

"Shut everything down," said Alverez, her hands flying over the control panels in her cockpit. "Except for the auxiliary power turbine, the radios, and the weapon systems. This site will give us the perfect cover from Legion sensor scans, so long as we don't create too much electronic activity."

"Julia, how long will we stay?" asked Sutter, once the postlanding procedures had ended.

"Until we get orders from Mitch. No one else matters, not even the Battle Station."

"But what if one of the other squads needs our help? It'll be more than an hour before the first F/A-99s arrive."

"They'll have to fend for themselves as best they can," said Alverez, irritated. "We all knew that when we went into this mission. So don't act so surprised about it now."

"Yes, I understand . . . Ju-Julia?"

"*What* is it now?"

"I think there's someone out there," said Sutter in a small, trembling voice. "And I think he's watching the ship."

"Damn it, Jeff. I thought you said this place was uninhabited." Alverez replied, fighting off the paralyzing fear Sutter's warning created by using anger. "Lynn, where is this guy?"

"Lieutenant, I swear there was no one here," said Taylor, bringing both turrets back on-line. "The infrared barely picked up any animals."

"He's off on our left, Julia," Sutter answered, "and behind us."

By releasing her shoulder straps, Alverez could turn just far enough to see a figure standing at the edge of the crash site. He appeared somewhat taller than a normal man, and while the auroral light was too weak to make most details stand out, she could see a ridge of spikes on his head. However, what unnerved her the most was the way he stood motionless, like a predator waiting for the prey to take flight in panic.

"He's just within the firing arc of the tail turret," said Taylor. "Want me to nail 'im?"

"No. Not yet," said Alverez, fighting to control her fear. "He hasn't made a move on us."

"Hell, he hasn't moved at all since Lynn spotted him. What gives with this guy? It's spooky."

"What do the sensors show?"

"Infrared, nothing," Taylor answered, reading off what one of his CRT screens displayed while he relayed the data to the pilot's cockpit. "Motion detector, nothing. And the tail turret's laser tracker shows he hasn't moved a centimeter since being spotted."

"Kill it, Julia," Sutter implored. "Before it attacks or reports us to the Citadel."

"I'm not picking up *any* radio transmissions from this area, Lieutenant." Taylor quickly scanned his electronic surveillance system panel and found only its status lights active. "We're the only ones talking here."

"Give me a close-up with the aft gun's camera," said Alverez. "I'm beginning to think this creature's more than inhuman."

On her cockpit's center display screen the silent and so far motionless figure appeared and grew until its head and shoulders filled it. The dim auroral light needed to be enhanced for any detail to become visible. First and most obvious was the creature's face, frozen in what appeared to be scream of agony. It took a few seconds for Alverez to realize not only were the creature's eyes lifeless, everything else about it was.

"Good God, it's a statue," Alverez finally concluded. "A damn statue."

"Now why would the Dark Legion wanna set up something like this?" said Taylor, studying the same image. "To scare people?"

"Maybe that's exactly why they erected it. Or perhaps it marks the site of some great victory of theirs over mankind."

"Some victory this was. Shooting down an unarmed, ci-

vilian plane ain't much of a challenge. This isn't something
I'd celebrate."

"Perhaps that's exactly what it is to them," said Alverez.
"Remember, the Legion isn't us. So don't go around expecting them to act or think like us."

"And what are we going to do about this thing?" Sutter
responded, the tone of her voice no longer fearful.

"Leave it alone. We're practically sitting in the shadow of
a Legion base, so we're not gonna attract attention by
knocking over one of their statues. If you want, we'll fly in
a street gang and let 'em vandalize it later."

"When I initially spotted them, Corporal, I thought they
were helicopters," said Private Renya Ozawa, pointing first
at the observation tower's main screen. "Now, I don't know
what they are."

"Don't feel ashamed, Renya-san," said Momoko
Watanabe. "Unless you've spent a lot of time here, you
wouldn't know what the Dark Legion has or is capable of."

In the days following the destruction of her reconnaissance warhead by the Legion raiding force, there had at last
been the influx of personnel and equipment she and the rest
of the outpost staff had repeatedly requested. While she no
longer had to do her watch tours alone, Watanabe knew far
larger reinforcements had been sent to the Mishima frontier
with Bauhaus, where a border clash threatened because Bauhaus tracked the raiding force back into Mishima territory.

"I'm confused, Corporal," Ozawa admitted. "Didn't the
Legion use helicopters on their last incursions?"

"Yes, they appear to have a good supply of human aircraft
and spacecraft," said Watanabe, stepping up to the immense
control and communications console. She turned most of her
attention to one of its auxiliary screens, where a computer
analysis of the Dark Legion's intercepting forces was just
ending. "However, they appear to use them only on operations beyond their territory. Inside it they prefer using their
own creations. Yes, they're using their ezoghouls."

"I'm sorry, their what?"

"Winged beasts. Biotechnological creations of flesh and
metal. They can carry almost any weapon imaginable and
are horrifying in combat—as we'll soon see."

While she spoke, Watanabe called up a reconnaissance file

from the computer's memory and displayed part of it on a data screen. She ran the final moments of a months' old warhead flight deep inside Citadel territory. Through the swirling clouds a centaurlike animal with furiously beating wings appeared.

Its powerful legs were tucked under its body, and its arms were outstretched. It held a Gatling gun–style weapon in one hand, which it fired at the wildly evading warhead. The other was empty, until it snatched the drone out of the air. The last image transmitted was of the ezoghoul's horned, malevolently grinning mouth, its reptilian jaws opening wide to engulf the drone. Then Watanabe turned to the console's tactical screen, where small clusters of symbols were about to be overtaken by larger forces.

"Is this what will happen to the Capitol Special Forces?" asked Ozawa, still transfixed by what had been displayed on the auxiliary screen.

"If they were flying Feline strike fighters or gunships, they would have a chance," Watanabe soberly observed. "However, they have only infantry weapons and jet chutes. I hope they'll all die gloriously in combat."

"I think one squad may be able to evade interception. Why would you want them to die?"

"Because capture by the Dark Legion is a far worse fate—a living death in the service of evil. I sincerely wish we could warn or help them, but this is of course against Mishima policy."

"What should we do, Corporal?" Ozawa asked.

"Order the rest of our warhead drones launched," said Watanabe. "And tell the cafeteria we'll take our meals up here. These Special Forces squads won't be the end of it, Renya-san. I suspect Capitol will continue with its assault on the Citadel. Tonight will be an even longer night than it usually is."

"This looks like it was once a Bauhaus system," said Venneti when he realized the base of the missile launcher he was working on had a vague hexagonal shape. "No wonder the Legion found it easy to destroy the defenses at Base Aquila."

"We'll do weapons identification at the debrief," Hunter advised. "Just hurry up and finish mining this thing. We have a lot more targets before we reach the inner defense zone."

"Finished, Captain. What detonation time do you want?"

"Set it for one minute before H-hour."

"The last one we set won't go off until ten minutes *before* H-hour," Shacker whispered in Hunter's ear. "What gives, Captain? I thought we were to knock out the net either on or just before H-hour. You're setting detonation times all over the map."

"It's to give the impression that a much larger force is out here than a single squad," said Hunter. "And that it's operating in this outer defense zone, instead of heading into the Citadel. I hope we can keep 'em guessing long enough for us to slip inside."

"Mitch, I'm picking up something on the operational channels," Rogers said quietly, cupping his hand over one of his earphones. "Distress calls."

His half-whispered warning cut through the other conversations and the background noise like a thunderclap. The rest of the squad fell silent as Hunter moved around the automated launcher to join Rogers. He briefly listened in on the transmissions with an auxiliary set of headphones, then ordered Rogers to switch on his radio set's external speaker.

"This is Sword Point to anyone listening!" Hogan shouted, his voice barely audible above the whistling wind and the growl of his jet chute engine. "My squad is under attack! We need reinforcements now! We need rein—"

Hogan's pleas were drowned out by an inhuman snarling and the snapping of skeletal wings. His screams and the transmission itself were cut short by a snapping sound; static mercifully filled the channel and the air around the launcher until Rogers shut off the speaker.

"From the earlier reports I heard, at least one of the other squads has been similarly attacked," he added. "We may well be the only pathfinder unit still functional."

"Is there anything we can do to help them?" asked Wendy.

"I'm afraid not," said Hunter. "And in the cold calculation of warfare, I hope their deaths will draw attention away from us. In that respect we can ensure that they didn't die in vain. Move out. Diane, you have the point."

* * *

"On the whole, sir, these reports are not good," concluded the senior coordinating officer after he gave Wood printed transcripts of the latest messages intercepted by the battle station. "Only one of our Special Forces squads has apparently evaded attack."

"And what about squad Trident?" said Wood when he realized they were not mentioned in the transcripts. "You've heard nothing from them?"

"Not since their departure from forward base Threshold. They could either be on schedule or brought down before even reaching their drop point."

"I can't believe Bamble and Sutter would go this long without sending in even the briefest progress report," said Hart, for once showing more concern than smug arrogance. "Perhaps the Colonel's right. Maybe they were shot down or crashed."

"Since their locator beacon hasn't been detected, I'll chose to believe they're on schedule," Wood responded, handing the sheets over to Hart. "And the rest of the operation continues as planned. Even if only one squad is still viable, they can still create enough havoc for it to succeed. Colonel, advise the air bases to begin launching their aircraft in ten minutes."

CHAPTER SEVENTEEN

"Is that it, Captain?" Parker asked quietly as the squad stopped at the edge of a small clearing.

"It's the only structure for hundreds of kilometers in any direction," Hunter answered. "It has to be the Citadel."

What had formerly been a glow on the horizon almost indistinguishable from the aurora australis had at last taken form and separated from the background light. To the naked eye the Citadel appeared as a single, squat spire rising from an increasingly deformed and stunted forest. Through the squad's night and sniper scopes, the huge complex appeared more detailed—and much more complete than the photographs shown at the briefing only a few hours before. Also visible was an antlike swarm over the structure and its immediate grounds; the construction crews were still hard at work.

"It makes my skin crawl just to look at it," said Parker, lowering her rifle and giving it to Halston so he could use its sight.

"We have to sneak inside that?" Venneti added, incredulous. "There must be thousands of creatures working on it."

"Tens of thousands," said Hunter. "And before we can sneak inside it, we have to cross this."

Hunter swept his hand over the terrain between the clearing they were poised to cross and the still-distant Citadel. The forest grew increasingly sparse and the clearings larger until, in its immediate vicinity, the landscape was nearly barren. And moving around the defiled terrain could be seen small groups of what appeared to be soldiers.

"From here on in is the inner defense zone," Hunter continued. "No more automated sensors, missile launchers, or observation posts. Now it'll be patrols of those creatures we were briefed on, necrotechnology hovercraft, and mine fields

in some of the clearings. Rogers, reset your motion detector
and EM scanner accordingly. From here on in we're to talk
as little as possible and avoid all contact with Dark Legion
patrols until H-hour. We'll cross this clearing at its narrow-
est point and only in pairs. Jake, you take the point. We're
still on schedule, twenty-nine minutes, eleven seconds to
H-hour."

"I'll miss the sensation this gives me," said Ragathol,
smiling serenely. "The flight from this planet to His Castle
will be a long one ... And even though the ship is capable
of it, it'll still be cramped. I must be prepared for that."

For what he expected would be the last time, Ragathol
stood in the center of his Nether Room, his legs spread and
his arms raised to its apex. The forces of the Dark Symmetry
washed his body with a liquid green light. It glowed much
brighter than it had at any other session and almost seemed
to dematerialize him. He barely heard Echmeriaz talking to
the other necromutant who entered his room. This time he
chose not to end the session prematurely; he let the forces
completely revitalize him before lowering his arms and
moving out of the stance.

"Who was that? And what news did he bring?" he requested.

"A messenger from Azurwraith," said Echmeriaz, turning
to face his Master. "He brought news of further human activity on the fringes of our Domain. The probing units he destroyed earlier appear to be part of a larger operation.
Capitol warplanes are marshaling at the farther range of our
sensors and are accelerating toward us."

"Is he preparing his defenses to stop them?"

"Yes, my Master. The grid is being energized as we
speak."

"Does he expect my launch will be delayed any further?"
asked Ragathol, a glimmer of concern edging into the serenity of his voice.

"His message to you is to proceed with your departure as
planned," Echmeriaz answered. "He'll let us know if it has
to be changed or delayed."

"I'm confident Azurwraith has the ability to destroy this
pitiful human attempt to assault us. Summon Caliqabaal and

Praecor to my presence. I wish to find out personally how their individual preparations are faring."

"Finish your meal later, Renya-san," Watanabe advised. "Here they come."

Ozawa nosily dropped his tray of fish cakes on the center's small table and rushed to the console. He eagerly scanned the main screen, but was unable to see any changes until Watanabe motioned to an auxiliary screen. On it he found the expected clusters of aircraft symbols, some of them skimming along the terrain's contours and repeatedly dropping out of radar coverage while others remained at considerably higher altitudes and cruised at slower airspeeds. The Capitol strike force had arrived.

"Impressive, Corporal. Thank you for alerting me," said Ozawa, bowing slightly in Watanabe's direction.

"We'll see if you're still thanking me in a few hours," she said. "Now our real work begins. Inform our commander of this development. I'll handle the warheads. This is the commander center to all drones, general cancellation order Viper. Commence Z-plan on my mark. Mark, mark, *mark*."

In the forty-five minutes since Watanabe had given the orders to launch more reconnaissance drones, the number airborne had grown from two to nine. They prowled the airspace just beyond Dark Legion territory at varying altitudes and flying various preprogrammed flight courses. The moment she gave the command to execute her new orders, the warheads broke away from their current headings and moved to preselected holding points.

As they did so they reduced airspeed, dropped to treetop height, and shut down most of their active reconnaissance and navigation systems.

"Excellent, all drones are responding perfectly," Watanabe observed when the last row of status lights changed to match the others.

"I'm sorry, Corporal," said Ozawa, bowing deeply after hanging up the telephone. "But I was able to talk only to the commander's adjutant. The major has retired for the evening and has left orders that he not be disturbed over trivial matters. Apparently I have not enough stature here to convince his adjutant that what we're watching is anything but trivial. I'm sorry."

"You needn't apologize for the arrogance of our officers, Private. From the sound of it, you'd think they'd want combat to take place only during normal business hours."

"And what should we do? Would the adjutant listen to you, Corporal?"

"Not likely," said Watanabe. "We're on our own, Renyasan. And I rather prefer it this way. There's no one to enforce corporate policy on us. Provided we do nothing excessive, we can make our own decisions. I want an update on the Capitol strike force. Let's see if we can better position our drones."

"Razides," Hunter whispered, nodding at the latest Dark Legion patrol they encountered. Then he signaled for the squad to remain silent.

Unlike the earlier patrols, which were seen only on the motion detector or through the sniper and night scopes, this one passed close enough to the squad's position to be seen without aids. They could also be heard, and while the Legionnaires made little noise beyond the clink of their body armor, the razides and necromutants breathed heavily and the ground seemed to shake under them.

This was especially true for the razides, grotesque humanoid creatures standing over ten feet tall. There were only a few of them in the patrol, which they commanded telepathically. Their glowing yellow eyes swept the terrain repeatedly like twin laser beams; when one of them stared repeatedly at the squad's position, they all believed they had been spotted. The razides wore no armor, their skin seemed thick enough to be armor on its own, and the weapons they carried were either Gatling guns or rocket launchers, which they seemed to handle as easily as a normal man would an assault rifle.

"God, I don't think even Bob Watts could handle these things," Halston said quietly after the patrol had moved by their position and was blending back into the night.

"Not without some major fire support," said Hunter, "or air support. Raymond, the radio."

"Who are you gonna contact?" asked Rogers, passing the handset over to Hunter. "H-hour is still nine minutes away."

"Julia. The Air Force will create a lot of havoc, but we need our own localized air support to get through these patrols. If she takes off now, she'll get here just after they make their initial attack runs."

"Lieutenant, I got increased EM activity in the radar frequencies," Taylor warned, watching the display change subtly on one of his CRT screens.

"Are they intensifying the scans in our area?" asked Alverez.

"No, it's an across-the-board increase. It looks to me like the whole defense grid's being energized."

"We're about nine minutes away from H-hour," Sutter advised. "Perhaps they've spotted the first waves of Felines?"

"Rapier, this is Battle Axe. Rapier, this is Battle Axe," said a distant, familiar voice above the aurora-induced background static. "Do you read? Over."

"Battle Axe, this is Rapier. You're weak, but we read you," said Alverez, surprised by the unexpected contact. "Do you need an evac? Over."

"Negative, Rapier. But we'll be needing fire support soon. Immediate dust off and follow the lead elements in. Contact us when you reach the inner zone. Battle Axe, out."

"Roger, Battle Axe. This is Rapier, out. Jeff, you check the weapons. I'll check the flight systems."

For nearly an hour the Cutlass had sat motionless amid the wreckage of the larger transport, and nearly silent, except for the muffled whine of its auxiliary power turbine. Now a deeper rumble shook the immediate area as its main engines were restarted. Minus its external lights, the gunship rapidly came to life and filled the air with the same fine ash it had kicked up on landing. Then it lifted into the air and rose just high enough to clear the trees surrounding the crash site.

"Lieutenant, request permission to be an art critic," Taylor asked, moments after lift-off.

"Permission granted," said Alverez. "Make it quick."

The helicopter's 15mm tail gun snapped down from the shallow recess it normally traveled in and swung toward the Dark Legion marker. With the ash cloud swirling around it, the statue was a relatively easy target for a lock-on. The two-second burst briefly illuminated the aircraft's aft fuselage and tail boom and spit out enough high-explosive and armor-piercing incendiary shells to blast the screaming figure into a widely scattered arc of rubble. By the time the ash

cloud finished dissipating over the crash site, the lead flights
of F/A-99s would be whistling past it.

"Hold it," said Hunter, just loud enough for everyone in
the squad to hear it, except for the point man. "Five minutes
to H-hour."

The squad stopped in the middle of the stunted trees they
were moving through and turned to the north. Shacker rejoined them a few seconds later and did not need to ask what
they were waiting for or trying to see.

"We're not even going to hear those first charges,"
Venneti advised, sensing the rise in tension among the others. "So don't expec—"

A novalike flash rose out of the darkened forest and became a boiling red fireball about the size of the sun. It was
still consuming the munitions in the first missile launcher
the squad had mined when a sharp clap followed by a prolonged rumble echoed across the terrain. It had yet to dissi-
pate when a second flared into existence a little farther to
the east.

"Excellent," said Hunter, smiling malevolently. "The
whole grid in this sector should be going down. The next
thing we hear should be—Damn, what's that?"

"Some kind of tracer fire, Captain," said Halston, responding to the bright green spurts of light being sprayed
out of the forest from several positions north of where the
squad had halted. "And from the looks of it, they're letting
loose with some heavy caliber stuff."

"Mitch, look," Rogers suggested, holding out the motion
detector to Hunter. On its view plate could be seen several
amoebalike masses moving in suddenly uncoordinated directions.

"They're confused," said Hunter. "They know there's an
enemy, but they can't tell where. It looks like they're trying
to shoot down the fireballs."

"Listen to them," said Wendy. Above the chatter of automatic weapons and thump of demolition charges going off
could be heard an inhuman wailing. It never let up and
seemed to roll ceaselessly like waves onto a beach. "It's that
screaming Capitaine Steiner told us about."

"God, you could go insane listening to it," Shacker remarked.

"At least they'll be easier to avoid . . . or locate," said Hunter, thinking for a moment. "I wonder."

"Wonder about what?" asked Rogers.

"If we could pull the same deceptions on these creatures as we've done on other MegaCorp forces? Advise me when you spot a small patrol, and we'll try to set up one of our ambushes. All right, we've seen enough. Move it out, there'll be plenty more fireworks for us to see in the future."

"Another three minutes and the lead flights will be entering missile range of the Citadel's outer defenses," Hart advised, watching the first groups of symbols rapidly approach the shaded area beyond the actual boundary to Dark Legion territory.

"I can read a tactical map just as well as you," said Wood, irritated. "Even if the net doesn't go down, it'll still be difficult for the Legion to intercept those planes because of their altitude. If they have to, they'll fight their way through the net on their own. That's why we put the defense suppression jets in the lead."

"Mr. Wood, we're getting EM fluctuations in the net," said the senior coordinating officer. "Something's happening!"

Wood turned back to the center's main screen as the nervous conversations he and the other officials were having died away. For several moments only the hum of electronics could be heard, then warning tones pierced the silence and a swarm of new symbols appeared on the screen. All were located inside Dark Legion territory, and all indicated either a loss of power, cessation of radar transmissions, or an explosion.

"They did it!" shouted General Sumner. "We got at least two holes appearing in the net! Colonel, advise the strike leaders. Commence primary mission plan. Destroy as much of the net as possible and attack the Citadel inner defenses."

"It looks as though Hunter's squad has been the most successful," said Wood, taking note of where most of the disablement symbols were located. Then he shot a laser-hot glance at Hart. "It appears as though my faith in them was justified, after all—and my confidence not misplaced."

"It appears, sir," was all Hart managed to say at first.

"And for the woman's sake we should all hope they'll continue to be successful."

"Yes, let's hope so. If Hunter is smart, he'll hold his squad back until the main attack elements arrive and enter the Citadel with them. Somehow, I think he'll find a way of sneaking into it all by himself."

On the main screen, formations of warplanes maneuvered to align themselves with the two partial corridors that had been opened in the grid. The moment they entered it, they broke into pairs and fanned out to attack more of its missile launchers, gun mounts, and radar sites. And at the forward bases along the frontier, the first symbols to appear from any of them in hours popped onto the screen and started circling. The Hercules assault transports and AH-19 gunships were taking off.

CHAPTER EIGHTEEN

"Lieutenant, triple-A on our port side," Taylor warned, as a swath of bright green tracers erupted out of the forest.

"I got it," said Alverez, swinging the Cutlass onto the target. "From the trajectory, I'd say they're going after the fighters. Too far for guns; switching to missiles."

In place of the Sidewinder series of air-to-air missiles they usually carried, the wingtip mounts were now equipped with Hellion antisurface missiles. From one of their shorter, larger-diameter launch tubes a Hellion burst through the transparent nose cap and arced toward the twin-barreled antiaircraft gun. It homed in on the infrared signature the hot barrels were creating. When it exploded over the mount, the prodigious ammunition supply was ignited, touching off a prolonged series of explosions visible for miles.

"Nailed 'em clean," said Taylor. "But I got even more antiaircraft radars coming on-line. Do we go after 'em?"

"No, the Felines have the Nemesis missile," said Alverez. "Let them go after the radars. We'll take out only targets of opportunity. Our real mission's with Hunter."

As the gunship turned back to its original heading, the lead flights of F/A-99 strike fighters thundered over it and broke into pairs. Almost at once they began unleashing Nemesis antiradar missiles and more Hellions. While they curved toward the ground, other missiles and additional tracer fire rose from it. However, their volume was not massive enough or sufficiently coordinated to either trap the fighters or overwhelm their electronic countermeasures.

In minutes the initial corridor Hunter's sabotage had created was rapidly expanding into a miles-wide swath cutting through the defense grid like a dagger. Far to the east a similar incursion was under way. If nothing hindered them, they would soon have the grid severed into two sections.

"There goes another one," said Taylor, the moment a distant fireball boiled out of the forest. "Those Air Force guys are pretty good."

"For all their bragging," Alverez noted before a jump in static on her headphones commanded her attention.

"Rapier, this is Foil. Rapier, this is Foil. Do you read me? Over," a familiar male voice asked.

"Foil, this is Rapier. We read you loud and clear. Is there something you need? Over."

"Affirmative, Rapier. We need a mission. Our squad was intercepted and slaughtered, and we're looking for revenge. Over."

"We're sorry about Hogan and his people," said Alverez. "They were good soldiers. We can always use a wing man. But remember, revenge is a dish best served cold. Over."

"I understand, Rapier. This revenge is too important to get hot and reckless about. We're coming in on your starboard side. Foil, out."

"I got 'em on the surveillance radar," Taylor advised, identifying a blip moving across his main CRT screen. "They'll be here in less than three minutes."

Almost exactly to the second of Taylor's estimate, a set of navigation and running lights flashed briefly in the aurora-streaked sky off the gunship's right side. The second Cutlass swung around its dark blue sister ship and settled into a position about a hundred yards off its left side and several dozen feet behind it. Enough distance separated the two aircraft so they could bob and weave independently to avoid ground fire and not risk collision.

The jets that had filled the sky around them minutes earlier were gone, spreading through the defense grid in an effort to neutralize a large enough section so the assault transports could fly it in relative safety. The succeeding flights of F/A-99s streaked past the slower-moving helicopters on a direct run for the Citadel and its inner defenses. With the exception of occasional tracer fire from an overlooked or newly activated antiaircraft gun, they were largely left alone.

"Proximity warning signals on drones Hiraga and Kongo," said Ozawa, deactivating the shrill beeping in almost the same moment they sounded. "All reconnaissance warheads are now inside Dark Legion territory."

"Excellent, Renya-san. Now keep watch on the others while I direct this one," Watanabe ordered, glancing at her subordinate as she hit the transmit button on one of the individual drone control panels. "Drone Akagi, change course and follow Cutlass-class gunships crossing in front of you on my mark. Maintain nominal safe observation distance at all times. Mark, mark, *mark*."

"Would it not be more productive to have the warheads trail the Capitol jets? Or wait for the assault transports?"

"Don't worry, we'll follow the flashier aircraft as well." Watanabe gave Ozawa a testy, irritated look, which immediately had him averting his eyes from her. "But these helicopters aren't the usual Grapeshots and Guardians we see around here. They're used exclusively by Capitol Special Forces and likely deployed the squads we saw earlier. Following them could be the most productive operation we'll perform tonight."

"I now understand. Thank you, Corporal," said Ozawa before he noticed one of the other drones had broken off its random search pattern and was orbiting a site deep inside Legion territory. "Look, drone Kirishima has discovered a new source of enemy activity."

On one of the console's auxiliary screens was an aerial view of what looked like a stone bunker. Its single entrance was open, and spilling out of it was not only a sickly yellow light, but a teeming horde of Legion troops. When Watanabe turned to the main screen, she found the bunker's location was in the inner defense zone, approximately where the computer estimated the Capitol assault transports would be landing.

"In a few more minutes there'll be thousands of them," Ozawa continued, "spreading across the landscape before the jets'll even notice them. What . . . what are you doing, Corporal?"

"Providing a way for them to be noticed," said Watanabe, lifting her finger off the auto record button on Kirishima's control panel. Now, none of its incoming data was being transcribed onto a laser disc. "Drone Kirishima, emergency cancellation orders Archimedes. Target site entrance. Execute maneuver Divine Wind. Mark, mark, *mark*."

"It's diving! Impact, fifteen seconds. What damage can it do? It contains no explosives."

"But it does contain something that is highly explosive." Watanabe tapped the fuel status meter on the Kirishima's panel until Ozawa noticed it. "The tanks are nearly full. Between that and the weapons those creatures are carrying, the results should be spectacular. And when the maneuver ends, you can help me delete my last orders to the warhead from the computer records."

On the auxiliary screen displaying the Kirishima's data feed, the image rolled and blurred in response to Watanabe's orders. When it stabilized, the bunker was again in the center of the screen and growing rapidly. In moments it had filled it, and the individual Legionnaires, necromutants, and razides teeming around it became identifiable. Then the image fluttered and dissolved into static as the status lights and readings on the drone's control panel went dead.

"Good God," Hunter blurted out when he felt the ground tremble under his feet. And seconds later the forest his squad was moving through was illuminated by a harsh orange light. "What the—hit the deck!"

Less than half a mile away, far closer than any previous explosion, a fireball split both earth and sky. The drone had managed to fly partway into the bunker before crashing. Its fuel tanks were ripped open instantly, and their contents were mixed with disintegrating engine parts. The resulting sheet of flame spread over the munitions and weapons stockpiled inside the bunker. In seconds they were igniting and chain-reacting violently.

The resulting detonation blew the roof off the bunker and rained it down on the surrounding countryside. Rocks ranging in size from marbles to basketballs pelted the area where the squad had taken cover; all the while the ground heaved from the continuing explosions at the site. The heat from the fires being generated in the bunker could be felt by the squad, and above the rolling thunderclaps they could hear the shrieks and wails of the Legionnaires.

"Listen to them," said Parker when the thunder died down to a rumble. "They never do stop, do they?"

"It sounds like they're coming closer," Venneti added.

"They are," said Rogers, rising to a crouch and sweeping

one area with his motion detector. "I got a small unit, Mitch. And it's moving into visual range, seventy meters."

"Heavy weapons, forward," Hunter commanded. "The rest of us will support you with grenade launchers. Ray, you detecting anyone else?"

"There's a couple of larger units at longer ranges. They'll probably come running when we open fire."

"That's exactly what I want. Plot us an evac route, Lieutenant, we'll need it. Prepare to fire on my signal."

Halston, Shacker, and Parker moved in the direction Rogers indicated and clicked off the safeties on their weapons. Hunter followed immediately behind them and signaled for them to stop near the clearing edge. He next motioned for the rest of the squad to take defensive locations along the flanks and rear of their position. They had just settled in when the Dark Legion patrol appeared.

Unlike most of the others they had seen, this one had only one razide, a few Centurions, and a swarm of Legionnaires moving around them. They moved in a steady run and appeared more intent on reaching the bunker area than on sweeping the landscape. The moment he saw that most of his squad had clear fields of fire, Hunter snapped his fingers.

The machine guns and sniper rifles barked loudly, and their muzzle flashes flared brightly in the semidarkness. The first to be hit in the patrol was the razide; Halston riddled it with a full burst of the new armor-piercing incendiary shells. They penetrated its thick skin and exploded among its metal skeleton and internal machinery. The creature managed to stay on its feet in spite of the multiple impacts and burst into flames as it tried to level its rocket launcher at the squad.

Next to fall were the two centurions, who had turned in the direction of the attack and were commanding the Legionnaires to charge. Shacker and Parker hit them with the same rounds Halston used, which blew the armor off their bodies and incinerated them in a similar manner. The moment they died, the surviving Legionnaires stopped their screaming and the assault. Massed rifle and machine-gun fire cut them all down in seconds, then the battlefield fell strangely silent.

"I got movement!" Rogers warned, swinging his motion detector rapidly. "Big time! Multiple directions!"

"Squad, mad time!" said Hunter. "Thirty seconds, then we evac! Leo, drop some Flamers here. Full timers!"

The entire squad stood in a circle and emptied their weapons into the surrounding terrain. They did not track any targets or draw any immediate return fire. For half a minute they put on a firepower display, then abandoned the position in the direction Rogers was pointing.

"Anything happening back there?" Hunter asked, changing a clip in his assault rifle as he ran.

"Yes, sir. The site's taking fire from two locations," said Harris, glancing over his shoulder. "Now three! And there goes one of Leo's specials!"

With each succeeding detonation of a napalm grenade, the volume of fire from the Dark Legion units intensified. It was only a matter of seconds before they were firing on each other. In the confusion of battle the telepathic orders to cease fire were not sensed or understood. And by the time the units had drawn close enough to be identified, they in turn were drawing attention—from arriving flights of F/A-99 fighters.

"That's it. Nail 'em good," said Hunter as he watched the strafing runs begin from where the squad took cover.

"How long are we gonna stay here, Captain?" Venneti requested.

"Just long enough to catch our breath." Hunter turned away from the air attack and glanced around until he got his directions. "The Citadel is that way, and we still have a good hike ahead of us."

"Shouldn't we wait until the assault transports arrive?" asked Rogers, sipping water from his canteen after he finished gasping for air, "and join in the general attack?"

"No. By the time those troops disembark, the Legion will be ready for a ground fight. I know it'll be dangerous, but sneaking into the Citadel will be easier during the initial air attacks. Which, from the looks of what's coming, should begin any minute now. Check your weapons. And if any of you are feeling tired now, let Wendy give you a booster shot. We won't have time for it later."

"I already sense what you're here to tell me is not good," Ragathol growled at the necromutant who hovered uneasily at the threshold to his Nether Room. "Enter and report . . ."

"My Master sent me to advise you of recent developments," said the necromutant, bowing respectfully to the creature seated on the basalt throne. "The probing forces he thought were destroyed have damaged part of our outer defenses and the human attack planes are exploiting it."

"Bring up a territorial map from the Command Nexus, Echmeriaz."

The map of Venus and its orbital traffic patterns were wiped from the wall screen and replaced with a tactical map of the Citadel and the surrounding area. On it were the symbols for hostile forces, the Dark Legion's, and something Ragathol had not expected to see, markers indicating battle damage.

"How ... how did they manage to do this?" he asked, clearly surprised.

"The humans are using equipment that deceives our sensors and confuses our ground forces," said the necromutant. "They've been more successful than we estimated."

"Deceive us ... How could these humans deceive us? We're the masters of the Dark Symmetry!"

"They'll not continue to do so for long, Lord Ragathol. Master Azurwraith promises this. To ensure your safe departure, he requests you delay lift-off until these intruders are dealt with."

"I'm blessed that your Master is so, 'concerned' about my safety," said Ragathol, the calm tone of his voice belying the sarcasm in his remark. "Tell your Master I'll wait ... though it had better not be for long. Otherwise, my flight plans will need to be changed, delaying my arrival at the Defiled Castle of He who we must obey."

"Yes, Lord Ragathol. I'll tell my Master," the necromutant promised, bowing again. "He's grateful for your cooperation."

"Why did you not grow angry with him, my Master?" asked Echmeriaz after the messenger had retreated from the Nether Room.

"Because anger would not have served me at this time," said Ragathol. "I wanted him to return to Azurwraith with my answer. Make a record of his defense of this Citadel. If it sustains heavy damage from the humans, then I might use his failure against him. Just as mine was used against me ...

If I use it right, I could return here as this Citadel's new master."

"We have another loss," advised an Air Force console operator. "Able Fox One-Nine. Its crew appears to be ejecting."

On the center's tactical screen a Capitol aircraft symbol changed from bright green to red and began flashing. A smaller symbol broke away from it—the cockpit pod had successfully ejected—then it faded out and was replaced by the marker for a downed aircraft, one of a growing number.

"Analysis," said the senior coordinating officer, moving over to the console. "What brought this one down?"

"Antiaircraft gunfire," said the operator. "And like the others, it appears to be either vehicle of infantry-based, not a fixed site mount."

"Send a pair of Grapeshots to rescue the crew—if they can survive that long in such a hostile land."

"Our fighter crews are going to have to learn not to go after such targets with auto-cannons," Wood observed, stepping over to the console as well. "It may be a glorious way to do combat, but its end isn't very glorious if we lose multimillion-value aircraft. Colonel, I want you to order the fighters to head for the nearest forward base as soon as they expend their external ordnance. The armament crews at the bases can have 'em rearmed in a matter of minutes."

"Yes, sir, though they may not like getting such orders from a Ground Forces colonel," said the coordinating officer.

"Then have General Sumner give the order." Wood turned and briefly pointed at the commanding officers, who were busy reading the reports their aides were handing to them. As he did so, he scanned the tactical screen yet again. "Sometimes service rivalry can be as bad as corporate protocol ... What are those two ships? They're moving a lot slower than the Felines, and the Hercules Fours are just entering the outer defense zone."

"They're two of the Special Forces gunships. We think one of them is from Captain Hunter's squad. Would you like them contacted?"

"No. Whatever they're doing, I have no doubt it'll help with the assault."

* * *

"Lieutenant, I still can't raise the squad," said Taylor. "I think the aurora might be giving us some trouble."

"I think what's happening on the ground may have more to do with it," Alverez replied. "There's enough noise going on down here to wake the dead—if the Dark Legion hasn't already done so."

Even through their helmets and the clatter of the rotor blades, Taylor and Alverez could still hear the muted sounds of explosions and gunfire. Unlike the strike fighters, which always stayed at least a few hundred feet above the ground, the slower-moving gunships were able to hug the terrain at often treetop height. They were largely ignored by the surviving defenses, which continued their frenzied efforts to bring down the higher-flying jets.

"Missile launch!" Taylor shouted. "Starboard side! Looks like they're launching a flock of 'em!"

"I got 'em. Too close for missiles, switch to guns," said Alverez. "Foil, this is Rapier. We're going after that active battery. Cover us. Over."

"Roger. We'll ride your tail, Rapier. Foil, out."

The Cutlass gunships broke hard to the right, with the blue one moving even farther into the lead. Half a mile ahead of them, a multiple-launch battery was still unleashing missiles at the flights of warplanes that were almost directly overhead. They broke formation and scattered frantically, ejecting flares and clouds of chaff in an effort to jam the Dark Legion weapons.

Taylor switched the forward turret to manual operation and placed the crosshairs floating on his tactical screen over the battery. The moment he pressed the button atop the control stick, a stream of tracer, incendiary, and armor-piercing shells burned into the darkness and scored hit after hit on the target. Even when Alverez swung the gunship past the target, he kept firing at it and the hatch that opened up in its base.

The launcher itself had just fired off all its missiles and did not explode when hit. What lay beneath the hatch proved far more volatile. It only took a few dozen shells flashing down it to start a fire. The initial explosion that followed blew the entire battery apart. Later ones occurred below the site and expanded the crater they repeatedly excavated.

"Rapier, gunfire, port side! Evasive! Evasive!"

Alverez pulled her Cutlass into an even tighter starboard turn and dropped it nearer to the ground. For a moment tracers flashed perilously close to the helicopter, until its wing man raked the area where the fire came from with its own stream of cannon shells. Alverez righted her ship just as she caught sight of two centaurlike creatures evaporating into secondary explosions.

"Watch it, Foil. These things just scored a hit," Alverez warned.

A thousand feet above them an F/A-99 lost its battle to evade one of the antiaircraft missiles fired by the battery. Its proximity fuse detonated it just under the aircraft, ripping it apart with a powerful blast and adding its fuel to the fireball. By the time the doomed fighter's wreckage finished hitting the ground, the rest of its squadron mates had re-formed.

"Rapier, this is Echo Sierra Lead. Thanks for the payback. Over," said the flight leader.

"Our pleasure, Echo Sierra," said Alverez. "When you guys hit the Citadel, be on the lookout for my squad. They'll be in the area. Over."

"We'll try, but that base still has most of its defenses intact. Echo Sierra Lead, out."

"Those things I shot up, were they ezoghouls? Over," asked the second gunship's pilot.

"I think they were," said Alverez. "Why?"

"How should I record them? As enemy vehicles destroyed? Or personnel killed? Over."

"We'll figure all that out at the debrief. Resume original heading and fall in behind me. Let's find my squad before someone like those things does. Rapier, out."

"I thought these ezoghouls had wings," Venneti said quietly. "How come they're not flying?"

"They're probably dangerous enough to a guy in a jet chute or even a helicopter," Hunter answered. "But I don't think even they could take on a Feline."

Hunter pointed his rifle's muzzle at a Dark Legion unit gathering at the entrance to another bunker. While a few razides and necromutants could be seen in it, most of the unit was composed of ezoghouls. They towered over the rest, even the razides, and easily handled the Gatling guns and other heavy weapons in their powerful hands. From the squad's position at the edge of a forest patch of stunted trees, they could hear the creatures snarl and hiss at each other in a language all their own.

"Captain, I think they've spotted us," Halston said in a hushed, nervous tone. "They're turning our way."

"Everyone keep down. Weapons ready," said Hunter, lifting his head just high enough to check on the other members of his squad and make sure they were still lying hidden in the tree line. "No, I don't think it's us they've noticed. I think it's something behind us."

"You could be right, Mitch," Rogers advised. "From the radio traffic I'd say there's a few squadrons of jets inbound."

"Captain, they're raising their weapons," said Halston. "What'll we do?"

"Stand by to fire. Target the ezoghouls only."

"Mitch, even if we all had machine guns like Ted's, they'd still outgun us," said Rogers. "Are you sure this is a smart thing to do?"

"The smart thing for us to do is call in Julia and evac Nova Miami," Hunter responded, raising his voice high enough for the sarcasm to be heard. "These creatures are probably targeting more fighters. If we can distract 'em, maybe our guys can have clean runs. Diane, Jake, you pull the triggers first."

"Got it, Captain," said Shacker, pushing the barrel of his rifle through the brush he was using for cover. "At this distance, head shots will be easy."

The bunker was some three hundred yards from the tree line. Creatures gathered at its entrance were either outlined in the pale yellow light spilling from it or the Citadel's massive foundation in the immediate distance. Parker and Shacker waited until most of the ezoghouls were aiming their weapons before opening fire.

They fired in unison, with Shacker's target taking a hit just above the left eye, blowing most of its head off. As its trembling body crashed to the ground, Diane's victim took a glancing blow to the same side of its head. The ezoghoul bellowed in pain and was sent spinning to the ground. The Gatling gun it held fired wildly into the air, the tree line, and finally the rest of its unit. A razide and another ezoghoul fell wounded, and while the rest opened fire on one of their own

kind to stop the carnage, they scarcely noticed the volume of
fire they were receiving from the forest.

While Halston's machine gun chattered its way through
the rest of the belt of ammunition it held, the squad's other
weapons spat out smaller caliber shells or grenades. An
ezoghoul was hit in the left side by an antiarmor grenade;
the resulting explosion tore it in half, finally getting the attention of the survivors.

They had just turned their weapons on the forest when an
ear-splitting screech ripped the air. All that was seen of the
F/A-99 was a blurred silhouette against the aurora veils and
the glow of its afterburners. The area around the bunker was
pelted with a rain of plastic spheres. An instant later they
detonated in a wave of lightninglike flashes.

"Keep your heads down!" Hunter shouted before he virtually buried his in the earth. He also tucked his arms in
against his chest to present the smallest possible target to the
coming storm of shrapnel.

Even though the fighter's objective was nearly a thousand
feet away, the antipersonnel cluster bombs it dropped were
highly indiscriminate area weapons. They filled the air with
triangular, carbide-steel darts. The ezoghouls and other creatures around the bunker were shredded by them. At the tree
line the darts had lost much of their velocity. Still, they
chopped apart the more exposed trees and clinked loudly off
the squad's battle armor.

"Captain, I think that did it," said Parker, scanning the target area with her sniper scope the moment the storm ended
and a brief, unnatural quiet settled over the terrain.

"I hope so," Hunter replied, rising slowly and checking
the newest scratches in his lightweight armor. "If we get any
more attention like this from the Air Force, it'll kill us. Anybody get hit?"

"I think I got nicked on the elbow," said Harris, examining a smear of blood on his glove. "I hope the Dark Legion
doesn't get any more dangerous than this."

"They probably will. Wendy, take care of him."

"Mitch, this is about the last cover we have between here
and the Citadel," Rogers observed. "It's still more than two
clicks away. How're we gonna cross that distance with this
kind of activity?"

"No one said it'd be easy," said Hunter. "But I think these guys might help us!"

Once again the air was split by the screech of turbofan engines at full power. More flights of F/A-99s swept in against the Citadel, unleashing a wave of laser-and-infrared guided missiles on it. Most were targeted against its gun mounts and missile launchers, but a few struck some of the unfinished sections, commencing the Citadel's destruction.

"All right, let's get moving!" Hunter continued, finishing the reloading of his rifle's grenade launcher. "The assault's beginning. We don't have much time between now and the arrival of the Hercules transports! This'll be the only chance we'll have to get inside that thing without a major fight! Move it!"

This time Hunter took the point and led his squad out into the barren terrain. More flights of strike fighters screamed overhead and challenged the Citadel's defenses with a variety of guided and unguided weapons. Unlike the first waves, which completed their runs relatively unhindered, these were met with artillery fire and a few missile launches—almost as if the Citadel itself was finally awakening to the fact it had come under direct attack.

With Legion attention turning to the air strikes, Hunter's squad found crossing the empty terrain intimidating but relatively easy. They watched the aircraft making the bombing runs almost as much as the Citadel itself. The first time they were forced to take whatever cover they could find was when a sharp bang echoed high above them.

They glanced up to discover an F/A-99 plunging out of a brief fireball. It righted just long enough for its cockpit pod to eject. Immediately afterward it increased speed, and obeying its final programmed commands, the fatally damaged aircraft plunged deep into the Citadel. When it exploded, it shook the entire fortress and the land around it.

"Did you feel ... of course you did," said Ragathol when he turned to Echmeriaz and noticed the look of concern in his eyes. "Find out what caused the tremor. Contact the Nexus directly ... I don't wish to wait for a messenger to bring me the answer."

Even several hundred feet underground, the fighter's impact was felt as a quakelike vibration. The Nether Room was shaken softly and briefly by it. Ragathol was stirred by the incident and rose from his throne. By the time he reached the console Echmeriaz was manning, the answer was coming in.

"The tremor you felt was caused by a human warplane," said the necromutant appearing on the console's lone view screen. "We damaged it, and it chose to plunge into our structure."

"What's the damage to the Citadel?" asked Ragathol, standing beside Echmeriaz.

"The resulting blast penetrated to the Nexus level, Lord Ragathol. We're unaffected, and we can work around the damage. We'll have to reroute power to overcome it. Unfortunately, this means Master Azurwraith is reducing the power levels to the hangar and flight facilities. Your departure will have to be canceled for the present time."

"Canceled . . . my triumph is to be canceled!"

Ragathol brought his fist down hard on the console, breaking its metal cover plate and damaging the electrical systems inside it. A loud sputtering and puffs of smoke erupted from it as the lone screen went blank, and even the wall screen dissolved into static snow.

"Master, what are we to do now?" asked Echmeriaz, watching the life flicker out of system after system on his console. "We're now unable to contact anyone."

"Accompany me to the hangar!" Ragathol stormed. "I'll personally take command of it! If necessary, we'll take the power we need to complete preparations and launch the spacecraft ourselves!"

"Good God. Head for the bunker!" Hunter shouted. "I don't care how far we're from it. That thing's gonna come down with a bang!"

In the moments following the crash, one of the Citadel's partially completed spires teetered to one side. For every degree it moved, it seemed to pick up momentum. Above the scream of jet engines could be heard the groaning of metal and the crunch of stonework. In the final seconds of its collapse, wind whistled around the spire; then it impacted with an earth-jarring crash. The clouds of dust it raised obscured part of the Citadel, and debris rained down as far away as the bunker the squad was hiding in.

"Captain, maybe we should use this moment to sneak inside?" said Halston, motioning to the tunnel entrance deeper inside the bunker. "At least we won't get hit by our own jets."

"We'll be doing enough tunnel fights once we're in that place," said Shacker, pointing to the fortress. "I'm not about to take a tunnel to get to the tunnels."

"No tunnel fights yet, Ted," Hunter advised. "It's likely we'll encounter Legion units somewhere in there, and we need to conserve our munitions for the time being. There'll be plenty of fighting for us once we're inside the Citadel. Leo, plant a charge at the entrance. Since we're not going to use it, let's make sure the Dark Legion can't either."

"Rapier, this is Foil. We got a couple of survivors from this one. Request permission to effect rescue. Over."

"Granted," said Alverez, glancing to the left and catching sight of the ejected cockpit pod deploying its main parachutes. "Get to it, you guys. From the sound of the earlier downing, those crews don't stand much of a chance if the Legion gets to 'em first. Over."

"Understood, Rapier. And we'll be on the lookout for your squad as well. Foil, out."

The trailing Cutlass broke sharply away from the lead ship and headed directly for the descending pod. In seconds the semidarkness swallowed it up, while the pod and its brightly colored parachutes were still readily visible. Because of its dark finish, the polar night even more effectively cloaked Alverez's gunship. Many of the Legion patrols it flew by never noticed it until tracer fire raked through them.

"Ground activity's getting kinda light around here, Lieutenant," said Taylor, switching between views from both the nose and aft turrets. "Think our guys were through here?"

"Could be," said Alverez. "Lynn, you getting any response from your transmissions?"

"No, Julia," Sutter answered, clicking off the transmit switch on the main cabin's terminal. "You think they're on another frequency?"

"If they were, it'd be the distress channels. And so far we haven't heard anyone familiar on 'em."

"Lieutenant, ground blast. Port side," said Taylor. "That

looks like an underground demolition blast. Not an artillery shell or a missile."

"I think you may be right," said Alverez. "Look sharp. We're investigating this one."

Minutes after the second gunship turned to the left, the lead one followed suit. Only it kept lower to the ground and reduced its speed as it approached the area it wanted to search.

"It'll take anyone at last a day to dig that out," Venneti commented, looking back and admiring his handiwork. "When I blow 'em up they stay blowed up."

"At least the Legion won't be able to use the tunnel to sneak up on us," said Hunter. "Or attack the ground forces when they arrive. Which won't be too long from now. C'mon, let's get moving before this place is swarming with troopers and Legionnaires."

"I think this place is swarming with something else," Parker warned. "I hear a plane, Captain, and it ain't no jet."

Mixed in with the cacophony of battle noises happening around them was the barest popping of rotor blades and the growl of suppressed turbines. The squad halted its advance and took what cover it could while it searched for the source of the noises. However, when the Cutlass was finally spotted, it was not because of anyone's sharp eyes, but its announcement.

"Battle Axe, this is Rapier. Battle Axe, this is Rapier," said a familiar voice, growing louder by the second. "Stand by for touchdown."

In the last fifty feet of its descent, the gunship activated its landing lights and side-slipped to the right before finding a level enough patch of ground. Its landing skids already extended, it raised clouds of dust on its arrival and immediately shut down all external lights.

"Julia, what are you doing?" Hunter demanded after inserting a plug from his communications headset into a jack normally used by ground crew. "We need ground support, but we don't need you sitting on the ground."

"One of the other gunships may have spotted an easier way to get you inside the Citadel," said Alverez. "Get inside, I'll explain on the way!"

"All right! Everyone in the 'copter and move!" Hunter

quickly disconnected his headset and began waving for the rest of his squad to enter the Cutlass. "This cab's got a fast meter!"

The main cabin doors slid forward as the squad ran from its scattered covering positions to it. In seconds they had all piled in it, and Alverez was gunning the engines to takeoff power.

"Lieutenant, some big door just opened in the Citadel," said Taylor, "and those Legion-things are pouring out of it."

"Activate your laser tracker and switch a Hellion to laser guidance," Alverez ordered. "Put the missile as far up that hole as you can."

"Will do. Arming Hellion."

Seconds before the helicopter lifted off, another of its wingtip-mounted launch tubes ejected a missile. It flew toward the Citadel, maintaining a stabilized, ground-skimming altitude while the gunship rose high into the air. In the last stage of its flight, the Hellion switched to laser guidance and homed in on the coherent light being reflected from the portallike entrance in the Citadel's base.

Already there was a constant stream of Legionnaires, Centurions, and razides pouring out of it. Few paid any attention to the stubby, short-finned projectile, even when it flew inside the tunnel. The strike fighters and lone gunship became their immediate targets, even though most of their weapons did not have the range to reach them.

Only a few had even started to fire when the Hellion exploded deep inside the tunnel. Many of the creatures charging for the entrance were blown out of it, and the structure in the immediate blast area caved in, effectively blocking the tunnel for any additional forces to use.

"Interesting effect," Watanabe noted, watching the entire sequence on one of the console's auxiliary screens. "A single missile has stopped a mass assault that would've required an entire artillery battery to destroy."

"In a sense it's very similar to what we did with the Kirishima," said Ozawa as he scanned the rest of the screens displaying warhead visual feeds.

"You're learning fast, Renya-san."

"But why, Corporal, did the Legion choose to meet a single helicopter landing with such a large ground force?"

"They probably thought it was part of the infantry assault we all know is coming," said Watanabe, turning her attention to the tactical screen, where the large formations of Hercules transports and AH-19 gunships were just entering the inner defense zone. "And now both Capitol's forces and ourselves know what those troops could face. I see Capitol is redistributing its air assets accordingly. We should do the same."

"What do you mean, Corporal?" Ozawa asked.

"Bring all drones into the Citadel inner defense zone. We'll establish patrol patterns for them, and we had better be prepared to use them."

"Julia, this is Mitch. What's this 'easy way' you've discovered into the Citadel?" Hunter asked after connecting his headset to the gunship's intercom. "If there is one."

"There is, I promise," Alverez replied. "We're working with Hogan's Cutlass, and they just discovered that the protective dome over the launch pad was hit during a strafing run and has partially collapsed. If we could finish the job, maybe it'll be a direct way into the Citadel's interior."

"We'd be a little more likely to find Lorraine Kovan if we entered that way," said Wendy. "If you'll recall, we were briefed that the Legion may be trying to take her off the planet."

"It may make our task a little easier," Hunter admitted. "And the Legion certainly wouldn't expect it. Julia, this'll be like flying in a grain silo. Think you can do it?"

"Sounds just like some of the VR games I use to play," said Alverez. "I never crashed in any of them."

"All right, we'll do it. But remember, this is reality, not virtual reality. Leo, Diane, open the compartment behind you. If we're going to descend into hell, then we better do it fully armed. Pack as much munitions as you can carry, we'll need it."

Wheeling into a hard left turn, the Cutlass stayed low to the ground and skimmed close to the Citadel's outer walls. Unlike the jets it drew no defensive fire, which had grown increasingly sporadic and disorganized after repeated strikes. It briefly circled the location where the second gunship was rescuing the fighter crew, then the two rejoined and flew to-

ward the Legion's launch facilities. Behind them the lead
flights of Hercules IV transports were just coming into view.

"God, the architect to this thing has to be a mental patient," said the lieutenant at the observation blister. "Sergeant, did you ever see the like?"

"Maybe in a spook movie," said Watts. "I gotta admit,
I'm impressed."

"You think we can take it, Sergeant?" asked the private
standing next to Watts.

"Well, this time the Air Force and the Special Forces
seem to be doing their job. They don't need the infantry to
rescue 'em this time. Just finish the job."

Without warning the cargo deck's low lighting changed to
a soft red to develop everyone's night vision. A nervous
murmur of voices swept through the soldiers; everyone
knew they were only minutes from landing.

"Listen up, troopers!" said the platoon's captain, walking
down from the cockpit's access steps. "Take your disembark
positions. Sergeant, I suppose you'd like to be in front?"

"Guys in front always have the best fields of fire," Watts
answered, grabbing his machine gun and moving closer to
the tail ramp. "Of course I do, sir. C'mon, kid, stick close to
me."

"Sure thing, Big Bob," said the private, following closely
in the sergeant's wake. "That fortress looked pretty huge.
You think we'll make it?"

"If you'll learn not to get reckless and remember who
your best friend is, that rifle is, not me, the lieutenant, or
your buddies. Don't let it down, and it'll never let you
down."

A hard rumble shook the troop carrier as the soldiers finished moving to their disembark positions. The fore and aft
pairs of vertical lift engines were being restarted, yet another
sign that the huge aircraft would soon be landing. Also per-
ceptible was the sensation of deceleration; the pod-mounted
main engines were not only being throttled back, their ex-
haust nozzles were being deflected as well. With the transports reducing speed, the AH-19 gunships were at last able
to jump ahead of them and sweep the designated landing
zones of any remaining Legion forces.

* * *

"We move any more ammo into this cabin, we'll throw the ship outta balance," said Venneti, noticing how little was left in the aft storage compartment.

"That'll be enough," Hunter advised, punching up the external camera views on the overhead terminal. "Finish loading yourselves. We're almost in the target area. Julia, this is Mitch. Circle the launch facilities when we reach 'em."

What had once been almost the sole aboveground features of the Legion base were now dwarfed by the Citadel and stood in its shadow. They had received some attention from the F/A-99s; a service tower was down and the segmented dome over the launch pad was damaged. Several of the wedge-shaped sections had collapsed, but most of the dome remained intact. As instructed, Alverez and her wing man began orbiting the complex on their arrival.

"I can't see anything inside it," said Parker, trying to look through the dome's collapsed sections. "I wonder what's below it?"

"We're soon going to find out," said Hunter. "Julia, this is Mitch. Blow the rest of it in."

In response to the command, the nose turrets on both helicopters cut loose on the dome. With sustained bursts the 20mm Gatling guns chopped apart what was left, which fell inside a deep, circular shaft.

"My God, it must be at least a hundred meters in diameter," Shacker estimated after the last segment had fallen in.

"And who knows how deep it is," Hunter added. "Julia, this is Mitch. You think you can fit the ship in there?"

"If there's no obstruction, there shouldn't be a problem," said Alverez.

"Then take us in. And tell your wing man he's to stay in this area for as long as he can. I don't want anyone or anything coming in on top of us."

"Will do, Mitch. Stand by for descent. Julia, out."

"Hand me a few more rifle grenades," said Hunter once he swung the terminal around for Sutter to use. Of the munitions he received, he loaded the first ones into his rifle until its launcher was full, then added the rest to the Harker combat harness he wore under his armor. "I know you all feel overloaded. But I think we're going to need every grenade and bullet we're carrying when we reach the bottom of that pit. This isn't a game, a computer simulation, or an exercise we're entering. And it probably won't be like any battle we've ever fought either. The hell we're descending into will be mankind's fate if this operation doesn't succeed."

CHAPTER NINETEEN

"Master Ragathol ... we were not expecting you," said Caliqabaal. "What do you wish?"

The necromutant's remark brought the work detail around him to a sudden halt. The tekrons, heretics, and other necromutants all turned in unison and bowed to the small entourage that had just appeared at the main hangar's aft portal.

"I wish to depart this world with the Receptacle," Ragathol growled. "How much preparation is there left before this spacecraft is ready?"

Unlike his previous visits to the hangar, this time the necromutant found it almost empty of the human aircraft and helicopters acquired by the Dark Legion. They had been moved into the various auxiliary hangars and bays to make room for the launch of the courier ship. It now stood on the transporter/launch vehicle, free of the stacking gantry and with only a few service towers to steady it. Fueling lines were attached to its huge roof and belly-mounted booster rockets; the frostlike coatings of ice on the lines indicated cryogenic propellants were still being pumped into them.

"Not much, my Master," said Caliqabaal. "We could almost take the Receptacle aboard now and leave. Except, we haven't the power to finish pressurizing the fuel cells on the ship and its boosters. Nor do we have the power to lift the pad to the surface."

"Shaguhl, can you tap into an electrical conduit and take the power we need?" asked Ragathol, turning to his lead tekron. Seconds later he had a telepathic response that briefly made him smile. "Excellent. Have a crew begin work on it immediately. Caliqabaal, what's happening down there?"

At the hangar's opposite end, a loud crashing caught everyone's attention. And it continued as more pieces of the launch pad's retractable dome fluttered down from the surface and impacted hard.

"The dome was damaged by an earlier attack, my Master," the necromutant answered. "It must now be giving way."

"Have a crew move the wreckage to another hangar. I'll not have it delay me."

"Prepare for descent," said Alverez, glancing out either side of her cockpit for a final check of the helicopter's position. "Jeff, what are you reading?"

"Radar altimeter indicates this shaft is at least three hundred meters deep," said Taylor. "Fire control radar shows it's straight-sided, no tapering and no obstructions. Wreckage at the bottom may make landing tricky."

"I'm not worried about that. We'll hover if we have to."

"Wait, something's happening down there. I got movement. I think we're gonna have a welcoming committee."

"Open fire," Alverez ordered. "Use the tail gun. Switch the nose turret over to me."

"We're down, Captain," announced the loadmaster. "Opening ramp!"

In the final moments of its descent, a heavy clunking shook the Hercules as its landing gear deployed. By comparison, the actual touchdown was quiet. Only when the transport settled off-level did everyone realize it had landed. By then, the tail ramp was opening and the first troops were charging down it.

"Fan out and form a perimeter!" the captain shouted. "There's gonna be a lot of planes arriving here in the next few minutes! Sergeant, check that structure! Make sure none of those creatures are in it!"

"Yes, sir!" said Watts. "Stay with me, kid!"

Running from the moment he stepped off the ramp, Watts was hundreds of feet in front of the other soldiers deplaning from the lead flight of troop carriers. While the others moved cautiously, Watts had taken most of the squad out to a bunker that had only been hit minutes before by the escorting AH-19s.

"Sergeant, what were these things?" asked the private,

trying to pick his way among the slaughtered Legionnaires. "They look like they've been dead for a lot longer than five minutes."

"From what the captain said, they probably were dead once," Watts advised, moving deeper into the bunker and scanning the bodies littering it for any signs they were still active. "But this Dark Legion couldn't leave 'em buried. Now we're gonna have to do the job all over again. What's that, kid?"

"The troop carriers, sir. They're lifting off."

Watts returned to the bunker's gaping entrance in time to see the last of the lead Hercules flight rise into the air on its vertical lift jets. Coming behind them was another four transports. They were just finishing their transitions from horizontal flight, lowering their landing gear, when green tracers erupted from the bunkers outside the perimeter line and the Citadel itself.

The Hercules nearest the Citadel tried desperately to evade, but was caught in a cone of fire. Its T-tail and one of its stub wings were chopped apart, causing it to roll to the left and hit the ground nose first. As it exploded and scattered its burning wreckage and bodies across the landscape, the three surviving transports managed to touch down safely, only to be swept with cannon and rocket fire until more Felines screamed in for revenge.

"Those guys better evac that ship fast," said Watts, nodding at the second Hercules to catch fire, "before it explodes."

"Sarge ... Lieutenant ... what's that noise?" the private said nervously. "I've never heard anything like it before."

"Well, it certainly ain't coming from out here." Watts turned and looked back into the bunker at the mouth of the tunnel he had only begun to investigate. The eerie yellow light that spilled out of it had grown harsher, and the inhuman wailing was growing louder by the second. "I think we're gonna have company!"

"Defensive positions everyone!" the lieutenant shouted. "Watts, Osborn, Gannon. Down in front! Everyone else, protect our back until the captain arrives! Whatever these things are, don't let up until you know they're dead!"

* * *

"Switching tail gun to night-vision targeting," said Taylor. "Give us a whirl, Lieutenant."

Hovering less than a dozen feet above the now-exposed shaft, the CFAH-4 Cutlass started to spin slowly to the left. Moments later its tail gun opened fire, the long bursts of tracers seemingly swallowed up in the depths of the shaft. Even though there was no visible response to the hail of shells, the helicopter dropped slowly into the shaft after it had completed its first rotation. Above it the escorting CFAH-3 continued to orbit the launch facilities defensively. Its guns and other weapons were silent, though they swept the area for any sign of Legion forces. Fortunately, all combat appeared to be happening on the other side of the Citadel.

For the horde of tekrons and necromutants who went to work on clearing the pile of debris, the storm of high-explosive and armor-piercing incendiary shells was unexpected. Because they brought no weapons with them, it was also a one-sided slaughter. Many were cut down just as they realized they were under attack, and still more fell as they ran for cover.

"Master, there's some type of gunship in the access shaft!" shouted Caliqabaal, running back to Ragathol's entourage.

"That's obvious. The humans are more brazen than I ever considered," Ragathol noted, looking past the necromutant to the bodies lying on the pad. "Arm yourselves and bring down these intruders."

"But, my Master, we have few weapons here. We're mostly workers and vehicle maintenance crews. Most of the armed units have gone to the surface to stop the main attack."

"I know *that*. In his wisdom Azurwraith has assigned few combat forces to me. Until I gather additional forces, you're to hold off these intruders with—Wait."

As Ragathol turned to leave, his gaze swept across the group of heretics led by Kyle Mortus. Since their arrival at the Citadel they had been under Ragathol's control and were assigned to spacecraft repair and preparation. When he discovered them, Ragathol smiled triumphantly.

"Excellent. Caliqabaal, arm these humans," he continued.

"They're the only ones who successfully challenged the Special Forces squad at Atlantis. Do you think you can hold these off?"

"Yes, my Master. We can do better than hold them off," said Mortus, stepping forward and bowing. "Give us the right weapons and we'll defeat them."

"Caliqabaal will see to your arming. On your lives, these intruders must not succeed in stopping me."

"Humans, these are weapons you can use," said Caliqabaal, opening a locker and displaying rifles that had not been warped and distorted by the Legion's black technology. "Hurry and arm them. I can hear the noise of the Capitol helicopter growing louder."

"Overall analysis of Dark Legion activity?" Watanabe asked when a flashing light near her seat indicated the computer had completed its assigned program. On one of the auxiliary screens the response immediately appeared.

Citadel air defenses are currently operating at less than 30% of estimated capacity. 89% probability that remaining Dark Legion Ground forces are massing for a counterattack on the Capitol beachhead. Insufficient data to predict outcome of Capitol assault at this time. End analysis.

"Does this mean the Dark Legion could win?" asked Ozawa, studying the same readout as Watanabe.

"There are more flights of Capitol strike fighters approaching the combat zone," she said. "And while their contribution to the attack wasn't part of the analysis, the future is still in doubt. We must do what we can to tip the scales in Capitol's favor. Drone Kongo, target east portal on Citadel structure. Program maneuver Divine Wind, attempt maximum penetration of target. Execute on my mark."

The target Watanabe had selected was one of the two main entrances on the Citadel's north face. Before the attack had begun, they had been the most complete on the fortress. The giant stone statues flanking them had only been in need of final detailing. Now they were scarred by bomb blasts and blackened by napalm strikes. The portal frames had suffered similar damage, but hordes of Legionnaires, Centurions, and other creatures still poured through them and came teeming down the stairs, trampling and crushing the bodies of those killed by earlier air strikes.

Only a strafing pass by F/A-99s or Grapeshots would attract defensive fire from the Legion forces. The hordes scarcely noticed the slim-bodied warhead as it streaked over them and flew inside the more heavily used of the two portals. Obeying its obstacle avoidance program, it managed to fly deep inside the increasingly narrow passageway, finally striking a roof support beam at high speed.

The instantaneous mixture of raw fuel and red-hot engine parts created a thunderous fireball that consumed the munitions of those it overtook. In turn they partly fed the explosion until it collapsed the passageway and blew out a massive plume of flame from the entrance. In the polar night's semidarkness it was visible for miles. And for a moment it even intimidated the thinking creatures among the Legion hordes.

"Altitude, fifty meters below ground level and continuing," Alverez called out, glancing at the altitude readouts on her Head-Up Display. "And so far, I'm not seeing anything threatening."

Still continuing to spin slowly to the left, the Cutlass was now over a hundred and sixty feet inside the shaft. Enough auroral light filtered down from above for Alverez and the others to see that the shaft had a nearly featureless surface. No compartments or passageways appeared to be connected to it, except at the bottom.

"Lieutenant, I got movement," said Taylor, studying the green-tinted image on his tactical screen. "A lot of it. I don't think I'll be able to counter it with a single machine gun."

"You want the nose turret?" asked Alverez.

"We better go with something bigger," Hunter advised, bringing up the same image on the terminal screen. "And fast. Arm a cluster bomb, set submunitions for two-tier detonation. Ten seconds and sixty seconds delayed action."

"You got it, Mitch. Jeff, are you ready?"

"Setting detonation times," said Taylor. "And the computer confirms the weapon is armed."

Seconds later, one of the gray pods mounted on the

gunships's stub wings dropped into the shaft. At approximately a hundred and fifty feet a compressed gas charge tore it open and scattered the spherical bomblets about the shaft. Many bounced off its walls before landing on the pad, where half of them detonated on impact. For several more seconds, until the flashes stopped, those on the gunship could see the shaft's bottom.

"Get down!" Mortus shouted. "That's a cluster bomb!"
The initial burst of explosions sounded like individual shotgun blasts. However, they rapidly built to a thundering crescendo that shook everything in the main hangar. The waves of shrapnel the bomblets unleashed shredded the necromutants and armed tekrons who were attempting to retake the pad. Some of their own munitions detonated along with the bomblets, adding to the destruction. The shrapnel reached far enough into the hangar to strike the courier ship and the transport vehicle it rested on. Fortunately, by then the jagged lengths of metal had lost much of their velocity and bounced harmlessly off their targets.
"Our forces are seriously depleted, human," said Caliqabaal, lifting himself off the floor. "And the helicopter is still descending. What do you suggest?"
"Set up defensive positions," said Mortus. "And wait for the gunship to land. Then we'll kill 'em all before they even make it out of their ship. We'll present our Master with victory before he can return with reinforcements."

"Sarge, these things don't die too easily!" the private said fearfully, hurriedly jamming another clip into his rifle while Watts continued snapping out quick bursts at the Legionnaires and other creatures.
"Tell me something I don't know!" said Watts. "Whatever you do, don't stop shooting 'em until they stop screaming!"
"Hold it, Bob! Hold it!" shouted one of the other fire support specialists. "I think we have killed 'em all. At least for this wave."
As the squad's weapons fell silent, an unearthly calm filled the bunker. None of the Legion casualties made any noise or moved, though many were burning. Outside the bunker the battle had moved beyond it. Covered by prowling flights of AH-19 gunships, Capitol ground forces were mov-

ing on the Citadel itself. Their progress was slow, mostly because of sniper fire and piles of Legion bodies on the battlements and stairs.

"Hey, what happened to the lieutenant?" Watts demanded when he turned and found the squad's medic tending to the officer.

"He didn't obey his own rules," said the medic. "He got hit; we'll have to evac him and some of the others if they're to live."

"Well, guess who that leaves in charge of this squad."

"You, Big Bob," said Osborn. "But before he advanced, the captain told me he wants us to stay here and cover this bunker, just in case these Legion things try to counterattack from the rear."

"Cover the rear?" said Watts, incredulous. "I haven't been part of a rearguard defense since I was the kid's age. And I ain't about to slide back into bad habits."

Watts nodded in the private's direction while he walked over to the stockpile of munitions left behind for the squad and selected more belts of 15mm shells. Those he hung on the external clips attached to his body armor.

"Bob, what're you doing?" asked Osborn. "You disobeying orders?"

"No. I'm reinterpreting them!" said Watts, entering the bunker and advancing through the field of Legion bodies to the tunnel's mouth. "Seems to me if we wanna keep these things from reappearing here, we should do it from as far inside this passage as we can. Call it a forward defense. Now is anyone gonna join me?"

"There goes the second wave of detonations," said Hunter the moment he spotted a new eruption of flashes below the gunship. "Get your rappel gear ready."

"For once couldn't we make a conventional landing, Captain?" Rogers asked, reattaching a metal clamp to his waist harness. "It would be easier."

"And under these conditions, impossible. There's too much wreckage on the pad for us to make a safe landing. If we have the time, we'll clear some of it and make a conventional takeoff. Everyone ready? Good. Julia, this is Mitch. Bring us to a hover at twenty meters and get ready for a rappelling."

Seconds later, the Cutlass stopped its descent and its side doors rolled open. The pylons over the side hatches snapped out again and dropped their lines. Hunter and three other members of his squad slid down the lines to the pad some sixty feet below.

Because the shaft concentrated the helicopter's rotorwash, they dropped into a whirlwind of dust and smoke almost too thick to see through. Had they not been wearing goggles, they would have been blinded, and as it was, they saw only the wreckage-strewn pad in the last moment of their rappelling.

They landed, detached their clamps, and spread out to cover the various entrances to the shaft. They were joined by the rest of the squad less than a half a minute later, who concentrated around the main hangar's entrance and waited for the helicopter to lift away. As the dust cloud gradually settled, Hunter signaled them to advance.

"The sound, it's growing weaker," Caliqabaal noted. "The war machine isn't landing. What's happening, human?"

"I . . . I don't understand," said Mortus, looking up from part of the stacking gantry that had been thrown down as a barrier. "Maybe they aborted the landing when they realized it was too dangerous."

"These are Special Forces, Kyle," said Dorr. "Just like what we encountered at the spaceport. And they don't give up. We may not see 'em, but they're out there."

"Yes. Shaguhl claims there are humans at the opposite end," Caliqabaal reported after turning to the lead tekron and receiving a flood of telepathic information. "There are only a few. We easily outnumber them. Advance now, and we can destroy them before our Master returns."

Caliqabaal filled his lungs with air and let out a long, shrill wail that echoed through the hangar. The other necromutants gave answering cries and, together with the remaining tekrons, moved out from their cover.

"What the hell was that?" Rogers asked when the attack cry reached their position.

"Never mind," said Hunter. "Check your motion detector. Jake, Diane, what are you seeing?"

"You're right, Captain. That is a *Gamma*-class courier

ship down there," Shacker reported, scanning the hangar's opposite end with his rifle's scope. "And it's stacked, ready to launch."

"There isn't much else in here," Parker added, doing the same procedure. "All the other planes and spaceships must've been moved to those auxiliary hangars. I do see parts of a vehicle assembly gantry, and there's movement around them."

"I got movement as well," said Rogers, sweeping the detector in a limited arc. "A lot of it. Several groups, and they're all moving this way."

"Let's use this cover and set up a cross fire while we still have it," Hunter ordered. "I want everyone to be careful using armor-piercing rounds. That courier's probably fueled. And no grenades, except for Leo's Flamers."

While Rogers pointed out the location of each Dark Legion unit, Hunter indicated where he wanted his teams to position themselves. As the dust storm ebbed and settled, the cavernous dimensions of the hangar became more apparent. It was the size of several sports stadiums, which was made even more apparent by the lack of any other aircraft or spacecraft except for the courier ship. Scattered across the hangar floor were pieces of the skeletal stacking gantry, a few tow vehicles, and roller-mounted shelves of tools. Among these the Legion units prowled, until the necromutants shrieked their attack cries once more.

"Let 'em have it!" Hunter shouted, training his M-50 assault rifle on the nearest group of hulking monsters.

A deafening barrage of rifle- and machine-gun fire filled the hangar, and at first the only necromutants and tekrons to fall were hit by the snipers and Halston. Then the napalm hand grenades began exploding. Blossoms of flame erupted in and among the Legion units, showering their members with burning jelly. In the hangar's semidarkness they became obvious targets; those who did not die from immolation were chopped apart by gunfire.

"Captain, I think they're falling back!" said Rogers, noting the pattern of movement on his motion detector.

"Let's keep up the pressure!" said Hunter. "Advance! Watch your flanks and watch each other!"

Moving carefully from their positions, the squad's teams kept firing on the Legion units and covered each other. Even though the units were retreating, some of their members continued to attack, and Hunter found himself facing a necromutant covered in fire.

"Die, damn it, die!" he shouted, emptying his rifle's clip into the doomed creature. It stumbled, but kept advancing, this time in the direction of the gunfire. Hunter feverishly worked the pump on his rifle's grenade launcher; when he squeezed the trigger again, a high-explosive grenade struck the necromutant in the chest and tore it apart.

"Captain, I thought we weren't supposed to use rifle grenades," said Harris after dodging the shower of burning flesh.

"Sometimes even I have to disobey my own orders. Leo, what do you have there?"

"I thought it was a dead Legionnaire or something," said Venneti, crouching beside a body obviously smaller than the necromutants and tekrons. "But it's someone. I mean, it's human. Or it *was* human."

"Never mind. I know what you mean," said Hunter, reloading his assault rifle and crossing over to Venneti's location. "Good God, it is human—not some reanimated corpse—but in this place?"

"He's probably a heretic," Wendy advised, joining the others. "As impossible as it may sound, for those like him, this hell may be their goal."

"Well, if this is where they'd like to be, then let's leave 'em all here. Spread out and pass the word. Be suspicious of any human we come across, except for Lorraine Kovan."

"Master Ragathol, we've been successful at holding off the humans," said Caliqabaal the moment he felt the nepharite's presence behind him. "And they've not damaged your ship."

"Because they probably know in destroying it, they would destroy themselves," said Ragathol as he reentered the hangar. "And you've not defeated them? I sense they are but one squad."

"I have few combat forces to command, my Master. The tekrons are dedicated, but their only skills are as workers. I've lost many and most of the necromutants under me. I see no reinforcements with you, my Master. Are we to receive any?"

"Soon . . . not what I wanted, but they'll do. Azurwraith is keeping all his Immaculate Furies around the Command Nexus, as if he expects Capitol ground forces to penetrate that far into his Citadel. However, I have more faith than he. I wish to view these intruders before they're consumed."

"Are you sure this is wise, my Master?" Mortus inquired. "These are Capitol Special forces."

"I know what they are," said Ragathol, giving Mortus an irritated look. "And I *still* wish to view them before they're nothing."

Both Echmeriaz and Caliqabaal tried to voice similar concerns, but were brushed aside by Ragathol. Glancing briefly at the spaceship it held, he moved past the huge transport vehicle and around the gantry sections until he was in front of them and had a commanding view of the rest of the hangar.

"Captain, I got movement near the transporter vehicle," Shacker advised, sweeping the hangar's opposite end from his newest position.

"Sure seems to be more of it down there than around here," said Hunter, moving over to his snipers. "What do you have?"

"More necromutants and tek-things. Wait, wait a second. I got some big guy with spikes coming out of his head. I think it's one of them nepharites."

"If you're right, that isn't *a* nepharite. It's *the* nepharite. Remember what Portius told us. They're the Legion's generals, and only one commands a Citadel. You think you can nail him?"

"At this range? You bet," said Shacker before glancing at Parker. "Take out one of those necromutants, Diane. The guy with the spikes is mine."

Neither Parker nor Shacker bothered to deploy the bipods on their SR-50 Improved M89. Instead, they balanced the heavy weapons on a horizontal frame piece to the gantry section they were using as cover. Additional sections and other obstacles made it difficult for Parker to take aim on one of the shorter necromutants. Shacker, however, had no such trouble lining up on the taller nepharite. In spite of the differences in their targets, both opened fire within seconds of each other.

* * *

"I don't need *those*," Ragathol growled, rejecting a heretic's offer of night-vision binoculars. "I see the intruders quite well. There are some now. They make good use of the available cover. They—"

Bright muzzle flashes among the group Ragathol pointed to caught his full attention. In an instant he knew exactly who the fire was directed at and dropped to the ground. The armor-piercing incendiary shells whistled past him barely a second later and impacted one of the transport vehicle's tractor treads. They easily punched through their rubber outer coverings, but smashed noisily into the thick steel plates. The holes started smoking as each shell's rod of plastic explosive ignited and burned the surrounding rubber.

"My Master, are you all right?" asked Mortus, crawling over to where Ragathol huddled.

"Of course I am," he said. "They'll have to do better to injure or kill me. Caliqabaal, what's affecting you?"

"I . . . I can feel them burning, my Master," said the necromutant, holding his chest and staggering to his feet. "I don't understand how the humans can do this to me."

Smoke curled out from around Caliqabaal's fingers. When it increased, he pounded his chest, as if it would extinguish the fires spreading through him. But his bio-mechanical systems were unable to cope with the damage even with his futile help. He stumbled into a gantry section and toppled it as he burst into flames.

"These humans must have better weapons than we've encountered in the past," said Ragathol after moving behind the relative safety of the transport vehicle. "It's no surprise that they now feel emboldened enough to strike out at us in our domain."

"Should we counterattack, my Master?" Echmeriaz requested, also seeking protection under the massive vehicle.

"No need. The nafai have arrived."

A rhythmic fluttering barely audible above the sounds of gunfire accompanied Ragathol's answer. In the hangar's back entrance a swarm of balloonlike creatures appeared. They were covered with finlike projections, the largest of which flapped like hummingbird wings to keep them airborne. Their large eyes glowed pale red in the hangar's low light, and their jaws appeared frozen in menacing grins, which exposed their interlocking sets of triangular teeth. The nafai flew past the legion personnel in irregular flocks. Their prey lay deeper inside the cavern.

"Captain, I got lots of movement now," said Rogers. "But it's not like anything I've seen before. I'm not reading individuals or groups. It's like a cloud."

"Is it a chemical attack?" Parker asked, reaching for her gas mask. "Should we break these out?"

"No, this gas sensor can detect agents down to three parts per trillion," Wendy answered, grabbing a bulblike device hanging out of her med kit. "And so far it isn't ringing on anything."

"Lieutenant, don't get out in front of us," said Hunter. "We don't know what you're reading."

"What could it be, Mitch?" asked Rogers. "It's not anything solid, and we've stopped drawing fire."

Though he kept to the available cover, Rogers had moved several dozen feet ahead of the squad. He swept continually with his motion detector, holding it in one hand and his Ironfist heavy automatic in the other. The increasing lull in gunfire from the Dark Legion forces caused him to move forward more aggressively. By the time the hundreds of sets of glowing red eyes became visible, he was out of effective coverage of most squad members.

"My God, they're alive," Shacker whispered as many of the eyes seemed to converge on Rogers.

"God, please! Help me!" he screamed. "Somebody help me!"

Dozens of nafai attacked him simultaneously, each making a slashing pass and carrying away what appeared to be a strip of clothing. And after the dozens came hundreds, especially when Rogers emptied his automatic in a wild burst. The nafai grew more frenzied in their attack, several attaching themselves to him as he collapsed.

"They're alive!" said Harris, leveling his submachine gun at the dimly visible creatures.

Even though a thick cloud of nafai swirled above Rogers, only a few were hit by all the rounds fired. Those either exploded or fluttered to the ground like leaves. Many of the rest streamed to Harris's position. The same thing happened when Venneti and Halston opened fire. Succeeding waves of nafai closed on them, often colliding with each other and various obstacles in their efforts to reach the soldiers.

"Fall back!" Hunter demanded. "Fall back, damn it, and stop shooting! They're attracted to it!"

The ground they had fought so hard to gain was now rapidly given up as the squad abandoned its positions and ran. The action appeared to confuse the nafai for a few seconds, then they wheeled around in their buzzing clouds and dove after their prey.

"Why are they going after anyone who fires a gun?" Venneti asked, catching up to Hunter.

"It's gotta be the heat!" said Hunter. "They must see infrared better than visible light!"

"Well, if it's heat they want, they'll get it!"

Venneti produced one of the Flamer grenades and set its detonation time at one second. He pulled its safety pin and heaved over his shoulder, arcing it high into the air. It detonated in midflight, producing a blossom of flame among the nafai clouds. Their response to it was like predatory moths to a freshly lit candle. They attacked the fireball, as well as their own kind who were caught in it and burned. Then the fireball burned out, and for a few critical seconds the nafai swarm wheeled around in a confused state.

"Everyone! Set your Flamer grenades at once second and toss 'em as high as you can!" Hunter ordered, twisting the detonation post on one of his grenades down to its minimum indicated time. "We need air bursts! Halston, stop firing your weapon! That's like using a cannon to hit flies!"

"Yeah, we both got something better than these, Theodore!" said Shacker, dropping his Improved M89 and reaching for a pistol grip just visible over his left shoulder. "Diane, grab your Street Blaster!"

The weapon Shacker pulled out of the holster mounted on his shoulder plate was barely eighteen inches long. Its tubular magazine was exactly the same length as its barrel, and its receiver was just large enough to contain the semiautomatic mechanism and move the shells from magazine to breech. The Street Blaster shotgun looked diminutive in Shacker's huge hands. But when he squeezed the trigger, it barked like a small cannon and unleashed a fountain of pellets on the approaching swarm. Nearly a dozen nafai either exploded from being hit or fluttered to the ground. It was an insignificant number compared to the waves of creatures. Fortunately, many of them were temporarily drawn off by another napalm fireball.

"That's it!" said Hunter. "Everyone, defensive circle! Break out your Street Blasters and riot ammo! Wendy, toss out some flares! Let's see if that'll confuse them!"

"They show remarkable cohesion," Ragathol noted, moving forward enough to observe the Special Forces squad trying to fight off their attackers. "In the past the nafai have inspired terror in human victims. These aren't fleeing in panic. They're different from most of the humans we've encountered."

"Master Ragathol, now is the time we should attack," said Mortus, stepping up to the nepharite. "In that defensive formation they're vulnerable. If we could get close enough, we'd kill them all in one action."

"Very good, heretic." At first Ragathol gave Mortus an angry stare. Then, as the plan was explained further, his serene smile returned. "Gather your people and move on the intruders. If the nafai can hold them there long enough, you'll destroy them."

"Hurry, damn it, hurry!" said· Hunter, slapping a clip loaded with green-capped bullets into his assault rifle. "They're returning!"

The lull in the nafai attack only lasted a few moments. Once the latest fireball burned out, they wheeled en masse for the squad's position, which had coalesced into a tightly packed ring. The reloading with antipersonnel munitions had only just ended when the swarm divided into several flocks and dove on their prey.

Their buzzing and chattering remained soft, but grew omnipresent, until the rifles and shotguns drowned them out. Every weapon emitted a hail of tiny pellets, even the submachine guns and rifles. They shredded the leading wave of creatures and caused the rest to back up and collide with one another.

The nafai became further disoriented as Wendy ignited flares and heaved them out of the ring. Like dogs chasing a stick, small groups would break off from the swarm and follow each flare. Wherever it landed they would cluster, trying to devour it until either it burned out or a napalm grenade bounced next to them and detonated.

Soon the air was thicker with smoke than nafai; and the rancid smell of their burning bodies even caused them to slowly disperse. Despite the weaker attacks the squad remained in its defensive formation. They stood so close the armor plates on their arms and shoulders would often rub together.

"Stay in position; I can still hear 'em out there," Hunter warned, the buzzlike fluttering drifting around with the smoke. "I'm hearing something, too, Captain," said Halston. "Only it ain't no flying piranha."

"All right. Everyone who doesn't have shotguns, reload with AP ammo." Following his own orders, Hunter pulled the last partial clip of green-capped shot shells from his rifle and stowed it. He had just finished reloading a clip of armor-piercing rounds when he heard footsteps beyond the defensive ring. "We got more company. Break rank and— Ow! Damn it!"

The muzzle flashes were barely visible in the smoke. What was more visible were the sparks from the bullets ricocheting off Hunter's breastplate. The force of the impacts and the pain they caused sent him tumbling to the ground. He managed to raise an arm to protect his face and felt a round glance off its armor before landing on his back.

In the seconds that followed the initial attack, the rest of his squad dove for cover and returned fire. The smoke was not thick enough to hide movement, but made aiming difficult. From the screams and crashing they heard, the squad could be sure of only one kill, until a charging figure seemed to materialize on top of them.

"We already defeated your kind once!" shouted Dorr. "This time you die!"

As he leveled his Bauhaus assault rifle at Wendy, his foot landed on a still-flapping nafai. Its teeth managed to bite straight through his shoe into his toes, causing him to scream, lose balance, and make a skidding crash into Halston.

"Too close for guns," he said, reaching for a scabbard strapped to his left leg, "switching to knives."

The survival knife Halston drew glinted dully as it flashed into Dorr's neck. It caught him just below his chin and plunged in all the way to its hilt. He could manage only a partial cry before his vocal cords were smashed, and he gripped the handle so tightly Halston had to fight so he could free his own hand. Dorr thrashed around and let out a few loud sputterings before dying.

"Mitch, are you all right?" Wendy asked, sliding over to where Hunter lay.

"I think so," he answered. "I'm gonna have to let Sherman know they also build good armor. Leo, there's another one!"

Dorr was still in his death spasms when another heretic seemed to magically appear. A burst of submachine gun fire caught him in the chest and threw him back into a gantry section. What he screamed was unrecognizable, except for "Kyle, help me!" With his death the other heretics moving in the shadows appeared to withdraw.

"How did they do that?" Venneti asked. "The last one got close enough to kill me with a penknife."

"Remember what Portius told us about heretics," said Wendy. "If their service to the Legion is exemplary, they're granted Dark Gifts. I think what we just saw were examples of those gifts."

"And did you hear what the first guy said?" Shacker questioned. "That they defeated our kind once before? These must be the heretics we encountered at the spaceport."

"If they are, then this is a grudge fight," said Hunter, getting off his back, but staying behind the available cover. "And we all know what those are like. So don't get carried away; stay professional and move out. I want everyone to look for Rogers. I know he's probably not alive, but we gotta confirm that and we need his gear."

"The nafai have failed," Ragathol snarled, glancing up at the hangar's roof and watching the scattered creatures dart around haphazardly. "It appears as though animals designed for mass attacks are unable to do so when their numbers fall below a certain level. In the future we must do some genetic reprogramming."

Clearly upset, Ragathol was able to maintain his serenity, until one of the nafai flew close enough to notice him, turned toward him, and hovered in front of his face. It emitted a soft chittering that sounded like pathetic whimpering.

The nephanite reached out as if to touch it. But when his arm finished extending, the creature started to shudder and screech in pain. Ragathol had opened a portal inside its body to the dark dimensions. The heat the portal generated cooked the nafai from the inside out. And when its body finally dropped to the ground, the brittle remains collapsed into ashes.

"The heretics appear to be meeting with some success, my Master," said Echmeriaz. "It's difficult to tell."

"Contact the Nexus again," said Ragathol, smiling at his small triumph. "Tell them we need more reinforcements. These intruders are proving more resourceful than anyone estimated. And do it directly; I don't want to wait for a dispatched messenger to return."

"Captain, over here," Redfield advised, motioning to where he and Halston stood. "Someone's crying."

Moving again between his teams, Hunter turned away from his snipers and approached his fire support specialist. Halston and his assistant were crouching next to a figure, the first they had encountered that was alive and not carrying a gun. As Hunter joined them, it tried to crawl farther under a gantry section.

"It's a woman, Captain," said Halston. "You think it's Lorraine Kovan?"

"No, she looks older and taller than Lorraine should be," said Hunter, laying down his rifle and trying to move forward.

"Taller? How can you tell she's taller from the way she's curled up?"

"Help me, please?" begged Monica Lewis in a scared, quivering voice. "Why did these people kidnap me? Who are they? Where am I?"

"Captain, d'you think they've kidnapped more than one person?" Redfield asked. "Maybe they got a bunch down here for experiments?"

"You all look so strong and handsome. Please protect me? Protect me from these things. Please, I'll love you forever if you'll do it."

As Lewis continued to plead, she moved out from her hiding place. What she said she almost purred. It made Hunter and the others forget where they were, that they were in the middle of combat. The deception continued until a thunderous explosion jolted them.

"What the . . . Diane, are you crazy?" Hunter shouted when he realized a hole had been torn in Monica's chest and the impact was lifting her off the ground. "You just murdered her!"

"Damn right I did," said Parker, a smoking Street Blaster in her hands. "Take a look at what she's holding."

As Lewis's body finished sagging to the floor, a metallic clatter sounded when her hand at last released the Aggressor automatic she had been pulling out from under her clothing. In a belated response to its appearance, Halston and Redfield pointed their weapons at the body.

"Protect me and I'll love you forever," Parker repeated, an edge of sarcasm in her version. "Get real, guys. How could you fall for a line like that?"

"It must've been some sort of Dark Gift spell," said Hunter, grabbing the heretic's automatic and pulling the clip out of it before tossing both away. "Apparently they can seduce as easily as invoke pain. We mus— God, are you feeling that?"

A sustained, quakelike vibration shook the huge hangar—long enough and severe enough to cause the stacked courier ship and external boosters to sway perceptibly, and for dust to filter down from cracks that had opened in the ceiling. It also caused the scattered gunfire the squad was drawing from the Dark Legion forces to briefly fall silent.

"C'mon, let's find Lorraine Kovan and get outta here," Hunter continued, "before our guys bring the whole Citadel down on top of us."

"What's the answer from the Nexus?" Ragathol asked, when his chief necromutant returned to his side. "When can I expect more reinforcements?"

"There will be no more, my Master," Echmeriaz said, hesitantly. "My exchange with them was cut off in midsentence with the sounds of explosions. I fear what we felt was the destruction of the Command Nexus."

"Yes, I register a disturbance in the forces of the Dark Symmetry." Instead of displaying anger, Ragathol gave in to an emotion he had rarely experienced before—apprehension.

"There can be only one answer for it ... Azurwraith has been killed."

"A nepharite, murdered? How is that possible?"

"We are not immortal. What I suffered on Luna should've been proof enough. My brother chose not to heed my experience and has paid for it."

"What will happen now to us, my Master?" asked Echmeriaz, fear growing in his voice.

"All will be anarchy! Chaos!" Ragathol shouted, holding his head as if it were throbbing with pain. "Coordination of the Citadel's defenses will collapse. I can feel the orderliness of the Dark Symmetry unraveling!"

The nepharite staggered as if under a physical assault. He turned and wandered far enough away from the massive transport to expose himself to hostile fire. Only after several rounds had passed close to him did Ragathol come back to his senses and return serenely to cover. By then the apprehension and pain were gone, and he was smiling triumphantly again.

"Yes, it's dangerous, but it can be done," he said to himself. Then he turned to Echmeriaz. "With the remaining force, you're to hold the intruders here and defeat them if possible. I'll retrieve the Receptacle and take her to my Nether Room."

"Captain, something's happening," Shacker warned, keeping his eye fixed to his scope's view screen. "That guy with the spikes is leaving the hangar. Damn, I almost had a clean shot at 'im."

"I hope it means the rest of the attack is going well, and he had to leave for a little crisis management," said Hunter, sliding up beside him and raising his night scope to his eye.

"We should try to keep track of him, Captain," said Wendy. "I suspect wherever he is, Lorraine Kovan will be. Remember, she was valuable enough to the Dark Legion for an entire Bauhaus base to be destroyed."

"You're right. Jake, make note of where this guy goes. If we get outta here, we'll want to follow him. Leo, what do you have?"

"A prisoner," Venneti answered, standing beside an unarmed man who was not wearing a uniform or body armor. "He didn't have a gun, and he surrendered as soon as we came upon him. I thought you might want to question him about what's happening."

"Good idea," said Hunter, lowering his rifle when he realized Harris was standing behind the prisoner. "Whoever you are, don't give me any garbage about your citizen rights. Answer my questions and you'll live. What was going on here before we arrived?"

"Our Master was planning to leave this world," said Mortus. "You've interfered with that."

"Who's your Master and what's he doing now?"

"Our Master is he who commands us. And he's awaiting your death, which I am blessed to give him!"

As Mortus finished his answer, Hunter felt a wave of pain sweep through him. It took away his voice and the ability to control his movements. He never felt gravity as strong as it suddenly became, and in spite of his efforts to fight it, he sagged to the floor. When he managed to raise his head, he discovered everyone else was similarly affected, except for Mortus.

"Die, unbelievers! None shall stand in the way of the Master!" he said, stretching out his hand.

"You first!" Hunter angrily replied. And for a moment the pain subsided. It was long enough for him to raise his assault rifle and squeeze its trigger.

The burst was not well-aimed, but at least part of it stitched across the heretic's stomach and chest. The impacts were enough to lift Mortus off his feet and send him tumbling over Harris's back. By the time he finished sprawling across the floor, the spell he had cast was ebbing away to an irritation.

"Captain, we got company!" said Parker, dropping her rifle and going for her Street Blaster again. "And Ted just capped off his belt!"

Hunter looked up in time to see Halston use his empty machine gun as a club on a sword-wielding heretic. Redfield had just enough time to reload his weapon before spraying two heretics who seemingly came out of nowhere. Hunter got an inkling of something closing on his back. As he turned, he caught sight of Venneti leveling his CAR-24 smg at him.

"Get your head down, Captain! Get your head down!" he

shouted, barely giving his commander time to comply before opening up.

With the CAR-24 smg muzzle less than a dozen feet in front of him, its deafening staccato was almost the only thing Hunter could hear. He thought he heard a curious spanging sound of bullets striking metal. It was not until he glanced over his shoulder that he could confirm the noise; the heretic sailing backward carried a bullet-scarred sword in his hands.

"Somebody stop 'im!" said Wendy, trying to hide behind an overturned set of tool shelves. "He's after me!"

The heretic had kicked the shelves out of the way and trained his rifle on Levin by the time a barrage of shotgun pellets and 10mm bullets shredded his upper body. She scrambled and rolled to get out of the way of the gruesome remains as they flopped to the ground.

"I never noticed it before, but short people do move faster than tall people," said Shacker, filling the unnatural quiet after the attack had ended.

"That'll be enough," Hunter ordered, stifling a small ripple of laughter. "Watch the perimeter. That may or may not have been the last of the heretics. Jake, Diane, sweep the area for movement before we advance."

"This is gonna become tiresome. We better find what's left of Raymond soon and salvage his equipment."

"Corporal, Drone Nagato has detected something unusual," Ozawa advised when one of the reconnaissance warheads prowling the Citadel area deviated from its random search pattern.

"It's those two Special forces helicopters again," said Watanabe, punching up the warhead's various camera views on one of her auxiliary screens. "Looks like they're orbiting the old launch pad area. I wonder why."

"They're directly over that open shaft. One even fired on a Dark Legion unit when it appeared in the area. I think something's happening inside the shaft. Where does it lead?"

"We believe to one or more hangars." Watanabe glanced up at the tactical screen and noticed the lack of any other activity around the launch site. "But we've never been sure. Looks like Capitol Special Forces are going to find out."

"Should we send the drone into the pad shaft, Corporal?" Ozawa asked. "It could easily fit down it."

"Compared to what we've been sending them down recently, of course we can," Watanabe slowly answered as she thought it over. "No. If we put a drone into the shaft, we might not be able to get it back out. This is a Special Force's mission, and they get touchy when you interfere with them. I've lost a couple of drones in the past because of it. Instruct Nagato to keep this area under surveillance at nominal safe distance. There's plenty of other activity for us to concern ourselves with."

"Captain, I think I've found Raymond," said Parker, her voice uncharacteristically weak and quivering. "What's left of him."

On the point again, she had moved the farthest into the hangar, more than two-thirds of the way into it, when she stopped and slumped against a portable power cart. Shacker was the first to reach her, followed by Hunter and the rest of the squad. What they found of Rogers was some armor and a tattered, blood-soaked uniform inlaid with bones and shredded flesh. Hunter quickly realized the sight was numbing his people.

"Jake, Diane, Ted, move forward and form a perimeter," he ordered. "Now. Move it. We'll take care of this."

"We always made fun of him," Venneti said quietly, somberly. "We didn't always take him into our confidence. But we never hated him, and he didn't deserve to die this way."

"Nobody does. Though I think in the future more soldiers will die this way in our battles with the Legion." Using his bayonet, Hunter cut out and otherwise dislodged as much of the equipment Rogers carried as was possible. "Most of this doesn't look like it was touched."

"Yes. I don't think those flying mouths have much of a taste for plastic and microchips," said Wendy. Using her canteen, she washed the blood off the gear Hunter was salvaging. "We got his motion detector, EM scanner, and the tracker for our emergency beacons. Is this all we take?"

"I think so. We'll have to leave this," Hunter replied, pulling a tactical radio out of Rogers's backpack and popping open its access panel. "But I'll make sure no one else can use it."

While the radio had an almost indestructible plastic armor case, its open panel made it easy for Hunter to use his rifle's butt stock to smash its sensitive, classified electronics into so much silicon rubble.

"Is there anything else we have to take?" Wendy added.

"Just one more thing," said Hunter. "I'm not going for his identity chip. Just the traditional tags."

Slipping his bayonet over the neck rim of Rogers's breast-plate, he probed what remained of the body until he fished out a thin, blood-covered chain. Hunter unlocked its clasp and slid it off the neck. He washed the chain and the gold-plated identity tag welded to it with water from his canteen before sliding it into an ammo pouch on his harness.

"I've never gotten used to this," he continued. "Thank God I haven't lost a lot of people from the units I've commanded. All right, let's move it. We're closer to that space-ship now so watch your fire. Jake, Diane, you got any movement to report on?"

CHAPTER TWENTY

"Mr. Wood, we finally have some information about squad Trident," announced the senior coordinating officer, stepping up to one of the civilians pacing the tactical center's floor. "This is a hard copy of the report."

The officer handed Noah Wood a freshly printed fax sheet, still warm to the touch. Wood smiled as he read it and started looking at the main screen as if to match what it said with what was happening.

"Have they been spotted, sir?" Hart asked. "Or have they actually obeyed some corporate protocol and reported in?"

"They were spotted, Mr. Hart," said Wood, giving the advisor a sharp glance. "One of our flights of F/A-99s were going to hit the Citadel's launch facilities when they got warned off by two Cutlass gunships. One of them was the dash-Four prototype, and it reported they were waiting to recover a squad that was in an underground area of the Citadel."

"They're actually in the Citadel's underground complex?" General Powers asked, unable to hide his surprise at the news. "Incredible. The Ground Forces have managed only limited penetration of a few tunnels."

"Yes, it appears as though the Special Forces have found a back door to this unassailable fortress. Your men are to be congratulated, General."

"What about their other objective?" asked Hart, trying to make himself heard and seen as the generals once again closed around Wood. "Was there any mention of her?"

"No. This was only a warning to the jets not to attack the launch facility area," Wood answered, showing the fax to Hart before handing it to Powers. "It has no message from Hunter. For that we'll probably have to wait until his squad evacs the hangar."

* * *

"Captain, I got movement. But I can't tell if it's on top of
the vehicle or just around it," said Wendy, slowly sweeping
the detector in front of her.

"Leo, Harris, sweep the transport pad," Hunter ordered.
"Switch from armor-piercing to antipersonnel rounds. Watch
for fuel leaks, and check on that spaceship's condition."

The multistory transporter pad now loomed above the
squad as they advanced on it. What had once been teeming
with activity now stood largely silent. All the tekrons,
necromutants, and heretics that had worked on the courier
ship were either dead or had retreated to the hangar's back
entrance.

For a few moments Hunter and the rest of the squad covered Venneti and Harris while they climbed an external lad-
der to the massive vehicle's first level. Once they
disappeared through an access hatch, the others spread out
and swept the rest of the hangar for Legion personnel. It did
not take them long before they found more.

"Human, die!" Echmeriaz roared, kicking away the cover
plates and gantry section he was hiding behind. He reared to
his full height and brandished the most suitable weapon he
could find, a welding torch whose flame was set for maximum width.

"Captain, watch it!" said Wendy, diving for cover. "Those
are fueling lines above him!"

"I know! I know!" said Hunter. "Right now I'd just like
to stay alive!"

Hunter backed up, then rolled to the left in an effort to
avoid the four-foot jet of flame the necromutant aimed at
him. As he hit the ground and rolled, he finally opened fire.
He struck the creature in the lower legs, shattering a knee-
cap, bringing it down.

Even then Echmeriaz continued to roar his defiance. He
pointed the blinding flame at Hunter, spoiling accuracy until
he was stitched with a burst of automatic weapons' fire from
another direction. Hunter could not see who helped him until
after he had emptied his clip and the necromutant no longer
moved.

"Wendy? From the sound of that Ironfist I should've
known it was you," he said.

"Well, I know you don't have those fancy rounds Ted and

the others do," Wendy answered, the heavy automatic in her hands still smoking. "So I thought you'd benefit from some major-caliber backup."

"Captain! Captain, over here!" Shacker cried out. "We got another prisoner!"

"What? Not another one," said Hunter, loading a new clip into his rifle and moving in the voice's direction. "What did I tell you we're to do with them?"

"Yeah, but this one's different! I know this guy!"

Just past the middle set of the thirty-foot-tall tractor treads, Hunter and Wendy came upon Shacker, who in turn was towering over a figure huddled next to the treads. It only took a second for Hunter to see the man was apparently unarmed and convincingly frightened.

"This is Denton Landis," Shacker identified, "of the Landis family?"

"You mean the family the district's named after?" Hunter asked, surprised at first. "Well, even the rich and powerful are taken with the Legion."

"Please! Please, just take me outta here!" Landis pleaded, shaking with terror. "This isn't what I wanted! Please, I'll tell you anything you want."

"The nepharite, where did he go? And we're looking for a woman the Legion kidnapped from a Bauhaus base. Where is she?"

"I'll tell you . . ." Landis made only a fleeting glance at Hunter's eyes; instead his attention was almost solely focused on his assault rifle, which Hunter moved perceptibly closer to his face. "Lord Ragathol is returning to his Nether Room. Down the hall, that way! The woman's there as well. She's being held in an Isolation Chamber. Now please, take me out!"

"I thought so," Hunter said grimly. "Nothing personal, but we've changed the corporate protocol on prisoners."

Straightening up, Hunter kept his rifle trained on Landis, who let out a thin wail when he heard the safety being clicked off. The burst of 10mm rounds caught the heretic in his stomach and chest. He screamed, then let out a painful whimper as he convulsed and died. Though Shacker was not surprised by the gunfire, it still made him jump, and it brought Diane running back to his location.

"What's going on here?" she asked.

"Enforcing our new rules on prisoners," said Hunter, finally looking away from the body. "What do you have to report, Corporal?"

"I think we've cleared the Legion from the hangar. There's personnel in the hall, but I didn't see any necromutants or Legionnaires—only those tek-things and what looked like medical personnel. None of 'em have made any move to retake the hangar."

"All their combat units must be on the surface, fighting the Ground Forces and Air Force. I hope it stays— What's going on?"

A long staccato barking echoed in the hangar, and moments later a body dropped off the back of the transport vehicle. Hunter, followed by Wendy and his snipers, crossed underneath it and reached the figure seconds after its hard landing. It was immediately obvious why its impact was so loud.

"It's a tekron," said Wendy. "I thought you guys cleared the hangar?"

"We only cleared the hangar," Shacker protested, "not this monster. The Captain assigned Venneti to do that."

"Leo, is your sweep finished?" Hunter asked, stepping out from under the huge machine and glancing up to its top level.

"Yes, sir. That's the last of 'em!" said Venneti, standing at the top platform's guard rail. "We cleared every room we could open, and we've taken a look at the courier."

"What do you have to report on it?"

"It's flight-ready and almost fully fueled. If our attack would've been delayed for just an hour, it would've been outta here and leaving orbit."

"No wonder the Legion didn't put up much of a fight around this thing," Parker concluded. "A couple of lucky shots and the whole place would've gone up."

"If that ship is fully fueled, then a lot more than just the hangar will go up," said Hunter, thinking for a moment. Then a smile crossed his face. "Leo! Can you rig demo charges to the ship and its boosters?"

"Sure thing, Captain," said Venneti. "But why?"

"To give this planet the biggest fireworks display it's ever seen. Plant your charges, set the detonation time for fifteen minutes, and wait until either we return or you can no longer hold this place. I'm going for the woman. Wendy, Jake, Diane, you're with me. Ted, you and Redfield are to stay here with Leo. Set up your defensive positions on the top platform. Be ready to abandon 'em when we return; we won't be long."

"Praecor, is the Receptacle ready for travel?" Ragathol asked curtly the moment he strode into the Isolation Chamber.

"Yes, my Master. She is ready," said the senior curator, motioning to the room's single bed and lone patient. "Is your spacecraft ready? The sounds of battle are growing more constant."

"No. I'll take the Receptacle from here by another means. Is she heavily sedated?"

As he spoke, Ragathol moved across the chamber to its bed. There he found Kovan still strapped down, though in a comalike sleep induced by the dark-colored drugs slowly dripping through her intravenous lines. He smiled as he studied her, especially when the flow of drugs was temporarily increased.

"There, my Master. This treatment will last for several hours," announced Praecor, laughing softly while he spoke. "If you cannot leave by spacecraft, how will you depart?"

"I'll take the Receptacle to my private quarters," said Ragathol. "There, where the forces of the Symmetry are strongest for me, I'll create a dimensional warp and take the Receptacle through its portal."

"But, my Master, such travel is dangerous, even for a nepharite. You cannot know where such a portal will take you."

"I realize its perils; I don't need you to tell me of them. Wherever I arrive, I can at least be assured it shall be in a Legion-held domain. Undo her feed lines and release her."

The intravenous tubes and cap of wires connecting Lorraine Kovan to the necrotechnology machines behind her were removed. When the leather straps were slid off her petite body, Ragathol slid his hands under her and lifted her off the bed with little effort. He turned and moved toward the Isolation Chamber's entrance, only to be stopped when Praecor stepped in front of him.

"And what is to become of us, my Master?" He giggled. "Do we return to the main processing chamber?"

"No . . . You're to stay here," said Ragathol, his anger momentarily becalmed. "More humans will be along soon for processing. You may have to use your Dark Gifts on them, but they'll be prime specimens."

"Processing. Yes, my Master. We'll await them."

With a final, malevolent look from him, the way was cleared for Ragathol. He walked into the vaulted hallway and discovered it was nearly empty. The hordes of tekrons, necromutants, Legionnaires, and all the other Legion creatures that filled it less than hour before were mostly gone. Most were drained off by the battle raging above ground; the few groups that remained in the hall moved without direction or purpose, having no Command Nexus to give them orders. A few approached Ragathol, but were quickly driven away by the aura of rage he gave off. This was not his Citadel to save; he had a more important task to devote his attention and powers to.

"God, it's like they cast the belly of some giant snake in concrete or rock," said Shacker, edging up to a corner of the main hangar's intersection with the hallway.

"If there's an entrance to Hell, it probably looks like this," Hunter responded, glancing up and down the hall and surprised to find it so deserted. "Odd, we must've caught them during a shift change."

"With so little activity, should we wait for Ted's diversion to start?" Parker asked, adjusting her sight's light-enhancement level to compensate for the hall's lower light level.

"Yes, there's no real reason to change our plans. And it won't be much longer."

Hunter checked his watch again, then glanced over his shoulder at the multistory transporter pad. Even though they were less than a hundred yards from it, dim lights and shadows were already shrouding it. The courier and its external boosters were partially hidden, and the movement near them on the pad's topmost level was scarcely visible anymore, until a stream of tracers poured out from Halston's newest position. His target was a small group of tekrons and a few necromutants. Several fell at once; the rest gave momentarily heavy return fire.

"All right, let's get moving," said Hunter, making one final check of his rifle's LED display. "Stay close to the wall and watch for the guy with the spikes."

One by one, Hunter lead his team around the corner and into the hall. In spite of the brief heavy weapons fire, the hall was relatively quiet—none of the shrieking or screams they had to endure earlier, just the muted thump and rumble of the battle happening far above them.

"Captain, this may sound weird, but I can feel vibrations coming up from below," said Wendy after the team stopped briefly at yet another entrance to a side room. "There must be a level below this."

"No doubt there is," Hunter answered, emerging from the room. "This one's empty, like the rest."

"Think we should investigate the lower levels?"

"Not unless that's where Kovan's been hidden. She's all we're after; this isn't a general recon mission. It's a miracle we've survived this far. If we keep our heads clear and stick to our objective, maybe we'll survive it completely."

"Captain, I got something moving," said Parker, halting her scan of the hall seconds after starting it up again. "Distance, six hundred and seven meters. And it's big."

"Jake, Wendy, do you confirm?" Hunter asked.

"I confirm. There's something down there and it's big," said Wendy, pointing her motion detector in the same direction Parker had her rifle trained.

"I got it, too," Shacker added, touching the magnification control on his scope. "Good God, it's an ezoghoul! I think it's wounded, and it's heading this way."

"Heading this way, like hell! It's charging us!" said Parker. "Captain!"

"Open fire," said Hunter, shouldering his rifle. "Fire at will. Wendy, break out your Ironfist."

At nearly two thousand feet, the creature was beyond effective range of Hunter's assault rifle, and in the dim lighting could scarcely be seen with the unaided eye. Only the sniper rifles and their scopes had the capability to hit it, and seemingly in unison their deafening blasts answered the creature's echoing cries. Their foot-long muzzle flashes also

gave it obvious aiming points, though because of its injuries
its return fire was too high and erratic.

The high-velocity, heavy shells caused the ezoghoul to
stagger every time it was hit. Hunter could see their flashes
when they struck the armor plate it wore. But it only seemed
to enrage the creature and provoke it into continuing its
charge.

"Captain, we're out!" Shacker warned when his next pull
of the trigger resulted only in the bolt clicking on an empty
chamber.

"Reload!" Hunter shouted. "And get outta the way!"

Still hundreds of yards off, the creature now loomed
larger—large enough for Hunter to see its eyes glowing with
a sickly light and close enough for him to feel the vibrations
of each footfall. He took aim at its horned, reptilian head
and squeezed the trigger. His rifle's thirty-round clip was
fired off in a single burst, the armor-piercing tracers forming
a continuous line of light. Most rounds did hit the ezoghoul
as it tried to twist and snake its head out of the fire stream.
One, however, struck it in the eye, finally bringing its charge
to a halt.

With a heavy thud the Gatling gun it carried hit the
ground and it bellowed in pain. Grabbing its head, the
ezoghoul reared onto its hind legs and even started flapping
its injured wings. For a few seconds it drew no additional
fire, until Hunter finished working the pump on his rifle's
grenade launcher and Wendy flipped the safety off her
Ironfist.

The first grenade hit the creature in its flank, where part
of its body armor had fallen away. The explosion caused it
to stagger, then its hind quarters dropped, as if its spine had
been severed. The next round struck the armor plate on its
left shoulder, and a burst of heavy caliber slugs tore pieces
out of its skeletal wings. Its deep roar became a pitiful
squeal and smoke poured from its body. They were the only
warnings the team got before the ezoghoul was peeled apart
by a fireball.

"Heads down!" said Hunter, dropping to the floor. "Incoming!"

The bio-mechanical detonation was powerful enough to
send the creature's body armor flying across the hall. It
clanged loudly when it hit the roof and sides. Pieces of burn-

ing flesh impacted with less noise, but were more numerous, causing the team to scramble to avoid getting hit.

"Captain, think we should take some of this back?" Shacker asked, pointing to one of the self-broiling lumps. "We could always tell Tim it's from a barbecue."

"I don't think he'd be fooled," Hunter replied. "Is anybody hurt?"

"No, but I think I'll get sick if I have to live with that smell for very long," Wendy admitted.

"I'm okay," said Parker after reloading her sniper rifle. "Next time we go up against these things, Captain, we better be armed with kitchen sinks. We had to throw everything at it but that."

"Keep it in mind for the debrief," said Hunter, using his rifle to help lever himself off the ground. "Let's keep moving. That nepharite has to be here somewhere."

"Captain, listen. Do you hear?" asked Wendy, and the moment the hall fell silent a soft giggling was heard.

"I do. Let's find out where that's coming from. Move it!"

"Ted, speak to me," said Venneti as he busily fitted a line of plastic explosive charges to the courier's belly-mounted external booster. "What's happening out there?"

"I think Mitch and the others had themselves a big fire fight with someone," said Halston, lowering the microphone on his headset so he could use it. "I saw some flashes and tracer fire. But I can't tell you much, other than I think the captain won."

"You seeing any other Legion forces?"

"Not since we chopped up that first group." Halston lifted his head above the makeshift barricade of metal floor plates around his position to give him a better field of view. "Everyone else has run into those side tunnels and entrances. I don't think they want a fight."

"They may also be going for reinforcements," Venneti concluded. "God help us if they do; we might not get outta this place yet."

"How much longer before you're finished back there?" asked Halston, looking over his shoulder at the courier ship and the huge boosters it was sandwiched between. At their bases he could just discern Venneti and Harris working under them.

"Another five or six minutes. We'll join you when we're done. Whistle us if we get any visitors. Leo, out."

"There's somebody in here, all right," Parker said quietly, stopping just short of the entrance to the room where the laughter came from. "I don't believe it, they're medical personnel."

The Isolation Chamber was better lighted than the hall, at least all its furnishings could be seen, as well as its staff. With Hunter directly behind her, Parker moved into the chamber. Both she and Shacker had slung their heavy sniper rifles over their shoulders and broken out their Street Blasters once again. Together with Wendy and Hunter, they swept the room and its occupants defensively, even though they carried no weapons and appeared to be the most human-looking of all the Legion creatures yet encountered.

"Yes, honored visitors? May I help you?" asked one of the placidly smiling staff. Like the others he wore a white gown that seemed almost iridescent. "Are you here for processing?"

Praecor walked slowly toward Hunter, holding his hands open to show he was unarmed. Part of the staff he commanded did the same with the rest of the team. Each selected a team member and approached with a smile and reassuring questions. The curator's talk blended into a constant, mesmerizing babble. It was also disarming, as the team members started lowering their weapons.

"We're . . . We're looking for a woman," said Hunter, raising his voice so he could be heard above the chanting of the curators—and to hear himself think. "Her name . . . is Lorraine Kovan. Have you heard of her? You must be keeping her as a prisoner?"

"We will find the woman," said Praecor, moving closer to Hunter, in spite of the rifle pointed at his stomach. "But first we must care for you. Processed? Yes."

"Hit the ground, troopers! I said, *Hit the ground!*"

The shouting was a cross between a jet taking off and a lion's roar. Compared to the mesmerizing prattle from the curators, it was shattering, and the team members retained enough of their training to respond. They all dropped to the floor as the Isolation Chamber exploded from a barrage of machine-gun fire.

Hunter looked up to see a bald-headed mountain of a man filling the chamber's entrance. The muzzle blasts from his M606 hid most of his features, but enough of his uniform and armor could be seen to show he was a Capitol soldier. He calmly raked the room with a continuous burst; Hunter marveled at the way he was able to maintain the volume of fire from so heavy a weapon and keep it accurate.

Above the thunder he heard hysterical cries and screams of creatures he had never seen before. The beautifully dressed staff that had been surrounding him moments earlier was gone. In their place were beings that vaguely resembled them, but their clothes were torn, their bodies decaying, and their skeletal faces frozen in hideous grins.

Even in death they grinned and continued to laugh. Praecor was among the first hit, but the last to die. After getting blown on to it, he slid off the chamber's lone bed, giggling contentedly, as if he were enjoying the pain inflicted on him. Around him lay the bodies of his staff and the sputtering, short-circuiting remnants of the necrotechnology machines lining the back wall.

"What . . . what happened to those people in the wonderful gowns?" Parker asked, rising to her feet and sweeping the carnage with her Street Blaster.

"Beautiful? What's she talking about, Captain?" asked the Capitol sergeant walking into the room. "Those things were uglier than my first drill instructor."

"These Legion creatures used their Dark Gifts on us, Sergeant," Hunter answered. "They seduced us. Thanks for saving us. It's likely most of us would've been killed."

"Don't mention it, Captain. I always knew us regulars would be rescuing you Special Forces types . . ." The closer the sergeant got to Hunter, the greater the light of recognition burned in his eyes. "I know you. You're Mitch Hunter. But I heard you were arrested. I thought you'd be as good as dead by now."

"Thanks for the concern. Sergeant?"

"Sergeant Watts. Robert Watts." As he identified himself, Watts came briefly to attention and remembered how to snap out a salute, which Hunter immediately answered. "One-Twenty-Third Mobile Infantry Battalion."

"Bob Watts? Big Bob Watts?" said Shacker, his jaw falling open. "*The* Big Bob Watts? God, wait'll Ted hears we met his idol."

"Where'd you come from, Sergeant?" said Hunter. "And why are you alone?"

"I led part of a squad down this tunnel we found near our Landing Zone," said Watts. "The rest either got killed 'cause they didn't listen to me, or turned back when they ran low on ammo. I wasn't through fighting, so I went lookin' for where the fight was and got lost. There must be miles of tunnels under this fortress. When I heard a big fight a couple of minutes ago, I came lookin' in this direction. That's when I saw you guys entering here."

"He probably heard us fighting with that ezoghoul," said Wendy, searching the chamber while the others made their introductions. "Captain, if Lorraine's as important to the Legion as we think she is, then this is the kind of room they'd keep her in. Just look at what we have. There's only one bed in here, and yet it had a big staff of these med-tech things. She was here, and I bet she's still close by."

"I thought we were supposed to be destroying this place, Captain? Not lookin' for someone."

"We'll destroy it, all right," Hunter promised. "But first we have to rescue a prisoner the Legion's holding. Wait a minute, Sergeant, where do you think you're going?"

"If it's all the same to you, Captain," said Watts, turning back for the entrance, "I'm here to destroy this place."

"You don't think you're gonna do it all by yourself?" asked Shacker. "Do you, Sergeant?"

"It won't take much power to destroy this place. Just one Watt!"

"Sergeant, if we find this woman, we'll find the nepharite," said Hunter, "the creature who commands this Citadel."

"Well, why didn't you say so in the first place?" Watts said, an eager smile on his face. "Just lead the way, Captain. Just lead the way."

"General, you look concerned," said Wood, noting the serious expression on Marcus Brown's face, where moments before there had been elation. "What's the trouble?"

"That last major explosion may have disorganized Legion forces, but it may also have increased their battle frenzy,"

Brown responded, looking up from the console screen he had been studying and the faxed reports he held in his hand. "The latest battle reports indicate the units we're encountering are fighting with suicidal fury. Our units are running out of ammunition, and their weapons are either melting or jamming. In some areas they've been forced to fall back."

"I have similar reports from the forward bases," said General Sumner, stepping up to Wood. "Munition stocks for the Grapeshots and Felines are running low. Many of their guided weapons are almost depleted from inventory."

"It sounds like we may have underestimated the resources it would take to defeat the Legion," Wood said somberly, glancing through the faxes Brown gave him. "Their fanaticism is truly unlike anything we've encountered."

"Should we order a retreat, Mr. Wood?" asked Hart, hovering at the edge of the group.

"Not yet. If we don't destroy this Citadel now, we won't have the capability to do so for a long time to come. The hell with corporate protocol. This attack continues until we're driven back, and not before it becomes financially unviable."

As they left the Isolation Chamber, Hunter's team fell into a preset search pattern. Parker took the lead, and Shacker covered the rear while Hunter, Watts, and Wendy Levin were strung out between them. The hallway now was completely empty except for them, though in the dim light it was difficult to see any figure beyond a few hundred yards and the cries and muted sounds of a distant battle were omnipresent. Next to each side entrance the team encountered, Parker would stop and attempt to scan it with the motion detector Wendy had given her. At the first few entrances she found nothing. Then she raised her hand and signaled a retreat from the latest one.

"There's someone in there all right," Parker whispered. "I couldn't get a good reading, but it's definitely occupied."

"Sling your rifles and break out your Street Blasters," said Hunter. "Load 'em with sabot rounds; we go in with stun grenades."

"Stunners?" Watts protested quietly while Parker and Shacker produced their shotguns and quickly reloaded them with armor-piercing sabot rounds. "We should go in shooting. Who do we have to be nice to?"

"The woman. We're not gonna rescue her by killing her—not when we've come this far to get her. Are we ready? Okay, Diane, let's do it."

Reapproaching the next entrance, Parker held a flash grenade in one hand, her Street Blaster in the other. When she was within a few inches of its edge, she armed the grenade and threw it in. It had scarcely started to bounce when a heavy volume of automatic weapons fire poured out of the entrance. The barrage continued until a blinding flash and an ear-numbing explosion overwhelmed it. The moment the light evaporated, Diane and Shacker were standing in the entrance, unloading their shotguns on the confused necromutants and heretics. They were immediately joined by Watts and Hunter, who opened up on the necromutants who had not seen fit to die when hit by sabot rounds. In seconds the firefight ended when the last of Ragathol's entourage toppled to the ground.

"Mitch, it's her!" Wendy shouted, moving into the Nether Room's antechamber the moment the firing ended. She quickly scanned the bodies lying in it while Hunter and the rest continued to cover them; in seconds she had found a brown-haired, petite woman slumped against a wall. "It's Lorraine Kovan, I'm sure of it."

"What's her condition?" Hunter asked, moving over to where Wendy was crouching. "Is she alive?"

"Yes, but she appears to be heavily drugged. With what, I couldn't tell you."

"Check and see if she's wounded. Sergeant Watts, I want you and the others to check these things and make sure they're all dead. I'm checking this."

Hunter pointed his rifle at the tunnellike entrance to the Nether Room. From where he stood, he could not see very far into it; in spite of this, he remained only long enough in the antechamber to change clips before slipping into the tunnel.

The moment he entered it, the ambient light dropped to nothing, almost as if a door had closed behind him. He felt the wall beside him, but could not tell how far he was walking or how long it was taking him. A few yards and an eternity later the light suddenly returned, an invisible door opened, and Hunter found himself standing in the Nether Room.

The first thing he noticed was its size, particularly its high, domed ceiling. The second thing was the nepharite and the shimmering window he stood in front of. On Hunter's entrance the window appeared to be a large plate of green glass mounted flush in the wall. Within seconds it had started to glow, then changed to black except for an outline. In the blackness a star field formed, and floating in it was a planet—a barren, lifeless-looking rock Hunter got only a brief look at before everything dissolved back to shimmering green.

"Human, you dare to interrupt me?" Ragathol raged, now facing Hunter; only Hunter could not recall seeing him turn. "You dare violate the sanctity of my residence?"

When he started to speak, Hunter trained his assault rifle on the nepharite, only to find he was unable to squeeze its trigger. No matter how hard he tried to concentrate, he was unable to make his body do what he wanted. He noticed the room was shifting on him, as if he were floating in it, and everything in it was changing shape. Hunter could feel his own body changing shape as well, slowly being crushed into some new form.

"You trespass on the very heart of the Dark Symmetry?" Ragathol continued, a contented smile on his face. "For that, human, you'll die!"

"I'm getting tired of hearing that," said Hunter, his anger burning through the spell and dissolving it. Instantly, the room and its contents returned to normal. He no longer felt he was floating in it or being crushed. And in the same instant he finally pulled the trigger.

Since the spell was still dissolving, the rifle seemed to literally explode in his hands. Its noise was deafening, its muzzle flashes blinding, and the recoil made it feel as though it were alive. In spite of this, Hunter was able to keep the weapon firing and pointed in Ragathol's general direction.

Part of the burst caught the nepharite in the chest and stomach area. Though he was taller and heavier than a human, the 10mm rounds caused him to stagger and roar in pain. The section of wall he had been trying to create a portal through started to glow bright green again and seemed to intensify with each hit he took. He tried to turn, but was thrown backward by the multiple impacts. He fell into the liquid green panel and was enveloped by it. Ragathol disappeared with scarcely a ripple; in an instant all that was left of him was the echo of his cry.

"All right, Captain, who're you firing at?" Watts asked, swinging his machine gun as he entered the Nether Room. "I want a few pieces of him."

"He . . . he was right in front of me," Hunter answered, finally releasing the trigger, long after the clip had been emptied. "I was shredding him, I'm certain of it."

"There ain't no one in this room except you and me, Captain. But I definitely heard someone talking to you before the shooting began, and screaming after it."

Watts circled the room until he stood in front of the wall section Hunter had been pointing his rifle at. Like the rest of the wall and ceiling it was carved from basalt. However, when he tried to touch it, Watts found the section too hot for his fingers.

"Damn, you could fry eggs on this," he continued. "What happened? Did he melt?"

"I think he was trying to open an interdimensional door," said Hunter, also stepping up to where the portal had been. "But now we'll never know what he was trying to do or where he disappeared to."

"Captain, Sergeant, you guys better get out here," said Parker, standing in the entrance. "I think we're gonna have company, real soon."

This time the Nether Room's entrance was nowhere near as long as Hunter remembered, or closed off by darkness. When he stepped back into the antechamber, he found Shacker lifting Kovan off the ground and cradling her in his arms.

"I think she's strong enough to be moved," Wendy reported. "What happened in there, Captain?"

"Ask me later," said Hunter, stopping just long enough to see that Kovan was alive before following his other snipers to the hall entrance. "Have you seen anyone, Diane?"

"No one yet," said Parker. "But they're coming."

Back in the hallway, the inhuman cries and wailing were more audible and even echoed slightly. No creatures or human could be seen, yet it was obvious there would soon be an army of Legion forces pouring out of the side tunnels along the hall's opposite side.

"All right, let's get outta here," Hunter ordered, briefly stepping back into the chamber. "I think these creatures are at last on to us. Set your Flamers to maximum detonation time. We'll use 'em as delayed action charges during our withdrawal."

"Flamers? What are these things?" Watts asked, watching the rest of the team members arm their grenades. "I never heard of 'em before."

"A prototype incendiary grenade," said Parker, showing him one.

"Ain't that something. You Special Forces types always have the real dangerous stuff."

"Of course it's dangerous," said Hunter. "It's a weapon. Diane, you take the point. Jake and Wendy, you're with me. Sergeant, you cover our backs. Now let's move it, and we better hope Leo's finished his mining."

As the team left the antechamber, the noise of the approaching forces had grown louder in the intervening moments. The wailing was sharper, and blended in with it was the clinking of armor and the stamp of countless boots. Instead of moving in a cautious sweep pattern, the team ran as fast as it could and still maintain unit effectiveness. They were nearing the main hangar's entrance when the first units finally appeared.

"Captain, we got those Legion zombies behind us," Watts advised. "Should I nail 'em?"

"No. Shooting will only attract their attention," said Hunter, glancing over his shoulder and catching sight of movement in the distance. "Start tossing your Flamers."

The clink and rattle of grenades landing on the hall's stone floor was the team's only answer to the Legion's appearance. Moments later, they reached the hangar's entrance just as the hordes of Legionnaires, razides, and other creatures pouring from the side tunnels were coalescing into a mob.

"Captain, what's going on out there?" Halston asked the instant he recognized the figures running into the hangar. "What's Jake carrying? And who's that with you?"

"Get down here and you'll have your answers!" Hunter shouted, motioning for his team to slow down once they rounded the corner. "I want everyone off that rig now! Leo, set your detonation time as I instructed, fifteen minutes! Now, let's hope our Com sets are strong enough to transmit a signal outta here. Rapier, this is Battle Axe. Rapier, this is Battle Axe. We need an immediate evac. Do you read? Over."

"Lieutenant, I'm getting a message from Captain Hunter," said Taylor. "I think he's asked for an evac."

"Switch it over to me. I'll handle it," said Alverez, changing her headset from the tactical air channels to the one reserved for Special Forces. She caught the tail end of Hunter's second transmission; while it was weak, she could understand it. "Battle Axe, this is Rapier. We read you. What do you want? Over."

"Evac, Rapier! Repeat, we need immediate evac!" Hunter answered, his voice fading in and out amid the static. "Advise Avenger they have fifteen minutes to evac the target area. We're blowing the whole Citadel! Over."

"Roger, Battle Axe. Prepare for evac. Rapier, out." The moment she signed off, Alverez was switching her headset back to the tactical air channel she had it on previously. As she did so, she glanced out her cockpit's port side, catching sight of the second Cutlass. "Foil, this is Rapier. I'm going in to get my squad. Will you advise Avenger to evac all our forces from the target area? Over."

"Understood, Rapier," said the second gunship's pilot. "But will those map watchers at the battle station listen to us? Over."

"Just let 'em know the advisory comes direct from Captain Hunter," Alverez replied. "Wish us luck. Rapier, out."

By pulling her continual left turn a little tighter, Alverez broke away from the other Cutlass and put her ship high above the open shaft. Once she brought it to a halt and stabilized it, she started lowering it back into the shaft. Less than a minute after receiving Hunter's order, the gunship had disappeared through the gaping hole in the ground.

"Wait a minute. I know you," said Halston after charging off the stairs and nearly running into Watts. "You're the legend himself. You're Bob Watts."

"We don't have a minute," said Hunter, taking a quick

head count of his squad. "You can ask him for his autograph later."

"Yeah, and I ain't no legend," Watts grumbled. "All the legends I know are dead guys. And I don't plan on being dead anytime soon."

"Captain, I set the charges just as you wanted," said Venneti, the last to come off the transport vehicle. "We got fourteen minutes, three seconds before everything blows. Say, where'd you find Big Bob Watts?"

"We'll explain it later," Hunter answered. "Right now we gotta catch a cab with a real fast meter. Diane, take the point. Watts, Ted, you cover the rear. Let's move it. This is an evac, not a jog."

The squad spent only enough time under the giant vehicle to gather its remaining teams before starting off for the hangar's opposite end. What had taken them so long and hard to capture earlier they now covered in a matter of minutes. They ran in as straight a line as possible, only moving to the left or right to avoid obstacles or the bodies of those they had recently killed.

Behind them they could hear the wailing and screams of the Legion hordes, building in intensity. Occasionally some of it would grow pitiful when one of the Flamer grenades would explode with a thump. Above the cries of their immolating victims could be heard scattered gunfire; the Legion was firing at imagined enemies and often hitting their own kind. Soon, if they kept up their current pace of advance, they would have real enemies to shoot at.

"Mr. Wood, we're getting a message from one of the Special Forces gunships," advised the colonel. "I think you should hear it before we decide to act on it."

The colonel escorted Wood over to a console whose operators were already being questioned by General Powers and General Brown. Even though he had not been asked to join them, Hart followed Wood at a discreet distance.

"Is it one of your people, General?" Wood asked as he reached the console.

"Yes, sir. It's Captain Hogan's pilot," said Powers, glancing up at the civilians. "He's relaying a message from Captain Hunter. We're to evacuate the target area immediately.

We got about fourteen minutes before he blows the entire Citadel."

"This time he's gone too far," Hart blurted out, continuing in spite of the sharp glances he got from Wood and the officers. "*We're* running this operation, not him. And since when did we give Hunter authorization to destroy the Citadel?"

"That'll be enough out of you, Mr. Hart," Wood said coldly. "If Hunter's found a way to destroy this infestation, then good. General Brown, evacuate all ground forces at once. Tell them to withdraw to the landing zones."

"As senior military advisor I suggest we wait until we can question Hunter personally before we do anything this radical."

"And as a senior stockholder I invoke executive privilege and relieve you of your duties. Lieutenant, escort this man from the center. General, commence evacuation. Coordinate air support with General Sumner to cover the withdrawal. General Powers, ask this pilot if he knows whether Captain Hunter has rescued the woman or not."

"Captain, I can hear the 'copter!" Parker shouted. "It's back in the shaft!"

"Then we don't have much time to do a little clearing," said Hunter as he reached the hangar's opposite end. "Jake, hand Lorraine over to Wendy. I want you, Leo, Harris, and Redfield to clear some of this debris to make a landing spot. Sergeant Watts, I want you, Ted, and Diane to cover us while we work."

Still littered with wreckage when its roof had been shot apart, the launch pad was unusable to the descending helicopter. Already the popping of its rotorblades echoed loudly as Hunter and most of his squad slung their weapons. Using sections of roof as shovels, they pushed the bodies of tekrons, necromutants, and smaller pieces of debris in order to create one clear area in the pad's center.

Shortly after they began their work, the chatter of machine-gun fire and the bark of Parker's sniper rifle drowned out most of the other noises in the shaft. The first Legion units had swept into the hangar's back entrance. Surprised by the volume of fire they received, those who were not cut down briefly retreated. When they came flooding back into the hangar, their numbers could not be stopped by just two machine guns, and their attack wail was deafening. Only at the launch pad was it drowned out by the gunship's arrival.

"Put your goggles down! Put your goggles down!" Hunter managed to say before the thunder of rotorwash and turbines overpowered everything else. He pulled his own goggles off his helmet and over his eyes just as the wash kicked up blinding clouds of dust.

It was almost impossible to see the Cutlass in the storm it created, impossible to tell it had landed except that its powerful external lights had stopped moving. The squad had to move within arm's length of it before they realized its side hatches were already open and both pilot and gunner were waving them in.

First to climb inside were Venneti and Parker, who in turn helped Wendy and Hunter move Lorraine in. The rest of the squad followed swiftly, though it was not until the hatches had rolled shut that Hunter was able to order a lift-off.

"Julia, this is Mitch! Get us outta here!" he said, the cabin so jammed he had to have Sutter work the intercom controls for him. "You got five minutes to get us as far away as possible."

"Roger, Mitch. I'm punching it," Alverez replied.

"What's that sound I keep hearing?" Sutter asked, as an intermittent, hollow *spang* grew more frequent.

"Gunfire," said Hunter. "The Legion horde's close enough to touch us. Let's hope they don't have anything sophisticated enough to penetrate our armor."

With a burst of turbine noise the Cutlass rocked and lifted off the pad. The inaccurate fire stopped almost immediately, though Hunter knew it would not cease for very long.

"Jeff, this is Mitch," he continued. "You still got that other cluster bomb?"

"Yes, Captain. It's still out there," said Taylor.

"Arm it and set submunitions for a two-tier detonation, instantaneous and forty-second delayed action."

"Setting detonation times, Captain. And the computer confirms the weapon is armed."

A moment later the last gray pod hanging on the gunship's stub wings detached from its shackles and dropped into the shaft. It had scarcely cleared the aircraft when its compressed gas charge tore it open, scattering the bomblets around the shaft.

Some of them exploded on contact with the shaft walls, unleashing their clouds of shrapnel with little effect. However, most survived the dispersal and landed on the pad, where about half detonated on impact, their shrapnel cutting to pieces the first wave of Legion creatures to reach the pad. Those who swarmed in after them had to contend with a near-continuous stream of shells from the helicopter's tail gun.

"Captain, I'm down to less than two hundred rounds on the aft turret," Taylor warned.

"Be careful with what you got, but keep firing," said Hunter, motioning for someone to push the overhead terminal down to him. "Julia, this is Mitch. How far to the surface?"

"Less than seventy-five meters," said Alverez. "Just a few more seconds and we'll be clear of this trap."

Enough auroral light was now filtering down from the surface for the Cutlass crew and passengers to see the smooth surfaces of the shaft wall, as well as the occasional green tracers flashing up from below. Moments later the tail gun ran through the last of its ammunition supply, which caused the main cabin to fall oddly quiet—until a dramatic increase in ground fire hit the aircraft.

"Damn, they keep this up and they'll shoot us down before we finish climbing out of this hole," Hunter advised above the clang and banging of rounds striking the fuselage and rotor blades, "new armor or not."

The barrage ended as rapidly as it had begun, with the second round of bomblet detonations. They swept the launch pad with a hurricane of shrapnel and blast effects. The dying and the dismembered bodies now littered it so deeply that the next wave of Legion creatures found it difficult to occupy the site with any speed. By the time the wave's first units had deployed, the Cutlass was leaping free of the shaft, and time itself had all but run out.

"Punch it, Julia! Punch it!" said Hunter. "Max out the engines. Let's see how fast you can push her."

Barely fifty feet above the shaft the Cutlass stopped rotating long enough to drop its nose and head away from the Citadel. Free of most of its weapons and fuel, it accelerated rapidly, even overtaking its wingman, which had a substantial head start. Behind them the ground forces retreated from the battered fortress as fast as they could. Many of its spires were down, and fires raged around it. In spite of this, the surviving Legion forces still put up a fierce barrage and even started retaking the areas Capitol had given up. Their counterattack caused the orbiting Hercules transports to back off and forced the F/A-99s still in the target area to continue their strafing runs to protect the now-exposed troops. The fighting continued at such an intensity that scarcely anyone took notice of the initial explosion.

In their rush to overwhelm and annihilate Hunter's squad, none of the Legion units who entered the main hangar bothered to check the transporter vehicle or the spaceship it carried. They swept around it like a torrent briefly encountering an obstacle. They were still surging forward when the charges placed on the external boosters detonated.

In an instant they and the courier sandwiched between them evaporated. They became a roiling fireball that flattened and smashed the huge vehicle beneath it and expanded in the next instant to fill the hangar. Part of the explosion traveled up the shaft and became a pillar of flame hundreds of feet tall, the first external sign of the Citadel's doom.

The rest of the fireball traveled into the adjacent hangars, down the back hallway, or through the massive cracks it had opened in the main hangar's floor and walls. They consumed whatever was combustible, sustaining what had become a living fire storm. Hundreds of explosions were set off—armed and fueled aircraft, munitions caches of various sizes, and finally, the fuel storage tanks and their processing facilities.

The pillar of flame had just started to die out when the area around the launch site briefly caved in, before mushrooming out in a sphere of light as bright as the sun.

"Corporal, look!" exclaimed Ozawa as the video feeds from the remaining drones lit up with the fireworks and their infrared and air pressure readings went off the scale. "No wonder the Capitol forces were evacuating!"

"No wonder, indeed," said Watanabe, her face brightening with astonishment, but the tone in her voice was one of satisfaction. "I heard rumors from the fighting on Mars that

these Dark Legion fortresses were indestructible. I'm glad to
see they're not."

"Should we recall our warheads?"

"No, Renya-san. Most will survive this, and our superiors
up the line will want the best data possible on this event.
I ... I just wonder if we will."

One of the closest manned sites to Legion territory, the
Mishima observation post was among the first to feel the
growing seismic shockwaves emanating from the Citadel's
destruction. On a planet where plate tectonic activity was
rare, the sensation of the observation tower swaying was un-
nerving to its crew.

"Corporal, what's happening?" shouted Ozawa, leaping
off his chair and grabbing hold of the console to steady himself. "Is the Citadel causing this?"

"I believe it is," Watanabe answered. "This is incredible ...
I don't think Venus has felt the like since our ancestors bom-
barded it with asteroids and comets to begin terra-forming it. I
think at last our superiors will finally be waking up!"

As the sphere of light rose out of the ground, its shock
wave spread out like a visible dome. Racing ahead of it were
the airborne strike jets, transports, and helicopters. Only the
F/A-99s escaped completely by hitting their afterburners.
The Hercules cargo lifters and gunships that were too close
to the Citadel were overtaken and battered around by the
shock wave; while those sitting at the landing zones were so
heavily damaged they were unflyable.

The sphere rapidly became a mushroom-shaped cloud as it
continued to rise, parting the clouds at higher altitudes and
blotting out the aurora's colorful veils. Its center cooled
from white-hot to red but kept boiling, consuming itself and
the thousands of tons of soil it had excavated. Eventually, it
would tower miles above the ground and eject enough material into the upper atmosphere to turn sunsets for the next
year a coppery red.

Below ground level part of the blast was channeled into
the tunnels and hallways running under the Citadel. Those
not collapsed or crushed by the earlier blasts carried the
flames to all its subterranean levels. There they found more
munitions and fuel stocks to feed off, as well as material in
the distortion chambers, weapon labs, and medical facilities.

More explosions shook the land even as the mushroom cloud continued to grow. In some areas the fires reached the surface and flared out of intact bunkers. In the Citadel itself they found still more material to consume and wracked the surviving structure with explosions. The few spires that had lasted through the air attacks and shock wave finally came down. In minutes the Citadel was reduced to a mountainous pile of burning debris. The heat given off by it was enough to incinerate anyone or anything standing within several hundred yards.

Most of the remaining Legion units were consumed this way, or were too stunned by the destruction of their home to either continue their attack or respond effectively when Capitol forces finally resumed firing at them.

"Good God, can you feel that?" Powers asked after the tactical center started to shake in a rhythmic manner.

"Yes. On Mars I've felt something like it many times," said Wood, a satisfied smile spreading over his face. "Only this time it's different. Now it signals the end of a Citadel, instead of some new activity by one."

"General, we're getting reports from the landing zones!" the Colonel shouted, motioning for Brown to join him at the primary communications console. "We have a lot of blast-damaged troop lifters. It's gonna take us longer to evac our people."

"How are the soldiers themselves doing?" Brown asked, moving up to the console.

"We have lots of popped ear drums and broken bones, but they're alive and mopping up what remains of the Dark Legion. They'd like to have a little help from the Air Force if we can get the crews to stop sightseeing."

"Tell them we'll get on it." Brown glanced back to where Wood and the other generals were still gathered and did some signaling of his own. "Varley, we need you to bark at your planes and gunships."

"Gunships," Wood repeated before turning to Powers. "General, see if you can contact squad Trident. Let's see if they were able to rescue the woman."

"I don't believe it. We're still in one piece!" Halston shouted. "I thought that last ride would've torn us apart."

"I think we can tell Dreamworks that this ship has passed its baptism of combat with flying colors," said Hunter while the Cutlass stopped its pronounced swaying and settled back into level flight. "Julia, this is Mitch. What does the target area look like?"

"Not much left of it," said Julia. "Just the world's biggest camp fire and one of those nuclear blast clouds we've seen in science-fiction movies."

"Captain, I'm getting a message from General Powers himself," Taylor advised. "They want to know if you've been able to rescue Lorraine Kovan."

"Tell them, yes. She's in a comalike state, but alive and physically uninjured." As he gave his response, Hunter glanced over at Venneti and Shacker, who together were cradling the petite, brown-haired woman while Wendy tried to take her blood pressure and pulse rate. "Ask them if they want us to bring her straight to the battle station."

"You think we have the fuel to make it that far?" asked Shacker. "I thought we'd land at one of the forward bases and turn her over to Intelligence."

"No. I . . . I think we'll be ordered to fly her straight to Athena," said Sutter. "In my briefing we were told she's *very* important to us. They'd want to get her into as high a security environment as possible."

"I think Lynn may be right," said Wendy. "If I were Noah Wood, I'd want to get her to the most secure place as fast as possible. And that wouldn't be a forward base."

"What's the matter with a forward base?" Watts added. "If it's good enough for us grunts, it ought t'be good enough for everyone else."

"Captain, I got our orders," said Taylor, his announcement ending the conversation. "You ain't gonna believe this. We're to fly all the way to Atlantis! The station's arranging for refueling tankers and fighters to escort us."

"The spaceport?" said Hunter, at first incredulous. "Well, it looks as though Leo was right this time. We will end up at Nova Miami."

"No, Captain, at least not all of us. You and the lieutenant are to escort Lorraine Kovan to Luna! Some of us will also be going with you; they'll figure it all out later. The station says they'll have a special courier outfitted and flight-prepped for us by the time we arrive."

"What's gonna happen to her once we get there?" asked Shacker.

"My guess is rehabilitative therapy," said Wendy, "if there's anything left to rehabilitate, and an extensive debriefing—if she can remember anything after the rehab."

"It looks as though this operation isn't gonna end just yet," said Hunter, looking over at Kovan again. "I hope she's as strong as I think she is. Her journey back to humanity is a long way from being over. Julia, this is Mitch. Set course due north, take the most direct route you can to Atlantis."

"Will do, Mitch," Alverez responded. "I'll take us to our optimum cruise altitude and reset our engines to max cruise speed. We'll make Atlantis in just over four hours."

"Roger, Julia. Make it a smooth flight. All right, let's get comfortable. Harris, open that hatch behind you. We'll put our weapons in first, then our armor. It may not make this place luxurious, but at least we'll have some creature comforts. Watts, that includes you as well. Safety your machine gun and stow it. This mission's a long way from over."

Climbing and slowing down, the Cutlass arced gracefully to the north, eventually settling on the most direct course for the Atlantis Spaceport. Above it flights of F/A-99s were already swinging around and closing on it to provide an escort. On the northern horizon the distant sun was no longer a glow behind the mountains. It was finally rising above them, bringing an end to the long polar night.

Behind the gunship lay the remains of the Dark Legion Citadel. Burning like a monstrous funeral pyre, it provided its own glow that almost rivaled the new sun. A thick, slowly roiling column of black smoke climbed into the sky, threatening to spread across it and blot out the dawn.

With many of the tunnels, caverns, and hallways collapsed under it, the Citadel's great weight could no longer be sustained. The area around it started to sag visibly. With an audible, mournful groan the land itself collapsed, almost as if it could no longer support the evil that had spread through it.

For several minutes the region trembled as level after level was crushed by those coming down on top of it. More explosions were touched off and in some cases blew debris out of the pit being created. When the collapse finally stopped, the pit was nearly a mile in diameter and over three thousand feet deep. The fire at its base would continue to burn for several weeks, until nothing of the Dark Legion's first outpost on Venus would remain. Humanity had its first triumph over the evil threatening to engulf it. But it was only the first, and would be short-lived.

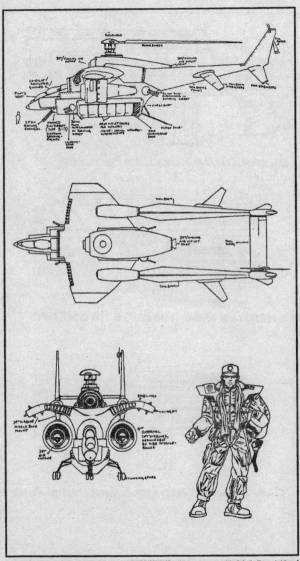

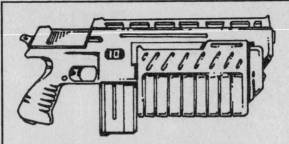

SHERMAN .74 MODEL 13 "BOLTER"

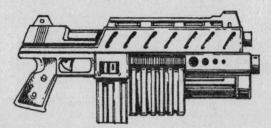

SHERMAN .55G MODEL 15 "IRONFIST"

CAR-24 WITH GRENADE LAUNCHER GL-240

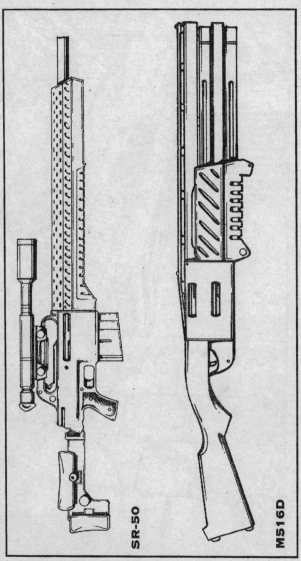

SR-50

M516D